MAQROLL

Alvaro Mutis

MAQROLL
THREE NOVELLAS

The Snow of the Admiral
*
Ilona Comes with the Rain
*
Un Bel Morir

TRANSLATED FROM THE SPANISH BY
Edith Grossman

HarperPerennial
A Division of HarperCollinsPublishers

The Library of Congress has catalogued the hardcover edition as follows:

Mutis, Alvaro
  [Novellas, English, Selections]
  Maqroll: three novellas / by Alvaro Mutis: translated from the Spanish by Edith Grossmann.—1st. ed.
    p. cm.
    Contents: The snow of the admiral—Ilona comes with the rain—Un bel morir.
    ISBN 0-06-016623-1 (cloth)
    1. Title.
PQ8180.23.U8A24   1992
863—dc20   92-52571

ISBN 0-06-092444-6 (pbk.)
93 94 95 96 97 CC/HC 10 9 8 7 6 5 4 3 2 1

CONTENTS

The Snow
of the Admiral

For Ernesto Volkening
(ANTWERP, 1908–BOGOTÁ, 1983)
*

In memory of, and in homage to,
his unshadowed friendship,
his unforgettable lesson

N'accomplissant que ce qu'il doit,
Chaque pecheur peche pour soi:
Et le premier recueille, en les mailles qu'il serre,
Tout le fretin de sa misère;
Et celui-ci ramene a l'étourdie
le fond vaseux des maladies;
Et tel ouvre les nasses
Aux desespoirs qui le menacent;
Et celui-la recueille au long des bords,
Les épaves de son remords.

Emile Verhaeren, "Les Pecheurs"

I thought that the writings, letters, documents, tales, and memoirs of Maqroll the Gaviero (the Lookout) had all passed through my hands, and that those who knew of my interest in the events of his life had exhausted their search for written traces of his unfortunate wanderings, but fate held in store a curious surprise just when it was least expected.

One of the secret pleasures afforded by walks through the Barrio Gótico in Barcelona is visiting the secondhand bookstores (to my mind the best stocked in the world), whose owners still preserve that subtle expertise, rewarding intuition, and canny knowledge which are the virtues of the authentic bookseller, a species well on its way to imminent extinction. Recently, as I was walking down the Calle de Botillers, I was drawn to the window of an old bookshop that tends to be closed most of the time but offers truly exceptional works to the avid collector. That day it was open. I walked in with the devotion of one entering the sanctuary of some forgotten rite. In attendance, behind an untidy heap of books and maps that he was cataloguing in an exquisite, old-fashioned hand, was a young man with the heavy black beard of a Levantine Jew, an ivory complexion, and melancholy black eyes fixed in an expression of mild astonishment. He gave me a thin smile and, like any good bookseller, allowed me to peruse the shelves while he attempted to remain as unobtrusive as possible. As I was putting to one side some volumes I intended to purchase, I unexpectedly came across a beautiful edition, bound in purple leather, of the book by P. Raymond that I had been seeking for

years and whose very title is promising: Enquête du Prévôt de
Paris sur l'assassinat de Louis Duc D'Orléans, *published by the
Bibliothèque de l'Ecole de Chartres in 1865. Many years of
waiting had been rewarded by a stroke of luck I had long since
stopped hoping for. I took the copy without opening it and
asked the bearded young man for the price. He quoted the
figure with that round, definitive tone of finality which is also
peculiar to his proud fraternity. Without hesitation I paid for it
and my other selections, and I left to enjoy my acquisition
alone, to savor it slowly, voluptuously, on a bench in the little
square with the statue of Ramón Berenguer the Great. As I
leafed through the pages, I noticed that inside the back cover a
large pocket, originally intended for the maps and genealogical
tables that accompanied Professor Raymond's exquisite text,
contained instead a quantity of pink, yellow, and blue sheets
that appeared to be commercial bills and accounting forms.
When I inspected them more closely, I saw that they were
covered by tiny, cramped writing, somewhat tremulous and
feverish I thought, in an indelible violet pencil occasionally
darkened by the author's saliva. The writing, on both sides of
the page, carefully avoided the original printed material on what
were, in fact, various kinds of commercial forms. A sentence
suddenly caught my eye and made me forget the French
historian's scrupulous research into the treacherous assassination
of the brother of Charles VI of France by order of John the
Fearless, Duke of Burgundy. At the bottom of the last page I
read these words, penned in green ink by a somewhat steadier
hand: "Written by Maqroll the Gaviero during his voyage up
the Xurandó River. To be given to Flor Estévez, wherever she
may be. Hotel de Flandre, Antwerpen." Since the book was
underlined and annotated in the same violet pencil, it was not
difficult to deduce that he had kept the papers in the pocket
designed for more momentous academic purposes.*

*As the pigeons continued to sully the noble image of the
conqueror of Mallorca, son-in-law to the Cid, I began to read
the variegated pages where, in the form of a diary, Maqroll
narrated his misadventures, memories, reflections, dreams, and
fantasies as he traveled upriver, one man among the many who
come down from the hill country to lose themselves in the*

half-light of the immeasurable jungle's vegetation. Many
passages were written in a firmer hand, which led me to
conclude that the vibration of the engine in the vessel carrying
the Gaviero was responsible for the tremor I had at first
attributed to the fevers which, in that climate, are as frequent as
they are resistant to all treatment or cure.

As with so many other pages written by Maqroll in testimony
to his contrary fate, this *Diary* is an indefinable mixture of
genres, ranging from a straightforward narration of ordinary
events to an enumeration of the hermetic precepts of what I
assumed was his philosophy of life. Attempting to correct the
manuscript would be both ingenuous and fatuous, and would
contribute little to his original purpose: to record, day after day,
his experiences on a voyage whose monotony and uselessness
were, perhaps, alleviated by his work as chronicler.

On the other hand, it seemed a matter of elementary justice
that the *Diary* have as its title the name of the establishment
where, for a long period of time, Maqroll enjoyed relative
tranquillity along with the attentions of its owner, Flor Estévez,
the woman who understood him best and shared the
exaggerated scope of his dreams, the intricate tangle of his
existence.

It has also occurred to me that readers might be interested in
having access to information related, in one way or another, to
the events and people Maqroll describes in the *Diary*. I have,
therefore, appended several accounts that appeared in earlier
publications but now occupy what I believe is their proper
place.

THE GAVIERO'S DIARY

*R*eports had indicated that a good part of the river was navigable up to the foot of the cordillera. It isn't, of course. We're in a flat-keeled barge driven by a diesel motor that fights the current with asthmatic obstinacy. In the bow, under a canvas roof supported by an iron framework, hang four hammocks, two portside and two starboard. Other passengers, when there are any, stay in the center of the boat on palm leaves that protect them from the burning heat of the metal deck. Their footsteps resound over the empty hold with a bizarre, ghostly echo. We stop constantly to refloat the barge after it runs aground on the sandbars that form without warning and then disappear, following the whims of the current. Two of the four hammocks are used by those of us who boarded in Puerto España, and the other two are for the mechanic and the river pilot. The captain sleeps in the bow under a multicolored beach umbrella that he moves according to the position of the sun. He is always semi-inebriated, a condition that he skillfully maintains by a process of steady drinking, which keeps him in a state of mind where euphoria alternates with a drowsy stupor he never overcomes completely. His orders have no bearing on our progress, and they always leave me perplexed and irritated: "Courage! Watch out for the wind! Into the fray, away darkness! The water is ours! Burn the sounding line!" and on and on throughout the day and most of the night. The mechanic and the pilot pay no attention to this litany, yet somehow it keeps them awake and alert and gives them the skill they need to avoid the constant dangers of the Xurandó. The mechanic is an Indian whose silence would make you think he was mute if it weren't for an occasional conversation with the captain in a jumble of languages that is difficult to translate. Barefoot, bare-chested, he wears greasy jeans that he ties under his smooth, prominent belly; a protruding herniated navel expands and contracts as he struggles to keep the motor running. His relationship to the engine is a clear case of transubstantiation; they merge, they coexist in a single endeavor: the launch must move ahead. The pilot is one of those beings with inexhaustible mimetic abilities. His features, gestures, voice, and other personal traits have been carried to so perfect a degree of nonexistence that they can never stay in our memories. His eyes are very close-set, and I can remember him only by recalling the sinister Monsieur Rigaud-Blandois in *Little Dorrit*. Yet not even this unforgettable reference works for very long, and Dickens's character vanishes when I look at the pilot. A strange bird. My fellow passenger under the canvas is a calm blond giant who chews a few words in an almost incomprehensible Slavic accent, and constantly smokes the foul tobacco that the pilot sells to him at an exorbitant price. From what I can gather he and I are going to the same place: the factory that processes the lumber that will be shipped along this route, and whose transport I'll supposedly be in charge of. The word "factory" produces hilarity in the crew, which doesn't amuse me at all and leaves me prey to vague doubts. A Coleman lamp burns at night, and a parade of large insects smash into it, their colors and shapes so varied I occasionally have the impression that the order of their appearance has been arranged for some mysterious educational purpose. I read by the light of the glowing wicks until sleep overwhelms me like a fast-acting drug. The thoughtless frivolity of the Duke of Orléans occupies me for a moment before I drop into an irresistible stupor. The motor changes rhythm constantly, keeping us in perpetual uncertainty: at any moment it may stop forever. The current is becoming wilder, more capricious. It's all absurd, and I'll never understand why I set out on this enterprise. It's always the same at the start of a journey. Then comes a soothing indifference that makes everything all right. I can't wait for it to arrive.

* * *

What I feared has finally happened: the propeller hit roots on the riverbed and bent the axle. The vibration was alarming. We've had to pull up on a beach of slate-colored sand that gives off the sweetish, penetrating smell of rotting vegetation. Until I could convince the captain that the only way to straighten the axle was to heat it, several hours were spent in the suffocating heat in a struggle to perform the most dim-witted, thoughtless operations. A cloud of mosquitoes settled over us. Fortunately, we're all immune except the blond giant, who endured the attack with an angry, controlled look as if he didn't know the source of his persistent torment.

At nightfall a family of natives—a man, a woman, a boy of six, and a girl of four—appeared unexpectedly. All of them were completely naked. They stood watching the fire with the indifference of reptiles. Both the man and the woman are absolutely beautiful. He has broad shoulders, and the slow movements of his arms and legs emphasize his perfect proportions. The woman, as tall as the man, has large, firm breasts, and thighs that round into narrow, graceful hips. Their bodies are completely covered by a thin coat of fat that softens the angles of their joints. Their hair is cut in a helmet shape, and they dress and keep it in place with the juice of some plant that dyes it ebony black and makes it shine in the last rays of the setting sun. They ask a few questions in a language that nobody understands. Their teeth are filed to points, and their voices sound like the quiet coo of a drowsing bird. It was dark by the time we straightened the axle, but it can't be put back in place until morning. The Indians caught some fish along the shore and went to the far end of the beach to eat. The murmur of their childish voices lasted until dawn. I read until I fell asleep. The heat doesn't let up at night, and as I lie in my hammock, I think for a long while about the foolish indiscretions of the Duke of Orléans and about those character traits that will be repeated in other members of the "branch cadette," who come from different stock but have the same disposition to felony, gallant adventures, the dangerous pleasures of conspiracy, greed for money, and unrelieved disloyalty. One might think further about why such behavioral constants appear so relentlessly, almost up to our own time, in princes of such diverse backgrounds. The water slaps against the flat metal bottom of the boat with a monotonous gurgle that is, for some elusive reason, comforting.

* * *

The family came on board the following dawn. While we struggled underwater to replace the axle, they stood on the palm leaves the whole day without moving or saying a word. The man and the woman have no hair anywhere on their bodies. Her sex swells like a freshly opened fruit, and his has a long foreskin that ends in a point. It resembles a horn or a spur, something totally foreign to the idea of sexuality, something without the slightest erotic significance. Occasionally they smile, which bares their filed teeth and eliminates any suggestion of cordiality or simple friendliness.

The pilot explains that it's common in these parts for Indians to travel the river in white men's boats. They usually offer no explanations, never say where they're going, and disappear one day as suddenly as they came. They're peaceful and never take anything that doesn't belong to them or share the food of the other passengers. They eat plants, raw fish, raw reptiles. Some come on board armed with arrows dipped in curare, the instantaneous poison whose preparation is a secret they've never revealed.

That night, while I was in a deep sleep, I was suddenly enveloped by a rank smell of decomposing mud and rutting snake that rose in a sweetish, unbearable stench. I opened my eyes. The Indian woman was staring at me, smiling with a provocativeness that was somehow carnivorous yet repulsively innocent. She put her hand on my sex, began to caress me, and lay down beside me. When I entered her, I felt myself sinking into a bland, unresisting wax that with immobile, vegetative passivity allowed me to move as I chose. The odor that had awakened me grew stronger as she drew closer; her soft body felt nothing like the touch of women. An uncontrollable nausea was rising inside me, and I finished quickly so I wouldn't have to withdraw and vomit before I reached a climax. She moved away in silence. In the meantime the Slav's hammock held two entwined bodies; the Indian was penetrating

9

the Slav and screeching quietly like a bird in danger. Then it was the giant's turn, and the Indian continued to make his inhuman sound. I went to the bow and tried to wash away the putrid stench of rotting swamp that clung to my body. I vomited with relief. The stink still invades my nostrils without warning, and I'm afraid it will stay with me for a long time to come.

They stood there in the middle of the boat, their gaze lost in the treetops as they chewed a mash made of leaves that resemble laurel and the flesh of fish or lizards that they catch with uncommon skill. The Slav took the woman to his hammock last night, and this morning the man was sleeping on top of him in his arms. The captain separated them, not for the sake of decency but, as he explained, slurring his words, because the rest of the crew might follow his example and that would surely bring dangerous complications. The trip, he added, was a long one, and the jungle has an uncontrollable power over those not born there. It makes them irritable and tends to produce a delirium not free of risk. The Slav mumbled some explanation I couldn't understand and calmly returned to his hammock after drinking a cup of coffee brought to him by the pilot. I suspect they've met before. I don't trust the obedient docility of this giant—the shadow of a sad, weary madness can be seen occasionally in his eyes.

* * *

MARCH 24

We've come to a wide opening in the jungle. After so many days we can finally see the sky and the clouds moving with benign slowness. The heat is more intense, but not as oppressive as that suffocating density under the green, shadowy dome of the great trees, where it becomes an implacable, persistent force that saps our strength. The noise of the engine dissipates into the air, and the boat slips along without our having to endure its desperate battle with the current. Something resembling happiness settles over me. It's easy to sense the relief in the others as well. But in the distance the dark wall of vegetation, waiting to swallow us up in a few hours, is beginning to take shape again.

I've used this peaceful interlude of sun and relative silence to

examine the reasons that impelled me to undertake this journey. I
first heard about the timber in The Snow of the Admiral, Flor
Estévez's place in the cordillera. I lived with her for several months
while I was recuperating from an ulcer on my leg caused by the bite
of a poisonous fly from the mangrove swamps in the delta. Flor
tended to me with distant but firm affection, and at night we made
love, hampered by my disabled leg yet with a sense of redemption,
of liberation from the old misfortunes that each of us carried like
an oppressive burden. I believe I've written elsewhere about Flor's
shop and the time I spent on the high plateau. A trucker with a load
of cattle he'd purchased down on the plains stopped there and told
us about wood that could be bought from a sawmill at the edge of
the jungle, sailed down the Xurandó, and sold at a much higher
price to the military posts under construction along the great river.
When the ulcer dried, Flor gave me money and I went down to
the jungle, although I had my doubts about the entire enterprise.
The cold in the cordillera and the constant fog moving like a
procession of penitents through dwarfed, shaggy vegetation, made
me feel an urgent need to sink into the burning lowland weather.
I'd received a contract to sail a freighter under Tunisian registry to
Antwerp, where certain adjustments and modifications would con-
vert it into a banana transport ship, but I mailed back the unsigned
papers along with some clumsy excuses that must have intrigued
the owners, who were old friends of mine, companions on other
adventures and misadventures that deserve to be recorded someday.

When I boarded the barge I mentioned the sawmill, but nobody
could tell me its exact location or even if it really existed. It's always
the same: I embark on enterprises that are branded with the mark
of uncertainty, cursed by deceit and cunning. And here I am,
sailing upriver like a fool, knowing ahead of time how everything
will end, going into the jungle where nothing waits for me. I am
sickened and depressed by its monotony, its climate worthy of an
iguana's cave. Far from the ocean, no women, speaking a language
of mental defectives. And in the meantime Abdul Bashur—my
dear comrade of so many nights on the shores of the Bosphorus, so
many memorable attempts to make easy money in Valencia and
Toulouse—waits for me and probably thinks I've died. I'm really
intrigued: these disasters, these decisions that are wrong from the

start, these dead ends that constitute the story of my life, are repeated over and over again. A passionate vocation for happiness, always betrayed and misdirected, ends in a need for total defeat; it is completely foreign to what, in my heart of hearts, I've always known could be mine if it weren't for this constant desire to fail. Who can understand it? We're about to reenter the green tunnel of the menacing, watchful jungle. The stink of wretchedness, of a miserable, indifferent grave, is already in my nostrils.

* * *

MARCH 27

This morning, when we stopped to unload some drums of insecticide at a settlement occupied by the military, the Indians went ashore. That's when I learned that my hammock neighbor is named Ivar. They stood on the bank chirping, "Ivar, Ivar," while he smiled as sweetly as a Protestant pastor. When night fell we were lying in our hammocks, the Coleman unlit to keep away the insects, and I asked him in German where he was from; he said Parnu, in Estonia. We talked until very late about our memories and experiences of places we both knew. As so often happens, language suddenly reveals a person entirely different from the one we had imagined. He strikes me as extremely cold, hard, cerebral—a man who feels absolute contempt for his fellow creatures, which he masks with formulas that he's the first to admit are false. Very dangerous. His comments on the erotic episode with the Indian couple amounted to an icy, cynical treatise by someone who has turned his back not only on modesty or social convention but on the most elementary, simple tenderness. He says he's going to the sawmill too. When I called it a factory, he began a confused explanation of what the installations actually contained, and this plunged me even further into despair and uncertainty. Who knows what's in store in that hollow at the foot of the cordillera? Ivar. Then, as I slept, I realized why the name was so familiar. Ivar was the cabin boy knifed to death on the *Morning Star* by a chief petty officer who insisted he'd stolen his watch when they went ashore to a brothel in Pointe-à-Pitre. Ivar, who could recite entire passages from Kleist and whose mother had made him a sweater that he wore proudly on cold nights. In my dream he welcomed me with his warm, innocent smile and tried to explain that he wasn't the other one, the one in the next hammock. I understood his concern immediately and assured him I knew that very well and there was no chance for confusion. I'm writing now at daybreak, when it's relatively cool. The long inquiry into the assassination of the Duke of Orléans is beginning to bore me. Only the most primitive, sordid desires can survive and grow in the irresistible flood of imbecility that washes over us in this climate.

But as I think of my recurrent failures, of how I keep giving destiny the slip in the same mindless way, I realize suddenly that another life has been flowing next to mine. Another life right beside me and I didn't know it. It's there, it goes on, it's composed of all the times I rejected a bend in the road or refused another way out, and the sum total of these moments has formed the blind current of another destiny that could have been mine, and in a sense still is mine, there on the opposite bank that I've never visited although it runs parallel to my ordinary life. Alien it may be, yet it carries all the dreams, illusions, plans, decisions, that are as much mine as this uneasiness I feel, that might have shaped the events of a history taking place now in the limbo of contingency. A history perhaps identical to the one I've lived, yet full of everything that didn't happen here but exists there, taking shape, flowing beside me like ghostly blood that calls my name yet knows nothing of me. The same insofar as I would have been the protagonist and colored it with my usual clumsy foundering, yet completely different in its events and characters. When the end comes, I think this other life, filled with the sorrow of something utterly lost and wasted, should pass before my eyes, and not my real life—its contents don't deserve the reconciliation of scrutiny, it isn't worth very much, I don't want it to be the sight that eases my final moment. Or my first? That's something to think about some other time. The enormous dark butterfly beating its woolly wings against the glass shade of the lamp is beginning to paralyze my attention, throwing me into an immediate, intolerable, disproportionate panic. I'm drenched in sweat as I wait for it to stop flying around the light and escape back to the night it belongs to. Ivar doesn't even notice my temporary paralysis as he turns off the lamp and falls asleep, breathing deeply. I envy his indifference. Is there a crack in some hidden corner of his being where unknown terror lies in wait? I don't think so. That's why he's dangerous.

* * *

We're stranded again on sandbanks that formed in minutes while we pulled ashore for repairs. Yesterday two soldiers came aboard who have malaria and are heading for the frontier post to recuperate. They lie on the palm leaves and shiver with fever, but they never let go of the rifles that knock with monotonous regularity against the metal deck.

I know it's naive and useless, but I've established certain precepts, one of my favorite exercises. It makes me feel better, makes me think I'm bringing order to something inside me. Remnants of life at the Jesuit academy, they do no good, lead nowhere, but they have that quality of benign magic I always turn to when I feel the foundations giving way. Here they are:

Thinking about time, trying to find out if past and future are valid and, in fact, exist, leads us into a labyrinth that is no less incomprehensible for being familiar.

Every day we're different, but we always forget that the same is true for others as well. Perhaps this is what people call solitude. If not, it's solemn imbecility.

When we lie to a woman, we revert to the helpless boy who has nowhere to turn in his vulnerability. Women, like plants, like jungle storms, like thundering waters, are nourished by the most obscure designs of heaven. It's best to learn this early on. If we don't, devastating surprises await us.

A knife in the body of a sleeping man. The bare lips of a wound that does not bleed. Vertigo, the death rattle, the final stillness. Like certain truths that life fires at us—insoluble, unerring, erratic, indifferent life.

Some things must be paid for, others remain debts forever. That's what we believe. The trap lies in the "must." We go on paying, we go on owing, and often we don't even know it.

Hawks screaming above the precipices and circling as they hunt their prey are the only image I can think of to evoke the men who judge, legislate, govern. Damn them.

A caravan doesn't symbolize or represent anything. Our mistake is to think it's going somewhere, leaving somewhere. The caravan exhausts its meaning by merely moving from place to place. The animals in the caravan know this, but the camel drivers don't. It will always be this way.

Putting your finger in the wound. A human occupation, a debased act no animal would be capable of. The inanity of prophets and fortune-tellers. A gang of charlatans, yet so many seek them out and listen to them.

Everything we can say about death, everything we try to embroider around the subject is sterile, entirely fruitless labor. Wouldn't it be better just to be quiet and wait? Don't ask that of humans. They must have a profound need for doom; perhaps they belong exclusively to its kingdom.

A woman's body under the rush of a mountain waterfall, her brief cries of surprise and joy, the movement of her limbs in the rapid foam that carries red coffee berries, sugar cane pulp, insects struggling to escape the current: this is the exemplary happiness that surely never comes again.

In the ruins of the Krak of the Knights of Rhodes, standing on a cliff near Tripoli, a nameless tombstone bears this inscription: "This was not where." Not a day goes by that I don't think about those words. They're so clear, and at the same time they contain all the mystery it is our lot to endure.

Is it true we forget most of what has happened to us? Isn't it more likely that a portion of the past serves as a seed, an unnamed incentive for setting out again toward a destiny we had foolishly abandoned? A crude consolation. Yes, we do forget. And it's just as well.

It turns out that stringing together these hackneyed words of wisdom, these inane fake pearls born of idleness and the obligatory wait for the current to change its mood, has left me with even less of the energy I need to face the crushing hardship of this hellish climate. Once again I read the names and biographical sketches of those who attacked the Duke of Orléans on his gloomy corner of the Rue Vielle-du-Temple, and learn of their subsequent punishment at the hands of God or men, for both were involved.

* * *

One of the soldiers died the day before yesterday. The sandbanks had just dissolved and the engine had started up, when one of the rifles suddenly stopped banging. The pilot called me to help him examine the body lying motionless in a puddle of sweat that was soaking through the palm leaves, its eyes staring at the thick jungle growth. His companion had taken the dead man's rifle and was looking at him, not saying a word. "He has to be buried right away," said the pilot in the tone of someone who knows what he's talking about. "No," answered the soldier, "I have to take him to the post. His things are there and the lieutenant has to make his report." The pilot said nothing, but it was clear that time would prove him right. Today, in fact, we pulled ashore to bury the body; it had swollen to monstrous size and gave off a stench that attracted a cloud of vultures. The king of the flock, a beautiful jet-black bird with an orange ruff and an opulent crown of pink feathers, had already settled on the framework supporting the canvas in the stern. A sky-blue membrane blinked down over his eyes as regularly as a camera shutter. We knew the others would never approach until he'd had his first peck at the corpse. When we dug the grave where the beach meets the jungle, he watched from his vantage point with a dignity not free of a certain disdain. And it must be noted that the beauty of the majestic creature lent the hurried funeral an air of heraldry and military arrogance in harmony with the silence that was barely broken by the slap of the current against the flat-bottomed boat.

We are traveling through a region of clearings so regularly spaced they seem man-made. The river is growing calmer, and the water's resistance to our progress is hardly noticeable. The surviving soldier is past the crisis and takes the white quinine pills with military resignation. Now he is in charge of both weapons and never lets them go. He chats with us under the captain's umbrella and tells us stories about the advance posts and how they get on with the soldiers across the border, about the bar fights on holidays that always end in several deaths on both sides, and how the dead are buried with military honors as if they had fallen in the line of duty. He has an uplander's cunning, and when he speaks he hisses the *s* and pronounces words with that peculiar rapidity which makes his sentences difficult to understand until we grow used to the rhythm of a language intended to conceal more than it communicates. When Ivar begins to ask details about the equipment and the number of conscripts stationed at the frontier post, the soldier half closes his eyes, gives a sly smile, and comes up with an answer that has nothing to do with the question. In any event he doesn't seem to like us very much, and I don't think he's forgiven us for burying his companion without his consent. But there's another, simpler reason. Like every person who has received military training, for him civilians are a kind of slow-witted obstacle that must be protected and tolerated; we're forever involved in shady deals and flagrantly stupid enterprises and we don't know how to command or obey, which is to say we cannot pass through this world without sowing disorder and unrest. Every one of his gestures tell us so. At bottom I feel envy, and although I'm constantly trying to undermine his unshakable system, I must recognize that it is what protects him from the silent ruination of the jungle, while the ominous signs of its effects on us become increasingly apparent.

The pilot prepares simple, monotonous food: rice cooked to a shapeless paste, beans with dried meat, fried plantains. Then a cup of something that passes for coffee but is really a watery slop of indefinable taste, with pieces of unrefined sugar that leave a worrisome sediment of insect wings, plant residues, and fragments of uncertain origin at the bottom of the cup. No one has alcohol except the captain, who always carries his canteen of aguardiente. He drinks with implacable regularity and never offers any to the other passengers. But it isn't the kind of liquor you'd want to taste, because judging by the captain's breath, it must be the worst bootleg cane liquor from some settlement in the interior, and its effects are all too obvious.

After supper, when the soldier finished his stories and the others had gone, I stayed in the bow hoping for a cool breeze. The captain sat with his legs hanging over the side and puffed on his pipe. Smoke is supposed to keep mosquitoes away, and in this case I wouldn't be surprised if it did, considering the filthy stuff he uses—its acrid smell bears no resemblance to tobacco. He was feeling communicative, which is rare for him, and he began to tell me the story of his life, as if the soldier's talkativeness had loosened his tongue by a process of osmosis that is very common when people are traveling. I couldn't help being interested in what I managed to understand of his disjointed monologue, spoken in a gravelly voice and filled with long, rambling circumlocutions that made no sense. Some episodes seemed familiar and might well have come from certain periods in my own life.

He was born in Vancouver. His father was a miner and later a fisherman. His mother was an Indian who ran away with his father. Her brothers chased them for weeks, and then one day his father arranged with a tavern owner he knew to make them drunk. When the brothers left, he was waiting for them on the outskirts of town, and that was where he killed them. The Indian girl approved of what her man had done, and they were married a few days later in a Catholic mission. The couple led an itinerant life. When he was born, they left him with the mission nuns. One day they never came back. When he was fifteen, the boy ran away and began to work as a cook's helper on the fishing boats. Later he signed on an oil tanker bound for Alaska. Then he sailed on the same ship to the Caribbean, and for a few years he made the run between Trinidad and the South American coastal cities, carrying airplane fuel. The ship's captain, a German with one leg who had been a submarine commander and had no family, took a liking to the boy and taught him the rudiments of navigation. From morning till night the German drank a mixture of champagne and light beer and ate sandwiches of black bread and herring, Roquefort cheese, salmon, or anchovy. One morning he was found dead, sprawled on the floor of his cabin and clutching the Iron Cross he kept under his pillow and showed off proudly during the high tides of his drunkenness. That was when the young man began a long pilgrimage through the ports of the Antilles that brought him to Paramaribo, where he set up housekeeping with a madam of mixed black, Dutch, and Hindu blood. Immensely fat and good-natured, she constantly smoked slender cigars made by the girls in the house. She loved gossip and managed her business with admirable skill. He developed a taste for rum with melted sugar and lemon, and ran three billiard tables located at the entrance to the establishment, more to distract the authorities than to entertain the clients. Several years passed; the couple got along and complemented each other in so exemplary a fashion that they became an institution, a topic of conversation throughout the islands. One day a Chinese girl came to work in the house. Her parents had sold her to the madam and used the money to establish themselves in Jamaica. They wrote two or three postcards and then were never heard from again. The new girl—tiny, silent, speaking no more than a few words of Curaçao pidgin—had not yet turned sixteen. She caught the sailor's eye, and he took her to his room a few times under the madam's tolerant, distracted gaze, but then he fell passionately in love with the girl and ran away with her, taking some of the madam's jewelry and the small amount of money kept in the billiard room cashbox. They wandered the Caribbean for a time and then sailed to Hamburg on a Swedish freighter, where he worked as a helper in the hold. In Hamburg they spent the little money they had saved, and she went to work in a Sankt-Pauli cabaret. Her number was a set of complicated erotic calisthenics performed with two other women on a small stage. The three of them spent many hours in an inexhaustible pantomime that excited the patrons but left them cold. They had robots' smiles on their faces and the unflagging elasticity of contortionists in their bodies. Then the Chinese girl did a routine with a huge Tartar suffering from giantism and a pallid clarinetist who made her musical commentary on the sketch assigned to the other two. One day the captain—that's what he was called by then—found himself implicated in a heroin-smuggling deal, and he had to leave Hamburg, and the girl, to avoid capture by the police.

Then the captain told an incomprehensible story that had something to do with Cádiz and the manufacture of signal flags that were altered almost imperceptibly to allow ships carrying illegal cargo to communicate with each other. I couldn't tell if the cargo was weapons, Levantine laborers, or raw uranium ore. Here too the story involved women. One of them talked, and the Civil Guard raided the shop where the altered flags were made. I didn't understand how the captain managed to escape in time, but he landed in Belém do Pará, where he traded in semiprecious stones and sailed upriver, engaging in all kinds of transactions. By this time he had fallen into hopeless alcoholism. He bought the barge at a military post where obsolete army equipment was sold at auction, and he sailed the intricate web of tributaries that crisscross the jungle in a dizzying labyrinth. Although he is enveloped in an alcoholic fog that dulls his faculties, for inexplicable reasons that escape all logic he has preserved both an infallible ability to orient himself and a power of command over his subordinates, who feel toward him a mixture of fear and unreserved trust that he exploits unscrupulously, and with cunning patience.

* * *

The climate is gradually changing. We must be approaching the foothills of the cordillera. The current is stronger, and the riverbed is narrowing. In the mornings the birdsong sounds closer and more familiar, and the smell of vegetation is more noticeable. We're leaving behind the cottony jungle humidity that blunts the senses and distorts our perception of every sound, smell, or shape. The breeze at night is cooler and lighter. Its dying, sticky breath once kept us awake. At dawn I had a dream belonging to a very special group that come to me whenever I get close to the hotlands, with their coffee plantations, bananas, swollen murmuring rivers, interminable rains at night. The dreams announce happiness and release a peculiar energy, an anticipation of joy that is, of course, ephemeral and soon turns into the inevitable atmosphere of defeat I know so well. But that flash of lightning, gone almost at once, is enough for me to foresee better days, enough to sustain me in the chaotic landslide of schemes and wretched adventures that constitute my life. In the dream I take part in a historic moment, a crossroads in the destiny of nations, and at the critical moment I offer an opinion, a piece of advice that completely alters the course of events. My participation is so decisive, the solution I propose so brilliant and just, that it becomes the source of a confidence in my own powers that sweeps away shadows and guides me with such intensity toward the enjoyment of my own plenitude that the dream's restorative power lasts for several days.

I dreamed I had a meeting with Napoleon in a Flemish country house in Genappe or its environs, on the day after Waterloo. The Emperor, in the company of several stunned aides and civilians, is striding around a small room containing a few pieces of rickety furniture.

He greets me absentmindedly and continues his agitated pacing. "What do you plan to do, Sire?" I ask in the warm, firm tone of someone who has known him a long time. "I will surrender to the English. They are honorable soldiers. England has always been my enemy but they respect me, and they are the only ones who can guarantee my safety and the safety of my family." "That would be a grave error, Majesty," I respond with the same firmness. "The English are a perfidious people without honor, and their war on the seas has been filled with sly trickery and cynical piracy. They are islanders, which makes them suspicious, and they see the rest of the world as an enemy." Napoleon smiles and answers, "Have you forgotten, perhaps, that I am a Corsican?" I overcome the embarrassment I feel at my slip and continue arguing in favor of an escape to South America or the Caribbean islands. The others join in the discussion; the Emperor vacillates but finally accepts my suggestion. We travel to a port that resembles Stockholm, and set sail for South America in a steamer that is propelled by a large side wheel yet still carries sails to supplement its boilers. Napoleon remarks on the strangeness of such a peculiar ship, and I tell him that in South America they have been used for many years, that they are very fast and safe and the English will never be able to overtake us. "What is this vessel called?" Napoleon asks, his curiosity mixed with distrust. *"Marshal Sucre,* Sire," I reply. "Who was he? I have never heard that soldier's name before." I tell him the story of the Marshal of Ayacucho and the treacherous plot to assassinate him in the mountains of Berruecos. "And is that where you are taking me?" Napoleon rebukes me severely, looking at me with open distrust. He orders his officers to arrest me, and just as they are about to seize me, a change in the sound of the engines leaves them perplexed as they stare at the thick black smoke pouring out of the smokestack. I wake up. For a moment I still feel relief at being free, and satisfaction at giving timely advice to the Emperor and thereby sparing him the years of humiliation and misery on Saint Helena. Ivar looks at me in astonishment, and I realize I am laughing in a way that must seem inexplicable and disturbing. We've come to the first, almost imperceptible rapids. The motor's efforts have redoubled. That was the noise that woke me. The barge rocks and pitches as if it were shaking itself awake. A flock of parrots crosses the sky with a joyful gabble that fades in the distance like a promise of good fortune and unlimited opportunity.

The soldier announces that we'll soon reach the military post. I thought I caught a flash of uneasiness and disguised uncertainty on the faces of the pilot and the Estonian. Something is going on between these two; they're partners in some crooked deal, some dirty business. I took advantage of a moment when the captain was reasonably lucid and they were talking in low voices with the soldier, the three of them lying in the bow and pouring water on their faces to cool themselves, to ask if he knew what they were up to. He gave me a long look and would only say, "They'll end up six feet under one of these days. People already know more about them than they should. It's not the first time they've made this trip together. I could settle accounts with them now, but I'd just as soon let somebody else do it. They're a pair of fools. Nothing for you to worry about." Since a good part of my life has been wasted in dealing with fools just like them, it's not worry I feel but weariness as I watch the approach of one more episode in the old, tired story of the men who try to beat life, the smart ones who think they know it all and die with a look of surprise on their faces: at the final moment they always see the truth—they never really understood anything, never held anything in their hands. An old story, old and boring.

* * *

APRIL 12

At noon we heard the whine of a motor. A few minutes later a Junker seaplane, a model from the heroic days of aviation in the region, was circling the barge. I didn't think any were still in service—a six-seater with a fuselage made of corrugated metal. The motor tended to sputter, and when it did, the plane descended to water level in case the engine failed. A quarter of an hour later it flew out of sight, to the relief of the river pilot and Ivar, who had been tense and guarded the whole time it was flying around us. We ate the usual rations and were taking our siesta when the Junker suddenly landed on the water in front of us and approached the barge. An officer in a khaki shirt, wearing no cap or insignia, climbed down to the floats, pointed to a spot, and ordered us to pull ashore. His tone was authoritative and boded no good. We did as he ordered and were followed by the Junker, its engine at half speed. We moored, and two officers with pistols in their holsters climbed down from the plane and immediately jumped to the barge. Neither one had insignias, but their manner and tone of voice testified to their rank. The pilot of the Junker still wore his tattered flying gloves, and on his shirt he displayed the silver wings of the Air Force. He stayed at the controls while the two officers ordered us to bring our papers and stand under the canvas in the stern. The soldier went straight to his superiors, one of them took the dead man's rifle, and the officer who ordered us ashore began to question us, not even looking at our papers in his hand. It was clear he knew the captain and the mechanic. His only question to the captain was where he was going. The captain said to the sawmill, and then he took refuge under the umbrella after a drink from his canteen. The mechanic went back to his engine. The interrogation of the pilot and Ivar was much more detailed, and as their answers became vaguer and their fear more evident, the other officer and the soldier trotted to a position behind the suspects to prevent them from jumping into the water. When the first officer finished with them, he came over to me and asked my name and the purpose of my trip. I told him my name. The captain didn't allow me to continue and answered, "He's coming with me to the sawmill. He's a friend." The officer didn't take his eyes off me and seemed not to hear the captain's words. "Are you carrying weapons?" he asked with the dry voice of a man accustomed to command. "No," I answered quietly. "No sir, even if it takes a little more time," he added, tightening his lips. "Do you have any money?" "Yes . . . sir, a little." "How much?" "Two thousand pesos." He knew I wasn't telling the truth. He turned his back on me to give an order. "Put those two on the plane." The pilot and the Estonian made some effort to resist, but when they felt the rifle muzzles against their backs, they obeyed meekly. They were about to climb into the cabin, when the officer shouted, "Tie their hands behind their backs, assholes!" "There's no rope, Major," the other officer apologized. "With their belts, damn it!" While the soldier covered them with his rifle, the officer laid his weapon on the floor of the cabin and tied the prisoners with their own belts. The grotesque postures they assumed to keep their trousers from falling produced no reaction in anyone. They were put in the seaplane behind the pilot. The major stood looking at us and then turned to the captain and spoke to him in a neutral, less military tone. "I don't want any problems, Cap. You've always known how to handle yourself here and stay out of trouble—just keep on like that and we'll get along like we always have. And you"—he pointed his finger at me as if I were a recruit—"you do what you came to do and get out. We don't have anything against outsiders, but the fewer who come here the better. Watch your money. You can tell that fairy tale about two thousand pesos to your mother, but not to me. I don't care how much you have, but you ought to know that around here they'd kill you for ten centavos to buy some aguardiente. As for the sawmill, well, you'll find out for yourself. I want to see you going back down the Xurandó pretty damn quick, that's all." He turned without saying goodbye and climbed in beside the pilot, slamming the door with a clang of ill-fitting metal that echoed along both banks of the river. The Junker moved away and then climbed slowly, painfully, almost touching the treetops, until it disappeared in the distance.

The captain hadn't seemed to hear the major. He continued sitting in the hammock, not saying a word. Then he raised his head in my direction and said, "We're saved, friend, saved by the skin of our teeth. I'll tell you about it later. I had no idea he was back in command of the base. He knows about everybody around here. They transferred him to the General Staff, and I thought he wouldn't be back. That's why I took a chance with those two. I don't know why he didn't nab us too. He's arrested lots of people for less cause. I'll see if I can get another pilot at the post. I can't do that work anymore. You know where the supplies are. I don't eat much, so you'll have to make your own food. Don't worry about me. The mechanic can take care of himself too. He can't do the cooking anyway because he has to take care of the engine. He brings his own food and fixes it his own way down below. All right, let's go." The mechanic returned to the bow to take the pilot's place. He backed into the middle of the current and continued upriver. As night approaches, I realize that the tension is disappearing, the rarefied, malignant atmosphere the pilot and Ivar created with their exchanges of looks, their whispers, their unsettling, corrupt presence. The mechanic's blind loyalty to the captain, his silent devotion to the task of maintaining an engine that should have been junked and sold for scrap years ago, give him an air of ascetic heroism.

* * *

APRIL 13

This contact with a world erased from memory by distance and the torpor in which the jungle buries us has, in a way, been encouraging despite the danger signs in the major's words and peremptory warnings. This very danger, in fact, returns me to the daily routine of the past, and the activation of my defenses, the alertness I need to face fairly predictable difficulties, are further incentives to shake off my apathy and climb out of the impersonal, paralyzing limbo I settled into with alarming willingness.

The vegetation is thinning out, becoming less dense. The sky is visible for a good part of the day. At night, close and familiar as they always are at the equator, the stars shine with a protective, watchful light that fills us with peace, with the certainty (fleeting, perhaps, but present in the restorative hours of night) that matters are following their course with the same fatal regularity that sustains us, time's human offspring, destiny's obedient children. I'm running out of the billing and customs forms I found in the hold, which the captain gave to me for writing this diary, my only escape from the tedium of the voyage. The indelible pencil is almost used up too. The captain claims I can get a new supply of paper and another pencil at the military base when we arrive there tomorrow. I can't imagine asking for so simple and openly personal a favor from the authoritarian major, whose voice still rings in my ears. Not the words but the metallic flat tone, as sharp as a gunshot, that leaves us defenseless, vulnerable, ready to obey blindly and in silence. I'm aware this is new for me, that I've never experienced anything like it, not at sea or in any of my various occupations and transformations on land. Now I understand how those incredible cavalry charges were accomplished. I wonder if what we call courage is simply unconditional surrender to the uncontrollable, neutral, overwhelming energy of an order issued in that tone of voice. More thought should be given to this.

* * *

Daybreak. We've arrived at the post. The Junker, tied to a small wooden dock, rocks with the current. This plane from another time, with its corrugated metal, painted black nose, radial motor, and half-rusted wings, is an anachronism, an aberrant ghost that I won't know where to place in my memory later on. The base consists of a structure built parallel to the riverbed, with a zinc roof and metal mosquito netting on wooden stretchers. A small headquarters is in the center, and in front of that a flag flies from a pole standing in the middle of a patch of leveled ground that soldiers under disciplinary action spend the day sweeping. The two wings of the building contain hammocks for the troops and small cubicles for the officers, with a single hammock in each. We were met by a sergeant who took us to headquarters. The major greeted us as if he'd never seen us before. He wasn't polite, and his military manner hasn't changed, but he maintains an indifference and a distance that alleviate our fear of awakening his animosity and, at the same time, indicate that his vigilance hasn't weakened but only moved away slightly to include other areas of the post's daily routine.

They put us up at the far end of the wing on the right. The mechanic preferred to return to the barge and sleep in his hammock beside the engine. We ate outside with the soldiers at a long table behind the building. Some river fish, and the chance to drink it down with beer, made the meal seem like an unexpected banquet. After we ate, the soldier who had traveled with us came over to say hello. We lit the cigars he offered us and smoked, more to keep the mosquitoes away than for the pleasure of tasting the tobacco, which was very strong. We asked about the prisoners taken away in the Junker. He didn't answer but looked up at the sky and then lowered his eyes to the ground with an eloquence that made further explanation unnecessary. There was a brief silence, and then in a voice that attempted to be natural he said, "Executions are noisy and you have to fill out a lot of forms, but this way they fall into the jungle where the ground is so marshy they dig their own graves on impact. Nobody asks questions and that's the end of it. There's a lot to do around here." The captain pulled on his cigar and looked toward the jungle, fingering his canteen like a man making sure he still has his charm against all misfortune. This summary method of eliminating undesirables was no news to him. As for me, I must confess that after the first chill down my spine I put the entire business out of my mind. As I think about it now, I realize that when life caves in on us, the first feeling to be blunted is pity. Human solidarity, so highly touted, has never meant anything concrete to me. We call on it in moments of panic when we tend to think about the help others can give us, not what we can offer them. Our traveling companion said good night, and for a while we contemplated the starry sky and the full moon, so disturbingly close we preferred to be in the room and rest in our hammocks. I'd asked our friend if he could get me some paper and a new pencil. In a little while he brought them and said, with a smile I couldn't decipher, "They're from the major. He wants me to say he hopes you use them to write what you ought to and not what you want to." It was clear he was repeating the message with an impersonal fidelity that made it even more sibylline. The stillness of the night and the absence of the noise of the motor, which I've grown used to, have kept me awake for some time. I'm writing in an effort to fall asleep. I don't know when we're leaving. The sooner the better. This isn't for me. Of all the places in the world I've been, and there are so many I've lost count, this is undoubtedly the only one where I've found everything hostile, alien, filled with a danger I don't know how to handle. I swear I'll never go through this again. I damn well didn't need it.

* * *

APRIL 15

This morning, as we were getting ready to leave, the Junker returned. It had left at dawn carrying the major and the pilot. The mechanic began to warm up the diesel engine, and the captain, with the new river pilot provided by the base, was loading provisions in the hold. A soldier called to me from shore. The major wanted to talk to me. The captain looked at me with suspicion and some fear. At that moment he was clearly thinking more about himself than about me. When I walked into headquarters, the major came out of his office. He made a gesture with his hand as if he wanted to take my arm for a stroll around the clearing. I followed him. His dark, regular features, adorned with a black mustache that he cared for meticulously but without vanity, wore an expression both ironic and protective, not quite cordial but inspiring a certain confidence.

"So you're determined to go all the way to the sawmills?" he asked as he lit a cigarette.

"Sawmills? I only heard about one."

"No, there are several," he answered, observing the barge with a distracted gaze.

"Well, I don't think that changes matters much. The important thing is to arrange to purchase the wood and then get it down-river," I said, while a familiar uneasiness came up through my stomach: it tells me when I'm beginning to stumble over the obstacles set up by reality if I've made the mistake of attempting to adjust it to the measure of my desires.

We finished our walk around the clearing. The major smoked with morose pleasure, as if this were the last cigarette of his life. Then he stopped, looked straight at me again, and said, "You'll manage one way or the other. It's none of my business. But I want to warn you about something: You're not a man who can spend much time here. You're from another place, another climate, another race. There's no mystery to the jungle, regardless of what some people think. That's its greatest danger. It's just what you've seen, no more, no less. Just what you see now. Simple, direct, uniform, malevolent. Intelligence is blunted here and time is confused, laws are forgotten, joy is unknown, and sadness has no place." He paused and exhaled a mouthful of smoke as he spoke. "I know you've heard about the prisoners. They each had enough history to fill many pages of an indictment that will never be filed. The Estonian sold Indians on the other side. The ones he couldn't sell he poisoned and dumped in the river. He sold weapons to the coca and poppy growers and then told us the location of their plantations and camps. He killed without reason, without anger. Just for the sake of killing. The pilot was no better, but he was smarter, and it wasn't until a few months ago that we could finally prove he took part in a massacre of Indians arranged to allow someone else to sell the lands they had received from the government. Well, there's no point in telling you any more about those two. Crime is boring too, and has few variations. What I wanted to say is this: If I send them under escort to the nearest court, it takes ten days. I endanger six soldiers, who run the risk of getting caught in a bribery scheme that can cost them their lives, or of being murdered by the criminals' accomplices in the settlements. Six soldiers are very valuable to me. Indispensable, in fact. They can mean the difference between life and death. Besides, the judges . . . Well, you can imagine. I don't have to spell it out for you. I'm telling you this not to excuse myself but to give you an idea of the way things are here." Another pause. "I see you've become the captain's friend, haven't you?" I nodded. "He's a good man as long as he has enough to drink. When he doesn't get his booze, he becomes another person. Be careful that doesn't happen. He loses his mind and is capable of the worst brutalities. Later he doesn't remember a thing. I've also noticed that you don't like barracks life or people in uniform. You're not entirely wrong. I understand perfectly. But somebody has to do certain jobs, and that's why there are soldiers. I've taken officer training courses up north. I was in France for two years on a joint military mission. It's the same everywhere. I think I know what kind of life you've led, and you may have had run-ins with my colleagues at one time or another. When we're not on duty, we're more bearable. Our work trained us to be . . . what you see." We were standing in front of the dock. "Well, I won't keep you any longer. Be careful. The pilot you're taking with you is a reliable man. Drop him off here on the way back. Don't trust anybody, and don't expect much from the Army; we're busy with other things. We can't worry about foreign dreamers. You understand what I'm saying." He offered his hand, and I realized it was the first time we'd shaken hands. We walked to the end of the dock. As I climbed onto the barge, he patted my shoulder and said in a low voice, "Keep an eye on the aguardiente. Don't let it run out." He waved goodbye to the captain and walked toward his office with a slow, elastic step, his body erect and a little stiff. We moved to the middle of the river and began to ride against the current and away from the camp, which was starting to blend into the edge of the jungle. An occasional flash of sunlight on the Junker's fuselage, like an ominous warning, showed us its location.

* * *

The new pilot is named Ignacio. His face is covered with pale wrinkles that make him look like a new-made mummy. When he talks he spits saliva through the few teeth left in his mouth, and he talks incessantly, more to himself than to anyone else. He respects the captain, whom he's known for a long time, and consequently he has a kind of friendship with the mechanic, to which he brings his conversation while the mechanic contributes his docile nature and inexhaustible talent for relating the life around him to the unpredictable behavior of the engine. Its sudden alterations threaten definitive, imminent collapse.

I was wrong to think that from now on the landscape and climate would become more and more like the hotlands. In the afternoon we entered the jungle again, the shadow created by the canopy of treetops and vines that crisscross from one bank to the other. The motor echoes like sounds in a cathedral. The incessant noise of birds, monkeys, insects. I don't know how I'll ever get to sleep. "The sawmills, the sawmills," I repeat in my mind to the rhythm of the water slapping against the prow. This was fated to happen to me. To me and nobody else. Some things I'll never learn. Their accumulated presence in one's life amounts to what fools call destiny. Cold comfort.

Today, during my siesta, I dreamed about places. Places where I've spent long, empty hours, and yet they're filled with some secret significance. They're the source of a message that is attempting to reveal something to me. The mere fact that I've dreamed about them is in itself a prophecy, but I can't decipher its meaning. Maybe if I list the places I'll discover what they're trying to tell me:

A waiting room in the station of a small city in the Bourbonnais. The train is due after midnight. The gas stove gives off too little heat, along with a swampy odor that clings to one's clothes and lingers on the damp-stained walls. Three faded posters proclaim the marvels of Nice, the charms of the Breton coast, the delights of winter sports in Chamonix. They only add to the sadness of the surroundings. The room is empty. The small alcove for the tobacco stand, which also sells coffee and croissants protected from flies by a glass cover on which suspicious traces of grease mix with the dust that floats through the air, is closed off with wire grating. I sit on a bench that is so hard I can't find a comfortable spot to fall asleep. I shift position from time to time and look at the tobacco stand, and at the covers of some crumpled magazines in a display case that is also behind the wire grating. Someone is moving inside. I know this is impossible because the stand is up against a corner where there are no doors. And yet it's increasingly clear that someone is locked inside. The figure signals to me, and I can make out a smile on the blurred face but can't tell if it's a man or a woman. I walk to the stand, my legs numbed by cold and the uncomfortable position I've been in for so many hours. Someone inside is murmuring unintelligible words. I put my face up to the grating and hear a whispered "Further away, maybe." I put my fingers inside the wire, I try to move the grate, and just then someone walks into the waiting room. I turn around and see the guard in his regulation cap. He has one arm, and the sleeve of his tunic is pinned to his chest. He looks at me with suspicion, offers no greeting, and walks to the stove to warm himself, clearly intending to demonstrate that he's there to prevent any infringement of station rules. I go back to my seat in a state of unspeakable agitation: my heart is pounding, my mouth is dry, and I'm certain I've ignored a decisive message that will not be repeated.

In a swamp where clouds of mosquitoes approach and suddenly move away in dizzying spirals, I see the wreck of a large passenger seaplane. A Latecoére 32. The cabin is almost intact. I go in and sit down on a wicker seat with a little folding table in front of it. The interior has been invaded by plants that cover the walls and ceiling. High-colored, almost luminous yellow flowers resembling guaiacum blossoms hang down gracefully. Everything of any value was stripped away long ago. The atmosphere inside is serene and warm, an invitation to stay and rest for a while. A large bird—its breast an iridescent copper color, an orange marking on its beak—flies in through one of the windows, where the glass has been missing for years. It lands on the back of a seat three places in front of me and looks at me with small, copper-flecked eyes. Suddenly it begins to sing in an ascending trill that comes to an abrupt halt, as if my presence won't allow it to finish the phrase begun with so much verve. It flies along the ceiling of the Laté looking for a way out, and when it finally goes, leaving the echo of its song in the plant-filled interior, I feel as if I'd fallen under the evil spells reserved for those who visit forbidden places. Something has struck the helm in the most secret part of my soul, and I couldn't have done anything to prevent it; it didn't even know I was there.

A battlefield. The action ended the day before. Looters in turbans are stripping the corpses. The humid heat weakens one's limbs, like fever with no delirium. Among the fallen are bodies in red tunics. The insignias have disappeared by now. I approach a corpse wearing wide, pistachio-colored silk trousers and a short jacket embroidered in gold and silver. These have not been stolen because the body is run through by a lance that goes deep into the ground and pins down the clothing. He is a high-ranking officer with a young face and a slender, sleek body. I know by his turban that he is a Mahratta. The looters have disappeared. A horseman in a red tunic approaches from the distance. He stops his horse in front of me and demands, "What do you want here?" "I'm looking for the body of Marshal Turenne," I respond. He looks at me in surprise. I know this is the wrong battle, the wrong century, the wrong combatants, but I can't correct my mistake. The man gets off his horse and explains with greater courtesy, "This is the battle-field of Assaye in lands that once belonged to Peshwah. If you wish to speak with Sir Arthur Wellesley, I can take you to him right now." I don't know what to answer. I stand there like a blind man trying to orient himself in a crowd. The horseman shrugs his shoulders. "I can do nothing for you." And he rides back the way he came. It begins to grow dark. I ask myself where Turenne's corpse can be, and at that moment I know it's all a mistake and there's nothing I can do. A smell of spices, of patchouli, of bandages that haven't been changed for days, of sun beating down on dead men, of recently oiled saber blades. I awake to the depressing certainty that I've taken the wrong road and will never find the orderliness, made to the measure of my longing, that was finally waiting for me.

I'm in a hospital. Around my bed is a curtain that screens it from the other beds in the room. I'm not sick and don't know why I've been brought here. I move the curtain to one side and see another curtain around another bed. A woman's arm moves it aside, and there is Flor Estévez, dressed in the kind of skimpy gown worn by patients who've had surgery. She smiles as she looks at me, while her breasts, thighs, and partially hidden sex are exposed with a candor not typical of her in real life. As always, her hair is as wild as the mane of a mythological beast. I go to her bed. We begin to caress with the feverish haste of those who know they don't have much time because someone is arriving shortly. As I'm about to enter her, the curtain is pulled back abruptly. Altar boys hold it open while a priest insists on giving me communion. I struggle to close the curtain. The priest keeps the host in a chalice, and an altar boy passes him a small silver box containing the holy oil. The priest attempts to give me the last rites. I look at Flor Estévez again, but she averts her eyes in shame, as if she had arranged it all for some purpose that escapes me. Flor dips her fingers in the oil and tries to rub my member while she sings a song whose sadness leaves me helpless, and I experience the awful deception of the inevitable outcome. All eroticism has vanished. I try to scream, as desperate as a drowning man. I wake to the sound of my own voice fading to a grotesque howl.

I'm engrossed in thinking about the message hidden in these visions. Night has fallen and the boat moves slowly. The pilot and the captain argue with a faint irritation that feels intimate and inoffensive. The captain is at the critical point of his drunkenness and resumes his senseless orders: "Find the wind, you stubborn old fool, find it or we're lost, damn it!" "Okay, Cap, okay, don't hassle me. If we're not moving, it's because we can't." The pilot responds with the patience of someone talking to a child. "Ignacio, you navigate like a snake with its head cut off—there's a reason they weren't using you anymore at the base. Steady on the rudder, damn it, it's not a soup spoon!" And so on for a good part of the night. It's obvious they really enjoy this. It's how they communicate. They're old friends, so old that everything's already been said. My siesta lasted too long and I won't fall asleep until daybreak. I read and write in turn. John the Fearless had no valid excuse. When he condemned the brother of the king of France to death, he condemned his own race to inevitable extinction. What a shame. Perhaps a kingdom of Burgundy would have been the appropriate response to the inexorable series of disasters that rained down on Europe.

* * *

As always, the possible keys to the visitations I experienced during yesterday's siesta have begun to reveal themselves today. They are my old demons, the stale phantoms that in different clothes, in another language, in a new twist of landscape, come to remind me of the constant threads that weave my destiny: living in a time completely alien to my interests and tastes, intimacy with the gradual dying that is each day's essential task, and the universe of eroticism always implicit for me in that task, my constant turning to the past in a search for the place and time when my life would have made sense, and a peculiar habit of always consulting the natural world and its presences, transformations, pitfalls, and secret voices, on which I still rely for the solution to my dilemmas and the final judgment on my actions, apparently so gratuitous but always obedient to their call.

Merely meditating on all of this has left me with a tranquil acceptance of the present that had seemed so confused and inimical to my affairs. Through an understandable error in perspective, I had been examining the present without taking into account those familiar elements revealed by yesterday's dreams. They were there, but I couldn't see them. I'm so accustomed to the prophetic quality of my dreams that although I haven't deciphered the message yet, I can already feel its beneficial, calming effect. I still don't understand Flor Estévez's actions: her initiative, her invitation to bed are so foreign to how she usually handles such situations. In fact, despite her savage appearance, her well-fleshed legs, her wild, disordered hair, her dark, rather moist skin, just slightly resistant to pressure as if it were made of invisible velvet, her full, sibyl's breasts partially exposed throughout the day—despite all these signs, Flor is a total stranger to flirtatious play and the sly erotic encounter. She erupts seriously, categorically, almost sadly, with the silent desperation of one who acts under the domination of an unleashed power, and she loves and takes her pleasure as wordlessly as a vestal. Perhaps Flor's provocative behavior in my dream is the result of my abstinence on this trip: the episode with the Indian was more disturbing then gratifying. It's more likely that it follows the classical confusion in dreams of traits and gestures belonging to different people. We can never be certain about the identity of the beings in our dreams. We never see just one person but a totality, an instantaneous, condensed parade of people rather than a single, definitive presence.

Flor Estévez. No one has been so close to me, no one has been so necessary to me, no one has cared for me with that secret tact buried in her wild, scowling aloofness so given to silence, to monosyllables, to simple grunts that neither affirm nor deny. When I talked to her about the lumber, her only comment was: "I didn't know you made money with wood. Houses, fences, boxes, shelves, whatever, but money? It's a fairy tale. Don't believe it." She went to the place where she hides her savings and gave me everything she had, without another word, without even looking at me. Flor Estévez, loyal and harsh in her anger, bold and sudden in her caresses. Absorbed, watching the fog roll in between the tall cámbulo trees, singing lowland songs, songs about fruit—joyful, innocent songs touched with a sharp nostalgia that remains forever in memory along with the tune and the transparent candor of their words. And here I am sailing up this river with a half-Comanche gringo drunk, a mute Indian in love with his diesel engine, and a ninety-year-old who looks as if he'd been born from the swelling bark of one of these gigantic trees with no name, no purpose. There is no cure for my reckless wandering, forever misguided and destructive, forever alien to my true vocation.

* * *

APRIL 20

We've entered another savanna, with small groves of trees and extensive marshes created by the floodwater. Flocks of herons cross the sky in regular formations that remind me of squadrons of reconnaissance planes. They circle the barge, land on the riverbank with impeccable elegance, and move in slow, prudent strides as they search for food. When a fish is caught, it struggles for a moment in the long bill, the heron shakes its head, and the victim disappears as if by magic. The sun goes down in a straight line over the featureless expanse of water gleaming through rushes and vines.

From time to time, as if to remind us of its imminent return, a small taste of jungle appears, a dense cluster of trees where you can hear the chatter of monkeys, the screech of parakeets and other birds, the regular, drowsy singing of giant crickets. The solitude of the place makes us feel defenseless, and despite the lethal stench that is always present to warn us of its devastating proximity, we don't really know what causes the feeling here and not in the jungle itself. I lie in the hammock and watch the scenery with apathetic indifference. The only variation I can detect is a gradual change in the light as the afternoon advances. The current offers almost no resistance to the boat's progress. The motor acquires an accelerated knocking rhythm, which is very suspicious given the engine's advanced age and demented unpredictability. All of this barely registers on the almost depersonalized surface of my mind. As always after one of my prophetic dreams, I've fallen into a state of marginal indifference bordering on muffled panic. I view this as an inevitable assault against my being, against the forces that sustain me, against the uncertain, vain hope, but hope after all, that someday things will be better and everything will start to work out. I've grown so accustomed to these brief periods of dangerous neutrality that I know I shouldn't examine them too carefully. That would merely prolong them. As with an accidental overdose of medicine, the effects will disappear only when the body absorbs the foreign substance that is poisoning it. The captain comes over to tell me that at nightfall we'll stop at a settlement for fuel and provisions. Remembering the major's recommendation, I ask about the condition of his canteen. He realizes I've been warned and answers with some annoyance: "Don't worry, my friend, I'll buy enough to last us the rest of the trip." He moves away, exhaling pipe smoke in the irritated manner of someone trying to defend an area of his inner life that has been trampled by strangers.

* * *

MAY 25

When we went ashore at the settlement, I never imagined I'd remain there for weeks, hovering between life and death, or that the entire aspect of the trip would change drastically into an exhausting struggle against total despair and attacks of something akin to madness.

The settlement is composed of six houses around a pasture trying to be a square. Two gigantic, incredibly leafy trees offer shade to the wretched inhabitants who gather there in the afternoon to sit on rough primitive benches hacked from tree trunks, smoking and commenting on the vague, always disquieting rumors that reach them from the capital. The only building with a zinc roof and brick walls is a school that also serves as a church when the missionaries come. It has one classroom, a small room for the teacher, and sanitary facilities that have fallen into disuse and are covered with mold and filled with indeterminate trash. The teacher was kidnapped by Indians over a year ago, and nothing more was heard about her until someone brought the news that she was living with a tribal chief and had no intention of returning. The military base keeps a meager complement of soldiers here, who sleep in hammocks hung in what was once the classroom. They spend the days cleaning their weapons and repeating a tedious litany of the minor miseries that nourish barracks life.

The captain provisioned his canteen, and we began carrying drums of diesel fuel to fill the storage tanks on the barge. The humidity, the unbearable heat, and too few hands made the work exhausting. Nobody wanted to help. The captain was drunker than ever, the pilot is so old he can hardly move, and the mechanic and I had to do it by ourselves under the indifferent gaze of the villagers, who are weakened by malaria and have the glassy, empty eyes of people who long ago lost all hope of escaping this place. On the afternoon of the first day I felt nauseated and had a dreadful headache, which I attributed to my having inhaled vapors from the fuel that we had to pour out with maddening slowness. The next day we continued the work. Rest and sleep seemed to have eased my symptoms somewhat, but at midday I began to feel an unbearable ache in all my joints, and shooting pains at the base of my skull immobilized me for minutes at a time. I went over to the captain to ask if he had any idea what was wrong with me. He looked at me for a time, and I could see by the expression on his face that it was serious. He took my arm, walked me to one of the hammocks in the school, helped me lie down, and had me drink a large glass of water with a few drops of a bitter, sticky, amber-colored liquid.

He said something to the soldiers in a low voice. It evidently had to do with my condition. They looked at me as if I were about to undergo a terrifying trial they were all familiar with. In a little while the captain returned with my hammock from the barge. He hung it at the far end of the room, away from the soldiers' hammocks, and almost carried me there, holding me under the arms. I realized I had lost all feeling in my feet and didn't know if I was dragging them or trying to walk. It began to grow dark. With the slight drop in temperature and an almost imperceptible breeze blowing off the river, I began trembling violently in a shiver that seemed to have no end. A soldier gave me a hot drink whose taste I couldn't recognize, and then I fell into a profound stupor that was close to unconsciousness.

I lost all sense of the passage of time. Day and night merged in dizzying confusion. Occasionally one or the other would stop for an eternity I made no attempt to fathom. The faces that looked at me were totally alien, bathed in an iridescent light that made them seem like creatures from an unknown world. I had ghastly nightmares about the corners of the ceiling and the seams where the sheets of zinc were joined. I kept trying to fit one corner into another by modifying the structure of the beams or realigning the rivets that joined the sheets so they wouldn't show the slightest variation or irregularity. I brought to these endlessly repeated tasks all the strength of will born of fever and maniacal obsession. It was as if my mind had suddenly become stuck in an elementary process of learning the space around me, a process that in ordinary life is unconscious but now had become the only purpose, the ultimate, necessary, and inevitable reason, for my existence. In other words, I was nothing else but that process, and that process was my only reason for living. As my obsessions persisted and became more frequent and at the same time more fundamental, I began to slip irreversibly into madness, an inert, mineral dementia in which I, or rather what I had once been, was breaking down at an uncontrollable rate. As I try to describe what I suffered then, I realize that words can't convey all the meaning I want to give them. How can I explain, for example, the icy panic I felt as I observed this monstrous simplification of my faculties and the immeasurable length of time I endured this torment? It's impossible to describe. Simply because in a certain sense it is alien and entirely contrary to what we usually think of as human consciousness: we don't become another being, we turn into another thing, a dense mineral composed of infinitely multiplying interior edges whose inspection and documentation constitute the very reason for our survival in time.

The first intelligible words I heard were: "The worst is over. It's a miracle he's alive." A khaki shirt with no markings of any kind, a swarthy face with regular features and a straight, dark mustache—someone was speaking from a distance that was incomprehensible, since he was just a few centimeters from my face, staring at me. I learned later that the major had come in the Junker. From the medical kit he always carried with him he had taken a medicine that they injected every twelve hours, and this apparently saved my life. They told me too that in my delirium I sometimes mentioned the name of Flor Estévez, and at other times I insisted on the need to go upriver and take San Juan fort, which was under siege by Captain Horatio Nelson just a few kilometers from Lake Nicaragua. It also seems I spoke in other languages that no one could identify, although the captain told me later that when he heard me shouting *"Godverdomme!"* he was certain I was out of danger.

I'm still weak, my limbs respond with irritating slowness, I eat without appetite, and nothing can quench my thirst. It's not a thirst for water but for some drink with an intense vegetable bitterness and a white aroma like mint. It doesn't exist, I know, but my specific, clearly identifiable longing for it does, and one day I intend to find the potion I dream about constantly. I write with enormous difficulty, yet at the same time, as I record these memories of my illness I free myself from the madness that came with it and did me the most harm. My improvement is steady and rapid, and at times I think it all happened to someone else, someone who was nothing but the madness and disappeared when it did. I know it's not easy to explain, but I'm afraid that if I try too persistently, I'm in danger of falling into one of those obsessive exercises—my terror of them is boundless.

This afternoon the mechanic came over and started talking to me in a rapid mix of Portuguese, Spanish, and some jungle dialect I couldn't identify. For the first time, and on his own initiative, he began a conversation with someone on the barge other than the captain, with whom he communicates in bare monosyllables. His face, with Indian features that one must scrutinize carefully to avoid a serious misreading of each expression, revealed an uneasiness that went beyond mere curiosity. He began by asking if I knew what disease I'd had. I told him I didn't. Then, as if astounded by an inexcusable ignorance that he considered extremely dangerous, he said, "You had ditch fever. It attacks whites who sleep with our women. It's fatal." I said I was under the impression that I was cured, and with somewhat cryptic skepticism he answered, "Don't be so sure. Sometimes it comes back." Something in his words made me think he was moved by tribal jealousy, the dark struggle against the foreigner, to make me suffer the kind of doubt that was fit punishment for my transgression against the unwritten laws of the jungle. In retaliation for his malice I asked what the whites who had habitual relations with Indian women did to avoid the terrible fever. "They always finish outside, señor. It's no secret." He reproached me with the same arrogance, as if he were talking with someone who wasn't worth too many details. "You have to wash afterwards with honey water and put a leaf of jimsonweed between your legs, even if it burns, even if it leaves a blister." He finished enlightening me as he turned away and went back to his engine with the air of a man who has been distracted from very important work by some unimportant piece of foolishness. At midnight I was reading when the captain came to ask how I was feeling. I told him what the mechanic had said, and he reassured me with a smile. "If you pay attention to everything they say, my friend, you'll go crazy. Just forget it. You're better now. What more do you want?" The smell of cheap aguardiente hung over the foot of the hammock as he walked to the bow, shouting his usual lunatic orders: "Half steam and look alive! Don't burn out my magnetos with your damned tapir grease, assholes!" His voice faded into the limitless night until it reached the stars, so close they had a delicious palliative effect.

* * *

MAY 27

The captain has stopped drinking. I noticed it just this morning when he joined us for our daily breakfast of coffee and fried plantain. After his coffee he always takes a long drink of aguar-

diente. He didn't today, and he wasn't carrying his canteen. I saw
a look of surprise on the mechanic's face, usually so impassive and
remote. Since I know the captain put in a generous supply at the
settlement, I don't think the reason is that he's run out of liquor.
I've been observing him all day, and I can detect no other change
except that he's also stopped giving those astonishing orders that
had become for me a kind of invocation necessary to the boat's
progress and the voyage in general. He didn't use the canteen all
day. At night he came to lie down in one of the empty hammocks,
and after a few preliminary remarks about the weather and the
possibility of really torrential rapids ahead, launched into a long
monologue about certain episodes in his life. "You can't imagine,"
he began, "what it meant for me to leave the Chinese girl in that
Hamburg cabaret. I never had much luck with women. Perhaps
the image I have of my mother is so different from the way white
women are that my dealings with them have always been condi-
tioned by my relationship to her. My mother was violent, silent,
and blindly devoted to the ancestral beliefs and daily rituals of her
tribe. She always thought whites were a necessary, unavoidable
incarnation of evil. I think she loved my father very much but
probably never showed it. My parents used to come to the mission
occasionally. They would stay a few weeks and then leave again.
During those visits my mother treated me with a gratuitous, almost
animal cruelty. She belonged to the Kwakiutl people. I never
learned a word of her language. I must have been marked for life,
because until I met the Chinese girl, women always left me.
There's something in me that they feel as rejection. I could have
spent the rest of my life with the madam in Guiana. Our affair was
based more on mutual interest than on sentiment. She was so
good-natured and easygoing, there was never any reason to quarrel
with her. In bed she displayed an unhurried, absentminded sensuality. Afterwards she would always burst into childish, almost innocent laughter. Everything changed when I met the girl. She penetrated a corner of my soul that had been kept sealed and even I
didn't know was there. With her gestures, the scent of her skin, her
sudden, intense glances that soon filled me with overwhelming
tenderness, with her dependence that was a kind of unthinking,
absolute acceptance, she could rescue me instantly from my confu-
sions and obsessions, my discouragement and failure, or my simple

daily routine, and leave me inside a radiant circle made of throbbing energy and powerful certainty, like the effects of an unknown drug that produces unconditional happiness. I can't think about all of this without asking myself how I could have left her for such trivial reasons, the kind of unimportant situation I had once faced very skillfully and settled almost effortlessly without ever being caught. Sometimes I wonder in desolate rage if I met her when it was too late, when I could no longer deal with so much life-giving joy, when the response that might have prolonged my happiness had already died. You understand what I'm saying. Some things come too soon and others come too late, but we only find out when there's nothing to be done, when we've already bet against ourselves. I think I know you well enough to suppose that the same kind of thing has happened to you and you know what I'm talking about. From the moment I left Hamburg, nothing has mattered. Something in me died forever. Alcohol and a passing acquaintance with danger have been the only things that gave me the strength to start again each morning. But I didn't know they could wear out too. Alcohol only provides a temporary reason for living, and danger disappears whenever we get close to it. It exists as long as we have it inside ourselves. When it leaves us, when we touch bottom and truly know we have nothing to lose and never did, danger becomes a problem for other people to deal with. Do you know why the major came back? That's why. I haven't talked to him about it, but we know each other well enough. While you were delirious in the classroom, we understood each other again. When I asked him why he had come back, all he would say was: "It's the same there as here, Cap, it's just faster here. You know that." And he's right. The jungle just speeds up the process. In and of itself it offers nothing unexpected, or exotic, or surprising. That's just the foolishness of people who live as if life lasted forever. There's nothing here, there'll never be anything here. One day it will disappear without a trace and fill up with roads, factories, people dedicated to working like mules for the empty thing they call progress. Well, it doesn't matter, I've never played that game. I don't even know why I mentioned it. What I wanted to tell you is not to worry. I didn't leave aguardiente, it left me. We'll keep going upriver. Like before. As long as we can. After that we'll see." He put his hand on my shoulder and stared at the current. He moved his hand away immediately. He didn't sleep but lay quiet and calm, with the serenity of the defeated. I write and then read, waiting for sleep. It always comes with the light breeze at daybreak. I'm certain the captain's words conceal a message, a secret sign that brings me a curious peace although it also tells me that the dice have been rolling for some time. The best thing is to let everything happen as it must. That's right. It's not a question of resignation. Far from it. It's something else, something to do with the distance that separates us from everything and everybody. One day we'll know.

* * *

MAY 30

In a curious way everything is becoming settled and calm. The dismal unknowns that loomed at the start of the trip have been clearing away, and now the outlook is simple and straightforward. The Indians left the barge and were forgotten. Ivar and his pal dug their own graves in the flooded earth of the jungle. The major has taken charge of us in a way that isn't explicit or even hinted at, but every day it becomes more evident. The captain stopped drinking and has entered a stage of peaceable dreaming, gentle nostalgia, harmless withdrawal. Day by day Ignacio seems to grow older and more like the protective jungle spirits. The mechanic has coaxed feats worthy of a cabalist from the motor. Along with the feeling that I've been saved by the skin of my teeth, convalescence affords me the tranquil security and invulnerable well-being of the chosen. I'm not oblivious to how precarious such guarantees can be, but as long as I submit wholeheartedly to their power, things file past in an orderly way and stay where they belong instead of attacking in an all-out assault on my identity. And this is why I can view even my relations with the Indian woman, and (if it's true) the fatal consequences I managed to escape, as trials I had to undergo in order to conquer the forces of this devouring, insatiable, vegetal universe which, I can see now, is simply one more place a man must visit to complete his passage through the world and avoid the torment of dying in the knowledge that he has dwelled in a limbo and turned his back on the splendid spectacle of life.

By the afternoon light, and even after I had to light the Coleman lamp, I continued reading Raymond's book on the assassination of the Duke of Orléans. There's a good deal to say about the matter. This isn't the time, and I'm not in the mood for that sort of speculation. But still, there's a curious lack of objectivity in the report on the crime submitted by the provost of Paris, and a concomitant lack of ill will on the part of the author who publishes and comments on it. The reasons for a political crime are always so complex, and the hidden, disguised motives mixed in with them so complicated, that recounting the facts in detail or recording what the people involved thought about it is not enough to form conclusions that are anywhere near definitive. The twisted soul of the Duke of Burgundy hides chasms and labyrinths infinitely more tortuous than anything the good provost can detect or Raymond attempt to elucidate. But what most attracts my attention, in this case and in all the others that have cost the lives of men who occupy an exceptional place in the chronicles, is the utter uselessness of the crime, the absolute lack of effect on the course of the shapeless, sightless magma that flows without definite purpose or reason and is called history. Only our incurable human vanity, the extraordinary narcissism of our claim to a place in the irresistible current that carries us, allows us to think that the assassination of a public figure can change a destiny that has been eternally charted in the infinite universe. But now it's my turn; I think I've exaggerated the true significance of the death of the Duke of Orléans. It's enough to trace the sordid envy and spite behind his assassination. Perhaps that's why the more I read the book, the less the issue interests me, and the more I assimilate it to the daily human spectacle wherever it may occur. In any one of the miserable hamlets we've passed, there's a John the Fearless, a Louis de Orléans, and a dark street corner like the one on the Rue Vielle-du-Temple, waiting for Orléans and his appointment with death. There's a monotony in crime, and it's not advisable to have too much to do with it in books or in life. Not even in their evildoing can humans surprise or intrigue each other. That's why the forest, the desert, the sea, do us good. I've always known it. Nothing new. I close the book, and a swarm of fireflies dances over the water, accompanies the boat for a while, and is lost finally in the distant swamps where the moon shines brightly and then hides behind the clouds. A cool breeze, the advance guard of an approaching squall, is carrying me gently toward sleep.

* * *

JUNE 2

This morning we passed a flat-bottomed barge very similar to ours. It was stranded in the middle of the river on sandbanks piled high with tree trunks and branches carried there by the current. It was heading downriver and had run aground during the night, when the pilot fell asleep. He's accompanied by a mechanic who watched, with resignation and indifference, as the pilot attempted to free the barge with a pole. While the captain tried to help by pushing against the side of their boat with our barge, I talked to the mechanic, who continued his skeptical observation of our efforts. I asked him about the sawmills. He told me they do, in fact, exist and are a week's travel away if we don't run into problems with the rapids upstream. He seemed intrigued by my interest in them. I told him I planned to buy lumber there and sell it in the ports along the river. He looked at me with a combination of bewilderment and irritation, and just as he began to explain something about the trees, the noise of our motor, accelerating and finally freeing the grounded barge, drowned out what he was saying. I shouted, asking him to repeat what he had said, but he shrugged his shoulders indolently and climbed down to start the motor while the rapid current was still pushing them forward. They disappeared around a bend in the river.

We continued upriver. I tried to learn more from the captain about what the other mechanic had begun to tell me. "Don't pay any attention," he commented. "There's a lot of stupid talk. You go and take a look and find out for yourself. I don't know much about it. The sawmills are real; I've seen them a few times and I've carried people who were working there. But they only speak their own language, and I haven't been interested in finding out what they do or what kind of business it is. They're Finns, I think, but they can understand a little German. But I'll say it again—don't pay attention to rumors or gossip. People here are very fond of making up stories. It's what keeps them alive in the settlements and army posts. They embroider and exaggerate and change them, and that's how they survive the boredom. Don't worry. You've gotten this far. Find out for yourself and then see what happens." I've been thinking about what the captain said, and I realize I've almost lost interest in the lumber. I wouldn't care if we turned back right now. I won't, through pure inertia. As if it were just a matter of making this trip, seeing the jungle and sharing the experience with the people I've met here, going back with new images, voices, lives, smells, deliriums, to add to all the other phantoms that walk with me, with no other purpose than to unravel the monotonous, tangled skein of time.

* * *

JUNE 4

The look of the current is changing radically. The bottom must be rough and rocky. The sandbanks have disappeared. The river is narrower and the first foothills are beginning to rise along the banks, exposing a reddish soil that sometimes resembles dried blood and then fades to a pinkish color. On these cliffs the tree roots are bared like recently polished bones, while their tops flower in an alternating rhythm of light violet and intense orange that almost seems intentional. The heat is increasing, but it no longer carries the suffocating, dense humidity that strips away all desire to move. Now a dry, burning heat envelops us and transmits intact the light that beats down on each object and endows it with absolute, inevitable presence. Everything is silent and seems to be waiting for some devastating revelation. The clattering engine is a blot on the rapt stillness all around us. The captain comes to warn me: "We'll be at the rapids in a little while. They're called Angel Pass. I don't know where the name comes from. Maybe it's because when you come downriver, this calm is waiting for you like a consolation and a promise that the danger is over. But when you travel upriver, the calm is deceptive, and that can be fatal for novices. This is where I always recite the prayer for travelers in mortal danger. I wrote it myself. Here. Read it. Even if you don't believe in it, at least it helps to take your mind off your fear." He handed me a paper in a plastic cover so smeared with the grease, mud, and grime that had accumulated with the passage of time and the touch of countless hands, that it was almost impossible to read the text, written on both sides of the paper in a haughty, angular, and defiantly clear feminine hand. I'll transcribe the captain's prayer as I wait for us to reach the rapids:

> High calling of my protectors, those who have gone before me, my constant guides and mentors,
>
> come now in this moment of danger, extend your sword, with firmness uphold the law of your purpose,
>
> revoke the disorder of birds and creatures of evil omen, wash clean the hall of innocents
>
> where the vomit of the rejected congeals like a sign of misfortune, where the garments of the supplicant
>
> are a blemish that deflects our compass, makes our calculations uncertain, our forecasts mistaken.
>
> I invoke your presence at this hour and deplore with all my heart the manacles of my equivocations:
>
> my pact with man-eating leopards in the mangers,
>
> my weakness and tolerance for serpents that shed their skin at the mere shout of lost hunters,
>
> my communion with bodies that have passed from hand to hand like a staff to ford a stream, and on whose skin the saliva of the humble is crystallized,
>
> my ability to contrive the lie of power and cleverness that moves my brothers away from upright steadiness in their purposes,
>
> my carelessness in proclaiming your power in customs offices and guardrooms, in pavilions of sorrow and on pleasure boats, in guard towers along the border and in the corridors of the powerful.
>
> Wipe away in a single stroke all this misfortune and infamy, save me,
>
> certain of my obedience to your bitter laws, your abusive haughtiness, your distant occupations, your desolate arguments.

*I give myself completely to the domination of your unobjection-
able mercy, and with all humility I prostrate myself at your feet*

*to remind you that I am a traveler in mortal danger, that my
ghost is worth nothing, that those who perish far from home are like
trash swept into a corner of the market,*

*that I am your servant and am helpless, and that these words
contain the unalloyed metal of one who has paid the tribute*

owed to you now and forever throughout pale eternity. Amen.

My doubts concerning the efficacy of so barbaric a litany were
certainly reasonable, but I didn't dare express them to the captain,
who had handed me the text with evident devotion and faith in its
preventive, protective powers. I went to the bow where he was
observing the whirlpools that were beginning to shake the boat, I
handed him the paper, and he put it in a back pocket where he also
keeps all the equipment for cleaning his pipe.

* * *

JUNE 7

We passed through the rapids without mishap, but in many ways
it was a revealing test of what, until yesterday, had been my image
of danger and the real presence of death. When I say "real," I mean
it wasn't the phantom we call up in our imagination and concretize
with elements taken from memories of the deaths we've witnessed
under a variety of circumstances. No. This was a matter of perceiv-
ing, with all the fullness of our mind and senses, the immediate,
unassailable proximity of our own death, the irrevocable cessation
of our existence. There, within reach, beyond defiance. A good
test, a long lesson. Come too late, like all the lessons that affect us
in a direct, profound way.

On the day the captain gave me his extraordinary prayer, the
mechanic decided we had to stop to overhaul the motor. When
you're going against the current in the rapids, an engine failure
means certain death. We pulled ashore, and he disassembled,

cleaned, and tested every part of the machine. It was fascinating to see the patient knowledge that an Indian from the most isolated regions of the jungle uses to identify with a mechanism invented and perfected in countries whose advanced civilization rests almost exclusively on technology. His hands are so skillful they seem guided by some tutelary spirit of machinery, one that is completely alien to this Indian with his flat Mongolian face and his skin as hairless as a snake's. He could not rest until he had meticulously tested each stage in the motor's operation. Then, with a slight movement of his head, he let the captain know it was ready to carry us upstream through Angel Pass. Night had fallen, and we decided to stay where we were until dawn. Beginning the ascent is not something one does in the dark. We set out the next day at first light. Contrary to what I supposed, the rapids were not created by rocks on the surface blocking the river's movement and making it more violent. It all takes place down below, where the riverbed is full of hollows, uneven surfaces, caves, eddies, faults, while at the same time the angle of descent grows steeper and the water, with constant changes in direction and intensity, pours down in a deafening whirlpool of crushing force.

"Don't lie in the hammock. Stay on your feet and hold tight to the bars under the canvas. Don't look at the current, and try to think about something else." Those were the captain's instructions. He stayed in the bow the whole time, clutching a precarious bridge and standing beside the pilot, who handled the rudder with abrupt movements in his effort to avoid the crash of water and foam that would loom suddenly like the back of some unimaginable beast. The engine was constantly out of water, the propeller whirling in air with runaway, uncontrolled speed. As we entered the ravine that the current had been gouging for centuries, the light turned gray and we were wrapped in a veil of foam and mist that rose from the turbulent whirl of water as it smashed against the polished rock surface of the channel walls. Night seemed to fall for hours. The barge pitched and shuddered as if it were made of balsa wood. Its metal structure echoed with a muffled rumble of distant thunder. The rivets that held the metal plates together vibrated and jumped, shaking the entire frame with the instability that precedes disaster. Hours passed, and we couldn't tell if we were moving forward. It was as if we had settled forever into the implacable roar of the water, expecting at any moment to be sucked down by the whirlpool. An indescribable exhaustion began to paralyze my arms, and my legs felt as if they were made of something soft and numb. When I thought I couldn't bear any more, I heard the captain shouting in my direction. He gestured toward the sky with his head, and a crooked, enigmatic smile appeared on his face. I looked up and saw the light growing brighter. Some rays of sun broke through the cloud of foam and mist and made it shine with the colors of the rainbow. The howl of the torrent and the rumble in the hull began to diminish. The barge was moving forward, its rhythmic rocking controlled now by strong, regular turns of the propeller. When the pitching grew even gentler, the captain squatted on the deck and signaled to me to lie down in the hammock. His striped umbrella had disappeared. When I tried to move, my whole body ached as if I'd been beaten. I managed to stagger to the hammock and lie down, a feeling of relief spreading through me like a balm accepted gratefully by every joint and muscle, every centimeter of skin that had been numbed and whipped by water. As I celebrated the joy of being alive, I was overcome by a slight drunkenness, a peaceful drowsiness. The river was widening again, and flocks of herons flew out of the rushes to settle on treetops heavy with flowers. Once again the dry, unchanging, motionless heat reminded me that there had been other afternoons like the one now drawing to a close in benevolent, unbounded calm.

I fell into a deep sleep that lasted until the pilot brought me a cup of hot coffee and some fried plantain in a chipped pewter plate. "You got to eat something, boss. If you don't get your strength back, hunger wins out and you dream about the dead." His voice had a fatherly tone that left me awash in childish, gratuitous nostalgia. I thanked him and gulped the coffee in one swallow. As I ate the slices of plantain, I felt the gradual return of my old loyalties to life, to the world that holds endless surprises, to the three or four beings whose voices reach me despite time and my incurable wanderlust.

* * *

The landscape is beginning to change. At first the signs are sporadic and not always very clear. Even if the temperature stays the same, the oven heat, as unmoving as a stubborn animal that refuses to budge, is sometimes rippled by light, cool breezes. These exotic gusts from another climate remind me of the veins in marble, alien in color, tone, and texture to the mass. The swamps are disappearing and in their place is a dense, dwarfed growth that gives off a mixture of smells like the odor of pollen kept in a container. Something like honey with a very pronounced vegetal accent. The riverbed is narrowing and deepening, the banks are taking on a muddy consistency that feels like clay, and the fresh, transparent water has a faint iron color. The changes are affecting everyone's state of mind. There's a relief from tension, a desire to talk, a gleam in our eyes, as if we knew that something long awaited was about to happen. In the last light of afternoon a lead-blue line appears on the horizon and becomes easily confused with storm clouds massing at a distance impossible to determine. The captain comes over and points at the spot I'm watching with so much interest. He makes a wavy motion with his hand, sketching the outline of a cordillera, and without saying a word he nods his head and smiles with a touch of sadness that makes me uneasy again. "The sawmills?" I ask, as if I would like to avoid the answer. He nods again, raises his eyebrows, and puckers his lips in a gesture that means something like, "There's nothing I can do, but you can count on all my sympathy."

I sit on the edge of the prow, my legs dangling over the water that splashes me with a coolness I would have enjoyed more on other occasions. I ponder the factories and what they conceal, sensing an unpleasant surprise that nobody has wanted to talk about in any detail. I think of Flor Estévez, of her money about to be risked in an adventure heavy with omens, of my habitual obtuse willingness to take on enterprises like these, and I realize that I lost all interest long ago. Thinking about it produces revulsion mixed with the paralyzing guilt of a man who knows his work is about to begin, while he is only looking for a way out of the commitment that is poisoning every moment of his life. A state of mind that's all too familiar. I'm well aware of the openings I use to escape the troubling discomfort of being in the wrong, and that keep me from enjoying what life offers every day in dubious compensation for my remaining stubbornly at her side.

* * *

A strange dialogue with the captain. Enigma flows beneath the words. That's why writing them down is not enough. His tone of voice, his gestures, his way of losing himself in long silences, helped to turn our conversation into one of those times when it isn't the words that communicate what we want to say. Instead they become obstacles, distractions that hide the true reason for talking. His voice from the hammock facing mine startled me. I thought he was asleep.

"Well, it's coming to an end, Gaviero. This adventure's almost over."

"Yes, it looks as if we're almost to the sawmills. I could see the cordillera clearly today," I replied, knowing there was more to his observation.

"I don't believe you're very interested in the sawmills anymore. I think the decisive thing this trip had in store for us has already happened. Don't you?"

"Yes, I do. Something like that," I said, giving him the chance to finish his idea.

"Look, if you think about it, you'll see that from our meeting the Indians to Angel Pass, everything has been linked, everything fits together perfectly. These things always happen in sequence and with a definite purpose. What's important is knowing how to interpret it."

"In my case you're probably right, Cap. But what about you?"

"Lots of things have happened to me along these rivers, along the great river. The same or almost the same as on this trip. But what intrigues me this time is the order in which they occurred."

"I don't understand, Cap. Naturally there's been one order for me and another for you. You didn't take the Indian to bed, you didn't get sick at the post, you didn't think you'd die at Angel Pass."

"When I meet someone who's lived your kind of life, who's undergone the trials that made you the man you are now, then being a witness and companion is as important as experiencing those things myself—perhaps even more important. The days I spent at the base sitting beside your hammock and watching your life slip away were a more decisive trial for me than for you."

"Is that why you stopped boozing?" My rather brutal question was an effort to make him be specific.

"Yes, that, and what it forced me to think about. As if I'd suddenly discovered I was playing the wrong game. It's bad enough to live part of your life in a role meant for somebody else, and even worse to find out when you no longer have the strength to make up for the past or get back what you've lost. Do you understand?"

"Yes, I think so. It's happened to me, too, lots of times, but only for short periods, and I've managed to recover and land on my feet." I was trying to change the direction our talk was taking and at the same time let him know I'd gotten the message.

"You're immortal, Gaviero. It doesn't matter that you'll die one day like the rest of us. That doesn't change anything. You're immortal for as long as you live. I think I've been dead a long time. My life is made as if scraps left over after cutting a dress had been patched together any which way. When I realized that, I stopped drinking. I can't go on fooling myself. When I saw you come back to life in that classroom and defeat the plague, I saw into myself very clearly. I saw my mistake and when it had begun."

"When you left Hamburg?" I asked, testing the ground.

"It doesn't matter. You know? It doesn't matter. It might have been when I ran away with her. When I left the Antilles. I don't know. It's not very important. It doesn't matter." I could hear the uneasiness in his voice, an irritation directed more at himself than at me, as if he hadn't expected to go this far when he began the conversation.

"Yes," I agreed, "you're right. It doesn't matter. When you come to this kind of conclusion, the beginning doesn't matter. It doesn't explain much."

A long silence made me think he'd fallen asleep. His voice startled me again.

"Can you guess who knows this as well as we do?" he asked in what might have been a joking tone.

"No. Who?"

"The major, man, the major. That's why he came back to the base. I've never seen him show so much interest in someone who was sick. Don't forget, he's seen his share of dying soldiers. He's not a man who's easily moved. You've seen him. I don't have to tell you. Well, the fact is he spent hours with me keeping watch over your delirium, following the battle you waged in that hammock, like an animal who's just been captured."

"Yes, I suspected something of the sort because of how he treated me when we said goodbye, and the things he said. He couldn't understand why I'd been saved, and that intrigued him."

"You're wrong. He understood as well as I do. He could see the immortality in you, and that baffled him so much it changed his character completely. The first chink I've ever found in him. I thought he was invulnerable."

"I'd like to see him again," I said, thinking out loud.

"You will. Don't worry. He's still intrigued too. When you meet again, you'll remember what I've told you." Now his voice was quiet, velvety, distant.

I understood that our talk was over. I was awake for a long time, turning over the hidden meaning that flowed out of the captain's words and dug deep inside me, working forgotten areas of my mind and setting warning lights everywhere. As if someone were cupping my soul.

* * *

JUNE 12

Ahead of us the cordillera looms on the horizon with overwhelming precision. I realize I'd forgotten how mountains make me feel, what they mean to me as a protective place, an endless source of challenges that strengthen me, sharpen my senses, awaken my need to defy fate and try to test its limits. At the sight of the mountain range misted over by the blue-tinged air, I feel a silent confession rise up from the depths of my soul and fill me with joy. Only I know how much it explains and lends meaning to every hour of my life: "It's where I come from. When I leave it, I begin to die."

Maybe that's what the captain means when he talks about my immortality. Yes, that's it—now I understand completely. Flor Estévez and her untamable dark hair, her rough, kind words, her body in disarray, her songs to soothe hooligans and babies whose helpless innocence only she can understand, with the wisdom of a childless woman who shakes life by the shoulders until she forces it to hand over what she demands.

The cordillera. Everything had to happen to bring me to this experience of the jungle so that now, with the marks of the trials I had to undergo in my passage through its soft, decomposing hell still fresh on my body, I could discover that my true home is up there in the deep ravines where giant ferns sway; in the abandoned mine shafts and the damp, dense growth of the coffee plantings covered in the astonished snow of their flowers or the red fiesta of their berries; in the groves of plantain trees, with their unspeakably soft trunks and the tender green of their reverent leaves so welcoming, so smooth; in the rivers crashing down against the great sun-warmed boulders, the delight of reptiles that use them for their lovemaking and their silent gatherings; in the dizzying flocks of parrots that fly through the air, as noisy as a departing army, to settle in the tops of the tall cámbulo trees. That's where I come from, and I know it now with all the fullness of someone who has finally found the place for his business on earth. I'll leave it again, I don't know how often, but I'll never return to the places I'm leaving now. And when I'm away from the cordillera, its absence will pain me with a new pain, with the burning desire to go back and wander the paths that smell of woodland and yaraguá grass, of soil that's just been rained on, of sugar mills grinding.

Night has fallen and I'm lying in the hammock. The cool breeze comes like a promise and a confirmation, carrying an occasional scent of fruits that had been erased from my memory. I approach sleep as if I were going to relive my youth, just for the brief space of a night now, but having rescued it intact, unscathed by my own clumsy dealings with nothingness.

* * *

Today I finished the book about the assassination of Louis de Orléans by order of John the Fearless, Duke of Burgundy. I keep it among my few belongings because I intend to reread certain details. It's clear there was a lengthy provocation on the part of the victim, who was supported by Isabel of Bavaria, his sister-in-law and most certainly his lover. The provost's modesty and the author's prudery don't permit them to elucidate a matter that seems of capital importance to me. The struggle between Armagnacs and Burgundians, especially its origin and the real reasons behind it, could be studied from very surprising angles. But this is something for the future. The archives of Antwerp and Liège must contain revealing documents that I'll have to investigate someday. I propose to do just that if I can still be of service to my dear friend Abdul Bashur and his associates. Abdul, what an extraordinary man he is: the warm, unconditional friend prepared to lose everything to help you, and the implacably astute businessman engaged in labyrinthine vendettas to which he's capable of devoting most of his time and fortune. We met in a café in Port Said. He was at a nearby table, trying to sell a collection of opals to a Jew from Tetuán who could not understand what Abdul was saying, or would not in the hope he would run out of arguments and sell the gems at a lower price. Abdul looked at me and, with the intuition of a Levantine who knows what language to speak with a stranger, asked me in Flemish for help in the transaction and offered me a percentage of the profits. I moved to his table and spoke in Spanish with the Jew. Abdul told me his terms in Flemish and I laid them out in Spanish. The deal was closed to Abdul's complete satisfaction. We stayed behind while the Jew walked away, fingering the stones and muttering oblique curses against all the seed of my ancestors. Abdul and I soon became good friends. He told me he was in the shipbuilding business with his cousins but that they were having a streak of bad luck. He was putting money together to go back to Antwerp and get the business on its feet. We wandered the Mediterranean until, in Marseilles, we managed to place an extremely compromising shipment that nobody else wanted to take a risk on. Our profits allowed Abdul to reorganize his company, and I sank my share in the lunatic venture of the Cocora mines, where I lost everything, and nearly lost my life. I've already written that story.

Later Abdul Bashur wrote to offer me a freighter under Tunisian registry, but I decided to try my luck with these sawmills that I now find promise little or nothing. As I recall all these events and projects from the past, I feel overcome by an indescribable fatigue, a torpor and loss of will, as if I'd spent ten years of my life here in these places of damnation and ruin.

* * *

JUNE 16

The day before yesterday at dawn I was awakened by a shadow obscuring the first ray of sun that usually shines in my eyes, and to which I've grown accustomed because it forces me to turn in my hammock without waking up completely and enjoy for another hour the particularly refreshing sleep that makes up for my restlessness at night. Something was hanging from the framework under the canvas and blocking the light. I awoke with a start: the body of the captain swung gently from the horizontal bar. His back was to me and his head rested on the heavy cable he'd used to hang himself. I called Miguel, and the mechanic came immediately and helped me take down the body. The purplish face had a wild-eyed, grotesque expression that made it unrecognizable. I realized only then that one of the captain's consistent traits, even in his most drunken states, was a kind of ordered dignity in his features that made one think of an actor who had once played the great tragic roles of Greek or Elizabethan theater. We searched his clothing for a note but found nothing. The mechanic's face was more closed and inexpressive than ever. The pilot came over to watch us and shook his head with an old man's resigned understanding. We pulled ashore when we found a place where we could bury the body. We wrapped it in the hammock that he used most often. The earth had the consistency of clay, and its reddish color grew more intense the deeper we dug the grave. The job took several hours. When we finished we were dripping with sweat and our limbs were aching. We lowered the body and covered it with earth. The pilot had made a cross of two guaiacum branches that he cut as soon as we landed and carved with fond patience while we worked the spades. With his knife he'd cut the words "The Kap" in painstaking letters on the horizontal branch. For a time we stood in silence around the grave. I thought about saying something but realized it would disturb our meditation. Each of us was recalling, in his own way and with his own collection of memories, the shipmate who finally found rest after living what he had called the life that wasn't his. We walked back to the barge, and I knew I was leaving behind a friend exemplary in his comradely discretion and firm, unflawed affection.

When the barge pulled out, I went to ask the mechanic about the rest of the trip. "Don't worry," he said in his barbaric but intelligible mix of languages, "we're going to the sawmills. I been the owner for two years. When Cap bought the barge at the base on the big river I put in this motor I been taking care of a long time just waiting for a chance like that. Later I bought it off him, but I never wanted him to leave. Where could he go and who would take him he drank so much? Those orders he shouted I think they made him feel he was still the owner and captain. He was a good man, he suffered a lot, who could understand him better than me? He called me Miguel. My real name's Xendú, but he didn't like it. He respected you a lot—sometimes he said he was sorry he didn't know you before. He said you could've done great things together." Miguel went back to his motor, and I leaned against one of the mooring posts and watched the current. It occurred to me again that we don't know anything about death, that all the things we say and invent and whisper about it are miserable fantasies that have nothing to do with the categorical, necessary, ineluctable fact whose secret, if it really has one, we take with us when we die. It was obvious the captain had decided to kill himself many days ago. When he gave up drinking, it was a sign that something had stopped inside him, something that had kept him alive and had broken down forever. Our conversation the other night comes back to me now with irrefutable clarity. He was telling me what he'd resolved to do. He wasn't the kind to suddenly say outright: "I'm going to kill myself." He had the defeated man's sense of decency. I didn't want to decipher the message, or more accurately, I chose to hide it in that corner of the soul where we keep irrevocable facts, the ones that no longer depend on us for their fateful realization. I think he must have been grateful for my attitude. What he said was to be remembered after his death and perpetuated along with his memory: he knew it would always be with me. He took his life so discreetly! He waited until I was sleeping soundly. It must have been just before dawn. He was obliged to use one of the crossbars. Any other method would have attracted our attention. That decency is in tune with the rest of his character and makes me feel he's even closer to an idea I have of men who know how to move through the world, through the corrupt, mindless mob. The more I think about him the more I see that I learned practically everything about his life, his way of being, his failures and his insistent hopes. It's as if I'd met his parents: his mother, the untamed Indian loyal to her man, and his father, lost in a dream of gold and unattainable happiness. I can see the fat madam at the Paramaribo brothel and hear her jovial laugh and the sound of her sensual, flat-footed walk. And the Chinese girl. The one I know best. There's a good deal to say about her and why he abandoned her in the great Sankt-Pauli sewer. It was a way to begin his death, to build it inside himself with one irremediable step, one incurable mutilation. I can't sleep. I've spent the night turning in the hammock, remembering, thinking, reconstructing a recent past in which I was taught lessons that will mark me for the rest of my life. Perhaps my own death is beginning now. I don't dare think about this too much. I want everything to fall back into place on its own. For now, the important thing is to get back to the uplands and take refuge in the blunt, wholesome safety of Flor Estévez. She would have understood Cap so well. But who knows, she has a sharp nose for losers and they're usually not to her liking. How complicated it all is. How many wrong turnings in a labyrinth where we do everything we can to avoid the exit, how many surprises and then the tedium of learning they weren't surprises at all, that everything that happens to us has the same face, exactly the same origin. I won't sleep tonight. I'll go have coffee with Miguel. I know where these tortured musings on the irremediable can lead. There's a dryness inside us we shouldn't get too close to. It's better not to know how much of our soul it occupies.

* * *

I'm now writing on stationery with an official letterhead, which the captain kept in a box along with customs forms and other papers relating to the barge. I realize it's an effort for me to continue this diary. It's difficult to establish how, but in some way a good part of what I've been writing was connected to him. Not that I ever thought he would read it. Nothing further from my mind. But it's as if his presence, his figure, his past, the way he survived at the very edge of life, all served as a reference point, a guide—say it once and for all—an inspiration, despite all the inanity the word has acquired in the mouths of fools. Since what I now record on these pages deals exclusively with me, with what I see and the things that occur around me, it suffers from emptiness, a lack of weight that makes me feel like just another traveler searching for new experiences and unexpected emotions—the sort of thing, in other words, that I reject most deeply, almost physiologically. But on the other hand, it's clear that all I have to do is recall his phrases and gestures, his lunatic orders, to feel the impulse again to go on scribbling. Last night, in fact, I had a revealing dream so rich in detail and substance, and so coherent, that out of it will surely come the subterranean energy to continue the diary.

I was with Abdul Bashur on a pier in Antwerp—he always calls it Antwerpen, in Flemish—and we were on our way to visit the freighter whose command he was going to entrust to me. We stopped in front of the ship: it looked like new, recently painted and all its catwalks and pipes shining and neat. We walked up the gangway. A woman was scrubbing the wooden deck with unsettling energy and dedication. The rounded forms of her body were emphasized each time she bent over to scrape at a stain that resisted the brush. I recognized her immediately: it was Flor Estévez. She stood up smiling and greeted us with her usual brusque cordiality. Something she said to Abdul indicated they already knew each other. Then she turned to me and said, "We're almost finished. When this boat leaves port, it'll be the envy of the world. There's coffee and somebody waiting for you in the cabin." Her blouse was open. Her dark, full breasts were almost completely exposed. With some sorrow I left her on deck and followed Bashur to the cabin. When we walked in, there was the captain at a desk covered with disordered piles of papers and maps. He held his pipe in one hand and greeted us with the brisk, vigorous handshake of a gymnast. "Well," he said as he scratched his chin with the hand that held the pipe, "here I am again. What happened on the barge was only a rehearsal. It didn't pan out. We've worked very hard here, and whether we sell it or decide to operate it ourselves, buying the boat was a brilliant move. The lady thinks we should keep it. I told her we'd see what you two thought. And really, Gaviero, she's been waiting for you very impatiently. She brought the things you left in the uplands and wasn't sure if anything was missing." I said we'd already spoken with her. "Let's go then," he said. "I want you to see everything." We went out. It began to grow dark very quickly. The captain walked ahead to show us the way. Each time he turned around, I could tell that his face was changing, that a sad, forsaken look was settling more and more firmly on his features. When he reached the machine room, I saw he was limping slightly. Then I was sure it wasn't him anymore, that we were following someone else, and in fact, when he stopped to show us the boiler, we saw a defeated, slow-witted old man mumbling some incoherent explanation totally unrelated to whatever he was pointing at with his trembling, grimy hand. Abdul was no longer with me. An icy wind blew through the hatchways and rocked the ship, whose impressive solidity had vanished. The old man moved toward a stairway that went down to the depths of the hold. I stood looking at a ramshackle collection of instruments, rods, and valves that hadn't been used in a very long time. I thought of Flor Estévez. Where was she? I couldn't imagine her connected with the sordid ruin that surrounded me. I ran toward the deck, longing to see her, tripped on a step that gave way under me, and fell into emptiness.

I woke drenched in sweat, my mouth filled with the bitter taste of rotten fruit. The current is stronger and rougher. A mountain breeze comes like an announcement that we've entered a region completely different from the ones we've passed through so far. The pilot, with his eyes on the cordillera, is cooking an insipid-smelling mixture of beans and yuca that reminds me of the jungle and its climate of exhaustion and mud.

* * *

Today I had a conversation with the pilot that helped to clarify, at least partially, the enigma of the sawmills. In the morning he brought me coffee and the inescapable fried plantain. He stayed there, waiting for me to finish my breakfast, obviously wanting to tell me something.

"Well, we're almost there, aren't we?" I observed, giving him the chance to say what he had on his mind but didn't dare say because of that distance where old people hide to avoid being hurt or ignored.

"Yes, señor, just a few more days. You never been up there, right?" There was a touch of curiosity in the question.

"Never. But tell me, what's really in those factories?"

"Some men came from Finland to install the machines. That's three sawmills, set up a few kilometers apart. The soldiers guard them, but the engineers left. Some years ago now."

"And what timber did they plan to cut? I don't see enough trees around here to supply three installations like the ones you're telling me about."

"I think there's good timber at the foot of the cordillera. I heard about it one time or another. But it seems they can't get it to the mills."

"Why not?"

"I don't know, señor. Really. I couldn't say." He was hiding something. I saw a shadow of fear cross his face. His words weren't spontaneous and easy anymore. He'd lost his desire to talk, and as far as he was concerned, he'd already said enough.

"But who does know? Maybe the soldiers can give me some information when we get there. What do you think?" I didn't expect to get much more out of him.

"No, señor, not the soldiers. They don't like people asking questions, and I don't think they know much more than we do." He began to move away, picking up the empty cup and plate.

"And suppose I talk to the major?" I had touched a delicate nerve. The old man stood still and didn't dare look at me. "I'll talk to him if I have to. I'm sure he'll tell me what I want to know. What do you think?"

He walked slowly toward the stern, muttering and staring into the distance.

"Maybe he'll tell you something. Us folks around here, he never tells us nothing and he don't like us to stick our noses in. Talk to him if you want. It's up to you. I think he respects you." As he mumbled these words, he shrugged his shoulders with the resignation, especially pronounced in him, of old men faced with inevitability and the foolishness of others. I remembered his behavior when we cut down the captain's body, and then at the burial. He didn't want to participate in the destructive games of men. He had lived so long he must have found the sum total of human folly not only intolerable but completely alien.

There were no great surprises in what the pilot told me. I've put two and two together, and I've been convinced for some time that the trucker in the uplands and the people I talked to when I came to the jungle described an enterprise that is nothing but an illusion composed of scraps of rumors: vague miracles of wealth within reach, the kind of lucky break that never really happens to anyone. And I'm the ideal person to fall for it, no doubt about it. I've spent my whole life setting out on this kind of adventure and finding the same disillusionment in the end. Although I console myself eventually with the thought that the reward was in the adventure itself and there's no reason to search for anything but the satisfaction of trying every one of the world's roads, they all start looking suspiciously alike. And yet they're worth traveling if only to stave off tedium and our own death, the one that really belongs to us and hopes we can recognize her and take her as our own.

Growing discouragement and lack of interest, not only with the factories but with the trip itself and all its events, difficulties, revelations. The landscape seems to match my state of mind: the vegetation, almost dwarfed and intensely green, has a smell of concentrated pollen that seems to stick to the skin; the light filters through a thin mist that confuses one's sense of distance and the size of objects. A steady drizzle has been falling all night, soaking through the canvas and running down my body in lukewarm drops of something that seems more like sap than rainwater. Miguel the mechanic talks constantly about his problems with the motor. I've never heard him complain before, not even when we had to face the rapids. Clearly he misses the jungle, and this country affects his mood and weakens his connection to the engine, as if he were suddenly defenseless and the motor were challenging him like a stranger, an enemy. The pilot continues to stare at the cordillera. From time to time he shakes his head like a man trying to banish a disturbing idea.

Not the best frame of mind for continuing these entries. I know myself fairly well, and if I keep sliding into this chasm, I can end up with nothing to hold on to. In the solitude of this country, with only these two ruins of the jungle's devastation for companions, there's a risk of not finding the slightest reason for staying alive. The drizzle came with the afternoon light. The mist evaporated and at times the air was as transparent as if the world had just been made. The pilot signaled from the bow to show me, straight ahead, there at the foot of the craggy mass of mountain, a metallic reflection shining in the last rays of the sun with a golden hue that reminds me of the domes of small Orthodox churches on the Dalmatian coast. "There they are. That's it. Tomorrow night we'll be there if all goes well." His slow, uninflected voice sounded as if it came from a ventriloquist's dummy. I found myself wanting the trip to go on indefinitely, wanting to put off the moment when I would have to face the troublesome reality of those huge structures whose brilliance is fading as darkness approaches, bringing with it the noise of crickets and flocks of parrots searching the foothills for shelter for the night. I've started to write a letter to Flor Estévez with no other purpose than to feel her near me and listening to the lunatic story of this voyage. I'm confident I'll give it to her one day. For now, the relief I feel in writing the letter is surely a way to escape this slide toward the nothingness that is overwhelming me and, sadly, is more familiar than even I imagine when I recall it as something gone without leaving a trace.

"Flor, my lady: If the pathways of God are mysterious, the ones I take here on earth are no less incomprehensible. Here I am, a few hours away from the famous factories, the ones the

driver carrying the Llano livestock told us about, and I still
don't know much more about them than what he said on that
night of confidences and rum in The Snow of the Admiral,
which is, by the way, where I would like to be now, not here.
In fact, I have good reason to believe it will all come to
nothing, at least according to the rather vague pieces of
information I've been receiving as I sail up the Xurandó, a river
with more whims, bad habits, and contrary moods than the
ones you display when the upland closes in on itself and it rains
all day and all night and even the blankets feel wet. The other
night I dreamed about you, nothing I can tell you now because
I'd have to fill you in on the other people in the dream whom
you don't know, and that would cover many pages. I'm writing
a diary, whenever I can and on whatever paper I can find, and I
record everything, from my dreams to our mishaps, from the
character and appearance of my traveling companions to the
changes in landscape as we move upriver. But getting back to
the dream, I should tell you that in it, or rather by means of it,
I've come to realize your growing importance to me, how your
body and not always docile spirit preside over my life and its
misfortunes and the ruin where it takes shelter when I've grown
sick of wandering and miscalculation. By now this should come
as no surprise. I know your talents as a seer and hermetic oracle.
And so I won't even take the time to tell you in detail how, in
this hammock, I need to feel your turbulent body, need to hear
you howl in love as if a whirlpool were swallowing you up.
Such things should not be written, not only because it does no
good but because, in memory, they suffer from a certain rigidity
and undergo such startling changes that it isn't worth expressing
them in words. I don't know how things will go here. What I
do know is that the cordillera is there in front of me, its aromas
and whispers are reaching me. All I do is think of the
place—it's clear to me at last—that is my real home on earth.
Your money is still safe and I suspect it will come back to you
intact, which is what I truly want. I've thought of telling you
something about the jungle and the people who live here, but I
think you'll find out more about them in my diary if I can get
it and its author safely back to you. I've seen death twice, each
time with a different face and chanting her spells so close to me

I didn't think I'd return. Strange, but this hasn't changed me at all. It only taught me that the lady has always watched over me and kept track of my wanderings. The captain (I hope we'll soon be talking about him at length) told me that even though I'm obviously going to die one day, for as long as I live I'm immortal. Well, that doesn't sound right. Of course, he said it better, but that's basically the idea. The most striking thing is that I had the same idea, but about you, because I think that inside The Snow of the Admiral you've been weaving, building, raising the landscape around you. I've often been convinced that you summon the fog and drive it away, that you weave the giant lichen hanging from the cámbulo trees and direct the course of the waterfalls that appear to burst from the heart of the rocks and tumble over ferns and mosses of the most startling colors, intense copper to the tender green that seems to shine with its own light. We've talked so little despite the time we've been together that perhaps these things come as a surprise, but they were what really made me decide to stay with you on the pretext of healing my leg. Speaking of which, it's still numb in places although I can use it to walk. I'm not very good at writing to someone like you whom I carry deep inside me and who wields so much power over the most secret corners and convolutions of the Gaviero, who, if he had met you sooner, would not have roamed so far or seen so much of a world that brought him so little profit and even less wisdom. A man learns more with a woman like you than by taking to the road and dealing with people who leave only the sad wake of their disorder, the miserable limits of their ambition measured against the ludicrous extent of their greed. The reason for these lines has been just to talk with you a while to calm my fears and feed my hope. I'll stop now and say goodbye until we meet again in The Snow of the Admiral and drink coffee in the front passageway, watching the fog come in and listening to the trucks drive up the mountain with their motors straining, identifying the drivers by the way they shift gears. This isn't all I wanted to tell you. I haven't even begun. Which doesn't matter, of course. With you it isn't necessary to say things because you already know them, you've always known them.

Many kisses and all the longing of one who misses you very much."

* * *

Today at dusk we reached the first sawmill. What we saw as right in front of us wasn't as close as we thought. The Xurandó makes a series of wide curves here that alternately move the brilliant aluminum and glass structure away and then bring it back again, turning it into a mirage—an impression that is heightened by how unexpected such architecture is in this place and climate. We moored at a small floating dock secured by yellow cables and impeccably maintained gangways made of light-colored wood. It reminded me of the Baltic. We came ashore and approached the building, which is surrounded by a barbed-wire fence over two meters high, with metal posts painted navy blue and placed every ten meters. We waited for some time by the sentry box at the entrance, and finally a soldier came out of the main building, arranging his clothing as if he'd been sleeping. He told us that the rest of the staff had gone hunting and would return tomorrow at dawn. Moved by an unexpected curiosity, I asked him what they hunted out there, and he stood looking at me with that astonished expression so characteristic of an ordinary soldier when he doesn't know how to hide something from civilians and finally decides to lie—a thing he would certainly never do with his superiors. "I don't know. I've never gone. Possum, I think, or something like that," he answered as he turned and walked toward the building. We went back to the barge to eat supper, get some sleep, and try again the next day. And again, in the fading afternoon light, the enormous metal structure was surrounded by a golden halo that made it look unreal, as if it were hanging in midair. It consists of a gigantic hangar, similar to the ones used for zeppelins, flanked by a small structure that apparently serves as a warehouse, and a row of three barracks, each containing four rooms, for the men who guard the site.

The hangar is built on an aluminum framework, with large, wide windows at the sides and front, and a dome on which a series of broad, tinted-glass canopies help keep out the sun. I remember seeing similar structures not only along Lake Constance and the shores of the North Sea and the Baltic, but also in ports in Louisiana and British Columbia where they load lumber cut into planks and ready to be shipped all over the world. The outlandish presence of a building like this on the banks of the Xurandó, at the edge of the jungle, is made even more startling by how meticulously it is maintained. Every centimeter of metal and glass gleams as if they'd just finished building it a few hours ago. A sudden loud noise indicated that a turbine had been switched on. The entire complex was illuminated by what appeared to be neon lighting, but much more subdued and diffuse. The light didn't reach the surrounding area, which explained why we hadn't seen it from a distance. The impression of unreality, of an unbearable nightmarish presence in the equatorial night, at first kept me awake and then visited my intermittent dreams, and each time, I found myself drenched in sweat, my heart racing. I knew I'd never have the chance to meet anyone who lived in this inconceivable building. A vague uneasiness has been taking hold of me, and now I'm trying to write in the diary so I won't look at the floating Gothic marvel of aluminum and glass lit by that morguish light and lulled by the gentle hum of its electrical plant. Now I understand the reservations and evasions of the captain, the major, the others, when I kept wanting to know what the sawmills really were. There was no point. The truth is impossible to communicate. "You'll see." That was what they all said in the end, refusing to go into detail. They were right. Once again Maqroll makes port at another of his extraordinary, unprofitable insights. It's hopeless. It will never change.

* * *

JUNE 24

This morning I went back to the sentry box. A guard listened to my request to speak with someone and closed the window without answering. I saw him talking on the phone. He opened the window again and said, "No visitors allowed at these installations. Good morning." He was about to close the window and I hurriedly asked, "The engineer? I don't want to talk to any of the guards, just to him. About lumber sales. Even if it's just by phone, I'd like to tell the engineer my reason for coming here." He looked at me for a moment with neutral, expressionless eyes as if he had heard my words through a distant loudspeaker. In a voice that was just as flat, almost energyless, he said, "There hasn't been an engineer here for a long time. Just soldiers and two sergeant majors. We have instructions not to talk to anybody. There's no point asking again." The telephone gave a frenetic ring. He closed the window, picked up the phone, listened intently, and finally nodded; he'd received an order. He opened the window a crack and said, "You have to remove the barge before noon tomorrow and stop asking to see somebody. And don't come back to the sentry box. I can't talk to you anymore." He slammed the glass shut and began to look over some papers on the desk. I felt immersed in another world, as if I'd sunk down to the depths of an uncharted, hostile ocean.

I went back to the barge and talked to the pilot. "I was afraid of this," he said. "I never tried to talk to them or go up to the gate. Those soldiers aren't from any base around here. They're relieved every so often. They come from the edge of the cordillera and they go back the same way, cutting across the mountain. Now you tell me what to do. Tomorrow noon we have to get out of here. I don't think it's a good idea to be stubborn." I suggested visiting the other factories further upriver. "No point in trying. They're all the same. Besides, we're running out of diesel. We'll have to go back at half speed and use the current. If we don't find fuel in one of the settlements, let's hope we have enough to get back to base." I lay down in the hammock and stopped talking. I was filled with a vague frustration, a silent irritation with myself and all the delays, negligence, and thoughtlessness that had brought me to this point and could have been avoided so easily if my character were different. We'll go back downriver. Crushed by irresistible despair I lay there trying to swallow the rage that swelled against everything and everybody. Knowing my anger was futile only increased it. At night, when I felt calmer and more resigned, I lit the lamp and wrote. The operating room light that floods the building, its aluminum and glass skeleton, the hum of the turbine, are becoming so intolerable that I've decided to leave tomorrow and get away from their devastating presence.

* * *

We left this morning at dawn. As we cast off and let the current carry us to the middle of the river, the subdued howl of a siren could be heard coming from the building. In the distance another answered, and then another even further away. The factories were telling each other that the intruders had gone. The arrogant threat, the unspoken menace in those signals left us silent and debilitated for a good part of the day. We moved at a speed that at first pleased and surprised me. Then I suddenly thought of Angel Pass. A shudder went down my spine. Maybe it was easier going down-river. But I felt I wouldn't have the heart to face the crashing water again, its deafening noise and whirlpools, the overwhelming power of its unbridled energy. Late in the afternoon we came to a vast stillwater that turned the Xurandó into a lake, its shores lost in the distance no matter which way we turned. I was falling into a sleep that I hoped would revive me and help me forget the hostile world of the sawmills. A distant hum grew louder. I was torn between drowsiness and curiosity, and as sleep began to gain around, I heard a voice calling, "Gaviero! Maqroll! Gaviero!" I woke up. The Junker from the base was slipping through the water alongside us. The major stood on the floats, his hand extended for a line that the pilot threw to him. He caught it on the second try and brought the plane close to the prow. "We're going ashore!" he ordered as he made a gesture of welcome with his free hand. He looked thinner, and his mustache wasn't as straight and neat as it had been. We moored the barge and secured the Junker to the prow. The major jumped on deck, as agile as a cat. We shook hands and went to sit on the hammocks. With no preliminaries and no questions about the trip, he came right to the point. "A patrol found Cap's grave. I went there last week. Some animal had tried to get to him. I had them dig deeper and we filled the top half with stones. In the jungle you can't just bury the dead. The animals get them in a few days. So you're on your way back? I can imagine what it was like. There was no point trying to warn you. Nobody believes you when you try to explain. Each man has to experience it for himself. What will you do now?" "I don't know," I answered, "I don't have many plans. I want to go back to the cordillera as soon as I can, but I don't know if there's a road on this side. But I wouldn't like to leave and still not know what's going on with those people in the factories. They say the machines are intact. I'm never coming back. Why don't you tell me?" He looked at his hands as he brushed away the leaves and mud left by the line. "All right, Gaviero," he began with a faint smile, "I'll tell you. In the first place, there's no mystery. The installations revert to the government in three years. Someone very high up is interested in them. He must be pretty influential because he could arrange for the Marines to guard and maintain them. And it's true, they are intact, but they were never put in operation because of an armed uprising in the timber area." He pointed to the mountain range. "Who's behind it? Not too hard to guess. On the reversion date, when the mills are turned over to the government, it's very possible the guerrillas will disappear as if by magic. Do you understand? It's very simple. There's always somebody smarter, isn't there?" Again that tone, that mixture of mockery and protectiveness, assurance and world-weariness. Before I could ask the question, he said, "Why didn't I tell you? We're big boys now, aren't we. I let you know as much as I could. Now that you're leaving and will certainly never come back, I can tell you everything. It's good you left when they told you to. Those people don't fool around. They say things only once. Then they open fire." I expressed my gratitude for his having given me as much warning as prudence would allow, and apologized for my obstinacy in pushing ahead. "Don't worry about it," he said. "It's not the first time. The business is very tempting—nothing harebrained about it. Except for what I told you: There's always somebody smarter. Always. It's just as well you're taking it philosophically. It's the only way. Well, now I have a proposition to make: If you want to go to the uplands, maybe I can help. Tomorrow, if you like, we'll fly to El Sordo Lagoon. It's in the middle of the cordillera. There's a village on shore where trucks leave for the uplands. Settle up with Miguel. I'll come at dawn tomorrow, and we can be there in an hour. What do you think?" "I don't know how to thank you," I answered, moved by his interest. "I really don't have the strength to go back to the jungle or face the rapids again. I'll pay Miguel and expect you tomorrow. Thanks again. I hope this doesn't put you out too much." "I told you the first time we met—you're not the man for this country. No, it's no trouble. The commander commands. The important thing is to know how far you can go, and I learned that when I was a second lieutenant. It's the only thing you have to know when you put on the braid. All right then, see you tomorrow. I'm leaving now because there's barely time to get back to base." He shook my hand, whistled to the pilot on the barge, and jumped onto the plane. He said something to the pilot beside him and looked at me with a smile more roguish than cordial.

This will be my last night here. I must admit to indescribable relief, as if I had drunk a potion that instantly restored all my strength and returned me to the world, the order of things that are mine. I talked to Miguel. He didn't mind settling now. I paid him and gave the pilot a good tip. I'm trying to sleep, but a wild excitement is churning inside me and keeping me awake. It's as if a great stone had been lifted from me, as if I'd been relieved of an overwhelming, painful, crushing task.

* * *

JUNE 29

The major came in the Junker at about seven in the morning. I picked up my gear and said goodbye to Miguel and Ignacio, who smiled the way old men do at the foolish stubbornness of others who repeat the mistakes they themselves have already made and forgotten. Miguel gave me his hand but there was no handshake. It was like holding a warm, damp fish. In his eyes I could see a distant, faint glimmer that revealed all the cordiality he was capable of feeling. At that instant I knew I was leaving the jungle. The mechanic not only is its perfect expression but is made of its very substance. He is an amorphous extension of that disastrous, faceless world. I climbed into the Junker, sat down behind the pilot and the major, and adjusted my seat belt. We moved in the water for a moment and then took off to the soothing vibration of the fuselage. I fell into a kind of trance until the major touched my knee and pointed to the lagoon down below. We landed gently in the water and taxied to a pier where a sergeant and three soldiers were waiting for us. The major climbed down with me. I said goodbye to the pilot, and then I realized he wasn't the one I had met before. He had one eye and a whitish scar on his forehead. The major left me with the sergeant and told him to find me a place to stay in the village until I located a truck going to the uplands. He gave me his hand and, with rather forced seriousness, cut off my attempts to thank him. "Please, from now on, think over your business ventures more carefully and don't take this kind of risk again. It's not worth it. I know what I'm talking about. You do too. Goodbye, and good luck." He climbed into the cabin and slammed the door, making the fuselage resonate with a familiar sound. The plane moved away, leaving a wake of foam that began to dissipate as the Junker disappeared into the low clouds of the cordillera.

Something has ended. Something is beginning. I saw the jungle. I had nothing to do with it, and I'm not taking anything away. Perhaps only these pages will bear dim witness to an episode that says little about my shrewdness and that I hope I'll forget very soon. In less than a week I'll be in The Snow of the Admiral, telling Flor Estévez things that surely will have little to do with what really happened. I can taste the aroma of bitter coffee on my palate.

Yesterday some Marines came to the village. They're part of the detachment that was relieved at the sawmills. They say the barge was wrecked at Angel Pass and the bodies of Miguel and the pilot haven't been found. The current must have carried them far downriver and washed them up on some beach in the jungle. The barge, stripped and battered, ran aground on a sandbar. Nobody came to claim it.

✳ ✳ ✳

Inside the binder that held the pages of Maqroll's diary was a loose sheet, written in green ink, with a hotel letterhead and no date. When I read it, I realized it was related to the diary, and for that reason it seems appropriate to transcribe it here. It may be of interest to those who have followed the Gaviero's story.

HOTEL DE FLANDRE ✳ *Quai des Tisserands No. 9 / Antwerp / Te. 3223*

. . . as we agreed. For three days we climbed a steep highway full of dangerous, carelessly engineered curves. At a certain point in the road I left the truck and rented a mule at the Cuchilla inn. For two days I wandered the uplands, looking for the highway that runs past The Snow of the Admiral. When I had lost all hope, I finally found it. I left the mule with the boy who had rented it to me and sat down in a gully to wait for a truck driving to the top. Two hours later an eight-ton Saurer came struggling up the grade like an asthmatic. The driver agreed to give me a ride. "I'm going all the way up," I explained, while he looked at me as if he were trying to remember who I was. We traveled all night. He woke me at dawn in a fog so thick it almost made driving impossible. "It must be around here. What're you looking for in this godforsaken place?" "A shop called The Snow of the Admiral," I answered as fear began to rise through my solar plexus." "Well," the driver said, "I'm going to stop for a while. You look around and see what you find. With this fog . . ." He lit a cigarette. I walked into a milky air so thick I could hardly see anything. The ditch beside the road helped to orient me, and in a little while I could make out the house. Letters were missing from the sign that hung by one corner from a rusty nail and blew in the wind. Everything was locked from the inside: doors, windows, shutters. Most of the glass was missing, and the building was on the verge of collapse. I went to the back door. Part of the balcony that used to extend out over a cliff had fallen in, and the thick wooden support beams, balancing on the edge of the ravine, were covered with moss and the droppings of parrots that rested there before flying on to the low country. It began to drizzle, and the fog cleared instantly.

I went back to the truck. "There's nothing left, señor. I knew the place but didn't know what it was called," the driver said with a compassion that wounded me deeply. "Ride with me, if you like. I'm going as far as La Osa coffee plantation. I think they know you there." I nodded in silence and climbed up beside him. The truck began the descent. A smell of burned asbestos indicated his constant working of the brakes. I thought about Flor Estévez. It would be very hard to get used to her absence. Something began hurting inside. It was the grinding of grief that would take a long time to heal.

* * *

Further information concerning Maqroll the Gaviero

COCORA

I stayed here to take care of the mine, and by now I've lost track of how many years I've been in this place. Undoubtedly a good many, because the path that led to the mine shafts and ran along the riverbank is overgrown with brush and plantains. Several guava trees are growing in the middle of the trail and have produced quite a few harvests. The owners and operators have probably forgotten all about it, and no wonder. They never found ore no matter how deep they dug or how many branches they made off the main tunnels. And I, a seaman for whom ports were mere pretexts for transient loves and brothel fights, who can still feel in my bones the sway of the crow's nest when I climbed to the top to watch the horizon and give storm warnings, to call out sightings of coastlines and pods of whales and dizzying schools of fish that approached the ship like a drunken mob, here I am, visiting the cool darkness of these labyrinths where a wind that is often warm and damp carries voices, laments, the unending, relentless toil of insects, the fluttering wings of dark butterflies, the screech of a bird lost in the depths of the mine shafts.

I sleep in what they called the Ensign's Gallery, the driest of the shafts, whose entrance faces a cliff that drops sharply to the turbulent river. On rainy nights I can smell it flooding: a muddy, sharp scent of bruised plants and animals broken against the rocks; a smell of anemic blood like the odor of women worn out by the hard climate of the tropics—the smell of a world coming apart precedes the drunken savagery of water rising in immense, devastating wrath.

I would like to leave a record of some of the things I've seen during my long days of idleness, for familiarity with deep places has turned me into someone very different from the man I used to be in the years I sailed oceans and rivers. Perhaps the acid breath of the galleries has altered or sharpened my ability to perceive the secret, intangible, yet rich life that inhabits these pits of misfortune. I'll begin with the principal gallery. One enters along an avenue of cámbulo trees whose hardy orange blossoms create a carpet that sometimes extends all the way down to the bottom. The deeper one penetrates the gallery the dimmer the light, though it shines with inexplicable intensity on the flowers blown far inside by the wind. I lived there for a long time and had to leave only because at the start of the rains I would hear voices, incomprehensible whispers like the prayers of women at a wake, yet the sounds of laughter and scuffling, which were in no way funereal, made me think of some obscene act prolonged endlessly in the hollow dark. I resolved to decipher what the voices were saying, and after listening for days and nights with feverish attention, I finally made out the word "Viana." At about the same time I fell ill, apparently with malaria, and could only lie on the straw pallet I used for a bed. For long periods I was delirious, and that lucidity, honed by fever beneath the superficial confusion of its symptoms, allowed me to begin a conversation with the women. Their honeyed attitude and obvious duplicity filled me with silent, humiliating fear. One night, obeying mysterious secret impulses made more intense by my delirium, I sat up and shouted words that echoed and reechoed against the walls of the mine. "Shut up, you bitches! I was a friend to the Prince of Viana! Respect the highest misery, the crown of those beyond salvation!" A dense silence that continued after the echoes of my shouts had faded away washed me up on the shores of my fever. I waited all night, bathed in the sweat of returning health. The silence remained, drowning out even the sound of humble creatures at their labor of leaves and secretions that weave the intangible. A milky light announced the dawn, I managed somehow to crawl out of that gallery, and I never went back again.

Another shaft is the one the miners called the Stag. It's not very deep, but through some quirk in the engineers' design an absolute darkness reigns there. Only by touch could I find my way around the gallery, which was filled with tools and carefully nailed boxes. These gave off an odor impossible to describe. It was like the smell of a gelatin made with the most secret distillations from some improbable metal. But what kept me in there for days on end, on the verge of losing my reason, was something standing at the very end of the gallery, leaning against the wall that marks the bottom of the shaft. Something that might be called a machine if it weren't for the impossibility of moving any of its apparent parts. Metal pieces of every shape and size, cylinders, spheres, all fixed in rigid immobility, made up the unspeakable structure. I could never find the end of it or measure the misbegotten thing, which was attached on all sides to the rock, its design of polished steel looming as if intending to be a definitive representation of nothingness in this world. One day, when my hands grew weary after weeks and weeks of feeling the complex connections, the rigid pinions, the frozen spheres, I ran away, horrified to find myself pleading with the indefinable presence to reveal its secret, the ultimate and true reason for its existence. I haven't gone back to that part of the mine either, but on certain hot, humid nights the silent metal presence visits my dreams, and the terror of it makes me sit up in bed with racing heart and trembling hands. No earthquake or landslide, however gigantic, can make this ineluctable mechanism in the service of eternity disappear.

The third shaft is the one I mentioned at the start, the one called the Ensign's Gallery. I'm living there now. A peaceful darkness extends to the deepest part of the tunnel, and the river, crashing against the stone walls and great boulders at the foot of the cliff, lends a certain joy to the atmosphere—a break, however precarious, in the endless tedium of my job as caretaker of this abandoned mine.

It's true that every so often gold prospectors come this far upriver to wash sand in their wooden pans. The acrid smell of cheap tobacco lets me know they've arrived. I go down to watch them work, and we exchange a few words. They come from distant regions, and I barely understand their language. I'm astounded by their infinite patience in labor that demands so much attention to detail and gives such poor results. The women of the cane planters on the opposite bank also come here occasionally. They wash their clothes in the river and pound them against the rocks. That's how I know they're here. I've had relations with a few who climb up to the mine with me. Hurried, anonymous encounters, less a matter of pleasure than a need to feel another body against my skin and fend off, even with that brief touch, the solitude that is consuming me.

One day I'll leave, follow the riverbank until I find the road to the uplands, and then I hope forgetting can help erase the wretched time I've spent here.

THE SNOW

OF THE ADMIRAL

When trucks reached the highest part of the cordillera, they would stop at a rundown shack once used as an office by the engineers during construction of the highway. The drivers of the large trucks stopped there for a cup of coffee or a glass of aguardiente to fight off the upland cold that often numbed their hands on the steering wheel and sent them hurtling into chasms where torrential rivers instantly swept away the wreckage of the vehicles and the corpses of their occupants. The twisted remains of the accident would surface downriver in the hotlands. The walls of the shack were made of wood, darkened on the inside by smoke from the stove where, day and night, coffee or an occasional slapdash meal was kept hot, but few drivers came in hungry because the altitude tended to produce a nausea that drove away all desire to eat. Colorful metal plates, nailed to the walls, carried advertisements for beer or analgesics, provocative women in bathing suits offering their fresh young bodies in a landscape of blue beaches and palm trees that was completely foreign to the frozen, glowering waste of the uplands.

The fog crossed the highway, dampened the asphalt that shone like unexpected metal, and disappeared into the tall trees with smooth gray trunks, vigorous branches, and sparse foliage that had been taken over by gray moss in which bright flowers grew, their thick petals dripping a slow, transparent honey.

A wooden board over the entrance bore the name of the shop in faded red letters: The Snow of the Admiral. It was run by a man they called the Gaviero. Absolutely nothing was known about his origin or past. Most of his face was covered by a thick graying beard. He walked with a makeshift bamboo crutch. A foul-smelling, iridescent wound on his right leg oozed continually, but he never paid attention to it. He waited on the customers, walking back and forth to the dry, regular beat of his crutch against the floorboards, a muffled sound that vanished into the desolation of the barren uplands. The man spoke little but smiled frequently, not at what he heard but to himself, a smile that seemed out of phase with the travelers' comments. A woman helped him at his work. She had a savage, concentrated, distracted air. Through the shawls and ponchos that protected her from the cold, there were hints of a body that was still strong and no stranger to pleasure. Pleasure filled with essences, aromas, memories of places where great rivers moved down to the sea under a dome of vegetation motionless in the lowland heat. She sang sometimes; the woman sang in a thin voice like the lazy call of birds in the great burning distances of the plain. The Gaviero would watch her for as long as the sharp, sinuous animal crooning lasted. When the drivers returned to their trucks and began the descent out of the cordillera, that song went with them; fed by empty distance and fatal abandonment, it left them on the brink of a longing beyond all appeal.

But something else in the Gaviero's ramshackle store made it memorable to the men who used to stop there and were familiar with the place: a narrow passage led to a back gallery that was supported by wooden beams and extended over a precipice half hidden by ferns. They went there to urinate, but despite their meticulous patience, they could never hear a splash. The sound was lost in the fogbound, overgrown depths of the ravine.

Phrases, observations, and sayings were written on the peeling walls of the passageway. Many were remembered and repeated throughout the region although no one ever really deciphered their purpose or meaning. The Gaviero had written them, and a good number were smudged by customers brushing against the wall on their way to that uncommon urinal.

Some of those that remained most tenaciously in people's memories are transcribed below:

I am the disordered creator of the most obscure routes, the most secret moorings. Their uselessness, their undiscovered location are what feed my days.

Keep that polished pebble. At the hour of your death you can caress it in the palm of your hand and use it to drive away the presence of your lamentable errors which, taken together, erase all possible significance from your vain existence.

Every fruit is blind to its gentler substances. There are regions where man digs out of his happiness the small, underground chambers of a discontent without reason or cure.

Follow the ships. Follow the routes plowed by worn, melancholy vessels. Don't stop. Avoid even the humblest anchorage. Sail up the rivers, down the rivers. Lose yourself in the rains that flood the savannas. Deny all shores.

Take note of the neglect that reigns here. Like the days of my life. That's all it was. It will never be otherwise.

Women never lie. Truth always pours from the most secret folds of their bodies. Our lot is to interpret it with an implacable paucity. Many men never can and die in the inescapable blindness of their senses.

Two metals exist that prolong life and sometimes grant happiness. Not gold or silver or anything else you can imagine. I only know they exist.

I should have followed the caravans. I would have died and been buried by the camel drivers and covered by the dung of their herds under the lofty tableland sky. It would have been better, much better. All the rest has truly lacked interest.

Many other phrases had been rubbed away by the hands and bodies that passed through the dark passageway. These seem to be the ones that gained most favor among the upland people. They surely allude to the Gaviero's earlier days and appeared in this place through the whims of a memory that flickers before it goes out forever.

THE ARACURIARE
CANYON

To understand the effect on the Gaviero's life of the time he
spent in the Aracuriare Canyon, one must consider certain
features of a place that is usually deserted because it is far from any
road or trail used by people from the low country, and because it
has a dismal reputation, which, although not entirely undeserved,
still does not correspond to its true image.

The river rushes down from the cordillera in a torrent of icy
water that crashes against boulders and treacherous shoals, creating
a frenzy of foam and whirlpools and the wild, furious roar of an
unrestrained current. It is thought that the river carries sands heavy
with gold, and prospectors often make precarious camp at its edge
and wash the earth along the bank, but so far there have been no
significant finds. Hopelessness soon overwhelms these outsiders,
and local fevers and plagues make short work of their lives. The
constant humid heat and a scarcity of food finish off those who are
not accustomed to the burning climate. Such undertakings usually
end in a rosary of humble mounds, resting places for the bones of
men who never knew rest or tranquillity in life. The river begins
to slow when it enters a narrow valley, and the water acquires a
smooth, peaceful surface that hides the dense energy of the current,
free at last from all obstacles. At the end of the valley looms an
imposing mass of granite split in two by a dark cleft. This is where
the river, in a silent rush of water as solemn as a processional,
penetrates the shadowy canyon. The interior, formed by walls that
rise straight up to the sky, their surface covered by a sparse growth
of lianas and ferns struggling to reach the sun, has the air of an
abandoned cathedral, a half-light disturbed from time to time by

sparrow hawks that nest in the narrow crevices of the rock, or flocks of parrots whose screeches fill the canyon with a nerve-shattering din that brings one's oldest longings back to life.

The river has created a few slate-colored beaches that glisten during the brief intervals when sunlight reaches the bottom of the canyon. Usually the water's surface is so serene that the movement of the current can hardly be detected. Only an occasional bubbling can be heard, ending in a vague sigh, a kind of profound complaint that rises from the depths and betrays the immense, treacherous energy hidden in the river's peaceful flow.

The Gaviero traveled there to deliver the instruments, scales, and mercury ordered by a pair of prospectors with whom he had contracted in an oil port on the coast. When he arrived he learned that his customers had died several weeks earlier and been buried by a charitable soul at the entrance to the canyon. Their names were written on a worm-eaten board in an improbable orthography that the Gaviero could hardly decipher. He entered the canyon and walked the smooth, broad beaches, where he occasionally saw a bird skeleton or the remains of a raft carried there by the current from a distant settlement further up the valley.

The warm monastic silence, its isolation from all human disorder and tumult, and an intense, insistent call impossible to put into words or even thoughts, were enough to make the Gaviero feel a desire to stay for a time, if only to escape the noisy traffic in the ports and the contrary star of his insatiable wandering.

With pieces of wood collected along the shore and palm leaves pulled from the current, he built a hut on a slate shoal that rose at the end of the beach where he decided to live. The fruits continually washed down by the river and the birds he caught without difficulty were his food.

The days passed, and with no particular purpose in mind the Gaviero began an examination of his life, a catalogue of his miseries, his mistakes, his precarious joys and confused passions. He resolved to go deep into this task, and his success was so thorough and devastating that he rid himself completely of the self who had accompanied him all his life, the one who had suffered all the pain and difficulty. He moved ahead in the search for his own frontiers, his true limits, and when he saw the protagonist of what he had always considered his own life recede and disappear, all that remained was the self engaged in the scrutiny, the act of simplification. He persisted in his effort to learn more about the new man born of his deepest essence, and a mixture of astonishment and joy suddenly overwhelmed him, for a third, impassive spectator was waiting for him, taking form and shape in the very center of his being. He was convinced that this self, who had never taken part in any of the episodes of his life, must know all the truth, all the pathways, all the motives, that had woven his destiny, which he could see now with naked clarity, and he realized suddenly that it was entirely useless and worthy only of rejection. But as he faced that absolute witness of himself, he also felt the serene, ameliorating acceptance he had spent so many years searching for in the fruitless symbols of adventure.

Until that confrontation, the Gaviero had gone through arduous periods of searching and testing and making many false discoveries in the canyon. The atmosphere with its resonance of a basilica, and the ocher blanket of water moving with hypnotic slowness, were confused in his memory with the internal movement that carried him toward this third, impassive sentinel of his existence, who did not judge, either to praise or condemn, who did no more than observe him with an otherworldly intensity that in turn reflected, like a mirror, the astonished passing of the moments of Maqroll's life. Serenity tinged with a kind of feverish pleasure invaded him, anticipating that portion of joy which we all hope to achieve before we die but which recedes as the years advance and the despair they bring with them increases.

The Gaviero felt that if the plenitude he had just attained could continue, death would lack all importance and be simply one more episode in the script, accepted as easily as one turns a corner or rolls over in bed while sleeping. For Maqroll the granite walls, the lazy flow of water, the smooth surfaces and echoing emptiness of the canyon, were like a premonitory image of the kingdom of forgotten men, the domain where death mingles with the procession of her sleepless creatures.

Since he knew that from then on the way things happened would be very different from what it had been in the past, the Gaviero delayed leaving, put off joining in the clamor of men. He was afraid to disturb his newly won tranquillity. Finally, one day, he tied some balsa trunks into a raft with vines, reached the middle of the current, and sailed downriver through the narrow gorge. A week later he emerged into the white light of the delta where the river empties into a calm, warm sea, and a light mist rises that makes distance more remote and expands the horizon into endless extension.

He spoke to no one of his time in the Aracuriare Canyon. What is written here was taken from notes discovered in the armoire of the miserable hotel room where he spent his last days before leaving for the marshlands.

THE GAVIERO'S VISIT

*H*is appearance had changed completely. Not that he looked older, more worn by the passing years and the harsh climates he frequented. He hadn't been away that long. It was something else. Something revealed in his weary, oblique gaze. Something in his shoulders, which had lost all their expressive movement and were held rigid, as if they no longer had to bear the weight of life or the prodding of its joys and sorrows. His voice had become noticeably muted and had a velvety, neutral tone. It was the voice of a man who speaks because the silence of others would be unbearable.

He carried a rocking chair to the gallery that faced the coffee plantings on the riverbank and sat down with an expectant air, as if the night breeze that would not be long in coming might relieve his profound but indeterminate misfortune. The water crashing against the great rocks provided a distant accompaniment to his words and brought an opaque joy to the monotonous recounting of his affairs, which had not changed but were submerged now in an indifferent, toneless chant that betrayed his present condition of hopeless defeat. He was a hostage of the void.

"I sold women's clothing at the Guásimo ford where upland women crossed the river on fiesta days, and since they had to cross the river on foot and their clothes got wet even though they hiked them up above their waists, they would buy something from me so they wouldn't have to walk into town looking bedraggled.

"There was a time when that procession of dark, powerful thighs, round, firm buttocks, bellies like the breast of a dove, would have excited me to frenzy. I left the place when a jealous brother came after me with a machete because he thought I was making advances to a smiling green-eyed girl when I was only measuring her for a skirt of flowered percale. She stopped him in time. A sudden disgust made me sell all my goods in a few hours and go away forever.

"That was when I lived for a few months in an abandoned railroad car on the tracks they never finished laying. I once told you about it. Besides, it's not important.

"After that I went down to the ports and signed on a freighter headed for fogbound, unmercifully cold places. To pass the time and relieve my boredom, I would go down to the machine room and tell the stokers the story of the last four Grand Dukes of Burgundy. I had to shout over the roaring boilers and clattering rods. They always asked me to repeat the death of John the Fearless at the hands of the king's men on Montereau Bridge, and the celebration of the marriage of Charles the Bold to Marguerite of York. Eventually that was all I did during our endless passage through fog and great blocks of ice. The captain forgot I existed until the chief petty officer went to him one day with the story that I wasn't letting the stokers do their work and was filling their heads with tales of bloody assassinations and outrageous attempts on the lives of great men. He'd heard me tell about the end of the last duke in Nancy, and who knows what the poor man thought. They put me ashore in a port along the Scheldt, my only possessions the patched rags on my back and an inventory of anonymous graves in the cemeteries on Mount Saint Lazarus.

"Then I dedicated myself to preaching and praying at the entrance to the Main River refineries. I announced the coming of a new Kingdom of God in which a strict, detailed interchange of sins and penitences would be established so that an inconceivable shock or a joy as brief as it was intense might be waiting for us at any hour of the day or night. I sold small sheets printed with litanies for a good death, in which the essentials of the doctrine were summarized. I've forgotten most of them, although I sometimes remember three invocations in my dreams:

> *ingot of life, shed thy scales*
>
> *wellspring of water, gather in the shadows*
>
> *angel of mire, cut thy wings.*

"I often wonder whether these lines really formed part of the litany or if they are the offspring of my mournful, recurrent dreams. This isn't the time to find out, and it really doesn't interest me."

The Gaviero abruptly halted the tale of his increasingly precarious wanderings and launched into a long, rambling, apparently pointless monologue that I remember with painful fidelity and a vague revulsion I cannot account for.

"Because in the end all these trades, encounters, places, have stopped being the true substance of my life, to such an extent that I don't know which are products of my imagination and which belong to real experience. By means of them, through them, I try in vain to escape the obsessions that are certainly real, permanent, and true, and that weave the final chain of events, the evident destination of my journey through the world. It isn't easy to isolate them and give them a name, but they are roughly these:

"To settle for a happiness like that of certain childhood days in exchange for a shortened life.

"To prolong solitude and not fear the encounter with what we really are, with the man who talks to us and always hides so we won't sink into inescapable terror.

"To realize that nobody listens to anybody, nobody knows anything about anybody. That the word is mere deception, a trap that covers, disguises, buries the precarious structure of our dreams and truths, all of them bearing the mark of the incommunicable.

"To learn, above all, to distrust memory. What we believe we remember is completely alien to, completely different from what really happened. So many moments of irritating, wearisome disgust are returned to us years later by memory as splendidly happy episodes. Nostalgia is the lie that speeds our approach to death. To live without remembering may be the secret of the gods.

"When I tell about my wanderings, my failures, my simpleminded deliriums and secret orgies, it is only to choke off, almost in midair, the animal screams, the piercing howls from the cave that would express more accurately what I really feel and what I really am. But I'm losing myself in digressions, and that isn't why I came."

His eyes took on a leaden stare, as if he were looking at a thick wall of colossal proportions. His lower lip trembled slightly. He folded his arms across his chest and began to rock slowly, as if trying to keep time to the sound of the river. A smell of fresh mud, of crushed vegetation and rotting sap, indicated that the waters were rising. The Gaviero was silent for a long time, until night fell with that dizzying explosion of darkness typical of the tropics. Intrepid fireflies danced in the warm silence of the coffee plantings. He began to speak, lost in another digression whose significance escaped me as he entered the darkest zones of his being. When he returned suddenly to events from his past, I could follow his monologue again.

"I've had few surprises in life," he said, "and none of them is worth the telling, but for me each has the mournful energy of a bell tolling catastrophe. One morning, in the stupefying heat of a river port, while I was putting on my clothes in a shabby room in a miserable brothel, I found a photograph of my father hanging on the wooden wall. He was sitting in a wicker rocking chair on the verandah of a white hotel in the Caribbean. During her long widowhood my mother always kept that photograph in the same spot on her night table. 'Who's that?' I asked the woman I'd spent the night with; only now could I see all the wretched disorder of her flesh, the animality of her face. 'My father,' she answered with a sorrowful smile that revealed her toothless mouth, and she covered her fat nakedness with a sheet soaked in perspiration and misery. 'I never knew him, but my mother, she worked here too, she always remembered him and even kept some of his letters, like that could keep her young forever.' I finished dressing and went out to the wide, unpaved street that was blasted by sun, blaring radios, the clatter of cutlery and dishes in the cafés and cantinas beginning to fill with their regular clientele of truck drivers, cattle dealers, and soldiers from the air base. I thought with faint sadness that this was precisely the corner of life I would never have wanted to turn. Bad luck.

"Another time I went to a hospital in the Amazon after an attack of malaria that was draining my strength and keeping me delirious with fever. The heat at night was unbearable, yet it saved me from the whirlpools of vertigo whose center was some trivial phrase or the tone of a voice I couldn't identify, the fever spinning around it until all my bones ached. In the next bed a trader who'd been bitten by a gangrene spider was fanning the black pustule that covered his left side. 'This'll dry up soon, this'll dry up soon and

I'll get out and close the deal. I'll be so rich I'll forget all about this hospital and the goddamn jungle that's only fit for monkeys and alligators.' The deal had something to do with a complicated traffic in spare parts for the seaplanes that flew the area with preferential import licenses, issued by the Army, which made them exempt from customs inspection and taxes. At least that's what I dimly remember, because all night the man babbled about the smallest details of the affair, and one by one they became part of the whirling crises of my malaria. Finally, at dawn, I managed to fall asleep, but I was besieged by pain and panic that lasted all day and far into the night. 'Look, here are the papers. They'll get all screwed up. You'll see. Tomorrow I leave for sure,' he said one night, and repeated the words with fierce insistence as he brandished a handful of blue and pink papers covered with stamps and captions in three languages. The last thing I heard him say before I succumbed to a long bout of fever was: 'Oh, what a relief, what joy. This shit is over!' The thunder of a gunshot woke me. It sounded like the end of the world. I looked at my neighbor: his head, shattered by the bullet, was still quivering, as mushy as a rotten fruit. I was moved to another room, where I hung between life and death until the cool breezes of the rainy season brought me back to life.

"I don't know why I'm telling you this. I really came to leave these papers with you. You'll know what to do with them if we don't see each other again. They're letters from my youth, some pawn tickets, and a rough draft of the book I'll never finish. A study of the real reasons that Cesare Borgia, Duke of Valentinois, went to the court of his brother-in-law, the King of Navarre, and helped him in the struggle against the King of Aragón. How he died at dawn, ambushed by soldiers in the outskirts of Viana. There are twists behind this story, dark areas I once thought were worth clarifying. That was years ago. I'm also leaving an iron cross that I found in an Almogávar ossuary in the garden of an abandoned mosque in an Anatolian suburb. It's always brought me good luck, but I think the time has come to travel without it. And here are the bills and vouchers that prove my innocence in that matter of the explosives factory at the Sereno mines. The Hungarian medium who was my companion at the time, and a Paraguayan partner and I—we were going to retire to Madeira on the profits, but they made off with everything, and I was the one who had to settle accounts. The case was closed years ago, but a certain urge for order made me hold on to these receipts, and now I don't want to carry them with me either.

"Well, I'll say goodbye. I'm going to take an empty barge to the Mártir Swamp, and if I pick up some passengers downriver, I'll have enough money to start again." He stood up and extended his hand with the gesture, part ceremonial, part military, that was so typical of him. Before I could urge him to stay the night and start downriver the next morning, he had disappeared into the coffee plantings, whistling a rather trite old song that had been the joy of our youth. I looked through his papers and found a good number of clues to the Gaviero's past life that he had never mentioned. Just then, down below, I heard the sound of his footsteps echoing against the zinc roof of the covered bridge that crosses the river. I felt his absence, and I began to recall his voice and gestures, and how much they had changed, and they came back to me now like an ominous warning that I would never see him again.

Ilona
Comes with the Rain

For my brother Leopoldo

Qedeshím qedeshóth,* *celebrated mad*
priestess, bronze, howl
of bronze, not even Augustine
of Hippo, a lecher and
sinner in Africa, would
have robbed the diaphanous
Phoenician of her body
for a night. I, a sinner,
confess my sin to God.

Gonzalo Rojas, "Qedeshím qedeshóth"

Son amour désintéressé du monde m'enrichit et m'insuffla une
force invincible pour les jours difficiles.

Maxim Gorki, Enfance

*In Phoenician: temple courtesan.

When Maqroll the Gaviero told stories about his life to his friends, he preferred those episodes adorned with a certain dramatic quality, a tension that could occasionally reach an openly lyrical mood or end in mystery with all its metaphysical, and therefore unanswerable, questions. Yet those of us who knew him well for many years also know there were specific periods of immensely troubled existence, which although not completely lacking in the characteristics so dear to the storyteller, tended to reveal a marginal aspect of his character that often brushed against, and even openly went beyond, the limits established by the penal code for the regulation of society. For Maqroll morality was a singularly flexible material that he often adjusted to current circumstances. He did not concern himself with what the future might bring as a result of the transgressions he forgot so easily, and crimes he may have committed in the past were in no way burdensome to him. Past and future, it should be noted, were not particularly weighty notions for his spirit. He always gave the impression that his exclusive and absorbing purpose was to enrich the present with everything he happened upon. It was clear, and others who knew him as well or better than I concur in this, that all the decrees, principles, rules, and precepts generally known as the law were of no great significance to Maqroll, who never gave them a moment's thought. They were something in effect outside the boundaries he had established for his own affairs, and there was no reason they should be allowed to distract him from his personal, rather capricious designs.

At flood tides of wine and reminiscence I heard my friend relate events in his life that were not the ones he summoned most frequently when attacked by nostalgia or, perhaps, what I would call a thirst for the unknown. Some of these episodes are recounted here in the voice of their protagonist. They seemed of interest for what they revealed of his other face, and I was very careful to return to them often with Maqroll until they, as well as the inflections of his voice and the digressions he was so fond of making, were fixed in my memory.

It goes without saying that I do not believe Maqroll kept these episodes to himself because he was ashamed or distressed by their frank marginality. I believe it was more a case of not wishing to implicate other participants in adventures they might prefer to conceal or forget for reasons of modesty and fear that, although not valid for the Gaviero, might be so for others. In any case I am aware of prolonging an unnecessary explanation, but the printed word is so definitive, so testimonial and compromising that it is difficult to simply release it, without precautions, to the scrutiny of possible readers. This was all I wanted to say. Now we will allow our friend to speak.

CRISTOBAL

When I saw the gray customs launch approaching with the Panamanian flag fluttering proudly at the stern, I knew we had reached the end of our troubled voyage. In fact, for the past several weeks every time we docked in a port, we had expected a visit like this one. Only the customary lax handling of bureaucratic affairs in the Caribbean had kept us safe until now. The launch made its way through still, gray water where unidentifiable pieces of garbage and decomposing dead birds were floating. The keel parted the oily surface, creating a slow wave that disappeared lazily a short distance away. We were far from the constantly changing turmoil of the open sea. Three officials dressed in khaki, perspiration staining their armpits and shoulders, climbed the ladder with unhurried pomposity. The man who seemed to be in charge, one of the blacks called Jamaicans because the Yankees brought their forebears here from the island to work on the construction of the canal, asked for the captain in an unshapely Spanish laced with Anglicisms. I led the way to the second bridge and knocked on the cabin door several times. At last a thick, weary voice answered, "Come in." I opened the door for the officials, closed it after them, and went back down to the foot of the ladder, where I had been talking to the first mate. The launch's engine purred with unexpected changes in rhythm, while an implacable heat fell from a cloudless sky and intensified the stink of rotting vegetation and mud from the mangrove swamps drying in the sun and waiting for the next high tide.

"It's all over. Now it's every man for himself and then we'll see what happens," said the first mate, looking toward the docks of

Cristóbal as if they held the answer to his disquietude. Cornelius was a short, plump Dutchman forever puffing on a pipe filled with the cheapest tobacco. He spoke an impeccable Spanish enriched with the most varied and picturesque curses. It was as if he had proposed to collect them during the years he sailed the islands, for they now constituted an authentic sampling of Caribbean scatology. When the voyage began, he seemed to treat me with a certain mistrust born of the irritability that afflicts seamen when they reach a position of command. They are always suspicious of any stranger who appears to be invading what they consider their domain. I managed to break down his initial reaction fairly soon, and we established a somewhat distant but cordial and solid relationship, maintained by our reconstruction of anecdotes and shared experiences, which would end in outbursts of laughter or die away against a backdrop of dreamy, defeated memory.

"There's no way Wito can escape impoundment. It's as if he'd been searching for it. If he loses the ship and this way of life, he won't mind. It will mean the end of a routine he stopped believing in a long time ago. All of this has been boring him to death for so long. At least that's what I assume from his attitude during this voyage. What do you think, Cornelius? You know him better than I do. How long have you two been together?" I was trying, without much conviction, to keep the conversation going while the obscure judicial ceremony that had threatened us for so many weeks was taking place overhead.

"Eleven years," answered the first mate. "What fucked up poor Wito's life was when his only daughter ran away with a Protestant minister from Barbados, a married man with six children. He left his parishoners, his church, his family, and took the girl to Alaska. Poor kid—besides being ugly, she's half deaf, too. That's when Wito began his crazy business deals. He took out mortgages on the boat and I think a house in Willemstad. You know how it is, you rob Peter to pay Paul. I'll bet those shits are here to fix him but good."

He shrugged his shoulders and puffed nervously on his pipe as he looked up at the cabin, where a discussion was going on whose outcome was perfectly predictable. In a little while the uniformed men came out. They put some papers in their portfolios and, saluting with a careless slap of hands against the visors of their hats, climbed down the ladder and onto the launch, which pulled away, cutting gently through the water in the direction of Cristóbal.

The captain appeared at the door of his cabin and called, "Maqroll, would you come here for a minute, please?" Now his voice was firm and steady. We went into the cabin, and he asked me to have a seat in front of the table that he used as a desk and where we had our meals. A weight seemed to have been lifted from his shoulders. He was a slim man of medium height, with sharp, foxlike features and eyes almost hidden by bushy, graying eyebrows. The first thing you noticed about him was the absence of any nautical traits. Not a single gesture identified him with the men of the sea. It was easier to imagine him as the headmaster of a boarding school or a teacher of natural sciences. His speech was slow, precise, almost pompous; he emphasized every word and paused slightly at the end of each sentence as if he were expecting someone to take notes on what he was saying. And yet behind that professorial air it was easy to detect a kind of emotional disorder, a need to hide something like a secret, painful wound. It moved those of us who had known him for some time to feel warm indulgence for the captain, though this never ended in deep or lasting friendship. Somewhere in his soul he bore the mark of the defeated that isolates them irremediably from other men.

"Well, Maqroll," he began, speaking more slowly than ever, "as you must have guessed, this has to do with the boat. It's been impounded by a bank consortium in Panama City." He seemed to be apologizing in advance, and gave me the uncomfortable feeling that he was going to make a confession I would have preferred not to hear. A small fan attached to the wall in front of us hummed as it slowly turned but did not cool the air heavy with the smell of sweaty clothing and stale cigarette butts. "It's finally happened," he continued, "the thing I've been afraid of for months. I've lost the ship and my house in Willemstad. The creditors will hire a crew to take the boat to Panama City. If you like, you and the first mate can go through the canal with them, and they'll pay you in Panama City according to the terms of the contract you signed with me. Now, if you prefer to stay here, they'll pay you just the same. All you have to do is let them know. Whatever you prefer."

"And what do you intend to do, Captain?" I asked, disturbed by the cool, calm way he was taking everything.

"Don't worry about me, Maqroll. You're very kind. I've made plans to . . ." He stammered in fleeting but visible embarrassment. ". . . to move on. Having you as a friend has been one of the finest things in my life. You've taught me lessons you're probably not even aware of, but they've helped me to endure, with varying degrees of success, and to hold on to what you call 'life's unexpected gifts.' There's a good deal to say on that subject, but I don't think this is the time for confessions. Besides, I suspect you know more about it than I do." He stood up rather abruptly and offered his hand, giving me a firm handshake into which he tried to put all the warmth he had avoided in his words. As I was leaving, he asked me to tell Cornelius to come up to talk to him.

Wito took even less time with the first mate than he had with me. When the Dutchman came back, I was engrossed in looking toward port, a dull depression growing inside me to match the prolonged silence of that dead muddy water. A silence that seemed to originate in the heat and increase as the afternoon stretched across the sky in a faint, luminescent, treacherous cloud. Cornelius leaned against the polished brass rail, his back to the ocean. He said nothing about his interview with the captain. He knew there was no point. It couldn't have been very different from what Wito said to me. Cornelius puffed at his pipe with the urgency of a man trying to rid his mind of an obsessive, wounding idea.

The shot rang out like the sharp, dry crack of wood. A pair of gulls dozing on the antenna flew away in an uproar of flapping wings and screeching that disappeared with them into the darkening sky. We raced up the ladder and into the cabin, where the strong smell of gunpowder caught in our throats. The captain, seated on his chair, was slipping to the floor. His eyes had the lost, glassy stare of the dying. A trickle of blood ran down his temple and joined two others streaming from his nose. His mouth smiled in a grimace that was completely alien to Wito's usual expressions. We felt a peculiar discomfort, as if we were violating the privacy of a total stranger. The body finally fell with a muffled thud, while the humming fan cut through the silence imposed by death when she wants to signal her presence among the living.

We radioed the harbor authorities, who lost no time in coming out in the same launch that had visited us earlier. This time there were three policemen in white uniforms and a kinky-haired mulatto doctor who made a clumsy effort to arrange his white coat, trying to achieve a moderately professional air that in no way suited his look of a happy-go-lucky cumbé dancer. The proceedings were brief. The police put the body in a gray plastic bag and dropped it into the launch like a sack of mail. Night had fallen by the time they left. The harbor lights went on in a blaze of gaudy neon. Music from the cabarets and cantinas was starting up the sad, raucous fiesta of the Antillean tropics.

We had met in New Orleans after being out of touch for many years. I went into a shop on Decatur Street with the presumptuous, misleading name Gourmet Boutique. It displayed a collection of pointless, silly objects, allegedly useful in the bar and kitchen, as well as foods and spices of the most varied origins and brands, all of them suspiciously similar in packaging to those sold as exclusives by certain shops in London, Paris, or New York. I wanted to buy candied ginger, a secret passion that I indulge even in my worst times of poverty. The price on the jar was so high that I went to the cashier to make certain it was correct, and there was Wito paying for two tins of Darjeeling tea, his favorite drink. Before saying anything we looked at one another and smiled with the complicity of old friends who know their mutual weaknesses and have caught each other in flagrante delicto. Wito insisted on paying for my ginger after the owner, in the Brooklyn accent that warns us we have everything to lose, gave his unctuous explanation for the outrageous price. Wito and I walked out together. After expressing the gravest doubts regarding the authenticity of both the tea and the ginger, my friend invited me to eat supper with him. He had a cook from Jamaica who was preparing a leg of pork with plums, a dish worthy of the highest honors. His ship was docked at the Bienville piers directly across from the shop where we had met. It was a freighter painted a furious yellow that I have seen only on the ruffs of toucans along the Carare. The bridge, cabins, and offices were white, and had needed a new coat of paint for some time. The name, too grandiose for the ship's modest tonnage and even more modest appearance, was the *Hansa Stern*. Susana, my friend's wife, had baptized it. In her youth she had lived for a time in Hamburg, and maintained her admiration for the great cities of the Baltic, glorifying them considerably in the process. Wito did not want to change the name out of respect for her memory. No explanation was necessary, but one of his typical character traits was a professorial and very Germanic need to explain everything with pointless precision, as if the rest of the human race needed his assistance to understand the world.

Winfried Geltern. His life deserves an entire book. It was so full of adventures, some of which he hurried over as if they were hot coals, that one became lost in their labyrinthine complexity. In the ports and coves of the Caribbean he was always known as Wito. It's impossible to say where the absurd abbreviation of that proud Viking name originated. In those places everything is eventually reduced to proportions that fluctuate between awkward travesty and a sad irony born of the island climate and the devastating, sordid poverty of the coast. With a certain sense of dramatic justice, his foxlike profile and air of a professor gone astray prevented the title of ship's captain from being added to his nickname. He was called Wito, just Wito, and he never let on that he knew how ridiculous the improbable diminutive was. Born in Danzig to a Westphalian family, he spoke all the languages of the world with disconcerting fluency. As if the sea were alien to his habits, his ideas and preferences, he never told stories or gave details about his life on board ship. His carriage was erect and rather stiff, and this worked wonderfully to emphasize his conversation, which he measured out with a watchmaker's meticulous exactitude. Wito often had moments of sardonic humor, and his paradoxes erupted without warning and were extinguished just as suddenly. One day I heard him say with absolute seriousness: "Weather is a purely personal matter. There is no such thing as a climate that is cold or hot, good or bad, healthy or unhealthy. People take it upon themselves to create a fantasy in their imaginations and call it weather. There's only one climate in the world, but the message that nature sends is interpreted according to strictly personal, nontransferable rules. I've seen Lapps sweating in Finland and blacks shivering with cold in Guadeloupe." When he concluded such statements, he would underscore his words with a repeated military bow, as if he had just pronounced judgment on the fate of the universe. One never knew whether to receive these paradoxes with a smile or with the conventional gravity of a disciple enlightened by the truth.

We ate in his cabin, and I had to agree that the arts of the cook from Kingston were as praiseworthy as his employer had promised.

Wito lit a cigarette made of black tobacco that gave off the acid stench of burning leaves, and over two cups of very strong coffee we began to talk about what had happened to us during the years we had not seen each other. When I finished, I told him I was going through one of those times when nothing turns out well. I was stranded in New Orleans and running out of the few dollars I had left after liquidating a lucrative business in deep-sea fishing equipment that I sold to people on Grand Isle in the Caymans. I had sent my SOS to friends on five continents but received no replies. It was as if they had all died. "Yes," Wito interjected. "Then you'll run into them in a bar somewhere and with a look of rehearsed surprise they'll ask, 'But where have you been? We thought you were dead.' " Well, the fact was I barely had enough in my pocket to pay my bill at a disastrous boardinghouse in a Turkish-Moroccan neighborhood where I had landed with a belly dancer, the niece of the filthy hole's landlady. The dancer lost no time in running away to San Francisco, and I stayed to endure, with relative patience, an endless rosary of accusations from the embittered aunt, who blamed me for the flight of the girl she called her innocent niece. An absolute jewel of a girl even more promising than the good lady suspected. In her possession were a minimum of ten extremely expensive watches that she had spirited away from patrons who came up during her dance to tuck a grimy five-dollar bill, or even some worthless South American currency, into the skirt or bra of her costume. Wito looked at me through the dense thicket of his eyebrows while a satisfied smile played over his harmless fox's face.

"Come with me," he said when my story was over. "I need a purser, and even though numbers are not your strong point, the work is so simple even you can do it. I had one but he contracted malaria and was hospitalized in Guiana. Merchant Marine regulations require a purser on board. You're the answer to my problem. But I have to tell you, Gaviero, things aren't going much better for me than they are for you. I began falling into debt about a year ago. I was managing to make my payments, but then suddenly everything became more difficult. There's no cargo, and every day another pirate airline with three old DC-4s transports freight at prices that make me wonder how they can pay for fuel."

"It depends on the cargo, Wito, it depends on the cargo," I explained, alarmed at his naïveté.

"Yes," he went on, "you're right, what a fool I am. Well, the fact is that the banks own two thirds of the *Hansa Stern*. But now I have good prospects for a load of copra from San Andrés Island to Recife, I think, and tomorrow they'll decide about a lumber shipment from Campeche to Houston. If both deals go through, the ship is free and clear, and we can take off for Cyprus and transport pilgrims."

That was where we first met, a good number of years ago, in circumstances that will be described in due course. Naturally I accepted Wito's offer, although I had serious doubts regarding the solid reality of the two transactions that were going to extricate us from our predicament. Something adrift in my friend's eyes was telling me that matters may have been much worse than even he could accept. But staying in New Orleans meant really hitting rock bottom. I felt a profound antipathy toward the city as it was now. The lively Creole port, with its wonderful music and bold, beautiful women from the four corners of the earth, had become a pretentious tart painted with local color as vulgar as it was false, her arms opened wide to tourists from Texas and the Midwest, a repugnant sample of the worst of the American middle class. All that remained was the river, majestic and constantly moving, which seemed to turn its dignified back on the lamentable spectacle of a city that had once been its favorite. I picked up my gear and left the landlady cursing at me in three Anatolian dialects while the cab pulled away and the driver, a gigantic black, laughed without understanding a word of the dire outburst pouring down behind me. In the purser's cabin I unpacked my few belongings, which all fit into a fairly disreputable seaman's bag. I was locking the door, on my way to supper with Wito, when I ran into Cornelius. I've already said what his initial reaction was. My long experience with Frisians gave me the confidence I needed to endure his withdrawn irritability during my first few days on board.

As I had suspected from the start, the business ventures were not what Wito had described. The Campeche lumber shipment shrank to a meager operation involving the transport of railroad ties from the Mexican port to Belize. A pittance. And the copra deal amounted to two trips between San Andrés and Cartagena, the disgusting stuff filling the air with an intense oily smell like the stink of bedbugs. Not enough to pay for the diesel we used. Then followed some equally significant cargo that clearly did not cover the costs of operating the *Hansa Stern,* a name that was becoming increasingly inappropriate and grotesque. Wito owed us almost three months' salary. He would make his excuses after supper, hiding his gray eyes behind the forest of hair that protected them. "I can take this painful liberty with you because you're my friends and understand better than anybody how these things are. But I can't pay the suppliers, the harbor authorities, and the rest of the crew with words and declarations of friendship. Something's bound to turn up, I'm sure of that, but I hope to God it's soon. I don't know what to do." He ran his hand through his graying crew cut with the gesture of a man trying to prove a geometrical theorem by some obscure, unconventional method. Cornelius and I always responded to his awkward excuses by attempting to encourage him and raise his spirits. Of course he didn't have to worry about us, we were all in the same boat—the joke didn't make him smile, of course, because we had repeated it so often—and before he knew it, we'd have the contract that would keep us afloat—at this point Wito didn't even notice the unlikely humor.

His capacity for magnifying possible business transactions had been visibly affected. Not that he sank into depression or despair. For him that would have been unthinkable. Quite simply, the internal mechanism that had sustained him for so many years jammed, and he was running in a kind of neutral. The rigidity of his gestures and postures was becoming more pronounced and his Baltic silences more prolonged. He no longer lingered at the table after a meal, recalling the old days: our meeting in Cyprus; his first voyage with Cornelius, who had been his wife's classmate in Rotterdam; our travels in the Adriatic with Abdul Bashur, our friend and accomplice in transactions that touched areas forbidden by law. He was manifestly taciturn. Now he said nothing over his cup of black coffee and, with increasing frequency, the tiny glass of raspberry liqueur that he drank in one swallow and refilled over and over again with an absent but courteous air.

Wito's wife came from a Jewish family in Amsterdam. They married when he was first officer on the *Murla,* a passenger ship in the Nord Deutsche Lloyd Bremen line. She always loved him as passionately as a fifteen-year-old. When Wito attained the rank of captain, she bought the *Hansa Stern* with money from an inheritance left to her in Aruba by a childless aunt and uncle. The ship had another name then, one more suited to its modest tonnage. Susana rechristened it, inspired by her memories of Hamburg. In the early days she often accompanied Wito on his voyages, and in the Antilles she was baptized Wita, which could have been predicted, knowing the island people. Her real name was Susana, and the nickname Wita made no sense, but it couldn't be helped and she accepted it with total indifference colored occasionally by a certain Jewish humor. Her appearance was strikingly different from her husband's: she had the physique of a Wagnerian soprano, a broad, smiling face, and the rosy complexion of a girl, which added considerable charm to her dark, expressive eyes full of tireless intelligence and energy. She treated me with the affection of a younger sister. She would always scold me with mock impatience:

"Ah, Gaviero! I don't know what you see in all this bumming around of yours from one place to the next. Why don't you get married and settle down somewhere?"

"Okay, I will someday. You help me find a wife," I would answer just to keep her quiet.

"No, that poor woman. You have more manias than an old rabbi and you get worse every day." And she would sit on my knees and pinch my ears, putting on a reproachful face.

I first met Wito in Cyprus, when Bashur and I were looking for a freighter to transport some unconventional merchandise, as Abdul and I, joking but cautious, had decided to call the shipment of weapons and explosives destined for a small naval station near Haifa. The operation was more than risky, and when we closed the deal, we asked Wito not to bring his wife. "If you're all going to be blown to bits, I want to be there too." She had made up her mind, and there was no dissuading her. The trip, filled with frightening moments, was peppered with delicious scenes of Wita feigning more panic than she really felt or exploding with glee when we got past a dangerous obstacle, whether it was a torpedo launch with a Union Jack in the stern or Egyptian planes buzzing us and sending signals it was better to ignore.

I was involved in the sale of the infernal Cocora mine when I heard that Wita had died in Willemstad of a carelessly treated case of typhoid. When she thought she was out of danger, she ate a basket of cherries that her parents had sent from Holland. I felt her absence as I've rarely been affected by anyone's death. She had an unusual talent for creating spontaneous joy, making it appear for no particular reason, because it accompanied her and her gestures, her laughter, because she loved people and animals, loved nightfall in the tropics and what she saw as the invariably childish and incomprehensible occupations and preoccupations of men. When we lose someone like her, we know that another portion of the meager happiness allotted us is gone forever.

Wito told me, in few words and without many details, about his daughter's flight with the Protestant minister. The girl was barely fifteen years old. She had not inherited Wita's rosy freshness but she did have her physique along with her father's rigid movements and something of his haggard coyote's look. She suffered from a hearing defect and a demonic temper. What hurt Wito most was the minister's Tartuffian hypocrisy, the honeyed piety with which he gained entrance to the house, taking advantage of the mother's absence and the girl's weakness. Wito forgave his daughter with the suspicious ease of a man who has rid himself of an unmanageable burden. When he recalled her, it seemed to be with silent reproach because she lacked all her mother's joyous virtues. Wito still loved his wife with a fervor incompatible with his age or the time that had elapsed since her death. Whenever he mentioned her, one had the impression that she was at his side. But recently even that familiar topic had begun to disappear from our dinner conversations. A chain of unthinking calamities and growing negligence, and a loss of will carefully disguised by strict adherence to an increasingly pointless daily routine, had finally brought everything to ruin.

My responsibilities had shrunk to almost nothing: a record of fuel consumption and expenditures; the payroll for fifteen sailors, a cook, and five mechanics; the buying and control of foodstuffs; an occasional incidental purchase. It took less than an hour a day. The rest of the time was spent in speculating, with Cornelius's help, on possible solutions to a situation that was becoming untenable. The Dutchman moved with a lassitude symptomatic of the inaction in which heavy men float when they have tended to their duties, which in his case amounted to going down occasionally to the machine room to supervise the work and, with increasing frequency, up to the bridge to relieve Wito, who spent more and more hours a day in his cabin staring into the darkness of his thoughts. We were all entering a state very close to controlled, sterile desperation. At one point I even thought that the impossible yellow paint on the *Hansa Stern* was the reason no cargo was waiting for us in any port. How could it ever have occurred to anyone to smear the dilapidated freighter with a color worthy of a parrot's tail, stripping away the little dignity that might have remained to this ship, built almost eighty years ago in Belfast, a veteran of numerous wars fought under the most anomalous flags. Only Susana Geltern, née Silverbach, who shared her husband's insouciance toward the things of the sea, could have done something like that. But blaming it all on the color was just another way of avoiding the problem. Clearly we had fallen victim to a devastating streak of bad luck. Each of our calamitous destinies had joined all the others with the force of a raging hurricane.

I've never thought that a transcendent sense of metaphysical fatality should be attributed to the times when misfortunes follow one another in catastrophic sequence. I've never believed in what they call bad luck if it's viewed as something ordained by a destiny we cannot change or redirect. I think it's more a matter of a certain order, external and alien to us, which imposes an adverse rhythm on our decisions and actions but in no way should affect our relationship to the world and its creatures. When a storm of bad luck vents its fury against me, I still enjoy the company of my drinking companions, the complicity of casual lovers, conversation with the wise, unflustered madams in houses of assignation, and the exchange of ideas with learned and highly esteemed friends in various parts of the world regarding the destiny of the great dynasties of the West, so often doomed by those fatal marriages that are arranged for clear political ends but then alter the course of history for centuries afterwards. In Puerto Rico, for example, I continue to ponder, with an eminent historian who is very dear to me, the consequences of the marriage of Marie of Burgundy to Maximilian of Austria. Losing oneself in these labyrinths may seem a sterile occupation to the uninitiated, but to me it appears much more practical and down-to-earth than charging blindly like a fool into external circumstances that conspire to complicate the purely utilitarian side of our life, which is surely less real and concrete given its fundamental, hopeless idiocy. In my case at least, nothing favors dynastic speculations more than the burning tropical heat that sharpens my senses and intelligence to the point of visionary delirium. It is then, when heat and humidity turn the night into a caldron, that sleep comes like a velvety, compassionate guillotine and leaves us on the shores of forgotten regions of childhood, or dark corners of history inhabited by figures whom we experience as ineffable, fraternal presences. In the weeks before we reached Cristóbal, I was visited over and over again by the recurrent dream in which I participate as a military and political adviser to the tall, dark, ascetically thin Palaeologus who rules Nicaea. Everything takes place with wonderful, spare efficiency. The successful conclusion of warlike undertakings and the signing of complex treaties occur within an order that might be called extratemporal and platonic, akin to the one that reigns both in the center of my being and in the golden flowering of the small empire on the shores of the Sea of Marmara. And this is why when my routine, daily affairs take an unlucky turn, as they did on the *Hansa Stern,* my affinity for the beings who populate history, and for the world that offers itself to my senses, still persists deep inside me. In fact, the more my practical difficulties multiply the more generously does that domain expand, along with my pleasure in the gifts that weave the essential warp and woof of my life.

Matters reached such a low point that during the second watch on a run to Martinique to pick up some Hindu families who were going to work in Guiana, Cornelius whispered to me in alarm, "Wito's paying for fuel with bad checks. You know you can't screw around with Esso. When we stop in Aruba for diesel, they'll be all over us. We're at the end of our rope, Gaviero, I'm telling you, the end of our rope." His predictions did not come true, or rather, they came true only in part. Two bounced checks were waiting for Wito in Aruba. He managed to cover them with money he obtained, as if by magic, three hours after a painful scene at the Esso refueling station. When we were back at sea, he confessed that he had pawned Susana's jewelry, which he had kept as a memento of love and good fortune, and the pocket watch his father had given to him when he passed his pilot's examination in Danzig. There could be no doubt about it now. This was the end of the rope so accurately predicted by Cornelius.

Wito suddenly had the idea of going to Panama. We never knew why. One morning, when Cornelius and I were on the bridge, he burst in, half awake and in pajamas, and in a thick, insomniac voice he ordered, "Change course, Cornelius, we're heading for Cristó-bal." And he went back to his cabin and the tea and toast with blueberry jam brought to him every morning by the cook. We didn't speak for a while. The first mate changed course and filled his pipe with a meticulous lack of enthusiasm. Then his only comment was: "Of course, now I understand, we're going to Cristóbal because there's no way we can get to Panama City. He doesn't have money for the canal. We'll have to go to Panama City by train and pay for the tickets ourselves." A dismayed laugh tried to force its way out of his habitual smoker's throat, roughened by the nameless, execrable tobacco he used. From that moment on we knew what to expect. The decision to dock in Cristóbal meant simply the end of the voyage for us. We were both filled with a sense of relief that soon changed to regret for having wasted long months in frustrated efforts to save the *Hansa Stern* and her owner. The asthmatic gasp of the engines and the muffled clang of the rods seemed to underscore our dejection.

Wito still followed his daily routine, more withdrawn each day in a kind of absence composed of resignation and indifference. At the table he exaggerated his courtesy, as if begging our pardon for any blame that might be his in the catastrophic situation we all shared without the slightest hint of reproach. We tried unsuccess-fully to convince him that we would stay on voluntarily, fully aware that the business was failing, and that over the years our intimacy with similar crises had made us immune to their conse-quences, but it was useless. He continued to withdraw and did not seem to hear what we said.

We reached Cristóbal at dusk, under a splendid sky in which the stars seemed to approach the earth in playful curiosity. The harbor lights tinged the sky with a rosy glow. We could hear the syn-copated noise of the bands whose spurious Afro-Antillean rhythms attempted to give some life to the cheap clubs and cabarets lining the streets. I was so used to that monotonous, depressing din, I confused it with the end-of-voyage mood that always brings with it a slight uneasiness, a vague fear of the unknown waiting for me when I touched land.

PANAMA CITY

After Wito's death I decided to go ashore at Cristóbal and continue on to Panama City by train. Cornelius stayed with the ship. The captain put in command of the *Hansa Stern* by the banks made him an offer he found more attractive than starting to look for work in a place he didn't know very well. We had looked through Wito's papers for some clue to his daughter's whereabouts. We wanted to let her know her father had died. All we could find was the address of the minister's church, and that was where we sent a telegram. The most likely outcome, however, was that the body would eventually be transferred from the morgue to an amphitheater in the Panama City Medical School to be used in anatomy classes. There was a certain macabre logic in this, considering the professorial manner and gestures that always characterized poor Wito from Danzig with his deliberate way of speaking, as if he were delivering a lecture he had memorized long ago.

The train ride took several hours. I made myself as comfortable as I could in a third-class carriage crowded with families and workers from the port. The unrepressed clamor began to make me drowsy: neighborhood anecdotes, tenement gossip, bloody tales, stories of terrible brutality, the shouts and cries of children—the eternal raw material of nameless, faceless lives, which always represents for me what sailors call "being on terra firma" and inevitably makes me feel overwhelming revulsion. The Zone's tropical landscape, the vegetation with its shining, dark metallic-green leaves, the heat coming in through windows open to catch an improbable cool breeze, the shouting passengers, all transported me to a European colony somewhere in Asia, and for a moment I could have sworn I was traveling across the Malay Peninsula between Singapore and Kuala Lumpur, where I had enjoyed periods of relative prosperity, thanks to the teak trade and other similar activities less easy to define. The characteristic rhythm of a moving train and the lightly swaying carriage lulled me into a half-sleep that left only a small part of my mind awake and alert, listening to the doughy, shapeless pronunciation of the language, the absence of sounds like *s* and *rr,* the piercing tones of the women's and children's conversation that reached me like the screech of birds disappearing into the banana plantations. "It's almost time," I thought, "to ask myself what I'm doing here and who the hell brought me here. The questions always arise from this feeling of endless tedium and vague fear when I know I'll be on land a long time. A bad situation, and I don't see it getting better any time soon. Panama City. I've never spent more than a week there, but I've visited it so often it's become familiar compared to all the dislocations of a life with no anchor or destination. Not a particularly attractive or interesting city, but it does create an exciting impression of total irresponsibility, of a place where anything can happen in the real, anonymous freedom to do whatever we want with our lives, and so it's like a sedative, full of agreeable but always unkept promises of unexpected happiness." But this time things were different. I would have to spend months on the isthmus, with its endless rainstorms and lethargic waves of temperatures hotter than a Turkish bath. I didn't know anybody. I'd always been passing through. No one I'd met had left a trace. An eloquent sign of this was landing here with Wito and Cornelius, neither one a true comrade of my fortunes and misfortunes. Hardly casual acquaintances, but strangers to the journey through the dark regions of life's adventure, that wild dance of rare joy shared with those we can truly call friends. I knew in advance I wouldn't find any of them in Panama City. The money I received when I left the *Hansa Stern* could last several months if I was careful. But I knew myself too well, and in a few weeks I'd be walking around with pockets as empty as my stomach. That didn't worry me. An opportune vodka and a woman never seen again were enough to redeem that moment when we think we've touched bottom. And they are not necessarily obtained only with money. I already knew how to get out of a tight corner when the inexorable trap seems to be closing. First one day, then the next, until one morning I set sail or devise some madness like the Cocora mine or the job in the Hospital de los Soberbios. It's all the same, it doesn't matter. What does matter is something else: what we carry inside, the wild propeller that never stops spinning. That's the secret, that's what must never break down. I fell into a deep sleep. When I awoke the train was pulling into the station. I suddenly felt that what I needed with desperate urgency was, in fact, an icy vodka. In the first bar I came to I would summon my tutelary gods, the blind counselors who appear only when we reach the state of grace that vodka provides with such wise, unswerving loyalty. There lay the redeeming answer, the revealed truth, the far shore where symbols shine bright and slow rituals are celebrated that dissolve every perplexity and drown every doubt.

I got off the train, surrounded by a concert of blaring car horns and the howl of a siren fading into the distance along with the last light of day. I hoisted my bag to my shoulder and walked toward the center of the city. The crickets were beginning their orchestrated calls, and neon lights went on with the vulgar, strident colors that make every night in every city on earth the same. I thought that before performing the ceremony of the vodka, which was indispensable for putting certain ideas in order and placating the various demons who come to haunt me whenever I leave the sea, I ought to find an inexpensive hotel. Along one of the narrow streets that lead from Avenida Balboa to Avenida Central, I saw the kind of place I was looking for. It had the unlikely name of Pensión Astor de Luxe. An old man with a graying Assyrian beard and the face of a Jewish coachman from the Vienna of Franz Joseph was dozing at the reception desk. His corpulent, imposing appearance was not suited to sitting behind a counter. It seemed a waste of his obvious energy. When he stood up to hand me the keys to the room, I realized he had an artificial leg. The unsettling creak of rusted springs created a sad impression of helplessness that was impossible to reconcile with the colossal Jew who faced me without a smile and wore the grim expression of someone living in a place where he doesn't speak the language very well. The room was on the fourth floor and looked out on the bay. A few stray gulls circled the almost motionless water, identical to what I had seen in Cristóbal. The filthy stuff filled my soul with the taste of failure and meanness, which did nothing to raise my spirits. Cars raced down the street at the lunatic speed that always takes me by surprise when I've been at sea a long time. Becoming familiar again with things on land requires a period of time that we never take into account when we come ashore. A dilapidated bed with defeated springs and a faded lilac spread spotted with stains it was better not to examine too closely, a precariously unsteady table, and a lithograph of a Saint Bernard watching over a boy asleep in the snow created that faceless, depersonalized atmosphere typical of all the hotels I've ever stayed in. The bath and two toilets were at the end of the hall. A gentleman in a top hat on one door, a lady from the 1930s on the other indicated with unnecessary eloquence for whom each cubicle was intended. I knew I couldn't face much more of the sordidness that had been accumulating for so long. I went out to look for a bar. Asking the Viennese coachman where I could find the closest one struck me as a complex linguistic operation. Besides, with someone like him it wasn't advisable to establish any bonds except those directly related to his work as concierge. After walking along the relatively quiet streets of a decaying residential neighborhood, I turned a corner onto a street where there were several bars, one after the other, each with its own neon sign and music playing at full volume. I went into the one that seemed the least noisy and asked for a double vodka with ice.

I became a steady customer at the bar, which turned out to be not only the quietest but also the one with the most faithful clientele. The owner was named Alejandro, but everybody called him Alex. He was a slender Panamanian with bulging eyes, one of those saloonkeepers who ask no questions but have an infallible memory for the preferences and alcoholic whims of their patrons. The ideal bartender. I decided to send my friends his address so that he could hold my mail. I didn't even look for a job. Experience had taught me that until one knows the secret rhythm of a city, looking for decent work is a waste of time. That frenzy I used to go into, pounding the pavements and hunting for work, was merely a sop to my conscience. I always ended up a garbage collector or a whorehouse porter, or unloading ships on the docks. And therefore this time, instead of sordid survival, I decided to take things easy and patiently explore the real escapes from a bad situation that Panama City had to offer. When prospects dimmed and doubts and discouragement began to churn inside, vodka could still calm the symptoms and keep me alert.

One Saturday, when my usual dose was not enough to carry out its rescue operation, I slowly finished the bottle and went to bed in an alcoholic fog. On Sunday morning I was surprised to see an enormous, naked black woman, with the hair of a Zulu warrior, asleep beside me. I shook her awake, and she lay there looking at me in astonishment and rage. Angry words in an Antillean dialect, a mix of patois and Grenadan English, poured from her toothless, thick-lipped mouth. I made her dress and got rid of her with a few dollars. As far as I could remember, I had left the bar alone and staggered to the hotel without a companion. I thought no more about it. A few days later I had too much to drink again, but without reaching the state I had been in before. And again the next morning I awoke to the half-imbecilic, terrified stare of a whore with hair bleached almost white and an emaciated body covered by tiny pink spots that were very disquieting. I got rid of her, too, this time without paying anything. I was certain I'd never seen her before. A third episode of the kind took place with an Indian who probably came from Tobago or another nearby island. She barely spoke Spanish and tried to attack me with a razor. I forced her into the hall and went back to my room. I called the desk to ask for clean sheets. The concierge answered and pretended he couldn't understand what I was saying. At that moment I understood what had happened and the origin of those visits. I dressed and went down to the desk. I asked for my bill, looked it over, and saw I had been charged for an extra person on the days the women had made their appearance. Without taking my eyes off his I ordered the one-legged concierge, slowly, calmly, and in very clear German, to remove the extra charges from my bill immediately and in my presence. And he did so in silence, with a solemnity that hid centuries of cynicism. Then I warned him that if he sent another woman to my room, I'd complain to the police and the health department and demand that they close his famous pensión de luxe. "It won't happen again," he said as he returned the papers to the wooden filing cabinet installed under the pigeonholes with the keys. "Don't worry. Must've been a mistake," he mumbled while his thick, moist lips tried to force a smile past the anger on his greedy coachman's face.

I told the story to Alex, who advised me not to have too much to do with him. "He owns the hotel and runs the whores on the block too. But that's not his most important business. He's involved in other things, and the cops have had their eye on him for a long time. The thing is he has influence higher up, and he spreads his money around, lots of money." I asked if I should move out and he said no, it wouldn't be much different anywhere else, the hotel was conveniently located, and people already knew me in the neighborhood, which was good for finding work. He was right. The concierge-cum-owner continued to treat me with the same impersonal coldness he used with everybody.

When I had lost all hope, I received a letter from Abdul Bashur. The stamps were Italian, it was postmarked Ravenna, and the news was in no way encouraging. He was trying to obtain an insurance payment for a ship he owned with his brothers and his brother-in-law, the husband of his older sister Jasmina. The insurance company was creating all kinds of difficulties in its effort not to cover the policy. The ship had been sunk by Libyan planes although it flew the Liberian flag. The company was trying to prove that this risk was not covered by the policy, and the Bashurs were spending every penny they had on lawyers, appraisers, and consular paperwork. Jasmina's oldest son had leukemia, and the cost of his treatment required greater and greater sacrifices. Still, Abdul was placing at my disposal some pounds sterling that he had in a bank in Panama City, the profits from a transaction a few years ago with the armed forces of a neighboring country. I clearly remembered the operation in which he and I had taken part, and I smiled at how discreetly he referred to the matter. Poor Abdul. He was a friend like few others, and the generosity he had shown me so many times, not only in business but in other, more delicate areas, could always move me to tears.

I was learning more about the city and realized that, as usual, first impressions had only been confirmed: it was a transient place, and for those passing through, it had the charm of a city that leaves no mark, that does not impose its secret, defining spirit or require any accommodation to the particular laws governing the unique routine that gives it life. For my purposes this was especially serious. It isn't the kind of city that offers the best opportunities to a man in my circumstances. Everyone is in transit. Weeks, even months can go by without finding anchor in definite work or beginning some venture, no matter how humble or limited. Furthermore, the more modest our goals the more difficult they are to achieve in the kind of race where no one pays attention to anyone else. Making the rounds of the lobbies and bars in the large hotels in the financial district and, at night, the clubs where people of every class, profession, and race attempt to shake off the overwhelming boredom of places they are forced to visit on business trips; in the charged, rather sordid air of the casinos, which, in those same hotels and elsewhere, offer a poor substitute for the passing desire for adventure and high emotion that Panama City awakens; in these, and in other, less respectable venues, I searched in vain for the opportunity that would pull me out of the quagmire into which I was sinking, slowly but irremediably. The shabbiness of my meager wardrobe, and other extreme signs of poverty, soon forced me to abandon those places. I had to be content with standing at the entrance and not going in. I did the same near the large stores to which travelers are attracted by merchandise that, for the most part, turns out to be seconds or brazen imitations of prestigious brands.

The rainy season came, settling over the isthmus with the unleashed force of a tornado and turning the streets into raging, uncrossable rivers. When I realized it was useless to go on looking for even a modest corner of the magic carpet that I always imagine flying close by, tempting us to climb on and escape to what the child in us secretly calls "the great adventure," when I knew there was nothing more I could do and the rain made my rounds impossible, I shut myself in my room at the pensión, allowing myself only less and less frequent visits to the bar. A curtain of rain fell into the filthy waters of the Pacific, and from my window the city seemed to dissolve, before my indifferent eyes, into fierce whirlpools of mud, garbage, and dead leaves spinning around the sewer openings.

On the day I spent the last dollar of the money Abdul had given me, the concierge, with a millenarian instinct for gauging such situations, called my room to say he wanted to talk to me when I came down. In the afternoon, before going to the bar, where in fact my bill was beginning to worry me, I stopped at the reception desk to face the Danubian coachman. In slow, halting, but very precise Spanish, words began to come out of the enormous bearded head that hovered over the counter as if it were an illusionist's table. It was clear I was at the end of my rope and wouldn't find any way out of my situation in Panama City. He knew the city very well. If I accepted, he could offer me something that would solve my problems, at least for the moment, and allow me to pay the month's rent I owed him as well as my tab at Alex's. The man knew more than I liked. When I came back from the bar, he continued, he wanted to come up to my room for a little chat. I agreed, and then I went to take shelter in the vodkas that would make conversation with the one-legged watchdog easier. I'd often received comparable offers in other crises like this one, always from people who bore an unmistakable family resemblance to the concierge. I could almost predict the broad outlines of his proposition. I came back to my room after midnight, and soon I heard the sound of his limping step. He sat facing me in a rickety chair. As he stroked his beard with a gesture that tried to be patriarchal but only made him look more untrustworthy, he explained his offer. The same old story. It involved going outside the law to earn the few dollars that would allow me to scrape by, not without some risk from the authorities. He had in his possession certain objects of value—watches, jewelry, cameras, expensive perfumes, liquor, wines with great names and renowned vintages—that some friends had left with him as collateral on loans. He didn't have to explain, obviously, that they were really goods stolen from customs warehouses in Colón or the storerooms of large department stores in Panama City. When he used the euphemism "collateral," an indefinable gleam flashed in his eyes, and the permanent smile on his thick lips froze into a vague grimace. My long years of wandering the Mediterranean had taught me to recognize the signs of petty swindling. I calmly let him speak, and when he finished I said he would have my answer in the morning. "Don't think about it too long," he said as he left. "There are other candidates, and they have more experience." I could have even predicted the way he said it, with that slightly menacing tone used with people who are up to their necks in water.

I didn't have to do much thinking. The next day I went down to the desk to tell him I accepted. "I knew you would," he replied, and he invited me into a dark, cramped space behind the cupboard with the pigeonholes and keys. This was where he slept. From under the rumpled bed that stank of concentrated urine and spoiled food, he pulled a wooden case, lined with crimson velvet and containing clocks, gold wristwatches, and perfumes in extravagant, unusually shaped crystal bottles. He told me the selling prices. If I could get more, half of the difference was mine; otherwise I'd only be entitled to fifteen percent of the sale. The places he recommended as most advantageous for making sales were the same ones I'd been visiting for weeks. The persistent torrential rains only added to the risk. "Stand under the canopy where the cars drop off and pick up passengers." Yes, I knew all that. No need to tell me. It wasn't the first time I'd be trying to waylay buyers for this kind of merchandise. The problem was that those were exactly the places where the police took shelter. I put the articles into my pockets and went out to begin the uncertain venture.

At first it was somewhat more profitable than I had expected. The prices were much lower than in the shops, and people took advantage of the opportunity with the impunity of tourists who ran no serious risk when they made their purchase. But the police, predictably, noticed my constant presence outside the hotels and cabarets, and they wasted no time in questioning me. I got out of difficulty with improbable excuses that I had to make more believable with small gifts. I convinced the concierge to share half their cost, and he agreed because of my relative success as an itinerant peddler of stolen goods. I brought my pensión bill up to date before the second month's rent was due. When I went to the bar to pay Alex, he said in a low voice, "Don't leave without talking to me first. It's important." A familiar uneasy sensation, a premonition of approaching danger, took away all desire for the vodka he had placed in front of me. I finally drank it down in one swallow and waited until the bartender could talk to me alone. A growing depression, a vague, inescapable despair, left my arms and legs feeling like rubber. At the pit of my stomach I began to sense a dense, paralyzing weight that shifted from time to time as if it were a knot of dozing reptiles. At last Alex went to one end of the bar, wiping a glass and motioning to me to follow. Then, looking around carefully as he spoke, he said, "They've been here asking for you. The police. You know, you can always tell they're cops even when they're trying to look like civilians. They know where you're staying and they smell some tie-in with the Jew. I don't know what you're up to, but be careful. They can be pretty rough here—they go out of their way to protect the image of Panama City as a safe place for tourists and people doing business. Move out of that hotel today and break with the owner. You can stay here. They're good friends of mine." He handed me a card for the Hotel Miramar in the old part of the city.

Convincing the Jew wasn't easy. He tried to downplay my fears and repeated, in what attempted to be a good-hearted tone, "I can fix these things, my friend, don't worry, don't worry." But it was precisely those few, honeyed words that made me decide to leave immediately. I returned the merchandise, paid my bill, and fifteen minutes later walked out with forty dollars in my pocket and a dead weight in the pit of my stomach, the ominous warning of disasters that, unfortunately, were all too familiar.

The Hotel Miramar was a little smaller than the Pensión Astor de Luxe, and its rooms a little cleaner. The owner, an Ecuadorian woman married to a Panamanian, was much more approachable and inspired more confidence than the sinister cripple with his coachman's beard. Alex had spoken well of me, and her friendly cordiality helped to calm my justifiable fears of having to deal with the police. An infernal racket came in through the window of the only vacant room. It faced a street filled with small bazaars whose indefatigably insistent Hindu owners stood on the sidewalk to draw customers inside. Each shop vied with its competitors by playing its radio or phonograph louder than every other shop's radio and phonograph, thereby demonstrating the virtues of the establishment to deafened patrons who bought the first thing the shopkeeper showed them just to escape his incessant talk, while he negotiated the price with awesome skill and stupefied them with music. Luckily, the silence at night was barely broken by a drunk's occasional bellow or the laughter of prostitutes waiting on the corner for an unlikely customer. It was then, when I was almost at the bottom of the abyss, that the redemptive miracle occurred. A ritual was being enacted, one that occurs with such punctual fidelity in my life that I can attribute it only to the impenetrable will of those tutelary gods who lead me through the obscurity of their designs by invisible but obvious strings.

ILONA

*O*ne afternoon, when I was engaged in a memory exercise that I hoped would be a temporary cure for panic and despair, the rain seemed to move away and a brilliant sun flooded the newly washed air. The exercise consisted of recalling moments of poverty and failure even more terrible and definitive than this one in Panama City. For example, among many other episodes, I remembered the time I was employed in the hospital at the salt-works. Along with a team of other workers, my responsibilities were to push a train of four or five of the cars used to carry gravel out to the end of the breakwaters. But instead of stones and pebbles we were transporting three or four patients in each car. They were going to take the sea air, which helped to heal the purulent sores that had incapacitated them for months. By some quirk, the water produced the affliction and only the air could help to alleviate it. At the happy prospect of relief the patients crooned the songs they sang to lull each other to sleep. Almost all of them had been blinded by the dazzling whiteness of the salt fields, and perhaps this was why their sense of touch had been so heightened that they enjoyed the healing quality of the air with an intensity we could not imagine.

While they sang their songs, we struggled to push the little train along rusted tracks rotted away by saltpeter. The wind blew at the sheets wrapped precariously around each patient. Many years ago I wrote something about this in a way that was certainly fragmentary, but perhaps closer to the events I was attempting to recall. In one of those comforting whims of memory my recollection of the saltworks was not painful. On the contrary, all I could evoke was the pleasure brought by the breeze to wounded, weakened bodies, the song leaving their throats like a benevolent murmur, the brilliant presence of a cloudless sky. However, with some effort I succeeded in remembering that we had only one meal a day, and the pay was so miserable we never had enough money to go to the port and forget our sorrows. Then I recalled the time I worked as a stoker on an unseaworthy old tub carrying hides from Alaska to a factory near San Francisco. We had been swindled into signing on for a year, lured by an advance that allowed us to drink for three consecutive days in the dim shelter of a tavern in Seward. Outside, the polar night continued in bone-chilling cold. On the second trip we asked for the rest of the salary we had been promised. The first mate showed us the contract. It was cleverly worded, and in it we had accepted as our only salary for the year the money we had drunk away in Seward. Three of us were stokers: the other two were a one-eyed Irishman, pickled in alcohol, who was constantly delirious, and a Yaqui Indian, silent and grim, who managed to break his arm on the second day out and, with that as an excuse, never touched a shovel again. The cargo gave off a fetid, sweetish smell that clung to our skin and clothes. I thought my days of wine and roses, if in fact I ever had any, had really come to an end. Luckily, after five months the damn ship collided with an ice floe off the Canadian coast. The Coast Guard rescued us and took us to Vancouver. The Seamen's Fund gave us enough money to last a few weeks. That was when a mad Canadian convinced me to give the Cocora mine a try.

That afternoon I brought to mind many other turnings in my life far worse than the crisis in Panama City, but obviously to no avail. I decided to take a walk and enjoy the good weather. I left the narrow streets with their Hindu bazaars, and was approaching the luxury hotel district, when without any warning the rain began and soon turned into a real downpour that threatened to wash away everything. I took shelter in the first doorway I came to, a small hotel with certain pretensions of luxury. In the lobby, along with the customary chairs and the tables holding out-of-date newspapers and magazines, there were slot machines lined up against the wall that opened onto the pool and main patio. Although the place seemed deserted, I tried to be inconspicuous. Not only was I soaking wet but my clothes had long since lost any chance at respectability.

I saw her from the back. She was playing a slot machine that was making noises and ringing bells, the signal that three figures had come up. I hesitated for a moment. According to the last I'd heard, she couldn't possibly be in Panama City. I walked over and she turned around with her characteristic expression, the look of happy surprise that appeared on her face at the slightest provocation. Yes, there she was. No doubt about it.

"Ilona! What are you doing here?" I managed to stammer.

"Gaviero, you madman! What the hell are you doing in Panama City?"

We embraced and then, without saying a word, we went out to the patio and sat at a small bar under a vine-covered canopy. She asked for two vodka tonics and sat looking at me for what seemed an eternity. Then, in a tone that suggested an almost pitying concern, she said: "I see. Things aren't going too well, are they? No, don't tell me now. We have all the time in the world to catch up. What worries me is finding you in exactly the wrong place. You should never have anchored here. Nobody gets out, especially if he's in the state you're in. You have to pass through, that's all. Just pass through. But tell me—inside, you know what I mean, deep down where you keep yourself, how is everything?" She looked at me as intently as a friendly sibyl, a woman with deep knowledge of the man she's interrogating.

"Down there," I answered in a voice whose joy and serenity surprised even me, "down there everything's fine. Everything's in order. It's the rest that's bad. On the outside. You're right, this is exactly the wrong place to be stranded, but that's the way it happened. I couldn't help it. I have two dollars in my pocket, and that's all I have. But now that I can see you and hear you right in front of me, I admit that all the rest is history, it's fading right now thanks to the vodka, and the scent of your hair, and the Triestine-Polish accent of your Spanish. I'm sinking into something very much like happiness."

"Things must be awful if they've made you sentimental and gallant. Anyway, it doesn't suit you." She laughed with the sarcasm she always used to hide her feelings. We were back to the normal tone of our friendship: humor that often turned macabre, a good-

natured recognition of the ties between us and the quirks of character that, while they did not separate us, always sent us off in
opposite directions.

With the money she had won she paid for the drinks, left a tip
worthy of a rajah, and stood up. "Come on," she said, "come and
dry your clothes and have a bath. You look like a Gypsy lover
down on his luck." I followed her to the elevator and we went up
to her room. She ordered me into a tub of hot water and put my
clothes in a hotel laundry bag. I shaved with the razor she used for
her legs. Through the open windows the heat felt wonderful after
the rain, which was moving out to sea, staining the water an ashy
gray. She lay down beside me on the wide bed and began to caress
me, while she whispered in my ear in a deep voice, imitating the
Benedictine monk who had once been our guide at the abbey at
Solesmes: "Gaviero you madman, Maqroll you screwup, Gaviero
you madman, Maqroll you ingrate," on and on until, entwined and
breathless, we made love between outbursts of laughter, like children who have just been miraculously saved from terrible danger.
Perspiration gave her skin a dizzying almond taste. Night fell suddenly, and the crickets began their nocturnal signals, the syn-
copated song that recalls the rhythm of secret, generous breathing
in the vegetative world. The odor of damp earth, of fallen leaves
beginning to rot, came in through the open windows. Music from
a Chinese restaurant next to the hotel reminded us of an episode
in Macao that we survived only by miracle. Neither of us mentioned it. There was no need.

Ilona. The woman was unforgettable. I've lived through so
much at her side, and so much more could happen in her company.
She was born in Trieste to a Polish father and a Triestine mother
whose family was Macedonian.

"Pronounce it right. Like this, look: Thessaloniki," and she'd
rest her tongue below her front teeth. Ilona Grabowska—*grande
famille* was her ironic comment. The name had undergone various
incarnations, depending on the circumstances. On one occasion I
met her in Alicante, where she was known as Ilona Rubenstein.
When I remarked that this seemed a trifle exaggerated, she cited
reasons having to do with a complicated transaction we had undertaken involving carpets to decorate a bank in Geneva, and in fact,
the last name helped our affairs in the most unexpected ways. She

was tall and blond. Her gestures were rather brusque. She was constantly arranging her short, honey-colored hair with a movement of her hand that identified her immediately, even at a great distance. When I saw her in the lobby, her hands were busy with the slot machine, which is what confused me for a moment. At the age of forty-five her slim, firm legs still gave her body the elasticity and balance of an adolescent. A round face and full, well-defined lips betrayed her Macedonian blood. Large, slightly prominent front teeth gave her a perpetually childlike, mocking expression. Her rather husky voice moved from deep tones to soprano range when she wanted to state something emphatically or recount an event that had particularly moved her. She never stayed with one man very long. But toward her friends, some of whom had been her lovers, she maintained absolute loyalty and an interest in what happened to them that often led to sacrifice on her part. She had no idea of the value of money and used it indiscriminately, regardless of the owner. And she had no attachment to things, which she could easily dispense with at a moment's notice. I once saw her take off a beautiful watch she had bought in Istambul and give it to the driver who had taken us across the Andes to Mendoza on a practically impassable highway. Foolishness is what infuriated her, the stupidity combined with pompous arrogance that is so common among people caught in the dull routines of the petite bourgeoisie and proliferates among bureaucrats, who are identical on all five continents. An unfortunate bank manager in Valparaíso who tried to lecture her on the impossibility of sending a money order abroad was suddenly assailed by a voice so loud it could be heard out on the street: "You go to hell and take your gold wire glasses and all your 'regulations regarding bank transactions' with you, you asshole!" and she turned her back on him after making a gesture with her arm that left the man even more stunned.

I met her in Ostend. I had gone into a crêperie to get out of the rain, one of those icy, persistent drizzles, typical of Flanders, that soak us to the skin in seconds without our even realizing it. She came in shortly afterwards. I was eating a ricotta crêpe at a small table pushed against the window, which looked out on the docks. Without seeing me she shook the rain from her hair and spattered me with water. "Oh, I'm sorry! I seem to have ruined your crêpe. Let's order two more and I'll keep you company until it stops raining." It was impossible to refuse an invitation made with such natural cordiality. We became friends. We lived together for several months, visiting the ports of La Mancha and Brittany, involved in a complex traffic in contraband gold—a plan devised by an Austrian who had been her lover and was now in the hands of the Zurich police. "He tried to involve me in some other idiocies in New York. He behaved like a rat, but the gold idea can work for a while." With those words she put an end to the matter of the Austrian and never mentioned him again. She had an ability to forget all about people who broke the unwritten laws she imposed on friendship and applied generally to all business relationships or any other relationships that life might offer. Eventually we settled in Cyprus, where we were joined by Abdul Bashur. He brought with him the idea of making slight modifications in the shape and color of Merchant Marine signal flags so that smugglers could communicate with each other and send warnings about the Coast Guard's activities. We tried it out with Wito's *Hansa Stern* and two Lebanese freighters, and it worked perfectly. Ilona had an affair with Bashur in which she adopted a protective tone, and my dear friend pretended to think it was the most natural thing in the world. Abdul, an expert in the most intricate, elaborate arts of guile that Levantines learn as children. Only Ilona could have managed it, but this all took place without causing the slightest friction among the three of us or damaging in any way the longstanding mutual affection that united Bashur and me. I moved to Marseilles for a time to promote the signal flag venture, while they went to Trieste to settle an inheritance she had received—an inheritance that soon disappeared in taxes and liens against the property. "I'm the one who thought I was going to inherit Miramar Castle at the very least," commented Ilona, "but all I got were the debts on the game warden's cottage," and she burst into her loud, cheerful laughter.

We didn't see each other again for several years, and then one day I ran into her on the ferry to the Isle of Man. The perpetual Scottish rain was falling, the rain that does so much for the greenery and attacks the bronchial tubes with deadly accuracy. We stayed in a modest boardinghouse in Ramsey, where I had a high fever and a case of laryngitis that silenced me, and she learned to knit impossible sweaters with sleeves that never matched. Abdul sent Wito to rescue us. We traveled to Rabat to heal my bronchial tubes and begin negotiating the matter of rugs for the Bank of Geneva. Then Ilona left for Switzerland, and months later we arranged to meet in Alicante. It was there I found her transformed into Ilona Rubenstein.

She was in the habit of appearing and then disappearing from our lives. When she left she did so without making us feel responsible or giving us any reason to think of ourselves as deceived. When she returned she brought with her a renewed supply of enthusiasm and that characteristic ability of hers to disperse any clouds that may have gathered over us. One always began all over again with Ilona. She was endlessly resourceful in finding ways out of bad situations, which always gave us the impression that, with her beside us, we were starting a new life with all obstacles providentially removed.

I told her about the *Hansa Stern* and Wito's death. "I knew it," was all she would say. "I knew it from the first moment I saw him. Life doesn't want to be treated that way, like a schoolgirl sitting at her desk." I told her about my efforts in Panama City to escape the tunnel in which I found myself trapped. She thought the story of the Viennese coachman was hilariously funny. "I know them," she said. "I can see him. They look at you as if you weren't going to pay. There were some in Trieste. I would see them when I went to school, holding my father's hand. They'd always tip their hats to him, and in those thick Russian bass voices they'd say very respectfully, 'Good morning, Count.' You know, of course, that my father wasn't a count, but in Trieste that's what everybody called him because he had the bearing and manner of a cavalry officer." When I told her about Abdul and the money he had given me just when he was having financial difficulties himself, she only nodded her head and smiled affectionately, as if to indicate that she knew our friend's generosity by heart. When I finished my story, which she had insisted on hearing before telling hers, Ilona stood up, went to take a shower, and came back wrapped in a towel. She sat facing me at the foot of the bed and began, a serious yet absent expression on her face. "My story is simpler, Gaviero, and less interesting. When what you called Operation Carpet was over, and you left for Peru on that idiocy of the Chiclayo quarries, I went to Oslo, where a cousin of mine was selling beauty products made from a marine algae base. One of those stories the French call *à dormir debout*. I spent two years there as her partner. Of course it failed. What an idea—to start that kind of business in a country where the night lasts half the year and women have schoolgirl complexions and bodies like artillerymen. In Oslo I met Eric Bandsfeld again, that Luxembourgian who wanted to marry me in Cyprus and you spent one whole night explaining to him that I'd never be anybody's wife, that I'd already devoted half my life to matters that had nothing to do with homemaking. Apparently you convinced him in spite of his incorrigible Saxon pigheadedness. This time his intentions were somewhat less ambitious, and I made two trips with him to Hong Kong. He was still involved in the pearl trade that had been so profitable when we knew him. The situation changed and he had to go into something else. He opened a vegetarian restaurant in Brussels. At first it was like algae creams in Oslo, but then the dieting craze caught on. Those women can use it. You know what they look like. Eric settled there permanently with a gold mine on his hands. I went to South Africa and opened a striptease club. I was trying to imitate The Crazy Horse. Everything was fine until the racial problems began. The authorities ordered me to get rid of two darling Haitians who pretended to make love while one of them talked on the phone. It was the hit of the show. I sold the place instead and came back to Trieste. Well, I won't tell you all the details. Two or three routine adventures, the kind you know won't work but you jump in anyway just for something to do, out of sheer inertia, because it can lead to something else. You know, our kind of thing. A year later I went to the Canary Islands with some guy who claimed to be the heir to a fortune in Tenerife. But he was no heir, he had no money, there was no fortune. Just a good-looking imbecile. A telegraph pole could make better conversation. But in the Canaries I met a Hungarian widow who suggested opening a boutique in Panama City with genuine designer clothes from the great houses, and very exclusive lingerie. No seconds, no fakes. She said that Panama City was ready for that kind of shop. More and more wealthy women from neighboring countries were pouring in every day, with demanding and very educated tastes. This wasn't the middle class who had always shopped here before. We agreed, so much so that we wound up in bed, where I must admit she was a genius. But she made the stupid mistake of really falling in love, complete with jealous rages, tears, and Magyar melodrama that scared away the customers and left me drained, without the energy to do anything. You know what the climate here does to the nerves: it muffles them, wraps them in a kind of foam rubber so that signals from the outside world are too faint and come too late. It was very hard for me to convince her I wasn't the person she had created in her overheated imagination, and that I certainly had no desire to live in a nightmare. My only purpose had been to have a good time, and nothing more. She ranted and raved. We sold the business. Two weeks ago she went back to London, determined to revive an old love affair with a Chilean woman, a pianist she had once tried to shoot. Luckily, she missed, but she had serious problems with the English police. And so here I am. In the Hotel Sans Souci: not too many luxuries, obviously, but not destitute either. Now, I have a proposition to make: We'll go to the Miramar tomorrow, pay your bill, and bring your things here. If there's anything to bring. Considering what you're wearing, I don't imagine there's much left. We'll form our usual partnership, divide what we earn with our well-known talents, and then we'll see. All right?" I didn't even have to answer. It was the same arrangement we had used before, either with my money or with hers. I knew it would work smoothly. It always did.

The next day we went to the Hotel Miramar, paid the bill, and I packed a couple of shirts, a pair of torn sneakers, and a pair of shapeless, oil-stained jeans that I kept more for good luck than with any intention of wearing them again. They were from my days in New Orleans and on the *Hansa Stern,* and I didn't want to discard them. Certain articles of clothing become good-luck charms. We imagine they protect us against disaster and so we never get rid of them and their alleged, but unproven, propitiatory powers.

Life with Ilona was invariably lived on two levels, or rather in two simultaneous and parallel directions. On the one hand, your feet were always on the ground, you were always intelligently but not obsessively alert to what each day offered in response to the routine question of surviving. On the other hand, imagination and unbounded fantasy suggested a spontaneous and unexpected sequence of scenarios that were always aimed at the radical subversion of every law ever written or established. This was a permanent, organic, rigorous subversion that never permitted travel on the beaten path, the road preferred by most people, the traditional patterns that offer protection to those whom Ilona, without emphasis or pride but without any concessions either, would call "the others." Woe to any companion of hers who betrayed the slightest inclination to accommodate to those models. Without hesitation she would cut all ties, all relations, all commitments to anyone who succumbed to such unpardonable weakness, and she would never again mention the person who had gone over to "the others," that is to say, who no longer existed. For those of us who had lived with her for a time, one glance was enough to warn us that we were approaching the danger zone. Abdul told a story that illustrates Ilona's principles very well. Once, when they were traveling together, Abdul wanted to send a postcard to his associate in a venture in which all the advantages had been the partner's, to thank him for his hospitality in letting them use his house on the island of Khyros for the summer. When he handed the card to Ilona so that she could sign it too, she looked him in the eye for an instant and went back to the bathroom, where she had been combing her hair. She didn't say a word, but Abdul tore up the postcard and threw the pieces into the toilet. The matter was not mentioned until several months later, when I met them in Marseilles. We were at the docks, eating lobster prepared with olive oil and garlic and accompanied by a modest Muscadet that was still reassuringly sprightly and direct. Abdul related the incident in a cheerful, mocking tone. Ilona laughed too, but when Bashur finished she sat looking at us like an angry Minerva, and her only comment was: "This Lebanese was in very grave danger with his courtesy *mal placée*. He was risking his head."

"I knew that right away," said Bashur, this time a little less cheerfully, taking a long drink of wine to hide the fleeting panic caused by Ilona's words.

The days passed tranquilly. The rains came less frequently, and we were beginning the splendid Panamanian summer that secretly, and very effectively, exhilarates me. One day I mentioned the matter of our finances and Ilona said, "Look, let's forget it for now. If we worry about it, you know very well we won't find the solution. Besides, there's no hurry. Yes, I know, this isn't where we want to spend the rest of our lives. Aside from that, there's no place like it. At least for us. The trouble with the kind of crisis you've just had is that it undermines the belief in luck and the faith in the unexpected that are essential for discovering a way out. Let things happen, they'll bring the hidden key. If you search for it, you lose the ability to find it." She was right. I hadn't realized until then how far I had fallen or how much the fall had hampered, even paralyzed, the mechanism that allows blind faith in our destiny—a certainty of good fortune that had often saved me from quicksands even worse than the ones I had just escaped thanks to Ilona and the rain that brought her, as always.

In the afternoon we made love with the slow, meticulous patience of someone building a house of cards. After the torrential, liberating collapse of the cards we reminisced about our friends, the places we had once enjoyed, the unforgettable food eaten in out-of-the-way corners only we knew, and the tempestuous bouts of drinking that invariably ended in a police station or a harbormaster's office. In either place everything was settled through an effective alternation of sophistries we had both mastered. We were overcome by uncontrollable laughter when we recalled that dawn in Antwerp in the office of the police commissioner, where a mild-mannered Belgian gendarme with a huge gray and copper-colored mustache looked at Ilona with astonished, sleepless eyes as she explained, very seriously, that I was her brother and that she had just rescued me from a psychiatric hospital to which I had been committed by the owners of the ship where I was second machinist. They were trying to keep the bonus I was entitled to when my contract expired. The poor Fleming scratched his head with a pencil as he observed us with an incredulity that from one moment to the next could lead to either a considerable fine or several days behind bars. Finally he told us to leave and never come back. Which we did, of course, at least in part. Not returning to Antwerp was unthinkable because at that time we were using the port as a base for our incursions along the Breton and Cantabrian coasts. And in this way, one afternoon after another, we relived the days we had shared with each other or with friends like Abdul, to whom we were joined in the unconquerable solidarity of those who do not want the world as it is offered to them but as they propose to make it.

If the agreement not to talk or worry about our finances was rigorously respected, we both knew that the account in the Indian

Trade National Bank was shrinking inexorably. There was no cause for alarm, but the moment would come when the amount on deposit would represent nothing less than our final hope for escaping Panama City. Before that happened, we had to find the magical solution that had always saved us and in which we, especially Ilona, had a faith very similar to the one that sustains the tightrope walker halfway across the high wire. Fleeting allusions, brief silences, remarks that touched the limits of the unmentionable, indicated that the matter concerned us both while, at the same time, we kept it from interfering with the rhythm of an endless vacation that we had imposed on our days. In the morning some hours of sun by the hotel pool, lunch at the House of Seafood or the Matsuei, where the selection of sushi was eminently respectable, in the afternoon a siesta and lovemaking that dissolved into happy memories, and at night the casinos at the large hotels, watching the eager Asians and South Americans who lost their money as if they were in Monte Carlo but behaved like unreconstructed barbarians. The night would end in some second-rate club where women took off their clothes in rather unimaginative ways and we tried to guess their nationalities, almost always without success: the "stunning Chilean" announced by the master of ceremonies turned out to be a well-traveled prostitute from a Maracaibo brothel; the "sensual Argentine" invariably confessed to being from Ambato or Cuenca and sometimes Guayaquil, always from Ecuador. Our wildest mistake was the night we bet that the "hot Uruguayan" was Colombian when she really did come from Tacuarembó. The variety of places was certainly limited, and the women on stage even more so. Our visits to that world grew less frequent, and we came to prefer a quiet bar at the Hilton or the Continental and the slow, steady consumption of cocktails whose original recipes we modified slightly. The unorthodox results were rated according to carefully selected criteria. That was the origin of the vodka martini we dubbed the Panama Trail, to which we added kirsch instead of Noilly Prat. It produced a slow euphoria that led us to glorify it as one of the most successful discoveries in our long careers as devout, confessed alcoholics faithful to a well-established doctrine of laboriously mastered tastes and rules.

The first, barely noticeable signs of the need to change a routine that was becoming intolerably long-lived began subtly enough but grew increasingly clear. Instead of going down to the pool we stayed in bed, prolonging an improbable sleep with caresses that were effective but, to some extent, had been summoned as a pretext for staying in the room. The bars did not offer the baroque density of possibilities expected by someone who has frequented Mediterranean ports. There comes a moment when the lack of a good blanc cassis or an authentic negroni can disturb one's spirit. Or when the desire for an arak with ice leads to a series of substitutes that only irritate a frustrated appetite. Before the situation reached a critical point that would have forced us to a drastic solution, Ilona had one of her inspirations.

VILLA ROSA

AND ITS PEOPLE

One afternoon we were on the terrace that extends the lobby of the Panama Hilton, drinking Tuborg beers obtained for us through a kind of sorcery, none too frequent in that hotel, by a waiter with whom we were on the best of terms. The heat shimmered on the pavement, deforming the shape of the taxis waiting for a passenger with the heart to go shopping under that punishing sun. Two minivans stopped at the entrance, and out stepped the entire crew of the Iberian Airlines DC-10 that stops in Panama City. We sat looking at the unmistakably Spanish types, so out of place in uniforms. "No uniform becomes a Spaniard," said Ilona, following some comment of mine. "They have too much character, they're too much like Romans from the time of Trajan, to fit into the kind of clothes the Saxons wear so well; if you've noticed, they all look so much alike that the monotony makes them anonymous. This head stewardess, for example—I'll bet her name is Maite, that she lives in Madrid and hates it, that she has one brother in the Merchant Marine and another who's a professional jai alai player." I said that perhaps she was exaggerating somewhat. In any event there was no way to verify her conjectures. I would not be the one to ask the tall, elegant brunette with the suntan and the broad shoulders about such personal matters. Ilona smiled vaguely without paying much attention to me. She had suddenly acquired an air of concentrated absence, the unmistakable sign that she was beginning to weave one of her famous schemes. We finished our beer and went to the Matsuei to try a good Buta Dofu instead of the all too familiar sushi. We said little during the meal and even less when we returned to the hotel. We lay naked in the bed, the windows open in hope of an unlikely breeze. I knew from Ilona's silence that this wasn't the time for lovemaking. I fell into a deep sleep induced by the Hilton's beer and the Japanese restaurant's sake. When I woke it was growing dark and the crickets had begun their undecipherable evening messages. Ilona was in the shower attempting to sing a Polish song, substituting an approximate humming for words she had forgotten. She came out wrapped in a towel decorated with Egyptian hieroglyphics that she had bought in the Ben-Rabí Bazaar but, as it turns out, was made in San Salvador. "The quality is excellent regardless," she said with the conviction of someone who cannot resign herself to having been deceived. She sat at the foot of the bed, as she always did when she wanted to propose something serious, and while she brushed her hair, she began to lay out the plan she had formulated during lunch and perfected while I was asleep.

"Maqroll," she said, "I know how we're going to get out of here with plenty of money and not too much work. I mean without too much work we don't like or that isn't worth doing. Pay attention and don't interrupt. When I finish you can tell me what you think. Listen—the idea is to set up a house of assignation staffed exclusively by stewardesses from the airlines that make stops in Panama City, and from other well-known lines. No, don't make that face. I know what you're thinking. Of course they wouldn't be real stewardesses. I'm not that crazy. We'll recruit girls who are willing to do the work and whose appearance would let them pass for real stewardesses. We'll have uniforms made. They'll receive some preliminary instruction: professional jargon, the company's routes, the people who make up a crew, anecdotes about their work and life on land. I have access to a mailing list from the boutique that Erzsébet Pásztory and I owned, and we can choose the first candidates from there. Some were already in the gallant life, as my father used to say, and others had a strong vocation. To attract clients, we can count on two sets of collaborators who are prepared to cooperate if we pay them regularly: the hotel bartenders we've subjected to our alcoholic heterodoxy, and the bellhop captains in the same hotels, many of whom already provide that service to guests. Yes, I know, it would all be done with absolute discretion, but sooner or later the police will make their appearance. In the boutique I acquired a certain amount of experience in this area. Some of the girls will have to be sacrificed on the altar of the establishment. Some strategically placed money will do the rest. We have to look for a house close to the hotels and in a district that's residential but already has some shops and restaurants, a few nightclubs. I've seen several streets near this hotel that fill the bill. We'll look carefully. Yes, the owners will complain when they find out what it's for. I'd prefer ones we can talk to frankly. Traffic in and out of the house would be perfectly discreet. Two, at the most three girls at a time. No dancing, of course, and we'd control the volume of music in each room. The girls will dress in the house, before the clients arrive, and the clients will always have to make an appointment by phone. The girls won't get out of their cab or their car in front of the house but at the nearest corner, always one at a time, never in pairs, never with their boyfriends or husbands or whatever. At some point we can expect a complaint from the airlines. They won't get very far and I'll tell you why: The uniforms won't be exactly the same as the ones the real stewardesses wear. We'll make some changes. If the client asks any questions, he'll be told it's a new uniform that's being tried out on certain routes. The fee: the girl keeps whatever the client wants to give her, obviously. But when he arrives for his appointment, and before he goes up to the room, he'll have to pay the house a hundred dollars. The girl will also pay us a fixed monthly rate regardless of the number of clients she's seen. If a client falls for one of the girls, we'll do all we can to make it hard for him to have another appointment with her: she's been assigned another route, she's on vacation, she's attending a training course in Miami or Tampa—any excuse that sounds professional and logical. It's a matter of spacing out their meetings, not preventing them altogether. If the client wants to be with two women, he'll be told it's impossible because they're very careful about keeping their adventures secret and they don't want to be seen by other stewardesses, even if they're from another airline. That's our policy, but a client we know and trust can enjoy special privileges. Now it's your turn."

I was astonished to see how Ilona had planned every aspect of the operation. I had forgotten her talents in that area. I told her so, and all I could think of to add was something that really concerned much more than the actual mechanics of the business, which seemed entirely viable and indisputably sound.

"It terrifies me to think," I said, "that we'll be staying in Panama City indefinitely if this succeeds. I'm not going to be anchored here for the rest of my life. If Abdul can get his business going again, we have plenty of plans for the future. Besides, I'm getting tired of the place. Nothing happens here. I mean, everything happens, but nothing that interests me."

"I absolutely agree with you, Gaviero," replied Ilona, putting the brush down on the bed. "I'm not going to spend the rest of my life here either. You know me well enough to know that if *you're* getting tired, I've had it up to here"—she passed a brusque, emphatic hand across her forehead—"but this, as a matter of fact, is a question of getting enough money together to leave Panama City and at least profiting from the time we've invested here. You'll need a fair amount of money to start something worthwhile with Abdul. You know what his plans are. In his heart he's always dreamed of being a little Niarchos." I had to laugh at her incisive description of our good friend's ambitions. Incisive and ironic because, unlike us, Abdul would never leap from one venture to another without ever realizing his dreams—dreams we had long since stopped pursuing. It was clear that life always holds in store surprises that are much more complex and unforeseeable than any dream, and the secret is to let them come and not block them with castles in the air. But Abdul, like a good Easterner, remained faithful to his plans for greatness, which he spread out before us with captivating eloquence and conviction. But this was another matter. Ilona's project was unassailable. For the moment I couldn't think of any serious objection. We decided to embark on the adventure, fully confident it would serve our purposes well.

It wasn't difficult to find the perfect house. The owner was a widow well along in years. After talking to her for a short time, we realized she had a past rich in love affairs and erotic episodes in which convention had not proven to be a major obstacle. This gave us the confidence to disclose the use we planned to make of her house. She asked only if we were also going to live there. We answered that naturally we planned to live there in order to give it the appearance of any other respectable, quiet family residence. She asked us for three months' rent in advance since we did not have a guarantor to sign the contract. We agreed on everything. In a short while we had decorated and furnished the house in a style in which the obvious mixed with certain of Ilona's southern whims, making it quite livable. On the first floor there was a very large living room with a fireplace. In the middle of the tropics this made us very happy. "Only in America, Maqroll, only in America is such a charming aberration possible," commented Ilona, looking at the stone edging that, with lunatic extravagance, decorated this attempt at European elegance in an equatorial zone. From the living room one passed to a dining room that we furnished as a small sitting room where the girls would receive their clients. A folding door separated this more intimate space from the larger one. Two other rooms and a maid's room on the first floor were turned into bedrooms with private baths. Ilona and I would live on the second floor, in separate rooms connected by a single bathroom. We also shared a terrace overlooking an abandoned garden in the house behind ours. In another room, also located on the upper floor, we installed a very basic kitchen and a well-stocked bar. Ilona solved the problem of servants very easily. The owner of the house visited occasionally to observe the proposed modifications, and she approved with a smile that was both joyful and nostalgic. When Ilona mentioned the question of household help, Doña Rosa— that was the widow's name—told her to employ one of the two black women who worked for her. The maid would come every day to clean and do whatever additional tasks we might have for her on our floor. The solution was ideal. All we needed was someone to attend to the clients. A boy from the Hotel Sans Souci, whom we knew and liked very much, agreed to work for us.

Ilona had what I called "baptismal raptures," when she would invent names for people and places which then became definitive. The house was dubbed Villa Rosa. When I heard it, I must have looked surprised, because Ilona said, "I know it couldn't be more banal, but homage must be paid to the landlady and all her flying time. Don't you agree?"

I wasn't very convinced, but I knew it was useless to argue. The boy we hired, who had the very common name of Luis, was called Longinos. He was short, plump, dark, with very regular, somewhat effeminate features. At first glance the name Longinos didn't suit him at all, but in time all three of us grew accustomed to it. This was always the case with Ilona's baptisms. It took a certain amount of time to discover their indisputable and revealing precision.

When everything was ready, we moved to Villa Rosa. Ilona made contact with the alleged stewardesses. She spoke of an "immediately feasible basic plan," reminding me of politicians and especially of economists: when a name is given to a specific activity, it acquires irrefutable reality, an existence beyond all doubt. The question of the uniforms remained. I found the solution and always insisted on receiving recognition for this fundamental contribution. Longinos had many good friends among the bellhops in the hotels where the crews stayed overnight. He made arrangements with them to borrow for a few hours the uniforms that the stewardesses gave to them for washing or ironing. A seamstress who had made alterations at the boutique copied the dresses and introduced small changes, following Ilona's instructions. In a few days the supply of uniforms was ready. Then we started going back to the bars in the principal hotels. A delicate stage of the operation had begun. It is well known that the police stay in constant communication with bartenders, waiters, and bell captains, who are irreplaceable sources of information. Our task was to spark their interest with enough money to keep them from passing the information along to the authorities. We moved very cautiously. In a few days we began to receive the first calls. Our female staff was fairly well trained, and the business began, slowly, as we had foreseen, but with a solid foundation and no serious difficulties. Doña Rosa would visit us periodically. She enjoyed the anecdotes concerning what she called our traffic in flight attendants. I must confess I've forgotten much of what occurred there, perhaps because of the catastrophic ending, the effects of which I will never fully recover from. I have a rather confused memory of the entire period, and I can recall only some faces, the sound of certain voices, and one or two notable incidents. We started out with five girls. Each adjusted perfectly to the type of woman required by the airline she was supposed to represent. A blonde, born in Maracaibo to a Texan father and a Portuguese mother, spoke acceptable English and played a Panagra stewardess to perfection. A brunette with skin the color of tobacco, classic features, and straight hair pulled back in a chignon, which gave her a slightly Andalusian air, fit the presumptive KLM uniform very well. For her we invented parents in Aruba and a vague university career in Barranquilla. In fact, she was from Puerto Limón and jabbered a passable English. The Colombian and Venezuelan companies were much easier to arrange. With two Panamanians and a Salvadoran we managed rather well. All of them had met Ilona in the boutique, and even then had suggested to her the need to increase their earnings. They went out occasionally with some businessman they met in the bar at the Hilton or the Continental, but this wasn't enough to pay for their wardrobes and the other costs of maintaining the veneer of respectability that was indispensable for attracting generous clients. The Villa Rosa formula helped them solve the problem.

I remember our first major problem, solved through the providential cooperation of Ilona and Longinos. One night, around eleven o'clock, a client arrived who had called twice for a meeting with the KLM stewardess, but for one reason or another it hadn't been possible to arrange. That night, however, he had his appointment and arrived a little ahead of time. Longinos came upstairs asking for Ilona. His eyes were popping with terror. And for good reason: the client apparently worked for KLM. Longinos had known him for some time and had seen him with the crews who stayed at the hotel. Ilona went down to confront the situation. It was no easy matter. In fact, our guest had once worked in the freight department at KLM, but was no longer employed there. He had his own business in Colón as a customs agent. In the minutes that remained before the arrival of the supposed Aruban, Ilona managed to learn that this was a man burning with jealousy over an old, silent love from his days at the Dutch airline. He was searching desperately for the stewardess who had always refused his advances. He was sure she was the one coming to Villa Rosa, because a tarot reader had predicted it with vague allusions that the desperate lover interpreted in his own way. By means of a signal arranged ahead of time with Longinos, Ilona knew the girl was now waiting in the adjoining sitting room. She offered the client a whiskey, courtesy of the house, and left to talk to the girl. In just a few minutes she had her change her uniform and go back to the small sitting room. Ilona returned to the client and explained that his friend from KLM had canceled because she was attending a training session in Amsterdam. But a charming girl from Avensa, who was here for the first time, was waiting for him. The man said goodbye with tears in his eyes, overcome by indescribable confusion. He stammered a few words and paid for the appointment he had made.

This incident opened our eyes to the complications that could arise when clients were employees of the companies whose names we were using.

"We have to use the uniforms of airlines that don't have offices here. We'll say the girls are members of crews in transit who are going to pick up a plane that was damaged somewhere else in the Caribbean." Ilona always found instant solutions in which she put unlimited faith. I told her this would weaken the clients' interest somewhat and might arouse suspicions regarding the authenticity of what she called "our basic offer." She disagreed, somewhat compassionately. "Ah, Gaviero you innocent! You have no idea of the things men are ready to believe when it's a question of taking some girl to bed. If I were to tell you . . ."

One night the bartender at the Hotel Regina telephoned to say that we'd be getting a call from a very special client, an immensely rich blind Anatolian who managed huge sums of money for associates who trusted his infallible intuition for making extremely profitable investments in financial paper. He spent his life in airplanes, following the routes of his impulses. He wanted to be with two girls at the same time. He called a short while later and I spoke to him in my almost nonexistent Turkish. He replied in impeccable French. He confirmed his wish, and I said I would call him the next day to tell him the time of his appointment. I mentioned it to Ilona.

"There are two problems," she said, "that haven't even occurred to you, but they're critical. First, if he's blind, he'll come with someone who acts as his guide; this can be arranged if we have him wait in the living room while the girls take charge of the Anatolian effendi. Second, if he's traveled so much and has a weakness for stewardesses, he must know the uniforms by touch. That may be what gives him his greatest pleasure, especially if he's old, which seems to be the case. The blind are terribly untrusting. Any alteration in the uniform is going to arouse his suspicions. He may not buy the story about a new model being tested on some routes. But there's no point in worrying now. I'll be there when he goes to the small sitting room to meet the girls. Then we'll see. These Turks are the devil himself, but in Trieste we knew how to handle them; if not, they would have devoured us centuries ago."

The man arrived punctually at six, as we had arranged. He was accompanied by a woman who was clearly his sister: the same curly reddish hair, the same prominent eyes, hers bottle green and his covered by an iridescent, whitish film. He must have been well into his eighties, but he had that robustness of Levantines, who stop aging at about sixty-five. They often reach one hundred without changing, and die of cardiac arrest in their mistress's bed or behind the counter of their store. His sister was somewhat younger and never smiled. She asked for tea while her brother, accompanied by Ilona, went into the small sitting room. The two girls stood up. The effendi approached and, just as Ilona had predicted, ran his hands over them carefully, touching each of the buttons and insignias on the uniforms, lingering on their breasts and hips. When he finished his examination, he turned to Ilona with a slow, malicious smile.

"It's a nice trick. Very nice. If they're stewardesses, then I'm Ataturk. But they're pretty and young, with the kind of firm flesh you never see down here. And you, señora, you're from Trieste, aren't you? Or is it Corfu? No, Trieste." And he caressed Ilona's hands with a delicacy he hadn't used with the girls.

"Yes, I'm from Trieste," she answered. "How could you tell?"

"The accent, madame, the accent and your skin; only women from Trieste keep such soft, elastic skin. On Corfu too, but they have a horrible accent there. All right, let's go to the bedroom."

The girls led him there, one on each side, while he squeezed their buttocks and bellies, repeating in a deep hoarse voice that had a certain charm, "A very good trick, very good. *Ah, ces triestins, très malins, très malins!*"

Meanwhile Ilona served his sister endless tall glasses of tea, which pleased the woman very much. The only language she spoke was an Anatolian dialect we couldn't decipher. The man reappeared after midnight, escorted by the two girls, who were laughing at one of his jokes. He took his sister's arm and said goodbye to Ilona, kissing her hand with a very *fin de siècle* bow. The girls, two Costa Ricans recently recruited by Ilona, stayed for the coffee and sandwiches that Longinos brought them. They had a fine sense of humor and were bold, self-sufficient women, like many of their compatriots. They recounted in detail the erotic feats of their client. The vigorous old man's performance had been exceptional. They admired his unhurried harem wisdom. He hadn't believed the stewardess story. He'd had his doubts from the moment he made the phone call. But he took it as a joke and regaled his bedmates with a detailed analysis of the characteristics of each uniform used by the major airlines, which proved once again the accuracy of Ilona's predictions.

This episode led us to gradually stop using the names of well-known airlines. It was an unnecessary and potentially troublesome risk. Experience indicated that it wasn't even necessary to mention any particular company. Most of the time the clients were satisfied with assuming that the girls were flight attendants. The airline was really secondary. With the exception of the blonde from Maracaibo, the brunette with the Gypsy chignon, and one or two others who fit particular nationalities and companies, the rest of the personnel eventually used a formula whose paternity I am also proud to declare: it was enough to tell the client that the girl hadn't signed a firm contract yet with any airline and was traveling as part of her training at a flight attendants' school in Jacksonville. Ilona, as always, had been right; our clients were not interested in verifying the authenticity of the offer as long as the woman had a certain cosmopolitan air, no matter how superficial, and was as attractive as they had imagined after the sales pitch made by the bartender or the bell captain at the hotel. Predictably enough, the word soon made the rounds of travel agents, regional managers who were always passing through, auditors from North American firms, and wealthy husbands who traveled for more or less legitimate reasons. They circulated Villa Rosa's telephone number among themselves, which made participation by hotel employees less crucial, but we kept them on out of loyalty and good feelings for those who had helped us at the beginning.

As an act of simple justice, it is necessary to say more about someone who played an increasingly important role at Villa Rosa, making him an indispensable friend whose intelligent loyalty inspired more and more of our marveling gratitude. I am referring to Luis Antero, whom we called Longinos. He was a native of Chiriquí and had the singsong, lisping mountain accent, which emphasized his childlike appearance. He was an only child. Longinos had been four when his father, an employee of the electric company, was electrocuted while inspecting the transformer on an electricity pole just outside the city. The smoking corpse hung there all day, twisting in the wind like a contorted puppet. It was Longinos's earliest memory. He spent his childhood clinging to his mother's skirts. She had gone to live with her two unmarried sisters, who had pampered the boy so much that he was marked for life: beardless and plump, with gestures that had an undisguisable feminine quality, he wasn't homosexual but looked as if he were because he had unconsciously adopted many of the mannerisms and speech patterns of the women who raised him. He had an infallible knowledge of the most secret and complex convolutions of feminine behavior, to which he owed the extraordinary number of sexual conquests he had made as a hotel employee. His absolute discretion, never broken even in the most compromising situations, also contributed to his success. If the name of one of his presumed lovers was mentioned in his presence, he put on so convincing a look of innocent astonishment at such an improbable story that he could deceive anyone who didn't know him as we did, anyone not fully aware of his subtle, hidden artfulness. Soon after coming to Villa Rosa, Longinos began to feel so much fondness and admiration for Ilona that he knew what she wanted before she opened her mouth, and he did whatever she wanted with perfect efficiency. Our earnings were increasing admirably, and after a few months we began to share our profits with him. Little by little Longinos took charge of recruiting new personnel and managing the permanent staff. He treated the girls with a mixture of rigor and friendly complicity that was so successful it allowed us to disengage from that aspect of the business. At first Ilona had been very conscientious, but she lacked the necessary patience and tact to manage a staff of women for whom she had little affection. "They're like baby birds who never grow up," she would say. "It doesn't matter where they're from. It's the effect of the tropics, and Latin machismo, and their lack of breeding. I always find it hard to tell the class they belong to because they have one characteristic in common: they're all hopelessly ill-mannered, and so malleable and capricious they're unpredictable. It's not that they lie, it's that they don't know how to reach the truth. They're always on route. *Elles me tapent sur les nerfs.* But Longinos manages them marvelously and gets things from them that I never could."

As Ilona came to depend more on Longinos, we had more time to spend together. We returned to making love in the afternoon and spent the night devising plans and imagining wonderful ventures, helpless with laughter at ourselves and our unrealistic projects. Ilona had lost weight and her full, firm breasts became more prominent. She didn't wear a bra, and this gave her a youthful air that suited her splendidly. A golden serenity had settled over her, which led to an economy of language that made her judgments even more definitive and her definitions more accurate, if that was possible. She called Longinos the Vizier of Mytilene, and following that logic, the Venezuelan blonde became Bilitis and the brunette from Puerto Limón Doña Refugio, a name she didn't seem to find very funny although she never said so. She would only frown with her heavy, dark, beautifully shaped eyebrows. Villa Rosa became La Maison du Maltais, a memory of an old French film with Marcel Dalio and Vivianne Romance that had marked us both when we were adolescents. I remembered it as one of my earliest experiences of sexual arousal.

Thanks to Longinos we were able to resolve, without too much difficulty, the pathetic and delicate episode of Señor Peñalosa. It is certainly worth telling this story in detail. It has the combination of tenderness, sorrow, and foolishness that distinguishes those classic tales in which we can recognize ourselves as the mad, hopeless dreamers who charge full tilt against something we call reality but can never precisely define.

One morning we were having breakfast on the little terrace, surrounded by large rubber and Indian laurel trees that grew in the untended garden next door. We had never seen anyone in the dense vegetation we had christened "the isthmian jungle." The absence of inopportune observers allowed us to leave the windows open when we made love in either Ilona's room or mine. After two discreet knocks Longinos said he had to talk to us. The hour meant it was something extraordinary. He always slept very late since he never went to bed before four or five o'clock in the morning. We told him to come in, and then he told us what was troubling him.

"A gentleman just called who says he's a guest at the Continental. He wants an appointment for tomorrow."

"Fine," I answered. "You arrange it. What's the problem?"

"The problem, señor, is that the man sounded very confused and uncertain. He asked questions that mean he's either a cop or he's never tried anything like this."

"For God's sake, Longinos," Ilona interrupted, "if he were the police, he wouldn't have hesitated for an instant, he would have sounded completely natural. You know what they're like."

"You're right, señora, but I don't know what to think. He sounded like a priest or something. I told him to call again in an hour. What should I say?"

"If he were a priest," answered Ilona, "he wouldn't have hesitated either, or let you know he was confused. Make him an appointment with Our Lady of Cali. I think I know what the problem is."

Longinos was much calmer when he left.

"That client's a timid man, Gaviero, a timid man," Ilona said. "I know them like the back of my hand. They're a mess, they complicate everything and stumble through the world like blind burros."

I agreed and thought there was no reason for alarm.

Our Lady of Cali was a very thin, very quiet blonde with an innocent face and pale blue eyes that she always lowered when anyone spoke to her. She hissed the letter *s,* as nuns usually do, and claimed to be from Cali, in Colombia. I think this was to take advantage of the city's reputation for having the most beautiful women along the Pacific coast and its environs. We concluded that she probably came from the Andean mesa but didn't admit to it because she thought, and rightly so, that this wouldn't add much to her monastic persona. According to comments made by some clients, she demonstrated a Babylonian skill in bed. They always asked for another appointment with her. Ilona had baptized her with that rather profane but, as always, fairly accurate name. The man arrived punctually the next day at four o'clock, an unusual time for appointments at Villa Rosa. Longinos came to my room and asked me to go downstairs.

"I think the señora is right. But it wouldn't hurt for you to take a look at him. People like him never come here."

And in fact, our guest represented a world where Villa Rosa belongs to the category of the unthinkable. Small, thin, with regular features and a straight, obviously dyed little mustache that did not match his graying blond hair, Señor Peñalosa immediately introduced himself with disarming candor. He wore gold-rimmed glasses and had those rather automatic but slow gestures typical of men who live with numbers and accounting books. He carried a dark brown briefcase with his initials in gold—no doubt a gift from his company for some recent anniversary. "Your first twenty-five years with us, my dear Peñalosa": the rote phrases of a manager who, for those same twenty-five years, must have kept the poor man in a perpetual hell of uncertainty and humiliation. I asked Peñalosa to take a seat. We began one of those superficial conversations about the weather and the high cost of everything in Panama City which at least can soothe one's nerves. For he was truly in the clutches of uncontrollable panic. He didn't know where to put his briefcase, or his hands, or his feet. At last, when he was a little calmer, he resolved to speak frankly.

"Look, señor, this is the first time in my life I've ever thought of doing, what shall I call it, something naughty like this. I'm chief auditor in an accounting firm that offers its services to the airlines. I got in last night and the bellhop who carried my luggage told me about this place where, it seems, stewardesses come to spend some time with respectable, discreet gentlemen. He gave me the telephone number and I decided to call. Let me tell you that I've always had an enormous weakness for the young ladies in that line of work. I fly a great deal in my own country, but this is the first time I've traveled abroad. I came to audit the books in an airline office that opened last year in Panama City. I'm married and have two daughters, one ten, the other twelve," and out of his wallet he took a color snapshot of his two girls sitting on bicycles in front of their house. In the background stood a woman with somewhat blurred features who smiled with the good will of the resigned.

"Very nice-looking girls. Thanks," I said, returning the photograph. I was about to add that this wasn't the place to show off his family. But I knew that any observation of the kind would have destroyed him. An abnormally long silence was interrupted by certain sounds from the adjacent sitting room. Our Lady of Cali was coming in to wait for Peñalosa. I broke the rules of our establishment, but I felt I ought to tell him something about the girl, for our guest had once again fallen victim to an uncontrollable panic, surely caused by the clear proximity of what had been his dream for all those years of repressed and passionate erotic fantasies.

"She's a very serious, very discreet girl who doesn't come here too often. She trains flight attendants for Panagra, and she's just passing through Panama City. Tomorrow she has to go back to work in Miami. You can have absolute confidence in her discretion, Señor Peñalosa. Don't worry about that. Make yourself at home. I'll send you two some whiskey."

"Thank you very much, señor," he answered, a little calmer again, "but I never drink. I don't know if I should. You're very kind."

"I think you should," I replied in a tone I hoped was authoritative. "There's nothing like a good drink of Scotch at the right time to break the ice."

Poor Peñalosa felt obliged to laugh, thinking I had made a joke. That hadn't been my intention, obviously. The auditor walked into the sitting room. Longinos introduced the girl, and I went upstairs to tell Ilona about our conversation.

She made some comment about the unpredictable reactions of timid men in these circumstances, but I didn't pay much attention. After midnight Longinos came to the door again.

"Señor Peñalosa says he'd like to spend the night with her. What do you think, señor?"

"Consult with the señora," I said. "I don't think there's a problem, but it's better to know what she thinks."

Just then Ilona came into my room.

"He'll have to be charged double for the night, and tell him he has to vacate the room first thing tomorrow. I don't want him here all day."

"He's already paid, señora. I told him that what he paid already was for just a couple of hours, and he came up with the money right away. But something's bothering me."

"Now we have everybody worrying about that poor idiot," said Ilona with evident irritation. "Let him do what he wants. Leave him alone and be done with it. Forget that fool or we'll all wind up like him."

"Señora," an imperturbable Longinos insisted, "the problem's not with him. It's his briefcase. It's full of money, and he pulls it out to pay for drinks. They're finishing their second bottle of

Dewar's. And he's given the girl over two hundred dollars."

"You should have started with that, boy," Ilona said in the calm, opaque voice she always used when there were premonitions of danger. "Gaviero, you have to go down and see him. Tell him we don't want any trouble. He has to give us the briefcase with the money and we'll keep it in the safe up here. We'll give him a receipt. When he leaves he can settle his bill and that'll be that. But he shouldn't be flashing all that money downstairs. Other clients are coming in now and we can't have any problems. I told you, these timid types, the respectable ones, good fathers, model husbands, they're dangerous as hell."

Señor Peñalosa agreed to everything and gave us the briefcase in exchange for a receipt that he wrote himself in an impeccable bookkeeper's hand even though he was already tight. The next morning Longinos woke us with the news that our guest wanted to stay in the room, and in addition to Our Lady of Cali he wanted us to please call the girl who lived with her.

"Matildita"—it seems that was Our Lady's name—"Matildita here tells me her roommate is a lovely girl and completely trustworthy," added Longinos, imitating Peñalosa's voice.

"I know who she is," Ilona called through the bathroom doors we always left open. "Call her, but tell her if she gets drunk like the last time, we'll throw her out. She's the one who got so rowdy with that guy from São Paulo who had the two bottles of raw rum and almost destroyed everything."

Three days went by. Peñalosa stayed in the room and his bill grew steadily. He asked for champagne to celebrate the arrival of two Salvadorans who had joined Our Lady of Cali and her friend. Everything was perfectly calm. The man never lost his composure. He called his roommates "the ladies who are my flight attendants." His face was shining with beatific happiness and unexpected, endless joy, and we were touched by his expression. The very foreseeable ending was not long in coming. One afternoon three individuals, looking unmistakably like executives with a great future in their company, came to Villa Rosa. I led them into the living room and prepared myself for what they had to say. They had come for Peñalosa. They were with the airline whose audit he had been in charge of. The money in his briefcase was intended for deposit in a Panama City bank that had no branches in other countries. It was meant to be used for making several urgent payments. They had called the hotel three days ago and couldn't reach him. The next day they found out he hadn't returned to his room. After a few discreet inquiries that morning, a bellhop told them about the telephone number he had given to Peñalosa. One of them, in fact, had arranged an appointment with Longinos and then canceled. Peñalosa, they said, was an absolutely trusted employee. He had been with them for thirty years. He had never worked anywhere else. He had started as an accountant. His conduct was beyond reproach, with never a slip. Peñalosa himself boasted that he was always faithful to his wife, that he had been a virgin when he married. Then I explained what our attitude had been toward him, and I reassured them about the briefcase. I showed them a copy of the receipt we had given Peñalosa and said the money was at their disposal. They paid his bill. It came to more than two thousand dollars. Then they indicated that they wanted to speak to Peñalosa and have him leave with them.

"If you'll permit me," I said, "I suggest you let me talk to him first and explain the situation. The man has been drinking for three days and he may very well lose control, although up until now he's behaved very correctly."

They agreed and stayed in the living room to wait for my report.

When I walked into the room, after knocking and saying who it was, the scene was both touching and grotesque. Peñalosa in his shorts, surrounded by his girls, some naked and others in underclothes, allowed himself to be caressed with the complacency of a pasha. I told the women to get dressed and go to the next room. I had to talk to the gentleman alone. They obeyed without delay. Peñalosa sat looking at me with a face where sorrow was giving way to devastating panic.

"What is it, señor, what is it? The ladies haven't done anything, I assure you."

I said that wasn't the problem. Three gentlemen from the company were waiting for him outside. They wanted him to go with them. On the verge of tears, he stammered vague excuses and explanations. He wanted to stay here forever. His life had been an interminable lie, a miserable act of cowardice.

"Nobody ever told me this existed, señor. I had no idea. Do you understand?" And he began to cry uncontrollably. The tears ran down the gray bristles that had aged him ten years in three days. "I don't want to go, señor. Don't let them take me. I want to stay here. You've all been so kind."

I got him dressed while I tried to convince him that it was impossible to grant his request.

"You'll come back again," I said in an effort to console him.

"No, señor, I'll never come back. I don't even know if I'll keep my job. But it's all right. It's ended, I know that. Thank you very much for everything."

He walked out, dragging his feet. I didn't want to go with him to the living room. Longinos accompanied him with that impersonal courtesy he had learned in the hotels and knew how to use in this kind of situation.

The episode of Señor Peñalosa put an end to my tolerance of a life for which I felt a growing dislike. Ilona had also reached a critical point of impatience with running the business. The endless traffic of women whose rather elementary lives were in conflict with ours had turned into a suffocating routine. We were being enveloped in a kind of insipid film made up of trivial stories, calculated meanness, professional jealousies, and a narcissism that each of them fed with the supposed preferences of the clients. Even so, Ilona, with a woman's natural, sympathetic solidarity and a tolerance I've never had for that gossiping harem atmosphere, had a higher limit of endurance for what I was beginning to find unbearable. She knew it, and with affectionate understanding she tried to make it easier for me to endure, but that life was clearly coming to an end.

During a breakfast on the terrace that lasted all morning, we resolved to face the situation squarely and end it. We agreed to wait for the first rains before leaving Villa Rosa. Ilona had the amount of our total profits—she had always taken care of that task, which was beyond my talents and inclinations—and we agreed to divide it in thirds, making Bashur an equal partner. To help him out of his difficulties, we also agreed to send our friend his share immediately. We would put our two thirds into a joint short-term certificate of deposit. What we earned from now until we left would pay for our trip and allow us to give Longinos enough to start some small business that would make him independent. The rains would come in a little more than two months. Making these decisions and putting a limit on our time in Panama City and our life in Villa Rosa produced a growing, restorative sense of relief in us.

"It will be interesting to find out," said Ilona, "why we've been so affected by something we never considered an affront to our very personal ethical principles. This disgust comes from somewhere else, some other place inside us."

"I think," I said, "that it's more a question of aesthetics than of ethics. That these women prostitute themselves with our consent and assistance doesn't concern us at all. What isn't easy to bear is the kind of life it pays for: very lucrative, of course, but hopelessly monotonous. In our Catholic Western world, prostitution and marriage are viewed as diametrically opposed. In fact, when we observe one of them as closely as we have, the antithesis dissolves and is transformed into a kind of aberrant parallelism. But I don't think we have to be so philosophical about it. Finding out that prostitution is as conventional as marriage, we've only confirmed the path we've chosen; our wandering and our desire never to reject what life, or fate, or chance, or whatever you want to call it, offers along the way—at least that keeps us from falling into a dreadful, resigned acceptance."

Ilona applauded with glee.

"Bravo, Gaviero! When you decide to think about something, you're right on target. The trouble is that in a little while everything goes topsy-turvy again, but that doesn't matter if you know how to set things right. We'll leave when the rain comes. You'll be sure to lose yourself in some mine in the middle of the cordillera, or go down into the canyon of the first river you come to, and you'll spend your time contemplating your navel and dividing yourself into three parts, like a Buddhist monk."

"Go to hell," I said, "and give me more tea. When you get the bright idea of opening a boutique in Terranova, I'll come and rescue you. You're not so bad at thinking up lunatic schemes either."

She came and sat on my lap, mussed my hair, and whispered in my ear in a Provençal accent, *"Ne t'en fais pas, Maqroll, on sortira d'ici passablement riches et ça compte quand même."*

A few days after this conversation on the terrace, the fateful messenger walked into Villa Rosa, the one the gods send to remind us that it's not up to us to change even the slightest portion of our destiny. She arrived in the shape of a woman with the Slavic and obviously fictitious name of Larissa. The dice had been rolling long before our decisions on the terrace. We learned that very soon.

LARISSA

Larissa arrived one morning around noon. She had been sent by Alex and the blonde from Maracaibo, who had already told Ilona something about a woman born in Chaco, of uncertain background, but who had traveled a great deal, spoke several languages, lived very quietly, and was tremendously good-looking. Longinos brought her to the terrace, where we were in bathing suits, enjoying the sun. The first thing that attracted my attention was a certain resemblance to Ilona. The same straight nose and protruding, well-delineated lips, the same build and long, shapely legs that gave the impression of elasticity and strength, of unassailable youth. But when I looked more carefully, I realized that the resemblance was purely superficial and vanished under close scrutiny. She wore her deep black hair in a wild, unruly style that reached almost to her shoulders. It was as if they both came from the same region but had nothing in common except a fleeting resemblance. Larissa had a husky voice, and her speech was fluent. She was extremely intelligent and seemed to possess that very rare faculty of focusing on the essentials, on what was lasting and true, and disregarding all the rest. We soon realized how mistaken that impression was. She looked into her interlocutor's eyes but not at the person. I mean that more than merely looking, she seemed to be searching, with secret, patient astuteness, for the other being who is always with us and comes to the surface only when we are alone, to deliver certain messages, dissolve certain fragile truths, abandon us to unspeakable perplexity. That is what Larissa was looking for, that is where she patiently delved in her effort to discover what we hoped and believed could never be found.

While she was giving us routine reasons for wanting to work at Villa Rosa, routine explanations of her relevant experience in Singapore, Stockholm, and Buenos Aires, her facility for languages, and other minor details, I noticed that Larissa had captured Ilona's attention, which was not at all usual. We asked if she would like something to drink, and she requested very strong coffee. She sat on a canvas chair in the shade of the immense cámbulo that grew in the garden next door. Some of its branches extended over our terrace, and the blossoms were falling around her. She was soon surrounded by an aura of intense orange. I had the impression that this effect was created as part of a secret ceremony whose significance escaped me. Her husky voice came from the shade with a sensuality that made me think of an avid pythoness questioning the future of helpless passersby. She caught me by surprise when she said to me, "I often go to a bar you visited a great deal last winter. We were never there at the same time. I mean, we were once, but you didn't see me. Alex has spoken of you. He told me you were staying at the Pensión Astor. I live nearby and know the owner. I don't know how you managed to get free of him. When you're caught in the web he weaves to trap you in his rotten trafficking, it's very difficult to escape."

"How did you manage it?" I asked, trying in turn to catch her off guard.

"I've never needed him, and I'd never get within reach."

The lesson was a little hard to swallow. Ilona looked at me with fleeting but visible alarm. I though the best thing was to take it as far as I could. I was learning what kind of person I had to contend with.

"At a certain moment I found myself obliged to work for him. But thanks to our mutual friend Alex, I escaped in time and went to live somewhere else."

"Yes," she said as the cámbulo blossoms continued to fall around her, "the Hotel Miramar. The Ecuadorian's a good person. I spent a couple of weeks there while they were making some repairs at the place where I live."

It was clear I should be quiet. Without a rivalry being established between us, or even any obvious friction, one of those subterranean but unmistakable differences of character made a confrontation with this informed, wary woman from Chaco ill-advised and pointless. If she was going to work with us, it was better to maintain a neutral territory where we could move without any problems. Ilona, who evidently was following our conversation with interest, changed the subject and steered it with great naturalness toward certain details related to the uniform Larissa would wear and the story that had to be invented regarding her work as a stewardess.

"I wouldn't want to wear a uniform," she said with such vehement decisiveness that we waited for an explanation. "You can say I'm a service inspector. That I travel regularly to verify compliance with regulations covering passenger service. I'll drop hints that I work for the Civil Aeronautics Board and have to travel incognita for obvious reasons."

Bringing in the CAB seemed foolish to me. I said that if we did, she'd be running the greatest risk. She agreed so readily that I was rather disconcerted. There was something in the woman that constantly eluded me. Not because she was trying to conceal it but because she belonged to a world I didn't know, and without being hostile it represented forces, currents, regions, that for me were terra incognita.

When Larissa stood up to say goodbye, Ilona did the same and accompanied her to the stairs. They crossed the bedroom, talking quietly, while Ilona put her arm around Larissa's shoulder in a gesture I had never seen her use with any of the girls. She wanted to seem the protector, but it looked more as if she were seeking support in someone stronger than herself.

At first Larissa's presence was not especially noticeable and brought no major changes in the routine at Villa Rosa. She often came in the morning to join us while we sunbathed on the terrace. She always kept in the shade, sitting on the chair she had used the first day, surrounded by the cámbulo blossoms that fell constantly around her, while we read or continued a conversation in which we usually recalled cities and places we knew. Larissa's opinions were always somewhat vague, as if they were surrounded by a fog that never gave her memories an exact outline or a definite shape. This, on the contrary, was one of the outstanding characteristics of Ilona's stories and recollections. In a single stroke she could evoke a city, a landscape, an island, a country. In the case of Larissa the vagueness even extended to her life in Panama City. We never found out where she lived. All we knew was that she didn't have a telephone. She would call from the bar we had both frequented, and that was where we left messages about the appointments we had made for her. Another of her peculiarities was that for the selection of her clients she established meticulous criteria regarding age, education, and origin. After her first few visits she explained, with her absent air and in her voice of a rutting baritone, "Please, I'm going to ask you not to make appointments for me with young clients. I prefer to be with mature men who've had at least some experience of other countries and don't have the rough, boisterous manners of Latin Americans. And under no circumstances do I want to see North Americans or Asians. I know it's not easy to find out details like these on the telephone, but if you can help me a little and Longinos cooperates, I'll take care of the rest in due course. I'll create my own clientele. There's a certain type of man I get along with very well, and they always come back." Ilona was about to say something, but Larissa didn't let her speak. "Yes, I know," she said with a smile that tried to be friendly but only seemed condescending, "perhaps I'm asking a great deal and this kind of request doesn't fit the house rules. I understand. But you'll see, soon it won't be a problem for you, while for me it's the only way I can do this work in a way that benefits everybody."

Ilona was silent. I continued to watch the clouds moving across the sky, blown by a breeze that announced the coming rains.

We found out from Longinos where our new acquisition lived. One day they called from the bar to say there was a letter for me. A few friends were still writing to me there. Longinos went to pick up my mail, and much later he returned and came upstairs to give it to me. He wore an expression that alternated between amusement and amazement.

"When I went for your letter," he said, "Alex asked me to take Señora Larissa a package that had been left there for her. It looked like women's clothing. He said it was supposed to be delivered to where she lived, not to the bar. I said I didn't know her address, and he looked at me as if he didn't believe me. Then, after hesitating a moment, he told me to go down to Avenida Balboa and then a few blocks north until I came to the ocean, and on a small beach with a kind of jetty made from the stones and cement blocks lying all around, I'd see an abandoned fishing boat leaning against the support wall. He said I should call to her from the sidewalk and she'd come out for the package. That's what I did. When I called her name, she looked out the porthole of the only cabin that seemed sort of livable and asked what I wanted and how I found out where she lived. I answered both questions, and she came out for the package. She was in her slip, and was mad as hell. 'Don't you go around telling everybody where I live. That's nobody's business. And don't ever come back here. You tell your bosses whatever you want. I'll talk to them myself. Now get the hell out of here, you miserable little shit!' She talked in a quiet voice, like she didn't want anybody to hear. But there was nobody around. What an angry broad. I'd like to know what kind of story she'll make up for you."

"Don't worry," said Ilona, trying to calm him, "it's not your fault. If she didn't tell them in the bar not to give out her address, that's her problem. Just don't go back, and that's the end of it."

Longinos left, and we didn't say anything for a long time. I had a clear memory of the wreck propped up on the little beach of shingle and concrete rubble. I had seen it every day from my window in the Pensión Astor. I recalled something I had forgotten but that struck me at the time: occasionally at night a dim light could be seen in one of the cabins adjacent to the bridge, which had collapsed. I also remembered the name of the boat. On a blackened bronze plaque screwed to a starboard railing, the word *Lepanto* was still legible. I was intrigued by the discrepancy between the sonorous, legendary name and the ruins of a humble coastal boat lying rusty and wrecked on a narrow beach that had been used as a dump for longer than anyone could remember. Longinos had mistaken it for one of the fishing boats that anchor at the other end of the bay, but certain elements of its design, the shape of the portholes and the two ventilation ducts still in place through some miracle of balance, made it easy to determine its origin. The boat came from the shipyards of Toulon, Genoa, or Cádiz. How it had landed here, wrecked against a seawall in Panama City, was a question I may have asked myself then but didn't think about later. Now the image of the *Lepanto*'s sad remains came to me out of the recent past, rescued from a charitable oblivion. A tormenting piece of evidence demanding to be deciphered with all the terror of the Delphic mysteries.

A few days after Longinos's visit Larissa asked to speak with us. She had just finished with one of her regular clients. She came up to our rooms looking tired and as if a controlled vexation could find no outlet that would justify it. Ilona gradually calmed her into a state of gentle exhaustion that favored conversation. My friend exercised remarkable influence on the inscrutable woman from Chaco: with a few chance words she imparted a tranquillity and peaceful equilibrium that could last for days. When Larissa was calm and disposed to explain the enigma of her residence, she began to speak. Her story contained corners, labyrinths, and ellipses bordering on a visionary world that lent itself to the kind of esoteric speculation I always protect myself against with a blind instinct for avoiding chaos, one of the faces of death that for me is least tolerable and most lethal.

"I boarded the *Lepanto* in Palermo," Larissa began. "I had lived there for several years as a companion to a Sicilian noblewoman, the Princess De la Vega y Hoyos, the last in a line of Spanish grandees who stayed in Sicily when the island was lost to the Spanish crown. The old woman watched over her small income with the frugality of one who knows she can fall into poverty at any moment. Brilliantly cultivated, she read all kinds of books in several languages, but preferred the classics and the great histories. She was a little mad. When she hired me, the princess had begun to be interested in spiritualism and a wide variety of esoteric experiments. With me she maintained a distant cordiality, due perhaps to her suspicions regarding my Latin American origins and her infrequent dealings with other people. She lived alone on a huge estate on the outskirts of the city. Once a week a gardener came to tend the park that surrounded the manor house, whose desolate, ruined appearance aroused intense melancholy. The old cook, deaf as a post, prepared two meals a day that were as deficient in imagination as in the most basic culinary sense. The princess had broken her leg in a fall down the main staircase, and for that reason she placed an advertisement in the paper for a companion. I went to see her, and she hired me. When the princess could walk again, she asked me to stay on. "I've grown used to you. If you go, I'll miss your company," she said with her typical mixture of distracted aristocratic insolence and the brusqueness of a solitary person who doesn't know how to treat other people. I decided to stay, although she paid me so irregularly I never knew exactly what my salary was or when I was supposed to receive it. I grew very fond of books as a result of reading aloud to the princess, always at night and in her room. Dawn often found me still reading to her. We would sleep all morning and take a stroll in the park after lunch. She told me old legends about her family. Complicated amatory exploits by the men of the house, whose fame for such deeds in Sicily was maintained with popular additions of a rather rustic crudity. One morning the Princess De la Vega y Hoyos was found dead of a massive heart attack. On drawing up the death certificate, it was discovered that she was ninety-four years old. I never imagined she was so old. I had thought she was a little over seventy. The notary responsible for settling her affairs presented me with a sum of money that she had left me in her will. It came to much less than my estimate of the amount she owed me, although I was so enmeshed in dates and partial payments that my records weren't very reliable either. The notary told me I could stay in the house until I decided what to do. I refused his offer. Without the company of the princess, the shabby solitude of the estate depressed me terribly. I went to the port to find a boat that was ready to sail. The destination didn't matter. There was the *Lepanto*. I spoke to the captain, a sly, foulmouthed man from Cádiz. After laborious discussion we finally agreed on the price of the passage. My accommodations were to be a corner of the hold where they had set up a temporary berth. He said he was sorry, but the only free cabin was being made into an office for some official of a shipping company that co-owned the boat. The *Lepanto* must have seen better days. When I went aboard, she looked as if a minor squall at sea would sink her. It seems her fragile appearance was deceptive, for I saw her face storms in the Gulf of León without suffering any damage. The captain said he was going first to Genoa and then to Mallorca, where I would disembark. I agreed, and went back to the estate to bring my few belongings, which were already packed. When I settled myself on the cot in the hold of the *Lepanto,* I never dreamed I'd still be living there today. The things that have happened to me in that place are of such a nature, they come from such dark, hidden corners of the unspeakable, that I can only tell you about them gradually. It's very late and what I have to say will take several conversations. For now, it's enough for you to know that

I do live on the wreck of the *Lepanto*. If you need me, please leave a message at the bar. I stop in there every day. I don't want anybody to come to the boat or try to get in touch with me there. I don't want to attract attention, and I try to be as inconspicuous as possible. Not many people know that anyone lives on the wreck. The light that's visible from time to time is usually explained as some couple who have gone there to make love. If people knew what was really happening, they'd never be the same."

After Larissa left, we were silent, assimilating and scrutinizing the portions of the story she had just told us, as well as what we could discern behind her final words, which made us feel a vague uneasiness that became almost unbearable as night fell and we were enveloped in the shadows of the abandoned garden next door.

"Let's go have a drink somewhere," Ilona suggested. "It's impossible here."

We visited several of the places we had frequented during our stay at the Hotel Sans Souci. The waiters and bartenders welcomed us with rather surprised cordiality. We returned home drunk with alcohol and exhaustion, but we hadn't succeeded in pushing away the gloomy disquiet caused by Larissa's words. In the days that followed we continued the process of liquidating the business. Bashur confirmed the receipt of the money we had sent him. In his words, he felt relief combined with gratitude—the kind of gratitude that, for his people, has the intensity and depth of a religious act. He was free of all his difficulties, and was outfitting a tanker to transport chemicals and dyes. It was not improbable, he announced with evident jubilation, that we would all meet again in Panama City. He would let us know about that when the ship was ready to leave the Antwerp shipyards. He had chosen the name: *Nymph of Trieste*.

"These Levantines are hopeless," said Ilona, disguising the tender feelings produced by Abdul's gesture. "When they abandon their Arabian nights, they dedicate themselves to throwing bombs and fighting in the mountains. I can't imagine you giving that name to any ship of yours, Maqroll."

I replied that first of all, my owning a ship was highly unlikely, and second, giving names to things and people was her job, not mine. We still hadn't decided what to do about Longinos. He was so attached to us, especially to Ilona, that we knew how painful the fact of our departure would be for him.

"I'll talk to him," Ilona promised. "Otherwise you'll end up taking him with you, and that's not the idea."

As always, she was right.

One night, a few weeks after our conversation with Larissa, she came to Villa Rosa for an appointment with one of her clients, the manager of a consortium of Scandinavian banks with offices in Panama City, a gigantic, mild-mannered Viking whose greetings were very ceremonious and who always seemed on the verge of falling asleep. As he was leaving he sent Longinos with a message for me. He wanted a moment to discuss a personal matter. I went down to the living room. The Norwegian remained standing, his straw hat in his hand, and his only comment was: "I don't think our friend is well. It's not medical. It's something else. Why don't you people talk to her? I'm sure you can help her."

That was all. He left as if he were hypnotized. The tropical night immediately engulfed him amid the noise of the crickets and the syncopated, inconsequential song of the great frogs hiding in the grass.

That same night Larissa continued her story. Just as I had been the first time I saw her, and now with the facts she had given us, I was disturbed by that tortured, shadowy area I felt lurking behind her presence, her words, her slightest gesture. But on this occasion there was a new element that I found extremely unsettling and did not know how to deal with: I saw that Ilona was more deeply enmeshed than I had realized in the grim net spread by Larissa. With alarming naturalness Ilona was breathing in the atmosphere that rose like lethal vapor from the presence of this woman who had come to Villa Rosa like a messenger from hell. This is why I find it necessary to transcribe her disquieting story in detail. I told Ilona about the fear expressed by the Scandinavian who had just been with Larissa, and she sent for her. We were on the terrace, enjoying the mild night breeze that cooled the air while it cleared the sky of clouds, bringing the firmament close and making it seem that the vast shining dome, alive with ceaseless activity, was within our grasp. Larissa arrived without delay, collapsed into the first beach chair she came to, and sat for a long time in silence. Her face showed extreme exhaustion. Her body took on a wan stillness, as if she were breathing her last. When she began to speak, we were intrigued by the husky firmness of her voice. It revealed a secret, intense energy originating in a place more secret, more untouched, more inconceivable than her failing physical presence.

"I should tell you everything from the beginning," she began. "The *Lepanto* had to remain in Palermo for two days after the departure date indicated by the captain. He was waiting for some papers from Palma de Mallorca that he couldn't sail without. Since I didn't want to go back to the estate and already had my things on board, I decided to stay on the ship. I slept very well the first night despite the odor of bilge in the hold. During the day I went to the port to buy some necessary toilet articles. I had to share a cramped bathroom with the captain, who had long since given up using it, and there were no towels or soap. I also bought some provisions to augment the food on board, which didn't promise to be very appetizing. I returned at nightfall. The captain tried to strike up a conversation whose purpose was all too clear. It seemed the right moment to let him know, once and for all, that he should forget any intentions of the kind, and that it was absolutely pointless for him to insist in the future. He listened, offered no serious argument, and we talked about something else. I asked him for a lamp to use at night. He said that at the back of the hold there was a switch for a light bulb that I probably hadn't noticed because it was hidden by a steel beam over the cot. When I went down, I realized I had to walk almost the entire length of the hold to turn the light on or off. I climbed back up on deck, and without waiting to hear my request the captain handed me a battery lamp. His impersonal, unpleasant manner indicated the resentment he felt at my rejection of his advances. But it was better this way, and I ignored his nasty mood. I fell asleep almost immediately and forgot to turn off the electric light. I had grown accustomed to the smell, and the gentle rocking of the boat moored to the dock helped me to enjoy a deep, restful sleep. I was suddenly awakened by a presence between the light bulb and my cot. I was still half asleep and thought it was the captain making another advance. The figure approached slowly and sat at the foot of the bed. What I saw woke me completely and shocked me beyond words. An officer of the Napoleonic Chevaux-légers de la Garde was staring at me. His steel-gray eyes were striking beneath the arch of graying eyebrows. He had a large, gray-blond mustache with carefully twisted ends, and two braids of graying hair that hung down from the shako, with its gold trim and regimental insignias. His strong hands, sinewy but well tended, were resting on his knees, lending an air of natural familiarity to the presence of this robust horseman. 'Don't be afraid,' he said in French with a Reims accent and a tone of command that was characteristic of military men accustomed to giving orders in the field. 'I only want to talk with you awhile. Excuse me for waking you, but I spend very long periods without talking to anyone, and your unanticipated presence here is a very pleasant opportunity for me.' I don't remember what I answered, but he transmitted so spontaneous and affable a need for company that we began to talk as if we had known each other for years. After he tried to reassure me about his unexpected appearance, he introduced himself with great courtesy. His name was Laurent Drouet-D'Erlon. He was a colonel in the Chevaux-légers de la Garde and first cousin to the general Count Jean-Baptiste Drouet-D'Erlon, who was very close to the Emperor. He was traveling on behalf of the count, on a mission about which he could give no further details. He was going to Genoa, where he expected to find certain news from the island of Elba on which, as I must know, Napoleon was being held by the allied powers. Then he would continue on to Mallorca. At this point it's important to explain something that's not easy to understand, and clearly hasn't been easy for me either—the logical impossibility of talking to an imperial soldier who referred to a present that was almost a century and a half in the past. I knew it was an unexplainable aberration, and at the same time, from the moment he began to speak, everything happened with a fluidity and logic that seemed unassailable. In other words, nothing in me resisted or was alarmed by an impossibility made possible by the warm plenitude flowing from this being from the past, a past that his mere presence turned into an absolute present. This acceptance, once perceived, became something that took place within the bounds of irrefutable normality, and that is the secret of everything that has happened to me since I boarded the *Lepanto*.

"We talked for the rest of the night. Or rather, he talked and I interrupted only to clarify certain facts and confirm my familiarity with places and events that I knew from my long hours of reading to the princess. It would be useless to attempt a detailed reconstruction of the life of someone like Laurent, with whom I have lived for so long. You never refer to the circumstances that are mentioned once and then become part of your life in common and are taken for granted. That first night he did not fail in his courteous but cordial formality, which eased our conversation and placed both of us in the situation of traveling companions who, in a happy coincidence that relieves the tedium of any sea voyage, get along well and enjoy each other's company. When the first noises on deck announced that day was breaking, the colonel stood and took his leave with a kiss on the hand that was more friendly than courtly. He went to the back of the hold and turned off the switch, leaving me in the half-light of dawn. I lay on the cot for many hours, trying in vain, obviously, to accommodate what had just occurred to the reality around me. I was certain that something in me had changed forever. I was afraid to go on deck and spend my last day in Palermo with a clear, vivid memory of the unthinkable, but at last I resolved to go up. The captain looked at me with misgiving and surprise. "I thought you were sick," he said, "and were going to spend the whole day down below. We're ready to eat. Would you like to join me, or do you prefer to go ashore and eat in the port?" I said I'd go ashore because I needed to stretch my legs and still wasn't very hungry. If we weren't on friendly terms, at least each of us knew the rules. That would make the trip more tolerable. Early the next morning we would sail for Mallorca. I ate in a tavern in the port and then visited the places in the city I had liked and which brought back pleasant memories. As night was falling I returned to the *Lepanto* and stayed on deck until supper. The bustling port distracted me until I felt stupefied and outside of time. The captain and I ate alone. We exchanged no more than a few words. I went down to the hold immediately after the meal and lay down. Around midnight, when I was going to leave the bed to turn off the light, I heard someone moving the switch at the back of the hold, and the light went out. Footsteps approached the cot. In fact, I was no longer astonished; I expected to see the visitor of the night before, who sat at my side and, changing the courteous, impersonal tone he had used before, launched into a long, feverish declaration of love more impassioned than anything I had known before. His hands began to move up and down my body in caresses that became more and more intimate and uncontrolled. We finally made love, he half dressed, I completely naked. His lovemaking was a series of assaults that were rapid and so intense they left me in beatific plentitude, but with less and less strength. Finally we slipped under the rough wool blankets, which still had bits of thistle and tiny twigs that lightly scratched our skin. He told me a good deal about his life. He had been captured twice by the Russians, once after the Battle of Austerlitz, and then in the Berezina Pass during the retreat from Moscow. On both occasions he was confined in the Crimea. He spent two years there the first time, enjoying the mild climate and warm hospitality of the Georgians. The second time, he was with the Duke de Richelieu, who served Czar Alexander I as governor of the region. In Odessa and Tbilisi the Circassian women, who offered their favors easily, initiated him into that peculiar, delicious rhythm that creates in the woman a kind of dependence similar to an opium addiction or a mystic's delirium. When the engines began to hum, announcing the departure of the *Lepanto,* the colonel said goodbye with a long, passionate kiss, dressed hurriedly, and disappeared once again into the vacillating shadows of dawn. A deep sleep until well past noon restored me after the night of excitement and pleasure. When I awoke we were far out to sea. The boat was rolling heavily, struggling against a sea agitated by the tramontane wind. The following night the lovemaking was repeated with no major variations except for the long silences of Laurent, who seemed to put all his energy and attention into enjoying my body, as if it were a feast that would be forbidden to him for some time to come. Before leaving he said he wasn't sure if he could return for a few days, but as soon as we were near the first port on our journey, he promised we would see each other again. And that is precisely what happened. I spent the night in a palpitation of longing that finally ended at daybreak in a sleep filled with visions of desire inventing the most absurd obstacles to its own satisfaction.

"Life on board moved within the routine tedium imposed by travel on small ships like the *Lepanto,* where one's interaction with others is limited to inane table conversation or comments on trivial incidents. Besides, I was engrossed in remembering the hours spent with Laurent. With unnatural fidelity, my skin seemed to retain the heat of his presence. Two more nights passed, and on the third a new surprise was in store. I was trying to fall asleep, to shut out the

light by pulling a corner of the blanket over my eyes, when someone again stood between the light bulb and my bed. I thought it
was my friend. I uncovered my face, longing to receive him, and
found myself looking at a man I couldn't identify at first. Then I
realized I had seen similar people in the paintings in the princess's
library. He was tall and slender, with pale, bony hands and a long
face that had a paleness too, part courtly, part ascetic. His deep
black eyes, with their long, almost feminine lashes, shone with
restrained, ceremonial intelligence. He was dressed in a tunic of
fine black broadcloth that hung down to the floor and had two
impeccably elegant notes of color: The fastenings from the collar
to the waist were a deep purple color beautifully edged in silver,
and the collar and hem of the habit were trimmed with a double
edging of silver enclosing a lime-green braid. He wore a high, stiff
hat of purple velvet over long, blue-black hair arranged with a care
not lacking in vanity. A golden winged lion hung from a chain on
his chest; one of its front paws held an open book on which were
written the words *"Pax tibi Marce Evangelista Meus."* With his
hands hidden in the long sleeves of his robe, he looked at me as if
trying to remember who I was. Suddenly he began to speak in
polished, perfect Italian. It was evident that he intended to avoid
any accent or word that might betray a specific region. He had a
deep bass voice, which was warm and serene and revealed an
extensive education at court. After begging my pardon for the
intrusion, he introduced himself as Giovan Battista Zagni, secretary
of the Judicial Commission of the Great Council of the Most
Serene Republic of Venice. He was traveling to Mallorca to receive payment of certain duties owed by the Bank of Mut for the
use of ports along the Dalmatian coast which belonged to the
republic. I invited him to sit at the foot of my bed. His tall figure
was commanding, and I preferred him at eye level so that our
conversation could be more natural and serene. He accepted with
a smile that showed his perfect teeth and made him look signifi-
cantly younger. Once again the same atmosphere of absolute familiarity was created that I had sensed when Colonel Drouet-D'Erlon
made his appearance. And again, with no effort or struggle, I was
able to reconcile the present in which I was living with the past
from which my unforeseen visitor had emerged. Matters moved
more quickly with Zagni. After a long hour in which he recounted

inconsequential events and wonderfully scandalous bits of gossip that had enlivened the hermetic society of Venice, he began to caress my knees, and then his hands moved between my thighs with the slow rhythm of a man who has devoted a good part of his life to wooing his flirtatious, intriguing compatriots. He behaved with the cautious certainty of someone whose gallantries and erotic digressions have never been repulsed. He unfastened the tunic with unhurried naturalness, removed his fine batiste underclothing, and lay down beside me under the blankets with movements that reminded me of certain religious ceremonies in which the priests seem almost motionless, but each gesture corresponds to a knowing calculation. We made love surrounded by the heady floral perfume worn by the official of the Most Serene Republic, a scent he had surely acquired along the Rialto in one of the small shops that sell Eastern essences. Before first light Zagni dressed with the same unhurried movements and took his leave with a kiss to my forehead, saying he would visit the next night. He indicated that only when we approached land would he find himself obliged to stay away until we were back at sea again.

"As if he suspected something, the captain of the *Lepanto* had been careful to point out to me that there would be several ports of call during the voyage. Given the condition of the vessel, the machinery needed frequent repairs to continue working. And so we had to stop in Salerno, then spend several days in Livorno, and in Genoa we had to wait a week for a replacement part for the axle shaft. After Genoa we stopped in Nice, and from there we headed for Mallorca in a storm that shook the boat so much it seemed about to sink. During the voyage my nocturnal visitors adjusted the routine of their appearances: it was Laurent the day before our arrival in each port, the time we were in port, and the night following our departure, and Zagni the whole time we were out to sea. My relationship with each of them became extremely personal and close. The colonel of the Empire told me of his campaigns in Germany, his time in Spain with Junot, his two long imprisonments by the Russians in the Caucasus, and his participation in a conspiracy in which his cousin, the general Count Drouet-D'Erlon, played an active role, to prepare the return of the Emperor, confined to the island of Elba. I had become so sensitive to his lovemaking that I ached for our arrival at the ports. My relations with Zagni had the nature of a religious ceremonial, something like a Byzantine aura, a golden magnificence that left me in a dream state, a slow delirium fed by the knowing caresses of the Secretary of the Council of Ten. With him, too, I always waited for nightfall like someone preparing herself for a celebration in which mystery and secrecy tempered any inopportune display of pleasure. Zagni never spoke of his personal life. He carefully avoided the slightest allusion to the responsibilities of his post, his daily family life in Venice, and of course, he never mentioned the names of relatives, allies, or simple acquaintances in the Most Serene Republic. Yet his obvious, rigorous precautions in no way interfered with the warmth and delicacy of his relations with me. He made me feel that we were accomplices in an unspecified, complex undertaking whose details and circumstances I was ignorant of, and which were of no interest to me because all my attention, all my senses were engaged in the knowing theory of his caresses. It would take hours, days, to recall the incidents of the voyage, their complex wealth of sensual experience, the rich incursions into a past lived as if it were unquestionably present. Besides, it isn't easy for me to talk about this for very long. When I remember in the presence of others, no matter how fond of them I may be, the fact of their presence, their attention and curiosity turns what happened into an unreal, unbearable nightmare for me. I'd rather tell you how the *Lepanto* ran aground on this coast and why I continue to live there. When we reached Mallorca, the captain began a thorough overhaul of the *Lepanto*. He explained that he wanted to sail to the Caribbean and use the vessel for trade along the Central American coast and in the islands. He said I could live on the ship until I found a new direction for my life in Genoa or somewhere else in Europe. He hinted that if I wanted to, I could travel with him to the Antilles. I wouldn't have to pay for my passage and perhaps I'd find some way to make a living over there. He made the offer with absolute prudence and emphasized that there was no hidden intention. What he wanted, he said, was to have company during the voyage and to prolong a friendship that he enjoyed. He admired my independence and respected my very particular, unusual way of moving through the world. I said I would give him my answer in a few days because I wanted to think it over. A smile of complicity passed over the captain's shrewd, olive-skinned face. For a moment it crossed my mind that he knew how I spent my nights in the hold. Curiously enough, this suspicion did not upset me at all. In some way the captain was part of it, a substantial part of the story even if my nocturnal lovers never mentioned the ship, or its owner, or the voyage, or anything that happened on board.

"That night Laurent, before he left me at dawn, said something that decided my destiny. 'Stay on the ship, Larissa. Don't leave us. Perhaps our visits will become less frequent the further we are from Europe. But we will always come back, and we will continue to exist only because of you.' I wanted to ask him a question that intrigued me: his use of the plural seemed to imply that he knew about the Venetian. I had never spoken of either man to the other. The colonel only raised his index finger to his lips, smiling affectionately as if he were telling a child to be quiet and go to sleep. I would not see Zagni until we docked at Mallorca. At that moment I knew I would have nothing to ask him. Laurent had spoken for Zagni as well, and his words needed no further clarification. And so it was that on the following day I told the captain I had decided to try my luck in the Caribbean and would accept his offer. 'I'm happy to hear it,' he answered very seriously and with no sign of complicity. 'We would have missed having you on board. We've grown used to your company. You're part of the *Lepanto*. We can't imagine it without you.' Again that plural. It may simply have referred to the crew and the ship itself, which he talked about as if it were an old friend. Yet I felt a vague disquiet that is difficult to describe and, I realized then, had accompanied me since I first set foot on the *Lepanto*. When we left Mallorca we had two days of terrible weather. As we sailed down the Málaga coast, it became calm again and the ship stopped pitching as if it were about to sink. One night, when the lights on shore were no longer visible, Zagni came to visit me. Before beginning the ritual of his desire, ceremonial, intense, and silent, he said with a formality that was obviously sincere and reflected his feelings, 'I see with immense pleasure that you have resolved to accompany us on this adventure to the Indies. It was my only opportunity to continue in the world. Perhaps I will not come to you as frequently as before, but that does not mean we will not meet from time to time. Gratitude, when it is absolute, cannot be expressed in words.' He began to caress me with the unhurried fervor of a man returning to life.

"As we moved away from the Mediterranean, after passing through the Straits of Gibraltar, the visits from my two lovers grew less frequent. But what puzzled me most and produced a piercing concern was the change, barely noticeable at first, in their demeanor. A change I cannot define. Their gestures were the same, their caresses unchanging, but each time they were less absorbed in the erotic rite to which they had accustomed me and which I could not imagine losing without losing my life at the same time. Both Laurent and Zagni were more chary of their words, which were losing their density and even their meaning. They didn't seem to be speaking to me in particular but to some imprecise creature barely connected to them by means of these erotic encounters, which did not lose their rhythm but no longer communicated to me the indispensable certainty that I was the one and only woman who participated in them. When we passed the Florida peninsula and sailed into the Caribbean, I waited in vain for visits from my friends. As we sailed out of Kingston, where we had to spend several days while repairs were made to the increasing number of leaks that put the *Lepanto* at risk, there was an announcement of an approaching hurricane. Zagni came to see me that night. In barely intelligible words he said, in a very cryptic way, that he didn't think he could endure. He lacked the strength to face the trial to come. It was the only time he mentioned Laurent's name: 'Colonel Laurent Drouet-D'Erlon is no longer among us. I have remained, perhaps because those of us born along the canals have a certain capacity to survive in this climate.' He caressed my breasts with the sadness of a man who will never again feel in his hands the warm body of a woman who gives herself in witness to the joy that is our compensation for the sorrow of being alive. Then he left with a clumsy haste that had never been present in any of his actions. The next morning the hurricane hit in a whirlwind of destruction and uncontrolled fury that carried us to Cristóbal, the *Lepanto* almost wrecked and its engines totally out of commission. The captain and his small crew went ashore. I lay on my cot, in the half-light of the hold, too weak to move, my body bruised and numb after the raging, implacable storm. The next day we were towed to Panama City. The owner had sold the *Lepanto* for scrap. The ship awaited its final destiny in the bay at the end of Avenida Balboa. They never came back for it. I went ashore to arrange my papers at the immigration office. I returned to the *Lepanto* and moved into the captain's cabin. I'm certain he thought I went ashore at Cristóbal without saying goodbye. A few weeks later another storm drove the remains of the *Lepanto* onto the beach of rocks and trash where it lies now. I couldn't abandon the ship. Against all probability I still hoped I would receive another visit from my friends. From the Venetian at least. I thought endlessly of them, reconstructing the hours we had spent together, the story of their lives, the heat of their caresses, their solidarity, their amorous complicity. When I had used all the money I had brought from Palermo, Alex told me about Villa Rosa and put me in touch with the Venezuelan woman. And that's how I came here."

Ilona had followed Larissa's story with intense concentration. At no time did she attempt to interrupt, and I was especially intrigued to see that her face didn't show the slightest trace of doubt or disbelief at the aberrant, improbable events Larissa recounted. Larissa left without waiting for our comments or questions, as if the mere telling of so unbearable an experience should have been enough to satisfy any curiosity, any interest one might have in her. We spent a considerable time not knowing what to say, until Ilona commented in a voice that came to me from a distance, the voice of someone who wakes from a devastating nightmare, "Poor woman. What it must have cost her to see her clients, what torture she must have suffered after every appointment. And worst of all, there's no way to help her. It's as if she were living on a far shore where our words can't reach her. And she wouldn't understand them anyway because she doesn't know the language. Each of us builds our own private hell, but she's had to carry the extra burden of others who weren't even alive. What an awful fate."

We decided to leave earlier than planned. Larissa's story had left us with a dull uneasiness we couldn't overcome. Longinos expressed his interest in keeping the business. He would give up the fiction of the stewardesses, which by now had almost disappeared. He spoke with Doña Rosa, who agreed to transfer our contract to him. She too had developed a visible fondness for the intelligent, discreet bellboy from Chiriquí, with whom she often had long conversations about managing the business for which Longinos showed much more vocation and talent than we did. His share of the profits allowed him to continue the establishment; he had long since taken charge, freeing us from an occupation we found less and less tolerable. The monotony of that routine was alien to our principles of perpetual displacement and rejection of anything that might mean a permanent commitment or an obligation to stay anywhere in the world.

As we continued our preparations for leaving Panama City and placing Longinos in charge of Villa Rosa, I was increasingly troubled by the manner in which Larissa's presence, and then her story, had influenced Ilona. The symptoms were not very evident, but for someone like me who knew her well and had lived with her for long periods of time, the change could not be ignored. Discussing it with her would have been both useless and inopportune. Ilona protected her independence jealously, and she had her own, very intelligent wariness when she shared confidences with the people she loved, those for whom she felt the friendship that is based on absolute trust, and on limits as strict as they are mutual. I knew that when the right moment came, she would discuss it with me. And that is what happened. A few weeks after hearing Larissa's story we received a letter from Abdul Bashur postmarked La Rochelle. He said that the *Nymph of Trieste* venture was making excellent progress. He had formed a partnership with two Syrian businessmen whom he had known since childhood. Vancouver was the final destination of their next voyage. And so he was planning to be in Panama City in the near future and would telegraph from the last port before they went through the canal. And then there were some remarks concerning our activities in Villa Rosa, which, while offending his Islamic puritanism, also awakened a mischievous humor that revealed his fundamental innocence and wit, hidden so well behind the arts of a Levantine merchant. Abdul's news lightened our mood considerably. We were overjoyed at the prospect of being with him again. But, on the other hand, his letter precipitated Ilona's uneasiness, as I expected it would. One morning, when we were having breakfast on the terrace, she brought up the matter with the reflexive intensity that she put into her words when it was a question of her feelings. As she served me tea with the ritual gestures she had brought to the occasion ever since we lived together for the first time, she said in her deepest voice, "I don't know what we're going to do with Larissa. I don't think she can stay here. But taking her with us would be a tremendous responsibility. What do you think?"

Her eyes were fixed on her cup as she poured tea with a slowness that betrayed her tense anticipation of my comments.

"I think," I said, after weighing my words carefully, "that this matter is more complex than your description of it. It's clear that if this woman goes on living in the wreck of the *Lepanto,* she will move quickly into hopeless physical and mental collapse. Her waiting time is over. At the edge of the abyss, of nothingness, she clutches like a drowning woman at a lifesaver, at the salvation represented by your friendship, your understanding, your interest in her inconceivable experience. But what I see, and the evidence terrifies me, is that instead of your pulling her out of the quicksand that swallows her up, she is pulling you in after her with a strength not even you can measure. Taking her with us would not solve anything, obviously. Besides, I don't think much will be gained by removing her from the *Lepanto.* She *is* that ship, she is so much a part of the wreck on the beach that no one knows where one ends and the other begins. The problem is not Larissa, who stopped asking herself questions or having any doubts a long time ago. The problem is you. Without gauging how much you've become involved, you've traveled so far with her on an unknown road that I don't know if you can still come back. Only you know that. I realize I'm not being much help. I don't know the extent of the bonds that join you to her. Not only their extent but their nature. I don't know. I don't know what to say to you."

Ilona had not tasted her tea, and she looked at me with alarmed, vulnerable eyes.

"No," she answered, "I haven't been to bed with her. If that's what you mean. That wouldn't matter very much. You know me well enough to know that those aren't the kinds of ties that can force me to change my life. It's something deeper, more terrible. It's a kind of heartbreaking sense of connection that makes me feel responsible for what might happen to her and, even worse and more incomprehensible, for what she has already suffered. Something in Larissa awakens my demons, those ominous signs in me that I learned to tame when I was a girl, to keep anesthetized so they don't come up to the surface and put an end to me. This woman has the strange ability to awaken them, but at the same time, when I offer her my help and listen to her with indulgence, I can pacify that murderous pack all over again. And that's why I don't know what I can do for her or how I can leave her."

My reply was that, as had so often happened before in our lives and in the lives of all human beings, the answer we are searching for, the way out of blind alleys, comes to us by chance in the unsuspected and unpredictable twists and turns of time. I knew it was a flimsy consolation I was offering her, that in her infallible lucidity she was thinking that around those corners time can also present us with the unimaginable horror of its machinations and surprises. We continued our breakfast in silence. It was clear that neither of us had much more to say. All we could do was go on with our plans to leave and not stop for something whose solution escaped us, perhaps because it wasn't in us to look for it, much less to find it.

THE END

OF THE *LEPANTO*

*L*arissa continued to visit us, but she had suspended all appointments with her clients. She spoke very little and was burdened by a fatigue that could not possibly be alleviated, an exhaustion that kept her on the verge of succumbing to a long, increasingly urgent desire to sleep. Longinos had taken over the business with so much efficiency and discretion that we began to feel as if we were his guests, always attentively cared for but completely removed from the life of Villa Rosa. The farce of the stewardesses was a thing of the past. From time to time we would cross paths with some beautiful visitor we didn't know, some elegant functionary from the world of banking or business who looked at us as if we were intruders he was discreetly avoiding. We put all our earnings together and deposited them in a joint account in a Luxembourg bank recommended to us by Abdul. We were only waiting to hear from him to set our departure date. I knew that for Ilona, Larissa's fate continued to be a lacerating, unanswerable mystery. One morning Longinos came upstairs to speak with me. I saw that he wanted to do this when Ilona wasn't present. I made some excuse and went down with him, and he whispered to me that Larissa wanted to see me. She'd be expecting me that afternoon on the boat.

When I arrived at the beach where the shapeless hulk of the *Lepanto* was lying, Larissa looked out the porthole of her refuge and invited me aboard. The cabin that had once been the captain's displayed devastating disorder and poverty. The unmade bed gave off an odor of cheap perfume and sweat. A faint smell of gas came from a small gas ring placed on what must have been the shelf for maps and navigational charts, and below that was a small tank of propane and some chipped, random kitchen utensils. The built-in closet, its doors missing, was barely covered by a piece of cloth. In it one could see articles of clothing that I recognized immediately as the ones their owner wore for her visits to Villa Rosa. Larissa was leaning against the porthole and looking at me with a distant air, as if she found it difficult to recognize me. There was no place to sit down. I remained standing as she began to speak in broken, disconnected phrases. She mentioned the approaching date of our departure, something about the new direction that Villa Rosa was taking. I answered with vague remarks, waiting to find out her reason for asking to see me. After a brief silence she fell onto the bed, covered her face with her hands, and spoke in a dull voice that attempted to hold back tears.

"Ilona can't go. She can't leave me here alone. I could never ask her. You can. Please, Maqroll, if she leaves me I have nothing left, nothing—you can see that," and she waved her arm at the cabin in a gesture of pathetic despair. I didn't know what to say.

"You talk to her," I suggested, knowing it would do no good. "I can't think of any solution right now. Come and see us and we'll all talk together. I don't know. I don't think I can be of much help to you."

She had covered her face again with her hands. When I finished speaking, her shoulders shook with desperation, as if she knew she was hopelessly lost.

I went home and told Ilona about my visit to Larissa.

"This has to be resolved quickly. Leaving her in suspense will make her suffer even more. I'll tell you tomorrow what I've decided," Ilona said with the firmness of a person who does not wish to prolong unnecessary pain.

We sat on the terrace waiting for the night to pass and bring us sleep. We remembered incidents from our undertakings with Abdul Bashur and, for the millionth time, evoked certain of his characteristics that especially moved us. Then we recalled the episode that depicted him best: his abrupt departure from Abdijan, where we had gone to close a deal involving the purchase of antique bronze figurines from the chief of a tribe in the interior, with the sole purpose of returning a portion of the immense profits he had made by transporting pilgrims from Tripoli to Mecca. "The

man who contracted the voyage," he explained, "is a holy innocent who accepted the first price I mentioned. I'm going to return
half the amount. Then I'll rest easy." We said that it could be taken
care of later, that his presence on the Ivory Coast was indispensable
because we didn't know much about antique African sculpture.
There was no way to convince him. He left that same night, and
ten days later he returned in a somber mood, an expression of
piercing guilt on his face. The patriarch had died and left no
relative in charge of his affairs. The Shiite community to which he
belonged refused to accept Abdul's money. "They don't understand my intentions," he said. "They think I'm trying to trick
them. I'm going to donate that money to the leprosarium in
Sassandra." And he did. The money would have allowed us to
double our profits from the sale of the bronze statues; we couldn't
afford to buy the most important piece, the one that would have
brought the most money in Europe.

That night Ilona tossed and turned in bed. I heard her get up and
go out to the terrace for some fresh air. It was clear she wouldn't
sleep. I dozed, and when I awoke she was stretched out on one of
the canvas chairs on the terrace. She looked so tired that I was
surprised by the serenity of her voice when she told me the decision she had reached.

"We're leaving, Maqroll. We're leaving here and I'm doing it
without any remorse. I'm not going to sink with Larissa. She's been
on the other shore for a long time now. It's not a question of
whether or not she can be saved. That doesn't depend on me or
on anyone else who still belongs to the world of the living. Who
knows how long she's been officiating at her own funeral. You
know I've never liked funerals, I've never gone to one. I'll talk to
Larissa when the time comes. I'm not going to think about this
anymore."

Knowing Ilona, I had no doubts regarding the firmness of her
resolve. Her loyalty to life always had something feline about it,
something instantaneous and reflexive in which reason played no
part. In fact, there was nothing more to say about Larissa. The
internal price that Ilona might have to pay did not matter. The dice
had stopped rolling. All bets had been made.

Longinos bought a small used station wagon and drove us to the
places we had frequented; they reminded us of my poverty-

stricken days and the prosperous times that had come with the appearance of Ilona. Larissa occasionally accompanied us. Although Ilona hadn't spoken to her, Larissa could guess what her verdict would be. On these outings she never mentioned the matter, and she didn't seem sadder than usual or more of a priestess to phantoms. The telegram from Abdul arrived on a Saturday afternoon. He would be in Cristóbal in a week and was expecting us on board the brand-new *Nymph of Trieste*. He was carrying bottles of the best Tokay. That part of the message was meant for Ilona, whose preference for Magyar wine was the object of frequent amusement on our part. What Abdul did not suspect, because we had kept it as a surprise, was that we would be sailing with him. On the day before our departure Ilona told me she was going to speak to Larissa. She was calm, but on her face one could see the rigidity of controlled pain that is accepted as the price we must inevitably pay to go on being who we are.

We had a light, cold lunch on the terrace. When we finished I went to lie down on the bed for a nap. Ilona said goodbye, and kissed me on the forehead.

"It won't be easy, Gaviero. You don't know how painful it is. It's like hitting an invalid. But there's nothing else to do. *Les jeux sont faits.*"

I saw her disappear through the door with the elastic stride of her long legs and the swing of her shoulders that endowed her with perpetual youth. I fell into a deep sleep. When I awoke it was almost dark. My head felt heavy with so much sleep. The heat had increased considerably, as it always does before the rain. It was the first storm of the season. Distant flashes of lightning lit up the sky with a brilliant and operatic regularity. The claps of thunder were barely audible, but it was easy to tell that they were coming closer. Suddenly Longinos burst into my room with a terrified expression, his face bathed in tears. He could scarcely speak.

"The señora, it's the señora—come with me."

He was trembling like a hunted animal. I threw on whatever clothes I could lay my hands on and we climbed into the station wagon.

"Let me drive," I said. "You're in no condition."

"No, señor," he answered, a little more under control. "You don't have a license. I can do it. Let's go."

He cried without stopping and couldn't explain anything to me. We reached the spot where the *Lepanto* had been. A group of curious bystanders stood around a small pile of ashes that the firemen were inspecting with the help of flashlights. The beams of light passed over twisted metal, stumps of charred wood that poked their way between the stones and the cement blocks blackened by fire. I went up to one of the firemen and asked what had happened.

"The gas tank that crazy woman kept in her cabin exploded. Nobody in their right mind would have done that! It all blew to pieces. Instant fire. We found her body. But it seems there was somebody else with her."

Suddenly he gave me an inquisitive look. Longinos interrupted: "No, he didn't know her. I did, I'll be here if I can help you with anything."

The fireman didn't seem to be listening and went back to his work.

"Here it is, here it is!" we heard someone shout from the rubble. A few seconds later a fireman passed in front of us, carrying something burned and shapeless in a sheet that he held by the four corners. From the sheet, dirty with mud and ashes, a pink liquid was dripping, barely staining the pavement. The fireman who had spoken with us came up to Longinos.

"Come later to the morgue to help identify the bodies. It won't be easy. They're almost completely burned. But maybe there'll be something: papers, some jewelry. Let me have your name and address."

Longinos gave him the information, and the official wrote it down in a notebook that he took out of his shirt pocket.

We stared, stunned, at the remains of the *Lepanto*. The bystanders were leaving. There were five or six of us left. I heard the unmistakable sound of an artificial leg on the pavement, and I turned around. It was the concierge of the Pensión Astor disappearing into the shadows of the street across the way. Then the full impact of what had happened hit me. It had all been so sudden that, until that moment, I had acted in a reflexive, absent way. Longinos took my arm.

"Let's go to Alex's, señor. Have a drink. You can't imagine how you look."

We went to the bar. Alex poured me a double vodka with ice.

He put his hand on my arm and in a compassionate voice that came from his very soul he said, "I know how painful this is, Gaviero. Count on me. If there's anything I can do. I'm your friend. You know that. Stay here awhile. As long as you want."

He went to turn down the volume of the music as much as his lively customers would allow.

A dull pain began to grow in the center of my chest. It was like a hedgehog swelling up, piercing everything, ceaselessly, relentlessly. Longinos sat beside me and looked at me disconsolately. I don't know how long I was there. After midnight Longinos took me to the Hotel Miramar. The owner, with sincere sympathy, gave me a room right away. I couldn't go back to Villa Rosa. Longinos didn't want to leave me alone, but I insisted that he take care of the legal matters. I also asked him to bring me some clothes, and the briefcase and suitcase that were in my room.

"I'll be right back, don't go anywhere. Wait for me, please," he said, visibly troubled at leaving me alone.

"Don't worry," I said. "Don't worry about me. I'm fine here. I don't want to see anybody. Come back when you can."

He left, somewhat relieved. I lay down on the bed, trying to keep my mind blank. It was impossible. With ravaging fervor the memory of Ilona invaded each moment of this unmoving, frozen, intolerable present. I couldn't get past the obsessive, inconceivable image of the pile of burned flesh that the fireman was carrying in the anonymous ambulance sheet, and the pink drops falling to the ground, mixing with the first drops of the rain that poured down now with the torrential fury of Panama's storms. Ilona dead. Ilonka, my girl, what a miserable blow against the best in life. Memories began to file by. With dry eyes, without the consolation of tears, I spent long hours in a final effort to keep intact, for one last moment, those images from a past that death was beginning to devour forever. Because what death kills is not the beings who are close to us, who are our very life. What death takes away forever is their memory, the image that blurs and fades until it is lost, and that is when we begin to die too. The absence of Ilona, when she was alive, was something I knew very well, something familiar. Her definitive absence was something so hard, so painful for me to imagine that I preferred to go back to memories. I could still find a refuge there, ephemeral and feeble but the only one I could turn to then to keep from falling into nothingness.

Longinos brought my clothes and papers. He had been to the morgue. A ring helped to identify Larissa. In the opinion of the firemen she had turned on the gas and let almost all of it escape. It was likely that the same person had lit some kind of flame. The explosion was so violent that it destroyed everything instantaneously.

"It was Larissa, señor. Bitch of a whore. I never trusted her. That woman was crazy. She laid a trap for Señora Ilona so she wouldn't leave. That's why she was so nice these last few days."

Poor Longinos was crying again with the candid yielding to grief of the primitive and the innocent, the only way to mourn the dead and find some relief from their absence. I told him to get some sleep. The next day he had to take me to Cristóbal to meet Abdul.

Very early the next morning Longinos was waiting for me in the lobby. First we went to the bank where we had our account, and I sent a draft in the amount of Ilona's share to her cousin from Oslo who was now in Trieste. She was her only living relative. Ilona loved her but had little patience for her conventional, bourgeois observations about not understanding how her cousin could lead the life she did. On the way to Cristóbal I told Longinos how I wanted our friend's remains to be buried. Her name, Ilona Grabowska, on a simple stone, and under that, in small letters: "Her friends Abdul and Maqroll, who loved her." We said nothing else during the trip. When we reached Cristóbal, a small tanker painted blue and orange was slowly approaching the dock. An ugly shooting pain in my chest announced the devastating task that was waiting for me: telling Abdul Bashur that Ilona, our friend, was no longer among us. On the prow of the ship one could read clearly now, *Nymph of Trieste*.

Un Bel Morir

For Jorge Ruiz Dueñas, an exemplary
friend and well-informed follower of the
Gaviero's affairs

Un bel morir tutta una vita onora.

Francesco Petrarca, "In Morte Laura"

Everything will vanish into oblivion
and the shriek of a monkey,
the creamy flow of sap
from the wounded bark of a rubber tree,
the splash of water against the moving keel,
will be more memorable than our long embraces.
"Un bel morir . . ."

Alvaro Mutis, "Los Trabajos Perdidos"

Accumulons l'irréparable!
Renchérissons sur notre sort!
. . . . Tout n'en va pas moins a la Mort,
Y a pas de port.

Jules Laforgue, "Solo de Lune"

Every man lives his life like a hunted animal.

Nicolás Gómez Dávila, "Escolios"

*I*t all began when Maqroll decided to remain in the port of La Plata and postpone indefinitely the continuation of his journey upriver. In this voyage to the headwaters of the great river, he had wanted to find some trace of those who had taken part in certain of his extraordinary adventures years before. Discouraged by the lack of information concerning his former comrades, and with a bitter taste in his soul at how the last few springs that fed the nostalgia which brought him such a great distance were drying up, he concluded it did not matter if he stayed in the humble settlement or continued upriver now that he no longer had a compelling reason to struggle against the current.

He looked for lodgings in La Plata and found a room in the house of a blind woman who was highly esteemed in the town. Everyone knew her as Doña Empera. After agreeing on the rent and the cost of other services such as meals and laundering his meager wardrobe, he chose a room with a rather unusual location. To create more space, the landlady had added two rooms that extended out over the river and were supported by lengths of railroad track inserted at an oblique angle in the riverbank. The structure was held firm by one of the miracles of equilibrium achieved by those who know how to take advantage of all the possibilities of guadua, the thick bamboo stalk that is supremely light and versatile in building projects. The walls, also made of guadua, were finished and sealed with the reddish clay found in the cliffs carved out by the water in the places where the riverbed narrows.

The room resembled a cage suspended over the gently murmuring tobacco-colored water that gave off a soothing aroma of fresh mud and of vegetation uprooted by the always capricious and unpredictable current. Doña Empera rented the other rooms to casual couples; her only demands were that they pay in advance for the number of days they planned to stay and keep their belongings in strictest order. She took care of the rooms, and in the most courteous but categorical manner she asked her guests to show her where they intended to keep each object. In this way she could clean and always follow the same order. When the Gaviero came to her house asking for a room, the landlady responded without hesitation: "I know you, señor. You've passed through La Plata several times but you've never stayed here. I've heard about you. Of course, nobody can tell me what your trade is or how you live. But that isn't what fascinates me. What intrigues me is that if women mention you, they never show rancor, but in their voices I can detect something like a fear of saying more than they should."

"People always talk too much, señora," said the Gaviero. He had passed through La Plata three or four times, looking for a place to settle for awhile, and the women he had met, casual lovers with anonymous faces and forgettable characters, were not worth Doña Empera's curiosity. "I never give them much to talk about, and maybe that's why they start imagining nonsense."

"Maybe," she replied, not very convinced. "What matters to me is that you're trustworthy and deserve my confidence. To hell with the rest. The blind know more about people than those who have eyes to see and don't use them. When we're deceived, it's because we want to be, we let it happen. You've been around and know what I mean."

Doña Empera took her leave, and Maqroll arranged his things and settled into his room. She returned when he was finished, and he showed her each object in its place.

"You haven't brought very much," she said, her curiosity touched with compassion.

"Only what's necessary, señora, only what's necessary," answered the Gaviero, trying to end the conversation.

"And those books, are they necessary too?" Doña Empera asked with that thin smile the blind use as an apology for their curiosity. "What are they about?" she insisted with an open interest that did not fail to intrigue the Gaviero.

"One is the life of Saint Francis of Assisi, written by a Dane; this is the French translation. The other, in two volumes, is in French too. It contains the letters of the Prince of Ligne. They can teach you a great deal about people, especially women." The blind woman's interest deserved, almost demanded, these details from the reader and owner of the books.

"My grandson used to read a lot to me, especially history books. I sold them when the federals killed him. They claimed he was a guerrilla because he was always reading. He did it mostly to help me pass the time. But those people don't ask questions; they come in shooting. They're always scared to death."

"Do they come to La Plata often?" the Gaviero asked, interested in the reference to the armed forces, with whom he had never had good relations anywhere in the world.

"No, señor. They haven't come down this far for a long time. Everything's very quiet now. But that doesn't mean anything. You never know with them."

The Gaviero said nothing and continued to set out his things and rearrange some of the rickety furniture in the room. The subject did not appeal to him. His connection to weapons had occurred in places completely foreign to this one, and with a very different set of people. Besides, all of that was in the past, one experience among the many that had contributed to the sum total of human folly. Before she left, Doña Empera made a kind of declaration of principles, or rather a statement of her rules regarding female visitors—an oral document that did not fail to fascinate him, for it allowed a glimpse of the landlady's sharp intelligence.

"If you want to bring a friend to spend the night," Doña Empera said, "I have no objection in principle. But since you've already seen what this town is like, and we've all known each other a long time, I would advise you, for your own sake, to talk to me before you invite anyone here. Don't take this as meddling in your affairs. I only want to avoid problems for both of us. I can tell you very useful things that will help you stay out of trouble. You know what I mean. Another thing: Be careful with your money. Don't let anybody think you're well-heeled; in a miserable village like this we're all drowning in poverty. All right, sleep well and good luck."

The tap of her cane moved away until it was lost in the back of the house. The Gaviero stretched out on the hard cot, where a light cotton mattress offered dubious protection against the bamboo strips of the frame. He heard the water flowing past with the monotonous energy of tireless routine. The murmur lulled him into a deep sleep, but the implacable afternoon heat, when the air stops moving and the mosquitoes come, startled him awake. He had not felt their sting for many years, but there was no way to escape their unmerciful buzzing.

Life in La Plata was like life in all the small settlements along the river. The principal event in the village was the arrival of the passenger boat, with its large bladed wheels painted ocher, or of the caravans of barges pulled by a sputtering tugboat. On these occasions the tavern, located among the other houses facing the river embankment that served as a square, acquired an extraordinary but short-lived activity. When the boats continued on their way, they left the town submerged once again in the torpor of a sauna, in a silence so profound it produced the impression that life had withdrawn forever. On some nights a record player disturbed the hushed darkness with the screeching, almost unrecognizable lament of a tango from the 1930s or a nasal song by Dr. Ortiz Tirado that told of love with all the melodrama of a fatal theatrical sin.

The Gaviero spent the days reading in his room and making carefully regulated visits to the tavern at the times when it was nearly empty. Doña Empera put him in touch with some of her friends, peasant women who came down from the mountains to make purchases in the only store in town, whose owner, Hakim the Turk, would press his attentions on them with urgent and always badly paid solicitations. The women tried to increase the meager sum of money they brought from the farm with extra earnings that would allow them to buy a fanciful adornment or a few meters of cloth. The blind woman's male friends provided them with the surest and most discreet transactions. Maqroll could not even remember the names of any of his transient one-night companions. Sometimes he recognized them by the smell of their skin or by their life stories; these were always the same, and they were told during the intervals between bouts of love-making. Each erotic encounter required him to follow an al-chemical process intended to preserve certain necessary areas of his memory, to keep them free of the faceless present and not allow them to lose their ability to save the Gaviero from the slow slide toward nothingness that so often tormented him.

One of the windows in his room reached to the floor and opened onto a swaying bamboo balcony that hung over the river. The Gaviero spent many hours there, leaning on the rail and contemplating the ever-changing, always engaging current of brown water that had no memory. On the opposite bank broad fields planted in cotton alternated with plots of sugar cane whose dark, steely tone contrasted with the white balls of inconceivable snow, imparting a vague nightmarish quality to the landscape. Behind the fields loomed the majestic cordillera, its peaks crossed by dizzying veils of fog or dense curtains of rain that fell for hours at a time. In the afternoons, following the rain, it was often possi-ble to see on the highest summits the emphatic, heart-stopping edge of the barrens, the inaccessible and solitary plateau. It was an orderly landscape. Dreamy and dense, it adjusted to the lazy rhythm of the rusty, abundant waters of the great river as it de-scended to the sea in a silence barely broken by the eddies bub-bling up around the great slate shoals that occasionally broke the surface. Maqroll spent many hours absorbed in this ceremonial pageantry that dissolved as night approached, accompanied by the feverish chorus of crickets and the screech of bats that just grazed the water and the roofs of the houses in their impetuous flight.

La Plata was a settlement similar to all the rest that lay dying along the great river, with no reason or definite purpose in their numbing, monotonous existence. A few houses with palm roofs. The army post and Hakim's store had zinc roofs, the first painted rat gray, the Turk's a raving, gratuitous strawberry color. The Gaviero had begun to feel a beatific serenity that troubled him because he felt it was alien to his inexhaustible wanderlust, whose absence might indicate a radical alteration in his being which he at first refused to accept. He always feared changes like these; in a way that was difficult to describe, he saw them as an omen of disastrous consequences, like the fall of a curtain for which he never thought himself sufficiently prepared. He was rudely awakened from these meditations on his balcony, and from his peaceful reading, by the news of a railway construction project along the Tambo Ridge, one of the highest and most inhospitable spots in the cordillera. In the mornings he could see the ridge, wrapped for most of the year in an impenetrable fog, from the balcony of his room. It had been pointed out to him by Doña Empera, who told him incredible stories about the place, tales of a deranged violence that sickened him with dark, undefined foreboding.

Maqroll's involvement with the railroad venture on the Tambo Ridge came about as the result of normal coincidence and an uncharacteristic nostalgia *à rebours*. Several months had passed since his move to Doña Empera's house. More than friendship, their relations had become almost familial. A woman of uncommon intelligence, she had developed a somewhat maternal affection for her guest, in which there was no small measure of curiosity about a man whose life was revealed to her in their long conversations at meals, and in certain jealously guarded pieces of information she had received before his arrival. The blind woman's secrecy regarding this information disturbed him. All he could learn was that it dealt with a time when he lived in the upland barrens beside a highway. This made him even more inquisitive, but Doña Empera maintained a rigorous silence.

Maqroll lived on a modest sum remitted by a bank in Trieste whose punctuality was subject to the most unexpected and outlandish irregularities in mail delivery. The checks were cashed by Hakim: he agreed to do so thanks to the intercession of the blind woman, who had a mysterious influence over him. From the beginning Doña Empera displayed the greatest understanding and patience when Maqroll's payment of his rent was delayed by

chaos in the post office. Before long she offered him small loans
to cover both the immediate cost of his transient loves and his
accounts at Hakim's store and the tavern, the latter bill the result
of a pressing need to forget what had long been pursuing him.
He sought refuge in the tavern, in fact, thinking that brandy
would make it easier for him to bear the attacks of despair
brought on, for the most part, by his growing awareness of the
effect of the passing years on his weary, incurably nomadic bones.
Predictably enough, the crises gave rise to more and more concrete fantasies about how his days would end, and these were
invariably accompanied by the increasingly radical destruction of
the feeble reasons that allowed him to go on living. His incursions into the tavern lasted for many hours and followed a routine of silence and marginalization, which both the owner and his
patrons learned to respect after Maqroll's first visit when, with
great circumspection, he sat at the most solitary table in a back
corner and asked for a double brandy. It did not matter if the
Victrola blared music that the Gaviero did not seem to hear. The
brandies followed one after the other while his eyes, vague and
opaque, were lost in an extraordinary internal landscape inaccessible to the others though devastatingly familiar to him. He spent
hours sitting there. When night fell he would ask for the bill and
either pay in cash if he had received the draft from Trieste, or
sign it in the broad strokes of his clear but somewhat childish
handwriting. Doña Empera, without mentioning anything to
Maqroll, had arranged for this accommodation of her guest with
the tavern owner.

No one approached the table where the Gaviero sat. Not even
the women he had met in La Plata, who came in to buy aguardiente for their men in the sierra. When boats or barge caravans
anchored in La Plata, the tavern would fill with thirsty, rowdy
men whom the owner, a serious, exceptionally strong black with
graying hair and beard, could control with just the expression in
his eyes. On one of Maqroll's early visits a tugboat mechanic, a
cross-eyed Hercules of black and Indian ancestry whom aguardiente had turned into a wild animal, stopped in front of the
Gaviero and challenged his isolation with stammering, slavering

words. Maqroll raised his eyes, looking at him with the weary imperturbability of a man who knows how to put an end to such situations, and said in a quiet voice: "Beat it, blubber lips. If you want trouble, you've come to the right place . . . and you won't like it."

The mechanic staggered off, sputtering vague curses aimed more at himself than at his unlikely opponent, who finished his brandy with a condescending smile and eyes that never left his adversary.

And for this reason the patrons were astonished one Saturday, when the Gaviero had begun drinking very early, to see a thick-set stranger, with an unkempt reddish beard and a ruddy face that exuded a suspicious geniality, go to the bar and ask for something the owner could not understand, and then, from his corner, to see the Gaviero raise his head and say in a loud voce: "Gin, he wants gin and water." And he spoke to the man in Flemish, inviting him to his table. As the newcomer walked in his direction, Maqroll pulled out a chair on the other side of the table. The owner himself carried over the gin and water, looking at the Gaviero as if trying to warn him about his guest. Maqroll took note of the warning and prepared to listen to the heavy-jowled stranger, who became entangled in an interminable monologue aided by emphatic movements of his short, plump, pink arms and a no less expressive rolling of his large, protruding, slate-gray eyes, in which any shred of sincerity that might have inadvertently escaped his inexhaustible eloquence was frozen fast. The man soon turned to Spanish, which he spoke with some fluency although he often had recourse to English words, especially at the end of his sentences. He introduced himself as van Branden, Jan van Branden, a railroad engineer by profession. The Gaviero, who had a long acquaintance with the people of Flanders, could not place his companion among the various types of Flemings he remembered. Van Branden also committed errors in the language of his alleged homeland, and used some terms more common to Holland than Belgium. But this was not unusual among Flemings who spent a good part of their lives in English and Dutch ports. In spite of these reservations the Gaviero, moved by nostalgia for the *vlaanderland,* had been caught in a tedious ambush from which he could not escape. His memories had conspired to cast an irresistible spell, and he continued to listen to the engineer's babbling with Benedictine patience until the stranger asked if he knew a place that rented rooms. They went to Doña Empera's house and, assuming he was a friend of the Gaviero's, she agreed to take the Belgian in, not without a certain reluctance. Van Branden said he would be in La Plata until the next boat, which is to say about two weeks.

He told the Gaviero that he was in charge of certain technical aspects of the railroad construction on the Tambo Ridge. He let it be understood in passing that Maqroll might possibly participate in some activity related to the project. Van Branden was the sort of man who accepted the civility of his new friend as something both natural and deserved, the kind who lets it be known that everyone can benefit from his valuable companionship, one of those for whom gratitude is as inconceivable as good manners. But Maqroll's memories of the *platte land* were too strong, and he established a relationship with the Belgian that was, unfortunately, based on a hopeless misunderstanding: Van Branden could never receive a satisfactory explanation of how the Gaviero had come to that lost corner of the cordillera along the muddy, treacherous river. And the Gaviero could not understand the presence there of the talkative engineer, even though van Branden wielded the pretext of the railroad with such convincing insistence. Maqroll guessed at the Belgian's confusion, and it amused him to think they were each plagued by similar questions about the other. But van Branden, certain he was exceptional, and above all suspicion, found no need to go into more detail concerning his own past. The two men overcame this tangle of reservations and got along, never going beyond certain unspecified but very evident limits whose infringement would have been unthinkable. They met in the tavern every two or three days. The Gaviero limited himself to nursing his brandy as long as possible while van Branden effortlessly consumed half a liter of gin mixed with water. He would resort to Flemish peppered with Anglicisms as his mean-spirited hostility to everything around them increased, although Maqroll ignored it. At about midnight they returned to the boardinghouse with slow, measured steps.

Doña Empera, of course, had informed van Branden of the behavior she expected in her house, and she must have made the usual offer to provide him occasionally with female companionship. "Women I know and trust" was her motto. When he was in La Plata, he received a weekly visit from a tall, ungainly older woman missing almost all her teeth, who came down from the sierra with two children, five and seven years old; they played along the riverbank while their mother tended to the engineer. Barely covered by a preposterous nightgown of dubious whiteness, she came to the window frequently to make certain her children stayed away from the water's edge. For his part, the Gaviero had begun to receive regular visits from a dark-skinned young woman with black, very expressive eyes and a strong, sinewy, but slim and well-proportioned body. Her name was Amparo María. There was something of a Circassian princess about her that he found extraordinarily attractive. The girl was discreet and spoke very little. In love she maintained a modest reserve, a kind of sudden distancing from the unleashing of her senses, which the Gaviero thought was in perfect harmony with his new friend's physical type.

It was understood that the blind woman's two guests avoided any discussion of their female companions. But one day van Branden broke this tacit agreement. He was returning to his room after saying goodbye to the woman, when he ran into Maqroll who was just leaving. He took him by the arm, something that visibly annoyed the Gaviero, and with a lecherous, porcine expression, his bulging eyes half closed, said unexpectedly, "These tropical women! What temperament, what charm! Don't you think so?" The Gaviero disengaged discreetly from the paw that was clutching at him and made no comment, contenting himself with the suggestion of a smile that neither accepted nor rejected the Belgian's words. It revealed instead a certain measure of amazement.

At about this time Maqroll accepted van Branden's proposal that he work for the Tambo Ridge project. The Belgian did not usually discuss the railroad. When he received correspondence, he would make some brief comment to his fellow lodger, always in a fleeting, imprecise way, about design plans for the track. But one day he invited Maqroll to the tavern for lunch. They were serving a fish stew that was available from time to time and was actually prepared by Doña Empera in her house. When it was ready, the tavern owner had it brought in and served to his patrons. In La Plata the stew had become a ceremony for marking any exceptional event. On this occasion, van Branden explained, it was the effective, concrete start of the Tambo Ridge project. The engineers and other personnel would arrive on the next boat, along with the first load of technical equipment and machinery. "I've thought of you," van Branden said as they attempted to eat a boiling hot stew in the tavern's already overheated atmosphere, "for a job that requires someone I can trust. I wouldn't offer it to any of the people I've met here. It's a question, my dear friend" (this new form of address alarmed rather than gratified the Gaviero; he knew his man), "of taking a mule train up to the Tambo Ridge; you'll be carrying crates of very delicate and costly machinery needed up there to make calculations for laying the track. I have an interesting sum available to pay for this work, which you could do with the efficiency and discretion the job requires." Maqroll disregarded the Belgian's conventional flattery. He said he did not have mules or the money to acquire them, and had not handled those animals since he was a boy and helped the mule drivers bring in sugar cane to the mill on the plantation. Besides, at his age he was not certain he still had the strength and stamina for such an undertaking.

Van Branden, very much in character, pretended not to hear, leaned across the steaming shad and its generous garnish of vegetables, placed his hands on the Gaviero's shoulders, and said with blatantly false enthusiasm, "Splendid, my friend, splendid. I knew I could count on you. You'll see, we'll get on just fine. Naturally you'll need an advance to buy the mules and the other things you'll surely need. That's no problem. Make your estimate and tell me how much it is. As for your total fee, as soon as I receive an approved budget from the company, and the report on how much equipment they plan to send up to the Tambo, I'll tell you the exact amount. All of that's arriving with the machinery and the engineers. We won't discuss it anymore. Let's celebrate with another drink." He called the waiter, ordered a brandy and a gin and water, and continued talking, this time in Flemish sprinkled with "of course," "you know," "you follow me?" and the other affectations in English that so irritated his companion. In all that linguistic salad there was a clear intention to conceal, to distract, to throw up a smokescreen in front of something that eluded the Gaviero each time he was about to grasp it.

The following week all the people and equipment arrived as van Branden had announced. That morning, by the time Maqroll awoke, the boat and a barge caravan with its tugboat were already sailing downriver toward the sea. The personnel had left immediately for the Tambo, "to take advantage of the coolness at dawn," the Belgian said, his eyes shifting as he let loose a torrent of explanations that the Gaviero had not asked for. What had not come was the budget. But that did not matter, he had enough money, they could settle the total fee later. With van Branden the subject of money took on an amorphous, slippery, forever unspecified quality. Somewhere in a corner of his unconscious mind the Gaviero already knew that payment for his work would be subject to the most unpredictable accidents. But he fell victim to a blind tendency, so typical of his character, to take on ventures that were built on air and justified by words, some flattering, others arrogant—ventures in which he invariably had to pay the piper. Van Branden's proposal and the all too familiar pattern made a suspiciously good fit. Maqroll would take the equipment up to the Tambo Ridge. He had seen it at daybreak, or on certain clear, calm afternoons, from the balcony of his room. Now, as he looked toward the imposing mountains, he realized the madness of making the climb with a drove of mules loaded down with unnamed and, according to the Belgian, exceedingly delicate instruments. And he had not stopped to think that the man had not yet shown him a single receipt or document, or anything written on stationery bearing the letterhead of the company that was building the project. But whenever he talked to van Branden, he was caught once again in the tangle of words and plans, detailed descriptions and imprecise memories of places they had both visited in the past, and he thought he saw everything clearly, simply, unobjectionably.

Not long after the Belgian made his offer, he again invited the Gaviero to the tavern to drink to the success of their plans. He gave him a sum of money sufficient, he said, to buy five pack mules with all their gear as well as a few other items Maqroll would need in the barrens, and to pay the wages of a mule driver, who, of course, would have to be completely trustworthy and come recommended by someone equally reliable. When the Gaviero took the money, van Branden asked him to sign a receipt written on a sheet of lined paper with no letterhead, naturally. Maqroll objected, pointing out that the sum indicated on the paper was larger than the amount he had received. The Belgian immediately offered a hurried explanation. "I'll give you the rest later. I'm having a few problems now, but don't worry. We understand each other. If it's not enough money, let me know. Everything will be settled before you make the first climb." A cloying look of complicity and an attempt at a smile wandered across his broad, congested face. Only his protruding eyes, like those of a rotting fish, remained inexpressive, tenacious, icy.

Maqroll began preparations for his trek to the barrens. The first thing he did was speak to Doña Empera. She could not understand why the tenant who had become her friend was undertaking such a venture. But in any case she resolved to give him the advice he asked for. For buying the mules, the best thing was to go to the Álvarez Flat, a coffee and cane plantation belonging to friends of hers who would sell him animals in good condition and at a fair price. All he had to do was mention her name to Don Aníbal Álvarez, the ranch owner. They had known each other a long time. For his part, Maqroll would see some familiar faces there. And at the flat he could also find a mule driver familiar with the region. This was indispensable. The barrens were not a place an inexperienced person entered casually; the vast, solitary expanses were sown with mortal dangers.

The Gaviero left the next day at dawn with Doña Empera's recommendations, her directions on how to reach the Álvarez Flat, and a small knapsack she lent him in which he carried the little he would need in the event he had to spend the night. The money for buying the mules was sewn into the waistband of his trousers. For the first hour he walked through fields of sugar cane. An irrigation ditch ran alongside the path, its calm, transparent water an announcement of the landscape that awaited him, the landscape of his childhood. The level ground ended and a steep slope began. He slowed his pace and had to rest several times at the side of the road. After so many years at sea, so many long stopovers in port, he had grown unaccustomed to this kind of effort. At the top of the slope the trail entered the coffee plantings, and beyond them loomed the nearby cordillera, bathed in a bluish halo highlighted by the colored patches of roofs and flowering orchards. Memories of childhood returned in a sudden flood of aromas, images, faces, rivers, instantaneous happiness. Once again he lived among the odors, laments, and songs that filled the thickets, the damp refuges adorned with anonymous flowers that were the only joyful note in the solitary gloom of the ravines. Rivers and streams poured down from the barrens and ran along the bottom of the cliffs; among the reeds growing on the banks of these torrents the haughty, nervous heron swayed, certain of the beauty of his silvery plumage and purple ruff. Maqroll had entered the coffee plantings on the foothills of the sierra. The green crowns of the coffee shrubs were protected by charcoal burners and cámbulos whose large, deep orange blossoms possessed the grandeur of the unattainable: the imposing height of those centenarian trees shielded the blooms from human curiosity until they fell to the ground and girls picked them up to put in their hair for a few hours before the flowers withered. Surrounded on all sides by coffee shrubs arranged in an order worthy of Versailles, Maqroll felt a flood of the unshadowed, unbounded joy that had characterized his childhood. He walked slowly to enjoy more fully this complete, unerring return to his only irrefutable happiness on earth. The restorative enthusiasm he treasured now would serve him later when he began the steep ascent to the inhospitable, treacherous ridge. The coffee plantings ended abruptly at the foot of a small hill topped by a natural mesa where the ranch house stood surrounded by orange and lemon trees, and erect mango trees with their dark, vigorous leaves. This miniature altiplano, called the Álvarez Flat, belonged to the family that had built the ranch and whose history he had learned from the blind woman. Twenty years ago three brothers had come to the plateau, fleeing the storm of political persecution in their region of the country. Mountain people, coffee planters, cane growers, cattlemen when the terrain and the grazing allowed, they were strong, taciturn, competent, and tenaciously astute in defending what was theirs. They came with their wives and children and some tenant families who had been connected to them since the time of their grandfathers. The oldest brother returned home a few years later. The youngest drowned in La Osa Gully trying to save a calf that had fallen into the ravine. The only one left was Don Aníbal, along with his wife and three children. All of them had worked with feverish persistence to wrest farmland from the wild, inch by inch.

When Maqroll reached the entrance to the house, a man was waiting for him at the top of the stairs that led to the gallery surrounding the building. Erect, tall, and slender, he had a lean, swarthy face with regular features and a distant, seigneurial quality that softened when it reached his eyes; dark, wary, yet cordial and sometimes playful, they contained all his affection. The Gaviero greeted him and said he had been sent by Doña Empera and lived in her house. The rancher invited him to the gallery, so wide it was more like a verandah, from which one could admire the imposing mass of the cordillera and the flowering extension of the coffee groves. Don Aníbal ordered coffee and in a friendly manner asked the reason for his guest's visit. Maqroll told him briefly of his business dealings with van Branden, and of Doña Empera's suggestion that he buy the mules at the Álvarez Flat.

"There's been talk from time to time," said Don Aníbal, "about this plan for a railroad on the ridge. I'm surprised at how suddenly the project has become solid enough to contract for the initial work and bring in engineers. I hadn't heard anything about it. As for the mules, I can sell you five. You can take three now. The other two will be here the day after tomorrow, and they're basically the same. I'll tell you right now they're not first-class animals, but none of them is ill-tempered. In La Plata you have to be careful and not let them eat banana leaves or grass along the river; it might make them sick. Just feed them grain while you're there. When you stop by here again on your climbs, I can give you enough fodder to last them up to the ridge."

Don Aníbal's direct, simple way of conducting his affairs captivated the Gaviero, who immediately established the rancher's spiritual kinship to those country men from the French Berry, the plains of Castile, Galicia in Poland, or the wild mountain peaks of Afghanistan, who live on the land, are intimate with it, and maintain a medieval, invariable code of conduct in which a large measure of innate, inflexible chivalry endures. Don Aníbal offered the services of a young man to accompany him on his first few trips and show him how to manage the mules and survive the barrens. His price for the animals seemed fair and at the same time made clear van Branden's bad faith, for it amounted to almost all the money Maqroll had left. He would speak to the Belgian when he got back.

He was still talking with the rancher when the coffee was brought to them, and Maqroll could not or would not hide his astonishment on seeing that the person carrying the tray, which was arranged with simple, austere charm, was Amparo María. The girl did not show the least surprise and must have known beforehand about his visit. Maqroll greeted her, not hiding the fact that they knew each other, and Don Aníbal reacted with the greatest naturalness. When Amparo María left, the rancher commented: "She's a very beautiful girl. Timid, serious, but loyal and very amiable. Her parents were killed when the violence broke out in our province. We brought her here and she lives with an aunt and uncle who care for her as if she were their daughter. My wife's very fond of her and wanted to take her to the capital when she went to register the boys in school, but Amparo María wouldn't go. Since she lost her parents the girl's been very fearful and apprehensive. It's understandable."

That was all he said. Just then a farmhand came to tell them the mules were ready, and they went to the stable. The Gaviero had complete confidence in the rancher's evaluation of the animals as he pointed out their defects and strong points in terms of the job they had to do. Don Aníbal suggested that Maqroll leave them on the ranch for now. He would send them down along with the other two mules and the driver who would accompany him up to the sierra. The Gaviero paid for the animals and prepared to return to La Plata. When he took his leave of Don Aníbal, the rancher said cordially, "You'll pass this way on your trips. Sleep here so you'll be well rested the next day. You can count on my friendship and any help I can give you." He extended his hand, which the Gaviero shook warmly.

He went out to the road. At the first bend Amparo María was waiting for him. With their arms around each other's waists, they walked a good distance not saying anything except for the most immediate, predictable comments on the landscape, the weather, and the shared intimacies joining them with bonds of tenderness that foreshadowed permanence. When they said goodbye at the start of the coffee plantings, Amparo María gave the Gaviero a kiss on the mouth that stunned him with the unexpected and, until that moment, hidden passion it revealed.

"Don't make that face, and watch where you're going or you'll fall into the ditch," said the girl as she laughed and showed her white Circassian teeth.

Maqroll walked to La Plata with the sensation of fluttering butterflies in his diaphragm that usually announced the beginning of a friendship with a woman to whom he gave himself completely. He had thought that at his age it would not happen again. The realization that it could eased the weight of his years.

The next day, after telling Doña Empera the results of his visit to the ranch and the good impression made by the owner and the people he had seen there (the tacit allusion to Amparo María was picked up by the blind woman, who made no comment but smiled with satisfaction), he went out to look for van Branden and found him on the dock, inquiring when the next boat was due. Maqroll invited him to have a beer, and the Belgian accepted reluctantly, looking at him suspiciously with rapid sideways glances.

"I have the mules," Maqroll told him. "The mule driver who's going with me will bring them down tomorrow or the day after. He can be trusted. Álvarez recommended him. Well,

I've used almost all the money and I need more, at least as much as you gave me before. Otherwise I don't think I'll be able to take this on."

Van Branden tried to dodge the issue with the most unseemly excuses. Then Maqroll told him firmly that he was quitting. He could find someone else just as gullible and trap him with his cunning. The Belgian changed his attitude immediately, took a wad of bills from his wallet, and handed them over without counting them, as if he were a banker weary of a troublesome client's pleading. The gesture was so false and theatrical that the Gaviero could not help smiling with open sarcasm. Van Branden injected several coughs to save the situation and said: "Well, that should take care of the first few trips. Much more than I estimated, but that's all right. I don't want you to distrust me in any way. When this money's used up, you let me know. But I repeat, it seems like more than enough to me."

The Gaviero began to count the money with an irritating slowness that made the Belgian's face flush with the purple color of his darkest days. When Maqroll finished he said, as naturally as if it were hardly worth mentioning: "Of course, I'll sign a receipt right now. That way everything will be clear, *mijn herr*. It should indicate that this is payment for the first three trips. All right?"

"No," the other man answered, resuming his attitude of an oligarch from the *Simplicissimus,* "no receipts now. This is a confidential transaction between the two of us. I trust you and have no doubt the feeling is mutual. We're both gentlemen."

Maqroll realized he would never get the better of this slippery character. He did not want to say anything more, and stood up. So did the Belgian, who looked at him with his ventriloquist's dummy's eyes where nothing registered, where everything lost reality and importance, and said: "Good afternoon, *mijn herr*. I wish you good luck." His mocking repetition of the Flemish words left the Gaviero unmoved. He had already taken the man's measure and classified him forever. In the course of his nomadic existence countless van Brandens had crossed his path, and his revulsion toward these people and their methods had long since changed into absolute indifference. When he met someone like van Branden, he recalled Sancho Panza's words without having to look them up in that splendid book: "Each man is how God made him, and sometimes even worse." When he returned to the boardinghouse, he discussed the details of their conversation with Doña Empera.

"But what can you expect from a rat like him?" she said. "Even the poor woman who comes to see him is a victim of his greed. He owes her money and always comes up with the story that one of these days he'll have her teeth fixed and send her children to the San Miguel boarding school. He has to pay his rent because he's afraid of me. He thinks I know more about him than I really do. It's just as well. That way I can keep him in line. Watch out for him. If he doesn't pay you every penny, just leave the things on the dock and let him deal with it the best he can. You'll see, he'll cough up the money soon enough."

The Gaviero felt a certain relief at the astute woman's vigilant solidarity. Great mother, protective sibyl, she would guard the rear while he climbed up to the barrens.

On the following day the driver brought the mules, and Doña Empera offered to keep them in a small stable behind her house. Everything was ready for the first climb. The driver sent by Don Aníbal turned out to be an animated, talkative, dark-skinned boy who knew the region like the back of his hand, and with tireless enthusiasm enjoyed demonstrating his knowledge of the marvels of the road as well as its hidden pitfalls and dangers. His name was Félix, but everyone called him Zuro, or Cornsilk, because of a lock of white hair that fell over his forehead. It was soon apparent to the Gaviero that without Zuro's help he would not reach the Tambo Ridge alive. In the first place, Félix showed him how to load the mules. They had picked up the crates in the warehouse on the dock, and the mule driver took charge of distributing them properly among the five animals so that the mules would not be hurt and could maintain their pace without becoming exhausted. He also informed the Gaviero about the stops they had to make and whom they could depend on for lodging. The first day's journey would bring them to the Álvarez Flat, where they would spend the night. The Gaviero had already traveled that stretch of road and knew that to reach the mesa where the Álvarez ranch was located, they had a four-hour climb up a trail washed out by the rains and strewn with large rocks ready to dislodge at the slightest touch and plunge with crushing force into a ditch or over the edge of the ravine. Then they had to cross the coffee groves that had brought back happy memories of the world of his childhood. The next day they would climb as far as an abandoned cabin built by miners looking for gold along the banks of the streams flowing at the bottom of the gorges. They would sleep there, and then, after a difficult day's trek across the barrens, they would come to the camp on the Tambo Ridge. As Zuro explained the coming ordeal and the character of those who lived in the area, the Gaviero realized that the undertaking was more arduous, more demanding than he had imagined. But his companion's good nature and joyful, determined spirit, and his intelligent assessment of the difficulties they had to face, gave Maqroll confidence that he could meet the challenge, which was what he needed then more than anything else.

When the mules were loaded and preparations were completed for the six-day journey—three days up to the Tambo and another three to return to La Plata—they left at first light with the blind woman's heartfelt good wishes. The ascent to the Álvarez Flat was not as difficult for Maqroll as it had been the first time, when he climbed alone and was not familiar with the road. When they reached the coffee plantings, he again felt undiminished fascination with that warm, welcoming atmosphere filled with the unmistakable colors of plants that seemed carefully selected to create an effect of natural yet ordered beauty. In reality humans had very little to do with it, for in the hotlands the climate was usually responsible for this paradisal harmony. Slowly, savoring each tree, each irrigation ditch with its clear water flowing silently along a bed of mud and swaying ferns, Maqroll crossed the coffee grove. As he began to climb the final, easy slope to the ranch house, Amparo María came out of the grove to embrace him. Zuro went ahead with the mules, for the girl did nothing to hide her joy at their meeting, and the mule driver surely knew of her trips to La Plata and her relations with

Maqroll. She was more beautiful than ever. Her black percale dress hugged her body, emphasizing the slender forms that seemed to be made of a substance in which tendon and bone had replaced and then acquired the molded softness of flesh. The curve of her waist, her firm legs, her hair twisted into a gleaming jet-black chignon at the nape of her neck, reminded him again of young flamenco dancers in Vejer de la Frontera and Cádiz. Amparo María, as sparing of her words as ever, leaned against him and looked into his eyes with the expression of a great, shy bird examining a room it has flown into by mistake. Little by little Maqroll had become painfully aware of the weight of his years and the intricate, tangled skein of his wanderings and misfortunes, joys and calamities. The only relief he found for that sorrow was to feel at his side this gentle, feline warmth accompanying him like a young Fate who preferred the path of indulgent tenderness.

Don Aníbal received them on the gallery, and while Zuro led the mules to the stable to unload and feed them, the rancher invited his guest to share with him a cup of steaming, foamy chocolate served with cassava biscuits fresh from the oven. They sat on rocking chairs, said no more than absolutely necessary, and looked at the overwhelming immensity of the cordillera on one side and the serene, flowering extension of coffee groves on the other. When night fell Don Aníbal told his guest that in view of the day's travel awaiting them the next day, it was advisable to go to bed early, for they would need all the strength and nerve stored up during sleep. The Gaviero agreed, not without first searching discreetly for some pretext to speak to the girl again. She made matters easier by coming to the room that had been prepared for him and Zuro over the stable, with a glass of milk for him to drink during the night. They talked for a long while under a gigantic ceiba that raised the vast marvel of its centuries-old branches near the stable. The young woman offered to ask Zuro to sleep somewhere else so that she could spend the night with her friend. Maqroll had to dissuade her, very unwillingly, and at last Amparo María agreed that the difficulties of the next two days' travel up to the ridge were overwhelming. She said goodbye quickly, as if she did not want to prolong a disappointment that was much deeper than it appeared on the surface. Maqroll went to his room, undressed, and lit a candle in order to read on the pallet that had been laid on the floor and which he found much more comfortable than his bed in La Plata. He knew that if he did not read, it would be difficult for him to fall asleep. A short while later the mule driver came in and, without undressing completely, lay down on the other pallet on the far side of the room.

Maqroll had brought Joergensen's *Life of Saint Francis of Assisi*. Usually he opened the book at random and began to read. Zuro was intrigued by what, for him, was extraordinary behavior, and he asked: "Are you praying? I thought you were tired."

"I can't sleep if I don't read for a while," answered the Gaviero, amused at his traveling companion's ingenuousness. "I'm not praying. I don't think it would do me much good, do you? But I *am* reading the life of a saint who loved animals, the woods, the sun, the streams, and the poor. He came from a very rich family and probably looked a little like you. He left everything for the sake of what he loved, and to offer up to God his love for all creation." Maqroll realized the explanation was so inadequate and fragmentary that it might give Zuro an incomplete, superficial impression of the Poverello. Zuro's response reassured him.

"Of course, if he liked animals and the woods and the sun, then he didn't need any money. I'll bet he even performed some miracles. God must have wanted to help him."

"Yes," replied the Gaviero, who marveled at the boy's spontaneous clarity of thought. "He performed a good many miracles, very admirable ones. I'll tell you about them another day. Let's go to sleep."

Zuro closed his eyes and began the regular breathing of someone falling into a deep sleep.

Amparo María woke them at dawn with fresh coffee and yesterday's biscuits. She was carefully dressed, her hair pulled back into the impeccable chignon. Ready to preside over a ranch fiesta, he thought as he drank his coffee. The girl left abruptly and returned to the house. The Gaviero did not have the heart to say goodbye either. She looked so beautiful that he could have stayed there forever and forgotten everything else.

The climb from the Álvarez Flat to the abandoned cabin took the entire day. The road gradually turned into the bed of a stream that flowed only after the rains. The mules had a difficult time trying to avoid the unexpected ditches that opened in front of them, and the treacherous rocks that came hurtling down to the edge of the ravine. Discouragement worked away at the Gaviero's soul: this ordeal would be repeated over and over again. Any profits he might make depended on the evasive van Branden and his no less phantasmal construction company. An old bitterness, one he had known for years, began to weigh on his spirit, making each step of the frenzied climb more onerous. But in one of his most characteristic responses, as he penetrated the steepest portions of the cordillera and experienced the aroma of perpetually damp foliage, the explosion of rich, unrestrained color, the thunder of water in the ravines singing its opulent descent in boiling crests of foam, an ancient, restorative peace replaced the weariness of the road and the struggle with the mules. The sordid deceptions he foresaw in the uncertain enterprise lost all reality and were buried in the resigned acceptance of his Islamic fatalism. The birds became increasingly numerous and varied, and their song, and the intermittent passage of flocks of parakeets flying in uproarious disorder over the tops of great cámbulos in brilliant flower and jacarandas still drowsy with the morning cold, confirmed the ephemeral certainty of redemptive plenitude. This alternation of states of mind tended to lead the Gaviero to meditations and reckonings nourished by the few but infallible books that accompanied him wherever he went.

As a consequence, all the van Brandens in the world only verified his ineluctable solitude, his impregnable skepticism when faced with the intractable vanity of all human enterprise, of everything undertaken by those unfortunate blind creatures who come to death without ever having suspected the marvel of the world or felt the miraculous passion which fires our knowledge that we are alive and that death, without beginning or end, a pure, limitless present, is a part of that life. He gave himself over to pleasure in the countryside, but he was aware that the various sensations piercing the numbness of his fatigue with wondrous, endless celebration were coming to him eroded by a torpid memory that the years had worn away.

Zuro climbed ahead of him, leading the first mule and frequently leaving the trail to avoid impassable stretches of road. The higher they climbed the stronger the wind blew. It began as a light buzzing in the ears, a breeze that barely moved the treetops and made the ferns tremble. Then the noise of the torrents in the ravine grew fainter or increased, depending on the intensity of the wind. By the time they reached the narrow, zigzag paths that hugged the cliffs, the wind was whipping around them with sustained fury. The vegetation became stunted, with thick, woolly leaves that grew around great trees whose gray trunks had a mineral texture and whose crowns, with their scant foliage, were hidden in fog stretching all the way to the peaks of the sierra. They had entered the barrens. Maqroll had not been in this landscape for a long time. Zuro said that up here, when travelers found themselves without shelter at night, they would use the thick leaves of the croton tree, called the friar bush in the mountains, to keep out the wind and numbing cold. It became more difficult for Maqroll to breathe. His temples throbbed and his mouth dried, making him feel a treacherous thirst. Just as he was about to suggest that they rest, Zuro said they would stop for a while. "We can't do anything now," he said. "We should drink as little as possible. Chew this slowly and it'll bring back your saliva." He handed him a slice of lemon. Then he cut another for himself and stretched out at the side of the road on a bed of friar bush leaves. Maqroll did the same, in silence. They lay there, taking deep breaths and waiting for their bodies to adjust to the rigors of the barrens. The lemon had an immediate effect, relieving the dryness and bitter metallic taste in his mouth that had been tormenting the Gaviero for some time.

When they started out again, the discomfort was much easier to bear. They reached the abandoned cabin as night was falling. The walls were made of stones set without mortar or cement, and the chinks were filled in with the same kind of leaf that had protected them when they slept on the trail. The slate roof was supported by thick, rough-hewn beams. A mud and bamboo wall that did not quite reach the ceiling divided the interior into two equal spaces, a stable and a sleeping room with a stone and brass fireplace in perfect working order. The place was relatively clean. The only trace of its previous occupants was a handful of cold ashes on the grate. There was a supply of wood beside the fireplace, and the rule was to replace what you had used when you left. Zuro prepared two beds of leaves and suggested they rest before eating or their heads would ache again after the meal.

"Not many people come this far. Most of them can't stand it," the mule driver began as Maqroll lay on his bed and looked up at the ceiling, feeling the healing warmth of the fire that Zuro had lit. "First the miners who built this shelter. They came looking for gold along the streams in the gullies. They didn't find much. After them a series of foreigners chasing the fairy tale of the mines. I don't think there are any mines in the barrens. And now the railroad men. They keep the cabin clean and more or less in order."

"But the ones who built it, where were they from?" asked the Gaviero, curious about the style of the cabin.

"Canada," answered Zuro. "They were good people, but when they came down to La Plata they would drink like crazy and get into terrible fights. Not even the Army could control them. Afterwards they'd sleep in the street with the dogs pissing on them. At dawn they'd buy what they needed at the Turk's and come back to the barrens as if nothing had happened. They were huge, with red beards that they never cut. They'd disappear up on the ridge, working the streams all day, shaking the sand in their pans, and looking for gold nuggets. When they found something, they'd shout until one of the others answered. They lived that way for two years, and then they took off, without paying their bill at Hakim's, after a fight that lasted all night and left four soldiers dead. They were never caught, and nobody ever saw them again."

After an hour's rest on the soft beds of leaves, they made coffee and fried plantain slices with scrambled eggs. The bread from La Plata was inedible. Zuro offered Maqroll some dry ground meat to mix in with the rest of his food. Maqroll thought it was delicious.

"It's important to eat, señor," the mule driver said sententiously. "The worst is coming tomorrow. Now, try to sleep and don't read too late. Up here sleep is the only cure for fatigue."

Maqroll smiled, amused by Zuro's protective, admonitory attitude. The boy did not know the countless nights he had spent in worse circumstances and even more inhospitable places. If he mentioned their names, they would mean nothing to the young mule driver from the Álvarez Flat: nights in Sar-i-Pul, the wind from the Afghan mountains whipping the tent with a roar that did not let up until dawn; nights in Kerala, the enchanted dance of swarms of fireflies extending the violet, funereal light, the air heavy with the fragrance of cinnamon and ginger; nights on the Guiana frontier, sinking into the fetid mud of the mangrove swamps; nights of danger and desperate hunger in Anatolia; nights of mosquitoes and fever in the Gulf of Veragua, where the rain comes down like an endless curse; nights in the *cayouns* at the edge of the marshes where the Mississippi deposits its weariness; nights of dead calm along the coast of war-torn Yemen; nights like this one in the barrens, like so many others that had been forgotten.

Maqroll lit the candle end that a foresighted Doña Empera had packed in the knapsack, and became lost in Joergensen's pages, in the harmonious Umbrian countryside where, in the middle of the twelfth century, the son of a wealthy family went off to search for God. Sleep gradually overcame him, until the book fell from his hands with a noise that woke him. He returned the volume to the knapsack and blew out the candle.

The Gaviero was dreaming. All his muscles relaxed, transforming exhaustion into a pleasant inebriation, a kind of benign intoxication that gave birth to a harmony of lucidity and joy comparable only to his memories of childhood, when everything around him was ordered and he felt a sense of well-being when he was awake similar to the one that came to him now in his dream. He was on the shore of Lake Maggiore, where he had come to walk along the path at the water's edge. Someone was supposed to walk with him. He did not want to lose any more time because he was sure that if he continued to wait, the extraordinary contentment he felt would suddenly disappear. He had to keep it intact as long as possible. He went down to the shore and followed the path; when the wind rose, the waves would lap at its edge, while on the other side there were shrubs that looked like laurel but gave off a strong sandalwood fragrance. He heard footsteps behind him and knew, without having to turn around, that they belonged to the person he had been waiting for. If he looked back, his exultant joy would turn into something he could not predict. He heard a woman's voice speaking correct Spanish, but with a heavy accent he could not identify. She was telling him about train schedules that did not coincide, long waits in railroad stations, endless inconveniences on her way to the lake.

"From Milan to Novara," she said, "everything was fine. But there, instead of connecting for Oleggio and Arona, I found myself going north. I got off at the first station, and when I went to change my ticket, the man behind the window, who looked like a priest, insisted that I show him my breasts. I did. It was the only way I could get back. My luggage was waiting for me in Novara. I boarded a train, and found out later that the last stop was Oleggio. I would have to wait six hours for a train that stopped in Arona, along the lake, where we had agreed to meet, so I decided to take the bus that stops just a few kilometers from Arona. Imagine my surprise when I saw you at the stop. There you were, Gaviero you madman, lost as always. You'll never learn, you with your air of a sailor who's been thrown off his ship."

Her final words produced an abrupt, devastating sense of desolation. It was Ilona, his friend from Trieste. Only she, Ilona the unique and incomparable, spoke to him that way, in that peculiar, unmistakable accent. Her voice, her firm, elastic step, her joyful white body burned to ashes in an absurd gas explosion in Panama City. He turned and saw a Spanish-looking woman with an aristocratic Moorish air who looked at him reproachfully, as if she held him responsible for the chaos on the railroad that she had been complaining about. "Ilona!" he said, unaware of his foolish mistake, his eyes filled with tears. She stared at him in amazement, as if he were a stranger who had suddenly spoken to her, then turned abruptly and walked away with a youthful, athletic step, swaying her hips in a rhythm that he knew was typical of Ilona.

He awoke, his chest heaving with sobs. The icy wind lashing the stone walls, and the intense odor of the leaves of his bed were a brutal return to a consciousness that was, for the moment, incomprehensible and alien. He slept again after a time, and then he was awakened by Zuro offering him a cup of coffee. With an absent, regretful air the Gaviero began to drink in slow swallows.

"Be careful about your sleep, señor," the mule driver warned. "You need it to stay alive. In the barrens altitude and exhaustion make you dream a lot. It's not good for you. You don't get your strength back, and they're never good dreams. Just nightmares. I know what I'm talking about: the foreigners who came to try mining all went crazy and tried to murder each other in the tavern or drowned themselves in the whirlpools in the river."

Maqroll did not reply to Zuro's warnings. He knew the boy was telling the truth. The dream about Ilona still troubled his spirit, rousing the sleeping demons that had not come to torment him for some time. Without saying a word he helped to load the mules and clean the cabin. Then they began the climb to the Tambo Ridge. When the wind became intolerable, the mule driver told him to place a layer of friar bush leaves between his undershirt and shirt to protect his chest and back. The effect was immediate. He retained all his body heat. What made the ascent a torture was the soil, a volcanic sand that gave way at each step, damaged the animals' hooves, and abraded the bottoms of their shoes. The resulting friction produced an unbearable heat and a sulfurous smell that burned the mucous membranes. Hour after hour they advanced three steps and slipped back two. They had to take shorter rest stops: night falls very early in the barrens, and climbing in the dark is suicidal. In the last light of day, along a desolate stretch of lava where the only sign of life was an occasional low shrub whose trunk bore a beautiful flower, like a pale funereal flame in the oncoming dark, they saw the lights. It would take them at least an hour to reach the camp. The full moon lit the way. As long as it was in the sky, they would have no problem.

Maqroll trudged on, lost in the memory of his dream. As is so often the case, with the passage of time the images, words, and hidden meanings became more precise and extensive, invading deeper and deeper areas of his being. The incomparable Ilona from Trieste, with her honey-colored hair and Macedonian profile, the wise, vigilant friend so steadfast in her affections, the only woman to perceive his penchant for vague undertakings that always caused trouble and always bordered on illegality. With just a few words she had known how to move him out of harm's way whenever he fell into those situations. As he helped to pull the mules out of pits of volcanic sand that buried them up to their cinches, he realized that the periods when they had lived together were the only times he had known anything approaching happiness, had enjoyed his nomadic mania without dreaming of unlikely El Dorados or dazzling fortunes. When they traveled together, it was she who chose the best itineraries and was careful to follow them, exercising no authority except good judgment that was used so naturally it went unnoticed, and a smile that always played about her lips and revealed her large, Thracian peasant's teeth.

Reflecting on the dark corners of his dream as they made the torturous trek through the barrens, Maqroll uncovered the key to many of his losses, much of his despair. He compared Ilona to Flor Estévez—that other memorable friend, who had cared for him during his recovery from a poisonous spider bite, in The Snow of the Admiral, her ramshackle shop at the side of a highway that crossed an upland barren like this one—and he realized that Flor, unlike Ilona, gave herself fully to his fantasies and would have joined her lover in the wildest of any that passed through his head. She had encouraged his senseless voyage along the Xurandó to search for unimaginable sawmills. He had left a good part of his health there, and when he came back for her, Flor had disappeared. But the signs in his dream made him realize that comparing the two women was absurd and fruitless. Desire was a constant spur to Flor Estévez; always achieved but never completely satisfied, it kept her relationships adrift in the midst of clamoring senses that clouded and distorted everything and never found an escape. It was like struggling in a tunnel with a swarm of delights that forever slipped from one's grasp.

When he returned to the present, they were in front of two railway storage sheds, two squat structures made of corrugated tin whose faded gray color blurred into the landscape. A team of laborers was supervised by a tall, lean man with an elongated profile like a hunting knife, who spoke with a marked Nordic accent and came toward them with a weary step not free of annoyance, looking at the Gaviero as if he were one more mule driver passing through. Then his attitude changed abruptly; apparently he had remembered something, and he greeted Maqroll and held out his hand with feigned courtesy. He switched to French and asked about the climb up to the ridge. In the same language, imitating his neutral tone, Maqroll gave some details and requested a receipt for the cargo that was already being unloaded inside the shed. The man smiled with a condescension that irritated the Gaviero. Tomorrow he would give him the papers; there was no hurry. He invited them to come in, taking it for granted they would spend the night. It was unthinkable for them to return now, to slide down the sandy slope in the dark until they reached the miners' cabin. Yet that was what Maqroll would have preferred. He walked into the warehouse to see how they had stored the crates. Two Coleman lamps lit the interior. There they were, carefully arranged boxes of varying sizes. On some the word "Fragile" was written in large black letters. At least ten trips like the one he just made had been needed to carry all of them up here. Van Branden had not said anything about that. Perhaps they had come by another route. The man who had greeted them—the Gaviero could not determine his nationality—paid careful attention to the handling of the crates that had just been brought in. When they were moved, the clink of metal could be heard, and each time this happened the man frowned with concern. Maqroll wondered why he had not heard the sound before. Perhaps it had been drowned out by other noises, by the wind in the barrens. Something else puzzled him: the name of the construction company did not appear on the wooden crates, on the papers where their arrival was noted, or anywhere in the warehouse.

When work in the storage shed was completed, Maqroll was invited to share a meal at a table set up in another, identical building connected to the shed by a small covered passageway that was also made of corrugated tin. Zuro stayed behind to eat with the laborers who had stored the boxes. A short, somewhat hunchbacked man with heavy graying eyebrows and a flat nose was already seated at the head of the table. He said he was a surveyor, a native of Danzig, whose nickname was Kraken. The taller man introduced himself as an engineer from Belgium. He mumbled his name so that it was difficult to hear. It was something like Martens or Harlens. The meal, consisting of canned food washed down with wine and beer of unusual quality for that region, passed with almost no conversation. A few trivial remarks about the weather or the difficulties of the climb led to brief dialogues that soon ended in dull, uncomfortable silence. Maqroll noticed that none of the dishes or flatware, or the piece of fabric that served as a tablecloth and had seen better days, bore any mark or sign to indicate its origin. But what intrigued him most was that the labels and all the brand names and lettering had been carefully scraped off the bottles of wine and beer and cans of tuna, sardines, and vegetables. No one lingered at the table. With a dry good night the two foreigners retired to their rooms at the far end of the building. They told Maqroll he could sleep in a hammock that the laborers would hang for him in a corner of the storage shed. When he went to the bathroom, Zuro was waiting for him, signaling that he wanted to speak to him alone. They went into a structure of rough-hewn tree trunks that was attached to the storage shed and served as an improvised stable for the visitors' animals. Zuro said: "Listen, they haven't laid a meter of track. The laborers don't know anything about a railroad or anything like that. Be careful, señor. I don't know why, but I think they're going to try to screw you."

The Gaviero was about to answer him when the supposed Belgian suddenly walked in, pretending to check the stable before he went to sleep. His expression meant, "I don't know what you're talking about, and I don't care." It was the look put on by people who do know, and do care. "Good night," he said with a faint smile that revealed teeth ruined by tobacco and neglect.

When he was in his hammock, wrapped in everything he could find and further protected by a mattress of leaves that Zuro had prepared for him, the Gaviero tried to sleep without reading first, trusting to his utter exhaustion. But sleep did not come. The previous night's visit by Ilona, disguised in a vague resemblance to Amparo María, had made him uneasy prey to an old anguish that had returned to undermine the little strength he had left and his diminished will to go on. At the same time, and inextricably entangled with her visit, he was troubled by the menace of the enterprise on which he was embarked. It was obvious now that van Branden had tricked him with a deception as clumsy as it was transparent. How could he have been taken in when he did not really need the money? He could have gotten by on the checks from Trieste until he found less murky, more solid work. Clearly he was losing his faculties, he was letting himself drift with the current, and if he allowed that to continue, it would be his ruin. He resolved to speak to van Branden on his return. He would try to get out of the deal by selling the mules and leaving La Plata as soon as possible on the first boat or caravan of barges going downriver. At last he fell into a deep sleep. At dawn Zuro woke him, saying that the mules were ready and they could leave right after breakfast. Nobody was in the sheds, the mule driver said; they had all gone out very early on the pretext of surveying the high end of the ridge. "Drink your coffee," he added, "and let's get out of here. I don't think they want us around much longer. They're very strange people."

Maqroll drank the coffee and they began the descent in a heavy fog blown in by the icy sierra wind that burned their faces and bit into their thighs like persistent teeth. They wrapped themselves in friar bush leaves and followed the trail, which was even more treacherous on the way down. The mules, free of their loads, tried to quicken the pace and slipped constantly in the shifting volcanic sand. An inconsolable panic could be seen in their eyes. Finally, slumping with fatigue, their faces and hands numb with cold, Maqroll and Zuro reached the miners' cabin. The shooting pains in their legs and the burning sensation on the parts of their skin they had not been able to protect from the punishing wind made it difficult for them to relax and rest. The beds of leaves that Zuro had prepared the day before were, fortunately, still intact. They lay down, overcome by exhaustion. Zuro had to rub the mules' hooves with the coconut oil he carried with him. "This keeps them warm. Otherwise nothing will get them up tomorrow." The Gaviero asked why they didn't use it too. "No, señor," the boy explained. "People heat themselves. You'll see, we'll be okay in a little while. What happens with mules is that they have thicker blood, and when they get cold, it's very hard for them to warm up again so they can rest." Maqroll had to accept the validity of Zuro's strange theory. He opened *The Life of Saint Francis of Assisi* and concentrated for several hours on the book that invariably relieved his sorrows. A smile crossed his face from time to time. Zuro looked at him in amazement, not daring to interrupt: for him the lives of saints were something forbidden and mysterious. It was better not to find out too much about them or try to get too close.

The next day they reached the Álvarez Flat. As always, the weather in the temperate regions raised Maqroll's spirits. He wanted to talk with Don Aníbal and learn more about the railway and the people connected to the project. The ranch owner received them with cordial expressions of concern for the difficulties they had faced on the climb up to the Tambo Ridge. Amparo María came to the stable when Maqroll and the boy were alone, unsaddling the mules. Zuro left discreetly while the girl embraced the Gaviero with an effusiveness she had not often shown before. With affectionate sobs she told him she had been very afraid for him, not only because of the punishing barrens but because of the people up there, who made her feel a gloomy, inexplicable wariness. The girl's warm, strong body, clinging to his with new and revealing intensity, transmitted a sense of peace and well-being that heightened the benign effect of the land of coffee and sugar cane; here he regained all his desire to live, all his love for the gifts of the world.

During the meal that was served on the gallery, Maqroll began to disclose to Don Aníbal the doubts he had felt on the Tambo Ridge. The rancher would not make any concrete response, clearly intending to discuss the matter when the others had gone to bed. Maqroll understood and waited. When the meal was finished, Don Aníbal lit a cigar, rocked in his chair, and sipped a cup of black coffee to which he had added a few drops of brandy. The Gaviero began to drink his coffee too, but added no liquor. Amparo María made an occasional appearance among the women who served the meal and now cleared the table, said good night, and retired to their rooms. After a silence Don Aníbal began to speak. The light of his cigar, moving in rhythm to his words, was all that could be seen in the darkness. Maqroll was ready to listen. He did not feel tired, and he was extraordinarily interested in what the rancher had to say.

"Look," Don Aníbal began, puffing hard on the cigar so that his face was visible for a moment, "there's not much I can tell you about that project. The idea of building a railroad over the ridge and across the cordillera has been talked about for many years. My father mentioned it when we came here. But then they began to build the highway along another route. It serves the same purpose, and everybody forgot about the railroad. Some Englishmen drew up the initial plans and did a little preliminary work. At first they were very serious and methodical. But then, in their spare time, a few of them began to wash the sand along the streams, looking for gold. It seems they found a few nuggets, and the rush was on. What they earned from that small amount of gold was much higher than their salaries. The railroad abandoned the project, work was suspended, and the area filled with prospectors. In some places there are still stretches of track and even some railroad cars that they used to store tools and canned food. That's when the Tambo sheds were built. The gold rush failed. After the initial excitement it seems none of the strikes was worthwhile, and mining was abandoned along with the railroad. Then, a few months ago, rumors began that the work would be resumed by a Belgian company, and there was a certain amount of activity in La Plata. Mule teams carried up crates similar to the ones you just took there. But it's very strange: the men on the ridge haven't built anything. They wander the mountains, apparently with no definite purpose, looking for who knows what. The ones who come to La Plata pay their debts fairly regularly, they travel up and down the river, sometimes they go up to the Tambo, but it seems they're after something else. That van Branden came through here. I haven't traveled, I've never even been to the capital, but I can tell you I didn't like anything about the man. To begin with, I don't think van Branden's his real name. Sometimes he makes mistakes when he says it, and his signature is a scribble that's never the same. Something tells me he's been here before, but using a different name. Maybe when the English were here. We were hospitable to him, as we are to any stranger, but it didn't take him long to realize we had our suspicions, and we never saw him again. They tell me he passes by here after dark. I don't know. One thing I can tell you: he's a very lucky man. The Army closed the post in La Plata and nobody's policing the area. If the soldiers were here, this so-called van Branden or whatever his name is would have to identify himself and state exactly what he and his people are doing here. I can guarantee that."

The Gaviero's uneasiness returned. His experience with the armed forces in these countries had been extremely instructive. When he sailed the Xurandó, he was witness to the kind of control they exercise and the methods they use to impose and maintain order. Personally, he had no complaints. On the contrary, they had saved his life when he was on the verge of death, victim of an apparently incurable disease that devastated the region. And they had rescued him on the return trip when he was about to face the rapids that killed his companions. But he had seen acts of summary justice that still made his skin crawl. All of this flooded his memory in an overwhelming torrent. He felt as if an old nightmare were about to begin again. With his diminished strength and increased years, the prospect terrified him. He did not want to think about it. Don Aníbal was aware of the

Gaviero's reaction and came to the rescue by telling him in detail about some improvements he planned to make on the ranch, forgetting or perhaps wanting to disregard the fact that in the years Maqroll spent roaming the seas and their ports like a perpetual fugitive, he had forgotten this world of his childhood. Don Aníbal stopped speaking, and they were silent for a long while, contemplating the starry sky that showered them with the tranquil consolation of our meager importance in the cosmic plan. Peace returned to Maqroll's spirit, and with it a desire for sleep. He turned to his companion and saw that he was nodding gently, the cigar in his mouth dropping ash on his white starched shirt. In a low voice he said good night to Don Aníbal and went to the small building adjoining the stables that was reserved for guests.

When he was back in La Plata, he learned that van Branden had not yet returned but was expected on the next boat. At least that is what he had said when he left, which did not necessarily mean it was true. Such statements, made to reassure his creditors and those involved in his plans, were no longer taken seriously by anyone. Maqroll prepared to wait. No new cargo for Tambo Ridge had arrived either. He resumed his sessions of talking and reading to the blind woman. He happily translated for her many pages of the two books in French he had brought with him. And she provided information about the area and the events that had occurred there over the past twenty years. The better he knew her the more he admired Doña Empera, whose intelligence and good sense seemed to deserve a better fate than being trapped in a wretched hamlet and running a boardinghouse in the midst of the chaos and intermittent violence that afflicted the region. It was, for example, a pleasure to hear how she judged certain actions of the prince of Ligne, whose true motivations lay carefully hidden in the clear, savory prose of his letters. The blind woman uncovered the truth that the great Belgian lord disguised, and interpreted it in everyday words. Doña Empera was almost always on target, and events usually occurred as she predicted. On these long evenings Maqroll forgot his difficulties and the physical ailments that, with unexpected insistence, had begun to remind him of the passing years.

During this time Amparo María visited him. When the girl

came to his room, he stepped out for a moment to speak with the landlady. He told her that he did not want to continue the affair, given the friendship and trust that now existed between him and Don Aníbal. He was afraid it would give rise to ugly gossip that would put him in an embarrassing position with the rancher, for whom he felt cordial respect. The blind woman reassured him, saying that the rancher tended to look the other way in such matters. On previous occasions the girl had come to the house with friends of Álvarez when they were in La Plata, either before or after a visit to the ranch. And furthermore, the girl was extremely discreet and reserved, which was to her advantage. If she was obliged to go back home, she would face a ticklish situation: an army lieutenant who tried to rape her had been found stabbed to death at the bottom of a gully. The case was never solved, but the Army tends not to forget things like that. Maqroll returned to his room, still plagued by doubts, but the desire the young woman awakened in him was stronger than all his prudence and fear.

They made love with a new intensity born, perhaps, of the shadows that were gathering around them. They lay on the precarious bamboo bed, watching the river as it flowed past the window that was barely covered by thin mosquito netting, and talked through the night. Behind her stern, fierce air Amparo María, the laconic brunette with the Gypsy waist, showed herself to be a creature mistreated by life whose lack of trust, and fear of being hurt, concealed a hunger for affection. This explained why her responses were so often sudden and brusque, and why, in the act of love, she held back at the climax. For Maqroll their lovemaking became a struggle to control his enjoyment of her body; its extreme, unsettling beauty opened vast possibilities that he had to negotiate with increasing astuteness. But Amparo María was tender and warm, with the spontaneity of those who live in hope of the caress, the loving word that will rescue them from the cage they have built for themselves. Adversity had prevented her from expressing these feelings with the hidden generosity that constituted the authentic core of her character. Her conversation unraveled in a kind of spiral, beginning always in long, apparently sullen silences and finally reaching a playful joy marked by child-like humor and unstudied candor. The two of them had formed a close friendship by creating a climate of trust and unreserved openness. This had been the work of the Gaviero, who guessed her real nature. At his age, he thought, he was lucky to hold in his arms a young woman whose characteristics and appearance recalled friends he had once had in small Mediterranean ports where a woman of her qualities was usually seduced, at some risk to one's life, in the obscure seraglios of Oran or Susa. On the threshold of old age the Gaviero was learning to accept what is inevitably given to us, with interest, in exchange for what might have been and is lost. Fate had brought him Amparo María. Twenty years ago he would have loved her, would have wanted to keep her on an isolated farm in Catania. Now, when he was weary, here in a country of horror and helplessness, she was his, a gift of the gods.

He mentioned some of this to the landlady, who answered with a certain touch of ironic resignation. "Yes, Gaviero. These things we're forced into by age, they happen to all of us. The bad thing is that they take us by surprise. They always start long before we realize we're doing them. You can imagine, the blind have to learn resignation from the moment we lose our sight. It's harder. Don't you think so?" Maqroll agreed without really grasping everything that Doña Empera meant to say, but what she said next reassured him.

"No, that isn't true. It's all the same, Gaviero, it's all the same. Life is like the water in this river: it levels everything, what it carries and what it leaves behind, until it reaches the sea. The current is always the same. It's all the same."

He could not or would not add anything to her words. They were too similar to what he had been telling himself for years. And his climb to the barrens had confirmed their truth and given him back his indifference, the old friend that saved him from the pain of serious misfortune and invariably closed the cracks through which he sometimes thought his soul might escape. It was a very peculiar indifference, identical to the one preached by the blind woman: while it kept him from defeat, it continued to offer him the gifts of the world that gave him his only solid reason for living.

Van Branden arrived on the next boat. By the time the Gaviero learned of his arrival, the Belgian was already at the back table in the bar drinking one large glass of gin and water after another. His eyes were bloodshot; below them a bitter discontent had drawn gray pouches inside the circles born of implacable insomnia. Conversation would not be easy. Maqroll informed him of the results of the first trip. Van Branden mumbled something noncommittal and then rebuked him for taking the young mule driver up to the ridge. "If you're going to use one of these shits, leave him in the miners' cabin. Don't make trouble for me with the people up there." The Gaviero preferred not to discuss the matter and moved on to what interested him: payment for his work. All he could make out in the Belgian's inconclusive rambling, which at times seemed intentional, was that there would be more crates on the next boat, larger and more fragile than the last shipment, that the money he had received was enough to pay for two more trips at least, and what the hell was he complaining about? Maqroll could not learn anything else. Van Branden clung to his drunkard's grumbling obstinacy, and everything was as vague as before. But a new element emerged from this meeting that set off a general alarm in the Gaviero—general but clear enough to awaken in him the old defenses that had saved him in so many corners of the world. He could glimpse a shadow of fear and contained panic behind van Branden's incoherent phrases. The haughty impunity assumed by the Belgian had given way to cowardly babbling, a loose tangle of obfuscation repeated with the circular insistence of a sly but inoffensive drunk.

Back in his room, with the balcony window partially opened to the gentle nocturnal flow of the river, the Gaviero tried to grasp the meaning of the fleeting danger signal awakened in him by the interview. It took him several hours to reach what appeared to be the obvious conclusions: the railroad, even if it existed, was a front for something else, some other purpose that was concealed because it was illegal; the two foreigners in the Tambo sheds and van Branden were partners in the conspiracy; the residents of La Plata and the people on the Álvarez Flat doubted the railway project and distrusted the men involved, who were suspiciously reluctant to show their faces at the ranch; the entire situation was possible due to the apparently temporary absence of any military authority in the region. That much was clear, and it was enough for him to take precautions on the imminent second climb. He would speak to Don Aníbal frankly about his conclusions. He was certain that the rancher, with his sound judgment and strict honesty, would be able to shed light on those aspects of the situation that were still murky. He counted on the mutual sympathy that was evident in his dealings with Amparo María's employer.

The new shipment reached La Plata two days later. It consisted of seven long crates, so heavy that each mule would be able to carry only one. Maqroll took the two left over to van Branden's room in Doña Empera's boardinghouse. Zuro was responsible for arranging the load so the mules would not be hurt and the crates would not slip off during the climb. It was not an easy task, but the mule driver demonstrated so much skill and persistence that finally everything was prepared to Maqroll's satisfaction. On a damp, fogbound dawn, the Gaviero said goodbye to Doña Empera, asked her to be absolutely discreet regarding the boxes left in her care, and began his second ascent to the Tambo Ridge. When they reached the midway point on the first day's climb, the coffee plantings were in bloom and the women were removing dead leaves from each shrub and pruning the central stalk, which sometimes grew too large and damaged the fruit. The warm air was heavy with the fragrance of the white blossoms that resembled an unexpected snowfall on the green domes of the coffee plants. The sound of the women singing and the noise of the water in the ravine as it rushed down from the sierra were, for Maqroll, a respite of pure, unsullied joy and forgetfulness. A morning in the hotlands that came to him as if by miracle from his childhood. The mountains still enveloped in a bluish veil of translucent mist, the trails zigzagging up the slopes and connecting the humble dwellings of the tenant farmers, seemed a vast, limitless domain, sheltering yet awesomely powerful. Its majestic presence recalled dreams that had come to him at sea to remind

him, he realized now, of his unqualified connection to this landscape and his wondrous memories of it. At a bend in the road,
just before the rise that led to the ranch, Amparo María was
waiting for him. She wore a long white smock that gave her the
air of a priestess, an effect that was heightened by the pruning
shears she held in her hand. The girl kissed him on the mouth
with a touch of defiance and whispered in his ear, tickling him
with her warm breath, "Don Aníbal wants to talk to you alone.
He says that when you come to the house, you should go outside
with him when he makes some excuse. But first let's rest under
that coffee tree I've just been working on; we'll be hidden and
nobody will see us."

The sweet promise of her invitation intensified his feeling of
excited contentment. He signaled to Zuro to go on without him,
and he followed the girl into the grove. She wore the enigmatic
smile of the Etruscan statuettes he had seen in a museum on the
Adriatic. Under the protective dome of azure-green foliage, Amparo María had prepared a bed of dry plantain leaves. She lay
down, stripping off her clothes in a sudden, emphatic gesture.
The Gaviero caressed her as he undressed slowly, silently. He
entered her in an act that felt like a sacred ritual. The girl's
feigned ecstasy became real, the result of her grateful admiration
for the stranger who carried the burden of his years and the desolate, consuming experience of unknown lands and their intox-
icating dangers and delights. They lay in each other's arms while
the sun, sifting through the leaves, moved along their bodies with
a dappled light that marked time's passing. When Maqroll finally
decided to go, Amparo María dressed as quickly as she had undressed. Her expression was serious and intense, as if she had
suddenly matured. She kissed the Gaviero passionately on the
mouth and ran to join her companions, who were leaving for the
midday meal.

By the time the Gaviero caught up to Zuro, the boy had already climbed most of the slope. "The mules are tired. We'll see
if they survive the barrens," he said to Maqroll, whose face must
have shown the serenity of the blessed because the mule driver
said in a bantering tone, "When you wake up we'll talk. Who
can think about the barrens in the coffee groves? Everything in

its own time, my grandfather used to say. He was a coffee grower. It wasn't for me, and here I am struggling with animals that come straight from hell. They're worse than ever today. The load is bothering them—it's not heavy but it's chafing their haunches." Maqroll walked on and said nothing. He had no response for Zuro, and he preferred to take refuge in a silence that would prolong the joy he had not expected to be granted again. He kept careful account of such visitations, and an inner voice told him they were coming to an end, that the moments of plenitude were about to be canceled out.

When they reached the Álvarez Flat, Don Aníbal, still wearing chaps, came out to receive them. He said he had been looking for lost cattle up where the ranch bordered the barrens. He invited the Gaviero to the gallery, ordered coffee, and then went to change his clothes. On his return they began to drink the large cups of steaming, aromatic coffee in silence. After a while the rancher suggested, very naturally, giving no particular weight to his words, "Why don't you come with me to the ravine? I want to show you some fruit trees I planted along the stream; they're producing very well and I think you'll find them interesting." The Gaviero agreed immediately, somewhat amused by the artificiality of the pretext, since Don Aníbal knew that Maqroll had little interest in matters so alien to his life as a sailor. They made the descent slowly, trying to keep their footing on the wet clay of the path. The rancher went into a small stand of trees growing beside the stream. The screeching of the parakeets was almost unbearable. He invited Maqroll to sit beside him on the large rock that broke the surface of a stillwater. He looked around and, with no preambles, began to speak.

"Well, my friend, this has to do with the railroad. Apparently you've always had serious doubts about the project. I wanted to confirm some of my own suspicions, and early this morning I went to the barrens. My excuse was the lost cattle, but I really wanted to talk to the herders who tend a flock of sheep I keep up there. They know everything that goes on. With what they told me, and the news I've been receiving from La Plata, I can tell you this: There is no railroad, not even a hint of a project like that. What they're storing in the sheds, and what you're transporting up to the Tambo, isn't machinery or precision instruments. Three times now men have come to the sheds in the middle of the night to take away the crates, or at least what's in them. Nobody knows where they go. I decided to warn you for two reasons. The first is that since I'm convinced you're not involved in this business, and because I like you, I wouldn't want to see you come to a bad end with that den of thieves. The second has to do with my own interests and the interests of my people. You can keep me informed about what's going on in La Plata and on the Tambo. Then I'll know about any danger in time to protect my ranch and my people from whatever may happen. It may be a while in coming. Maybe one or two more trips with your mules. The danger signs will come first in La Plata, not on the ridge, where I think they're overconfident. Send me your news through Amparo María; she's loyal and more observant than she seems. And I'll move immediately to avoid a tragedy here."

"Don Aníbal," replied Maqroll, "what is it exactly that you're afraid of? I'll be glad to tell you whatever I can find out in La Plata and on the Tambo. But I'd like to know what the threat is so I won't mistake trivial gossip for important information. I must say that everything in La Plata troubles me. Even a fool would be disturbed at what goes on there. I feel sincere affection and great respect for you and your people, and your confidence in me now draws me even closer and attests to your loyalty and sense of justice. But if you're not more specific about what the danger, it may be right under my nose and I won't see it."

"You're right, my friend," answered Don Aníbal. "I'll give you a little background. For years there's been turmoil in this region. Right now I don't know what may happen or who's behind it. It's not easy to keep track of these things; they twist and turn in the dark before they come to light. In Empera's house, in the tavern, on the docks, up on the Tambo, even in the miners' cabin, just keep an eye on anything new, anything out of the ordinary, any sign of a change in the lives of the people you deal with. I can't tell you more than that, not because

I'm keeping secrets but because I have no idea where the blow will come from. If I say it's a subversive movement, it will probably turn out to be army maneuvers, or a settling of accounts within the military or between different gangs of smugglers. I'm more interested in what you see in La Plata than in anything you learn on the Tambo. I already have people up there who keep a constant eye on things. This doesn't mean you should be careless about those two crooks hiding on the ridge. Don't let your guard down with them. But the river, my friend, the river is what brings the most terrible surprises. Nothing good has come down that river in all the time I've lived here. I know what I'm talking about. Let's go back now. I don't want anyone on the ranch to think you and I are plotting something. My poor people, their loyalty moves me and I feel responsible for what happens to them. We brought them here. Of course, you won't say anything about this to Zuro. He's loyal and very smart, but he loves to talk and that's made problems for me in the past. Don't distrust him, just his tongue. I guess that's all."

They climbed up to the ranch house and the Gaviero went to see to the mules. Zuro had unloaded them with the help of a farmhand, and the two of them were discussing the strange appearance of the crates. The Gaviero signaled to Zuro to stop the conversation, the farmhand left immediately, and the mule driver began to feed the animals. That night Maqroll and Zuro slept in the stable. Maqroll did not want any curious passerby to have access to the crates. The conversation with Don Aníbal had made him wary. He was tying together his conversations with van Branden and some of the blind woman's allusions, and began to see clear evidence of the dangerous minefield he was crossing.

They left before dawn for the cabin. The mules showed signs of weariness and grew increasingly resistant to Zuro's commands. Finally they reached the slope. The trail zigzagged along a precipice that deepened as they climbed. The path narrowed dangerously, hugging the steep cliff and its great protrusions of rock too large to be removed. The mules started trembling as they began the ascent, and then balked. "It's the load," said Zuro. "They can sense the danger in the unbalanced weight. We'll have to walk them one by one; if they all stop halfway up, there's no way to get back and we're bound to lose any battle with these animals. And to make matters worse, the ground's as slippery as soap with the rain."

The Gaviero proposed pushing on a little further. He did not want to be caught on the trail if they had not reached the shelter by nightfall. But halfway up the slope the mules refused to budge, and they put Zuro's plan into effect. The first mules were no problem. Maqroll waited further up the trail, and the mule driver led each one by the halter. As he was climbing up with the last animal, it shied at a bird that suddenly flew out of the rock wall. The path was so narrow that when the mule took a few steps backward, the weight of its load dragged it over the precipice. The animal fell in absolute silence into an abyss so deep that clouds covered the bottom, although the wind occasionally carried up the sound of the river that ran there. The mules noticed that their companion was gone, which made them even surlier. They were exhausted by the time they finally reached the barrens. Night was falling, and an icy torrent of rain suddenly poured down while lightning that seemed to be coming closer cracked all around them. The mules were trembling, and in the flashes of lightning one could see their eyes bulging with panic. It was almost midnight when they reached the cabin. They unloaded the animals immediately to help relieve their fatigue, and each man prepared his own bed with the friar bush leaves that were always kept in the shelter. When the Gaviero lit the candle he carried for reading at night, he saw a piece of paper on the rusty nail in the wall that served as a hook for clothes or gear. The note, in macaronic Spanish, was printed in block letters clearly intended to disguise the writer's identity. It told Maqroll to wait in the cabin and the crates would be picked up before noon the next day. Along with relief at not having to make the terrible climb from the barrens to the Tambo Ridge, he and Zuro felt the silent presence of hidden danger on which they chose not to comment. Each knew what the other was thinking. It rained all night with the persistence of those tropical storms that seem to announce the universal flood. In the morning they heated coffee and fried some slices of plantain, but the previous day's climb had awakened an appetite for more substantial food. They lay down again, trying to hold off their growing hunger with sleep. A banging on the door woke them with a start. They had both forgotten where they were.

The lean, acerbic engineer who had received them on the ridge came in with five other men. Five fresh mules were waiting outside. Without saying a word the laborers loaded the crates very carefully while the supposed Belgian checked the numbers on them against a list. "Two are missing," he said, glancing at the Gaviero with a combination of feline distrust and a barely disguised look of alarm.

"No," replied Maqroll, "only one's missing. It fell into the ravine along with the mule."

"Let me see," said the man as he compared the list again with the crates that had already been loaded. "You're right, only one's missing. But it amounts to the same thing. Where did the mule go over?"

"Right before the Santa Ana Flat. At the next to the last bend. We didn't even see it land. The clouds covered everything," Zuro hurried to explain. He knew the area better than the Gaviero, and he wanted to dispel the stranger's suspicions.

"You can tell that story to the man who hired you," the engineer said to Maqroll. "You're in for trouble. This cargo just can't be thrown away in the middle of the mountains. You'd better try to locate that crate and keep quiet about what you see if you do find it. If somebody else gets there first, steel yourself, because we don't fool around. All right, let's get going." Shrugging his shoulders he turned, started up the pack of mules, and disappeared into the rain that continued to fall with nightmarish tenacity.

When they were alone, Zuro said, "Don't worry. I know a way down to the bottom of the ravine. We'll leave the mules tied halfway down the slope. The trail's not far and we can be at the bottom in an hour. Then we'll see what this is all about. We'll bury the crate in a safe place and that'll be that. We can take this spade the miners left here."

Maqroll breathed a sigh of relief. Zuro's words restored his confidence in their ability to get out of this difficulty at no great risk. The engineer's warning had troubled him deeply. Nothing was more unsettling than intangible, vague threats by men on whom he was temporarily dependent. In this case, however, fear was not as great as repugnance at knowing he was at the mercy of someone who deserved neither respect nor gratitude. This was the kind of relationship he went out of his way to avoid.

The rain stopped. They led the mules down to the spot that Zuro had mentioned, and then left to find the path that would take them to the bottom of the ravine. At times the trail almost disappeared, but Zuro knew the way perfectly. The rain had made the clay soil so slippery that in some places they had to slide down the slope, holding on to plants that became taller and thicker the further down they went. At last they found themselves surrounded by intensely green vegetation so saturated with moisture it eased their respiration and relaxed the muscles that had contracted with cold and the exertions of the descent. By midday they had reached the torrent rushing past in a joyful turbulence of foam and whirlpools. The roar of the clear, icy water as it smashed into the walls of the ravine, the noisy flocks of parakeets startled by the intruders and darting out of the cliffs along with pairs of great birds that flew majestically into the distance—all of this gave the place a Delphic air, as if it lay outside of time and its corrosive labor. They walked along the river's edge while Zuro looked up to locate the spot where the mule had gone over the cliff. He stopped suddenly and pointed it out to Maqroll. But they were disconcerted when they saw no trace of the mule or its cargo. Zuro said that the corpse could have been carried by the current and trapped against some rocks, but the crate was a different matter. They soon discovered the bloated remains of the mule swirling around an eddy and crashing into large rocks; vultures stood on the carrion and pecked at it vigorously as they tried to keep their balance in the pounding current.

They decided to return to where they calculated the mule had fallen and resume the search for the crate. "Shit!" exclaimed

Zuro as he picked something up from the ground. "Somebody's taken it. Look." He handed the Gaviero a sliver of wood that they recognized immediately. They continued searching, and before long Maqroll picked up another clue that was even more worrisome. It was a piece of plastic label with some machine-printed words that had been smudged by water and rain, but on the lower edge the letters "Made in Czec . . ." were still legible. It was easy enough to guess the part of the word that was missing. Maqroll put the piece of plastic in his pocket and told Zuro they could go back for the mules. It would be imprudent to spend much more time in the ravine. The mule driver said that if Maqroll followed the river, it would not take him long to reach the Álvarez Flat. In the meantime he would bring the mules. Without a load they were easy enough to handle, and the climb up the slippery path was exhausting. The Gaviero agreed, though somewhat reluctantly. If Zuro was still on the trail at nightfall, the same men who took the crate might attack him. "Nobody dares to climb in the dark," the mule driver said. "I can take care of myself. Don't worry." "I'm not so sure," replied the Gaviero. "They had to come here last night for the box. They're not afraid of the slope." "No, señor," said Zuro. "They took the shortcut. That's a different story." The Gaviero gave in to Zuro's arguments, and they separated. As he made the descent, following the river, a wordless apprehension took hold of Maqroll. The presence of danger, unspecified but obvious, plunged him into an all too familiar state of mind: ennui, a weary tedium that invited him to admit defeat, to halt the passage of his days, for they were all marked by the kind of venture in which someone else always profited, took the initiative, forced him into the role of the innocent dupe who served other people's purposes without realizing it. When he felt like this a bitter taste filled his mouth, there was a painful throbbing in his temples, his stomach rumbled. It was fear, the old fear that pounced with feline regularity, the fear he had felt in the Cocora mine, that waited for him in the rapids of the Xurandó, that crouched, ready to spring, in the hold of the *Lepanto,* the fear he had felt in Antwerp and Istambul, the fear he had felt all his life, in a rosary of sordid disasters and occasional, confounding moments of incomprehensible joy.

No one he knew was at the Álvarez Flat. He was received in the kitchen by a woman with the face of a Chinese mummy, whose words formed awkwardly in her toothless mouth: they had all left, but Don Aníbal said he should come in and rest and wait for him because he had something to tell him, and he shouldn't go down to the port without talking to him first. The others were at the cleared field in the mountains and wouldn't be back until tomorrow. Amparo María was up there too. The old woman smiled with a complicity that the Gaviero found unpleasant. He did not want to stay in the kitchen to drink his cup of coffee, and he took it, along with a plate of food that had been warmed by the old woman, to the room they had prepared for him. After he satisfied the hunger that had tormented him all day, the Gaviero lay down, and as he fell into a deep sleep, he again saw the mutilated words on the label he had found in the ravine: *Made in Czec* . . . He knew what it meant, but he could not or would not go any further with his conclusions. There was no railroad. It was a front for another venture whose gears could crush him at any moment, with no warning—typical of how he was so easily, so gratuitously caught off guard.

A light knock on the door woke him. It was still dark. He had slept for many hours and had no idea of the time. He went to the door and there was Don Aníbal, wrapped in an oilskin cape that reached to the floor and was still dripping rainwater. He had just dismounted and his horse was tied to the gallery railing. Beside him stood Zuro, who had arrived at the same time as the rancher and was still holding the lead for the pack of mules.

"Hello, my friend." Don Aníbal greeted him cordially, but his tone indicated concern. "I'm glad you've rested, because before daybreak we have a little business to take care of not too far from here. I'm sure you'll want to join me. You can learn some things to your benefit and ours. They're saddling a horse and finding a cape for you. The rain hasn't stopped since yesterday. I'll meet you at the gate. I have to leave some instructions. Zuro will take care of the mules and bring you the horse. I'll see you soon."

Zuro followed Don Aníbal after greeting the Gaviero with a gesture to show that everything had gone well. Maqroll went back to the room to dress, and before long the mule driver returned with the horse and a rain cape. Apparently Don Aníbal had guessed that the Gaviero was a less than mediocre rider, and he had chosen a gentle mare for him that was rather hard in the bit but very docile. Maqroll mounted with some trepidation, and Zuro handed him the cape, which he put on without delay. The torrential downpour gave no sign of letting up. The Gaviero met Don Aníbal at the entrance to the ranch; they rode out side by side, traveling a good distance in silence. The rain fell in huge drops, making an opaque sound whose rhythm grew more and more rapid. Maqroll asked where they were going. Don Aníbal gestured that it was better to wait and talk later. Inside one of the pockets in the cape the Gaviero found an oilskin cap similar to the ones used at sea during a storm. He put it on and suddenly had the feeling he was in the middle of the ocean. The water beat on his face in warm, intermittent showers that made him drowsy. At last Don Aníbal moved his horse closer to the mare and spoke in a low, deliberate voice.

"We're going to a place in the mountains to meet someone who wants to talk to you. I've known this person a long time and trust him completely. Some facts ahead of time: This person told me about your mule going over with the load, and the effort you made yesterday to recover it. An accident that might have cost you more dearly than it did. The vultures circling the corpse led them to the mule. They took the box to a safe place and opened it. It was double-crated. The wooden part was smashed when it fell into the ravine. They found a Czech AZ-19 submachine gun, the most modern and deadly automatic weapon made, one that's in great demand on the black market. You'll hear more about that in a minute. The railroad charade has been exposed, if we still had any doubts about that. But this situation won't be resolved so easily. I know you had nothing to do with it and were used because you don't know the country. That, and my sincere friendship for you, make me certain of your innocence. But I think he's going to ask for your cooperation, which will make it easier for you to get out of the jam those men have gotten you into. I ought to tell you too that I have nothing to do with any of this; my only interest is the safety of my people as well as my own, and doing all I can to keep the ranch. My brothers and I put most of our lives into it, and I have to move very cautiously. Our time of peace is over. The Army's already here and there'll be plenty of bloodshed. We know what that's like. I'll try to protect the ranch, but I'm not prepared to die for it. I don't want to end up like some of my people have. Didn't anybody warn you when you came to La Plata that this was a powder keg ready to explode?"

"I gathered as much from certain things that Doña Empera and other people told me, but I didn't pay much attention," said the Gaviero. "I've always thought that the only people in danger in times like these are the ones who look for trouble. I've been in similar circumstances in other parts of the world, and my lucky star always protected me. Obviously I put too much confidence in it when I decided to stay here, but it really doesn't seem to make any difference. I'm not as young as I used to be, and I allowed chance to carry me along. I'm tired of so much wandering. These struggles to change the world: I've seen them end either in a miserable dictatorship bloated with simplistic ideology applied with no less primitive rhetoric, or in a profitable business for a handful of cynics who always pretend to be disinterested, decent people committed to the welfare of the country and its inhabitants. In either case the dead, the orphans and widows, become pretexts for parades and ceremonies as sickening as they are hypocritical. The great lie built on grief. I knew about the wave of terrible violence in La Plata. I didn't care. Finding a reason to live is what's hard for me, not dying. La Plata seemed the ideal place to call a halt, if only for a while, to the nomadic life I've grown sick of. The bamboo bed in the blind woman's house, the river that flows under my room and helps me forget on those fearful nights when memories crowd around and demand a settling of accounts, the strength and complicity of alcohol in the tavern, my refuge when the struggle with myself becomes too difficult: it's all I ask of a place where nobody knows me and I have no debts to pay. But my guardian devil forces me to start idiotic ventures and get caught up in other people's affairs, to become involved with them and feel I own a small portion of their destiny. That's how I fell into this railroad business. For the past few days I've told myself over and over again that I've run into men like van Branden and his partners on the Tambo in every corner of the globe. They're always the same, the same tricks used exactly the same way, without the least originality, always the same wolfish greed that deceives no one. I must confess that deep down I never really swallowed the story about the railroad, and that's exactly why I got involved. Maybe I was secretly hoping I could satisfy my sinister guardian angel and end up like that mule."

"My friend, I think you exaggerate," was Don Aníbal's reply. "I see you in a very different light, and I must confess in turn that I not only feel affection and respect for you but also enjoy your experiences and your stories. They're like lessons for me. Don't forget, I've been stuck in these mountains and haven't known anything but the ravines and this climate fit only for alligators. I realize that your experience with the men on the Tambo has made you relive other situations like it. I think we all have our regrets. You're seeing everything now in a gloomy, hopeless light. But I've heard you tell stories from a time when you surely felt very different from the way you do now."

Don Aníbal's response to the Gaviero was entirely sincere. He thought Maqroll's life was an example of one rich in passion and unforeseen moments of every stripe, one utterly different from his own life, which often appeared to him as a dull and meaningless routine. They continued to discuss the subject, each maintaining his own opinion. The devastating rain and ominous clouds gathering over their immediate future played no small part in the grim colors with which each described his own destiny.

The rain stopped suddenly and the sky cleared, revealing the brilliant marvel of a tropical night. Everything was illuminated by the faintly phosphorescent light of the stars reflected on the wet leaves and in the puddles, whose glassy surface was shattered into a thousand lights by the horses' hooves. They entered a small stretch of woods that must have been familiar to the rancher, who quickened his pace. Maqroll followed, bouncing to the gentle trot of the mare he tried to control with clumsy, fruitless tugs on the reins. They had ridden some distance when Don Aníbal turned onto a path that took them down a small rise and ended in a thick stand of trees that seemed impenetrable. He stopped his horse and waited for a signal, and when he heard a brief whistle, he gestured to the Gaviero to dismount. They tied their horses to nearby trees and Maqroll followed Don Aníbal, who entered the dense woods, walking slowly but with the assurance of someone who knows the way. A man was waiting for them in a narrow clearing, sitting on the fallen, moss-covered trunk of a tree that had been struck by lightning. He stood up to greet them in a firm voice that suited his field uniform and the captain's insignia on the collar of his olive-green shirt. He invited them to sit on the log while he remained standing, his arms folded across his chest. The dim light revealed a lean, pale face, with several days' growth of beard that made him look ill. His energetic voice and gestures dispelled that first, false impression, but in his large black eyes, with their shadows of tension and fatigue, one could see the fluctuating feverish gleam of a man who is struggling to stay as alert as his strength will allow. Don Aníbal hastened to explain the situation to Maqroll.

"Captain Segura would like to talk to you. I want you to know that he's been our friend for a long time and you can speak freely. I've already told him about you. What's said here will determine if you can escape the situation you've unintentionally become involved in." Turning to the captain, he added, "On the way here I told him about the contents of the crate. It goes without saying he had no idea what he was carrying. Now it's your turn, Captain."

The captain began to pace the small clearing, passing his hand over his face from time to time as if to drive away sleep or shake off his exhaustion. His words had a military rigor that endowed them with particular gravity.

"We know almost all we need to know about you, my friend. Don Aníbal guarantees your conduct and your innocence, no easy thing to accept in light of your trips up to the Tambo Ridge. I have only a few questions. First, I want to know how many foreigners you've seen in the Tambo sheds."

"Two men when I was there. One says he's Belgian and the other, nicknamed Kraken, claims to be from Danzig. I didn't see any other foreigner up there." Maqroll wanted to be as precise and impersonal in his answers as the captain was in his questions.

"All right," said the captain. "The one who says he's from Danzig is a German, born in Bremen. He has some accounts to settle in Punta Arenas. He killed two police sergeants there when he tried to escape the prison where he was being held for smuggling. The Belgian is actually Dutch and was the one who bought the weapons in Panama City. Now, tell me, have you seen anything in the miners' cabin that attracted your attention, anything strange or unusual? Someone else sleeping there when you two did? Traces of anyone using it recently? Anything like that?"

"No, Captain," answered Maqroll, "we haven't seen anyone, or any sign that anybody was there. The cabin is always kept fairly clean, and nothing was out of place the times we slept there. Wait—now I remember, yes, they left me a note on a hook, telling me not to go on to the Tambo, to wait in the cabin for them to pick up the load. And yesterday the Dutchman came with his laborers and took it all away on mules, very good-looking ones at that." The Gaviero was recovering his poise as he spoke. He felt a spontaneous confidence in the captain, who radiated the assurance of a man who knows the ground he is covering and the people with whom he is dealing. Moreover, it was evident that any suspicion he might have had about Maqroll had vanished.

"The man who hired you for this work is thickset, with bulging, bloodshot eyes and a florid face; he's a great lover of drink, or at least that's what he pretends, and he says his name is van Branden or Brandon. Is that right?"

"Yes, Captain, that's right. I don't think he drinks all he pretends to either. Another thing, he's oddly casual about money. He doesn't want receipts for the money he gives or any account of expenses. I could never get him to tell me the exact amount I'd be paid for my work."

"That's understandable," said the officer, the ghost of a weary smile on his lips. "The man doesn't keep very good accounts with the people who hire him either. They're very lax about money in the weapons business; the margin of profit for each intermediary tends not to be fixed. His real name is Brandon; he's an Irishman with a record as long as your arm. he was arrested in Trinidad for writing bad checks; the English want him for white slaving in the Middle East; in Saudi Arabia he was left for dead after a beating that was ordered by a sheik he had tricked into buying two virgins from Alicante who turned out to be two whores from San Pedro Sula. As I said, the list goes on and on. The charges against him here are more serious. I can tell you this: you're not very likely to see him again. Let's move along. Is there another shipment in La Plata for you to take up to the Tambo, or is another on its way, as far as you know?"

"I left two crates in Brandon's room in La Plata. They were just like the ones I brought up the day before yesterday. I haven't heard about any others due to arrive." Maqroll felt the officer's eyes boring into his. The captain continued his pacing, somewhat more nervously. With a slight change of tone he asked: "Who else knows about those crates? Does Amparo María know anything about them?"

A dull anger began to grow in Maqroll. This invasion of his emotions made him feel that he was at the mercy of the armed forces' unlimited power. He had spent his whole life trying to avoid them. He attempted to keep his response brief.

"I don't believe she knows anything. Unless Doña Empera's said something to her. Obviously the blind woman knows everything about my climbs up to the Tambo."

"I'm sorry, I have to insist on asking an extremely personal question, but it's very important to me to know what to look for. You can't imagine the kind of people we're facing or what they're capable of. Your private life is clearly of no interest to me, but I'd like to know what you've told Amparo María about your work for Brandon." The captain was making a visible effort to have his question sound as routine as possible.

"I haven't said anything to her directly. She knows what everybody else does: that I climb up to the ridge with a pack of mules carrying crates that contain machinery and instruments for the railroad project. I haven't told her anything about Brandon or the Tambo sheds. Now, Amparo María talks to Doña Empera, and Doña Empera does know many details; I've discussed them with her. Her knowledge of the area and its people has been very helpful to me." Maqroll did not want to say more about the owner of the boardinghouse for fear he would compromise her.

"Doña Empera only talks about what she knows she should talk about, and I'm sure she's been very careful not to say more than was absolutely necessary to Amparo María or anybody else. All right, now I'm going to ask you to help us with something else. I don't think it's any more dangerous than what you've already done. Please listen carefully. I want you to continue with your work as if you didn't know anything. Pretend you and I have never met. Take up the two remaining crates and any others that may arrive on the boat that's due any day now. It will be your last trip. When you stop at Don Aníbal's ranch on your way up, he'll give you my instructions. Don't try to find out anything else about this. In La Plata don't show any curiosity about what you're carrying. The less you know the better. If you fall into their hands and they suspect you're hiding something, all I can tell you is that no matter how much you've traveled or how much experience you've had, you cannot imagine what they're capable of doing to find out what you know. They've been in this business for years and forgot mercy a long time ago."

"And if van Branden comes back, what do I tell him?" the Gaviero asked with a pretense of innocence the captain, of course, ignored.

"If you really want to know what happened to Brandon, I'll tell you right now it's not a good idea to ask. You'll find out at the right time, or maybe not. What difference does it make? For now, all you need to know is that you won't be seeing him again. All right, let's continue. In La Plata live the way you have up till now. Any change would arouse suspicions. Go to the tavern, pretend you're looking for Brandon. The place is a center for smugglers, and those people are always hanging around. Go down to the docks to find out when the boat is due. Keep reading to Doña Empera, go on seeing Amparo María. Don't do anything that could indicate the slightest suspicion on your part. Just keep displaying absolute innocence, absolute ignorance of everything related to the country, this region in particular. You may see some new faces in port. They may approach you and try to find out what's going on up on the ridge. Just tell the story about the railroad and never deviate from it. Don't tell anyone that you plan to leave La Plata. In short, continue to be the man Brandon hired. Naturally, don't ever say that name or show signs of recognition if someone happens to mention it. Finally, I want you to know that I'm telling you all of this more for your sake than ours, which doesn't mean that one false step by you won't cost us many lives. We can't afford that luxury right now. Is everything clear? Do you have any other questions?"

"Everything's clear, Captain. I've been in situations like this before, and I know how to take care of myself and watch what I say. Don't worry about me or your men. I understand the risks I'm running and the ones you have to face." A slight resentment began to churn inside Maqroll. He had always been irritated by the inability of men in uniform to imagine that a civilian can understand and confront certain aspects of a world they think lies exclusively within their domain.

Segura was lost in thought for a moment, as if he were preparing a response to Maqroll's words, but then he raised his hand to his cap and with a laconic "Good night, gentlemen" he turned and disappeared into the forest. The splash of his boots on the wet ground grew fainter until it disappeared, leaving no clue as to the direction he had taken. It was as if the night had suddenly swallowed him up, with all his military arrogance, his soldier's inexorable destiny.

On the way back to the ranch Don Aníbal wanted to discuss various points that the captain had omitted. The plan to transport weapons from the marine terminal to La Plata had been known from the start. Military Intelligence had immediately identified the crates in the customs warehouses, and the General Staff decided to follow the trail all the way to the men who received the weapons. By tracking Maqroll they had gotten as far as the Tambo depot. In the meantime Military Intelligence had gathered information about the foreigners who came into the country under cover of working for the supposed railroad. Some years ago Captain Segura had been in command of the unit stationed in the area; his men had suffered heavy casualties, and he was put in charge of the operation intended to capture whoever came for the arms stored in the sheds. In Don Aníbal's opinion, the Army was putting too much faith in the captain's plan. The weapons in the barrens were so important and expensive that there might be many more smugglers than Segura believed.

"I've made only two climbs," said Maqroll, "and no matter how modern and powerful those weapons are, I don't think they're enough to arm many people, though it is true there were other crates in the sheds."

"You were carrying the most complex and delicate ones," explained the rancher, "but they'd already transported a good amount of ammunition and light weaponry."

The Gaviero noticed that his friend did not want to say much more about this, but he asked Don Aníbal one last question.

"Who did the transporting?"

"People connected to Hakim the Turk. They disappeared when they were paid. I rented them the mules. It was my mistake. But they didn't want to buy the animals and I didn't want any problems. You can't imagine the tightrope you have to walk to stay out of the violence that's been going on for so many years."

"But does that mean you had problems with Captain Segura?"

"No," answered Don Aníbal, "not with the captain, no. He knows me very well and understood my attitude. But I did have trouble with Military Intelligence; in this area it's run by the Marines, and I think those people detest me. They don't know the meaning of moderation. If you take part in any suspect activity, knowingly or otherwise, you're a candidate for execution, and with no preliminaries."

"It's good then that Segura came back," replied the Gaviero.

"I don't know, I don't know," Don Aníbal went on in a bemused tone, as if he were thinking aloud. "If his plan works, there won't be any problems for a while. If it doesn't, he'll bring tragedy to all of us. I don't know who's worse, the Marines or the smugglers. For years they've been fighting each other all along this part of the river, but in the end their methods are the same: they use cruelty without anger, in cold blood, but with a professional refinement and imagination that grow more and more terrifying. Their law is the law of conquest: whoever lives here is guilty, period. And both sides enforce the law on the spot and move on to something else. God help us." A deep sigh ended his remarks, and the two men continued to ride in silence.

The Gaviero was becoming aware of the quicksand into which he had fallen. With inexcusable naïveté he had walked into the very heart of the devastating nightmare, and it did not seem likely that he would emerge unscathed. He pondered each step that had brought him to La Plata, the way he had been caught in van Branden's net. Everything appeared so simple, so feasible. Yet the man's clumsy deceptions were so transparent, and at their very first meeting Don Aníbal had told him his suspicions regarding the so-called railroad project. With a good deal of alarm Maqroll viewed the evidence of how his proven defenses against this kind of danger had weakened. His undertakings had always borne the mark of the illusory, of what eventually vanishes into ashes and scraps of paper blown by the wind. But until now he had also been careful to avoid the danger of gratuitous brutality, to keep in reserve an eleventh-hour escape. Without his realizing it these faculties had surely been undermined by the passing years, and he had fallen into a pit where death had established its dominion and was preparing its harvest of grief and pain. In his bones he felt the hopelessness of the vanquished.

"I can imagine what you're thinking," his companion said suddenly, disturbed by the Gaviero's gloomy silence. "The situation's serious, but not desperate. Do what Segura told you to. He represents a guarantee for you, and he's a man of his word. I know him very well. And when it's all over, get out as fast as you can. It doesn't matter where you go, just leave the area. I'll find a way to escape with my people if we have to. I can't ask you to come with us. As an outsider with no ties in the country, you'd complicate our escape and be in even greater danger. Get to the ocean—that's your salvation."

"It always has been, Don Aníbal. It's never failed me. Every time I try something inland it's a disaster. But it seems I never learn. It must be my age." Maqroll spoke with all the sorrow of his thoughts and awareness of his failing powers.

They returned to La Plata the next day. Zuro took the mules to the stable to feed them and rub them down with coconut oil to counteract the exhausting effects of carrying a load that had pushed them to the limits of their strength, while Maqroll greeted Doña Empera and went to his room. He wanted to be alone, to bring some order to his spirit, troubled by what had occurred on the trip and the gloomy prospect before him. Some hours later the blind woman delivered him from his thoughts. She knocked discreetly on the door, and Maqroll was pleased to see her. He wanted to discuss certain aspects of the situation with the landlady; he trusted her intelligence and her knowledge of the people in the area, and her judgments were always well-informed and dispassionately objective. The Gaviero was lying on the bed, and she sat down at the foot of the cot and waited for him to speak. She had sensed his desire to talk to her when he told her to come in. Maqroll asked about the crates under van Branden's bed. She answered that they were still there. No one had seen them, and she had the key to the room. Maqroll told her everything that had happened, including his conversation with Captain Segura.

"He's a rigid man, but loyal and discreet," she said. "I met him when they were here the last time, a few years ago. We became friends, and every once in a while I introduced him to women I knew who still remember him very fondly. You can trust him, and you should, but always keep in mind that he's a professional soldier, and when it's a question of loyalty to the service, he won't hesitate to do whatever he sees as his duty. If he told you he believes in your innocence, it's because he really is convinced, and he'll tell that to his superiors. And that's a safe-conduct for you. Your next trip will be very risky. There are smugglers up there now, and with the Army after them things can turn ugly at any moment. But you have no choice. Don't even think about getting away now, because Segura would never forgive you." The blind woman made a gesture to silence the Gaviero, who was about to say something, and she went on. "I know that hasn't occurred to you, but I wanted to warn you anyway because I know my people. Don't talk about this to Zuro. Or to Amparo María either. Incidentally, she told me to say she's coming tomorrow to spend a few days with you. Both of them, in their own way, are loyal and very honest. The girl thinks very highly of you, as if you were a father. She also appreciates you as a lover; don't think your reputation as an unrepentant vagabond has lost any of its charm for someone like her, who dreams of a life where everyone notices how beautiful she is."

Finally the Gaviero asked about van Branden and the arrival of the next boat, and if there were new patrons at the tavern and Hakim's shop. Again the blind woman advised, with affectionate insistence, that he limit himself to what Segura had asked him to do. If there were any new developments, she would tell him. When she was about to leave, she turned and handed him two envelopes. "I almost forgot. They came yesterday. I think they're your checks." They were, in fact, the drafts from Trieste, and Maqroll asked her to hold them until he came back from his next climb up to the Tambo.

He soon fell asleep, sinking into a sweet, enveloping slumber that emanated from the corner of his being where his connection to life, the world and its creatures, was still intact. It was dark when he awoke. The river flowed beneath his room in a gentle murmur disturbed by the occasional rippling sound of a tree trunk carried downriver by the current or of an animal swimming to shore. The heat had settled in after several days of constant rain, and he had no idea of the time. The silence that reigned in the settlement led him to assume it was well past midnight. He lit the candle, opened Joergensen's book on the saint of Assisi, and began to read. The peaceful tropical night and the serenely flowing water helped Maqroll to enter the beatific beauty of the medieval Umbrian landscape. As he had so often in the past under similar circumstances, he lost himself in the world evoked by the Dane, erasing the senselessness of the present and creating a rather antagonistic distance between himself and its insistent actuality.

When the first light of dawn filtered through the cracks in the bamboo and mud wall, and the sounds of an awakening town reached his ears, the Gaviero fell into another deep sleep. He woke at noon, fully recovered from the fatigue of the climb. In the kitchen Doña Empera had a light lunch waiting for him, and a huge cup of strong coffee that brought him back to the world of La Plata, but without the dark foreboding born, for the most part, of exhaustion and hunger. Maqroll went down to shower in the improvised stall located under the house, facing the river. He took his time, relishing the muddy water brought up to the storage tank by a hand-operated pump. Along with the mud there were iron particles suspended in the river water, which gave him the sensation of being in a medicinal spring. This was the source of the tonic, curative effect of his showers in Doña Empera's house. He shaved the four-day growth of beard that made him look like a defeated vagabond who would awaken more suspicion than necessary in the townspeople. Wearing a clean shirt and khaki trousers that had been pressed by Amparo María during her last visit, Maqroll went down to the dock to find out when the next boat was due. He was told it would arrive in two days at the latest. He went to the warehouse to see if they had received a manifest for the new cargo. They said the telegraph was down, perhaps because of the rain. He thought there might be another reason, but chose to make no comment. The Gaviero went up to the square and stopped at the tavern to have a beer, but found it closed. He questioned several passersby, but nobody knew why. He had the impression they were trying to avoid an answer. He did not sense concern or fear so much as reluctance to offer concrete details, as if no one wanted to be quoted later as the source of information it was safer not to know.

The boat did not arrive two days later, and Amparo María did not come to see him when she had said she would. He spent interminable hours stretched out on the bamboo cot, looking at the palm leaf ceiling and lulled by the water that flowed with a hurried, constant murmur under the floorboards in his room.

Perhaps in his desire to preserve a certain internal harmony that he was accustomed to defending at all costs, he began to feel indifference toward everything connected to the little world of La Plata, the surrounding area, its people, all of them about to succumb to a whirlwind of violence and terror. It seemed far away, a distant place where chaos reigned, beyond his own life and the tightly woven events and memories that constituted the true, unalienable stuff of his existence.

In order to fill the void left by his estrangement from a present he preferred to ignore, Maqroll used the idleness of his days and a good part of his nights to evoke the past. Lying there in bed, his hands crossed beneath his head, his gaze lost in the indecipherable, changing patterns on the ceiling, he recalled, one after the other, the episodes summoned by memory with apparent capriciousness but evidently intended to reveal to him the hidden design of his destiny. Occasionally a bat disengaged from the ceiling, swooped low over his head two or three times, then returned to its place with a squeaking like unoiled metal. One of the scenes relived during those hours of idleness and waiting came to him with particular fidelity, as if it carried a more pronounced revelatory purpose.

He remembered a voyage he had made with Ilona to Nizhni Novgorod, which had been rebaptized Gorki, a word they never pronounced, not because of animosity toward the great novelist but out of devotion to the ancient name of Holy Russia's renowned border port. They were going to see a collector of antique icons, and had been granted Soviet visas thanks to the intervention of a London art dealer who was interested in acquiring certain pieces that were very possibly in the possession of the Russian expert. They traveled down from the city of Peter the Great to Rybinsk, and there they took a riverboat up the Volga to Nizhni Novgorod. The ship was a vessel of shallow draft but colossal proportions, with three decks of cabins and "all the modern comforts of river navigation comparable to those enjoyed by travelers anywhere in the world," according to the brochure they found in their cabin. It was one of those summers that settle over Northern Europe and seem eternal, immutable, and disturbingly clear: the sky was metallic blue, without the trace of a cloud or the sign of a breeze, and they were pursued by huge horseflies whose sting was more like a ferocious, invariably shocking bite. The fan in the cabin was out of order despite its shining appearance. The ones mounted on the ceiling in the dining room did not work either. The immobilized blades, covered with decorations of doubtful *fin de siècle* taste, constituted a kind of cruel joke on the stifling passengers who, when they attempted to open the windows in search of a breeze, found to their surprise that the complicated latches were broken, perhaps from the very moment they had been installed. In relatively fluent Russian Ilona dared to comment in a voice loud enough for the captain, seated a few tables behind her, to hear clearly. "If the revolution has not succeeded in allowing a window to be opened, one can only assume it is a total failure. These poor Russians will die of asphyxiation before they ever achieve socialism." The consequences of his friend's bold remarks soon made themselves felt. At the next meal dishes reached their table long after the other passengers had been served, and everything was cold. There was no way to have the waiter bring a simple glass of water. They decided to buy several bottles of vodka at the ship's bar and get thoroughly drunk in their cabin. They made love as noisily and scandalously as they could. Ilona howled like a she-wolf in heat and Maqroll bellowed like a Hasid in a trance, shouting the most outrageous phrases in every language he knew. The tension caused by the couple's erotic sound show created so much uneasiness among the passengers, most of whom were timid, disciplined functionaries on vacation, that the captain was obliged to retreat. Four days after Ilona's comment in the dining room, a complete tea was sent to their cabin with pastries, Caucasian marmalades, and other delicacies not found on the ship's menu. Later the first mate, a Ukrainian as obese as a pope, with hair the color of corn and the rosy skin of an altar boy, knocked at the door. Ilona opened it, wrapped in a towel. Blushing to the roots of his hair, the first mate stammered the captain's invitation to join him that night for dinner in his cabin under the stars. They accepted, intrigued at what that might mean. They went to the captain's cabin at the time he had specified, and found a splendid supper served on a private balcony overlooking the deck at the prow. Four fans cooled the air and kept away the flies. They could not remember when they had eaten so much beluga caviar or smoked salmon, washed down with the finest vodka, served in bottles frosted with ice, and ending with a Georgian white wine chilled to perfection. Relations were reestablished in an atmosphere of mutual cordiality that was maintained for the rest of the voyage. Though it was somewhat tempered by the captain's attitude, the passengers still showed hostility toward the foreign couple. The collector in Nizhni Novgorod turned out to be a mediocre forger whose ingenuous falsifications would not have deceived the most avid buyer from Wichita Falls. For the return trip they chose the train that took them to Helsinki, after a ferry ride in the company of a large group of Russian tourists who looked forward to drinking all the vodka in Finland and not missing a single one of the rather prudish nude shows at the bars in port. From Helsinki they sent a fairly tame erotic postcard to the captain of the ship that sailed the Volga and dazzled the people along the river with its opulent appearance, thanking him for all his attentions. It was concealed, naturally, in a discreet envelope. They never heard from him, and Ilona claimed that he must have been sent to Siberia, not because of the postcard, of course, but for the sumptuous suppers in his seductive cabin, with its silver flowerpots hanging from silk-covered walls and *fin de siècle* purple velvet easy chairs that recalled the furnishings in the Tsarskoye Selo.

His faithful memory of the details of this trip with Ilona confirmed the importance in his life of the beautiful, intelligent woman from Trieste whose macabre death in Panama City still caused him pain—a refusal to accept destiny which did not diminish with the passing years. On the contrary, at the first signs of age he mourned even more deeply the absence of his irreplaceable companion and joyful accomplice. The soothing effect of the memories evoked by Maqroll in a hazardous present soon disappeared. A short time later Amparo María came down to La Plata, her large, dark eyes wider and more startled than ever, her wary feline walk emphasizing the curve of her waist, her haughty air unable to conceal the cheap dark percale dress that clung to her body like a second skin. Maqroll knew the girl's humble circumstances, but the contrast between that poverty and Amparo María's proud bearing, her gestures worthy of an exiled queen, always took him by surprise, and the disparity brought him an intense excitement, as if she had prepared the erotic effect with a refined sense of decadence, which, of course, she did not possess.

Amparo María explained that she could not come on the day she had promised because Don Aníbal had given orders to make preparations for an eventual departure from the ranch. Everything was done in the greatest secrecy. They had gone several times to certain places in the mountains to store food, clothing, riding gear, and other items they would need for a long, uncertain journey. The girl looked thinner and darker. The work must have been exhausting. But more apparent than fatigue was her constant watchfulness, which made her movements even more deliberate and her breathing more rapid and agitated. They closed the door; she undressed and lay down beside the Gaviero. They did not speak for a long time. He admired the Gothic proportions of this body that reminded him of ecstatic angels by El Greco or the shapes of women half glimpsed in dark corners of Algiers or Damascus. They made love in silence, with ritual slowness, as if they were celebrating an ancient exorcism, as if this were "Qedeshím qedeshóth," the poem by a friend of Maqroll's that depicted a Phoenician temple courtesan. It was not the first time those visionary strophes, so familiar and revealing to Maqroll, had come to him and given a name to the heights of pleasure.

Amparo María stayed with the Gaviero for two days, not leaving the room except to eat in the kitchen with the blind woman. She spoke very little, even less than before, and displayed an affectionate tenderness that was, Maqroll sensed, a premonition of inevitable separation. The boat had still not arrived, which made Maqroll uneasy; until now it had always come on schedule. Amparo María returned to the Álvarez Flat one rainy morning. As she said goodbye, tears ran down her dark, smooth cheeks, taut against the high cheekbones in the firm yet delicate design of the face that so aroused the Gaviero. They agreed to see each other at the flat on Maqroll's next climb. "I'll wait for you on the road. I always see you coming long before you reach the house. Be careful here. You know." The girl knew more than she had let on. It was to be expected, given her friendship with the blind woman and their confidence in her at the ranch. This mature, restrained discretion suited the natural haughtiness of her beauty. In this, too, she was akin to women like Ilona or Flor Estévez who had been so decisive in Maqroll's life. When he realized the similarity, he felt a piercing nostalgia for the years in his nomadic, contrary existence when he had been allowed to enjoy to the fullest the companionship and fervent solidarity of those exceptional women.

Maqroll was awakened one day at dawn by the muffled whistle of the boat approaching the dock. He stayed a while longer in bed, as if trying to delay the moment he would have to face the hostile reality waiting for him, and decided to go down to the river in the hottest part of the day. Almost all the cargo for La Plata had already been unloaded. The Gaviero went to the warehouse and looked for a crate that resembled the ones he had taken to the Tambo. He found nothing and was about to leave, when the warehouse manager called to him. A mestizo wearing a sailor's hat that had once been white and was now an unidentifiable mix of grime and stinking sweat, the man knew him from the other times he had gone there to pick up cargo.

"Looking for something, my friend?" he asked with irritating familiarity.

"The same as always. Something sent by a man named van Branden," answered the Gaviero, looking into the purulent eyes examining him with malice and suspicion.

"Van Branden? Oh, sure. There are two crates here for you. They were unloaded before anything else. They're here in the shade. Have to keep them out of the sun, you know? They're for the railroad, right? Sure, sure. Come on, here they are." He pointed to two crates at the far end of the storage shed. Each word he said distilled a double meaning filled with hidden significance.

Maqroll picked up the boxes. They were not very heavy. In

addition to the wooden frame, they were wrapped in metallic paper with red markings that had been covered over with black paint in some places. The man did not give him a receipt, and his only comment was: "Be careful with them. They have to be kept in the shade, and they can't be banged around. It says here they should be delivered as soon as possible to the addressees on the Tambo Ridge. So now you know. Have a good trip." Everything was beginning to move with alarming speed. It was certain the man knew all about the farce of the railroad, and probably a good deal more about the cargo destined for the barrens.

The Gaviero decided to carry the two crates himself, without the help of the boys who came down to the docks whenever a boat arrived. As soon as he saw the crates, he knew what they contained. He had learned about explosives at the Cocora mine, handling them for over a year in the struggle to retrieve ore from blocked, exhausted tunnels. Although someone had tried to erase the printing, the packing and handling instructions clearly indicated TNT. Each crate probably held at least twelve sticks in protective gelatin and the same number of caps in a small cardboard container. No joke, he thought, if a mule walking along the precipice banged one of the crates into the rocks that protruded from the sheer wall and barely left enough room for the animals to pass. But despite this new risk added to old familiar dangers, his basic feeling was a certain indifference, a sense of relief at finally knowing what he would carry on his last trip and what was really behind the lie of the railroad. With everything clarified his spirit felt lighter, and he even took some pleasure in accepting the challenge. The serenity of a gambler holding on to his chips settled over him, renewing the taste for adventure that had been lost in the web of shoddy lies and deceptions in which he had felt himself trapped by van Branden, or Brandon, or whatever his name was. And certainly all the signs indicated that the wretched man was now *ad patres*.

Amparo María had said that Zuro could not accompany him on the first day's climb from La Plata to the Álvarez Flat because Don Aníbal had put him in charge of hiding provisions in the mountains in the likely event they would have to escape. Despite

Captain Segura's instructions, then, he had no choice; he would have to ask someone in La Plata to help him load the mules. Doña Empera, as always, came to his rescue. She hired the retarded son of the woman who owned the primitive bakery that supplied the region with a bread Maqroll always considered inedible. The boy worked as a messenger in the settlement although he spoke with difficulty. It was not easy to understand his messages, delivered in a shower of saliva and a weaving of his head that made the recipient dizzy. As often happens in such cases, the unfortunate creature was surprisingly strong, and this brought him respect in La Plata, where even the roughest stevedores on the dock were afraid of him.

The night before his departure Maqroll had a long conversation with the landlady. The risk he was taking on this final climb was clear. He left instructions in case he lost his life: she should wire the bank in Trieste that sent him the checks; keep the two books he was leaving behind, which some French-speaking guest could read to her eventually; burn his clothing and all the papers he kept in an oilskin pouch at the bottom of his suitcase, without showing them to anyone; tell Amparo María that knowing her was a final, splendid gift from the gods. Maqroll ended by settling accounts and paying his bill, and then he went to bed in order to be up at dawn the next day.

The blind woman woke him at first light to say that the boy had come to help with the animals. She had brought him a cup of black coffee and some yuca biscuits for the road. The Gaviero got up and went out to supervise the distribution of the crates and their placement on the panniers. Under the blind woman's direction the boy had already carried the boxes from Brandon's room down to the stable. The Gaviero showed him the two he had in his room and told him to handle them with utmost care. When the mules were ready and the crates of TNT had been covered with a layer of corn husks wrapped in a tarpaulin to protect them from the heat, the Gaviero paid the baker's son. He was sorry he could not take him along, at least as far as the Álvarez Flat, because he was very good at handling the animals, but in the event of a dangerous encounter he would be more of a hindrance than a help. The Gaviero was ready to leave, and he went to say goodbye to the blind woman. Maqroll began to speak, but Doña Empera interrupted him.

"You'll come back. I know. I still have something very interesting to tell you. When you come back. And then you should get out as fast as you can. It'll be a bloodbath. I'll take care of arranging everything. Now, take good care of yourself, don't do anything stupid, don't push yourself too hard, and keep your eyes open. I'll be waiting for you here. Goodbye." The woman hurried back to her kitchen, knocking her cane nervously against the wall to find her way.

When he was on the road, the blind woman's words came back to him, communicating the dark certainty that he would survive; at the same time her promise to tell him something that he would find especially interesting made him uneasy. He was afraid of unexpected news, piercing information that would disturb certain areas of his past he preferred, at least for the moment, to keep inviolate and shadowy. When the mules stopped to drink at a stream, just before the climb up to the Álvarez Flat, the landlady's promise was so present that the critical dangers of this last trip to the barrens receded into the background. Even his probable meeting with Amparo María and the pleasure of holding her in his arms were obscured by a fog of old melancholy.

At the ranch he found only a few old women, along with three or four sick children who could not travel; Don Aníbal and his people had left for the mountains on the previous day. Zuro would come for them and the children tomorrow so they could join the rest. One of the old women, who lived with Amparo María's aunt and uncle, came up to Maqroll and whispered: "The girl left a message saying not to forget her and to leave as soon as you can. She needs you but would rather know you're alive than being hunted down around here. And she says be careful."

He had feared that no one would be on the flat. He accepted their absence, however, thinking that it was better this way; his friends were safe, and this made him feel more prepared for the next, more dangerous stage of the trip. The women helped him unload the mules and gave him something to eat. He decided to sleep in the stable along with the cargo.

In the morning the same women helped him load the animals again. He gulped down a cup of coffee and started the climb to the miners' cabin. This part of the trip held the greatest risk: Both the Army and the smugglers were patrolling the area, but moving explosives through the narrow passes was a more immediate and certain danger. If they were banged into the cliff, with its menacing overhangs of rock, it would mean the end. He knew from his experience at Cocora that handling explosives, no matter how carefully it was done, could always bring fatal surprises. The cold only had to harden the protective gelatin and the movement of the mules would knock the sticks against each other, or the boxes containing the caps could open and they would begin to roll around the sticks, and then the risk of explosion would increase dangerously. When he was caretaker at the mine, he had often seen entire packs of mules fly into the air, along with their cargo and drivers, and the cause of the accident was never known. He remembered the last words of the old watchman who left him his job when he died. "Watch out for the dynamite, boy. It's like a woman—you never know why or when it's going to explode."

Furthermore, Zuro's absence made the task of getting the mules past the precipices overwhelming. He would have to see if he could manage it. In the meantime he began chewing on the wordless foreboding that he would never see Amparo María again. Since his last time with her, the days she had stayed with him in La Plata, the girl had joined Ilona and Flor Estévez in a kind of benevolent trio, complicitous and loyal, necessary and gratifying, who filled his days with meaning and exorcised the demons of tedium and defeat whose attacks he feared as he feared death. Each in her own way, through one of those quirks of fate so frequent in the Gaviero's life, had been torn from him as suddenly and violently as animals lose their mates. What linked him to the girl from the Álvarez Flat had more to do with her extraordinary bearing and the ancient beauty of her Mediterranean features than with any trait of her character, whose rather absent, restrained sweetness contrasted with Flor Estévez's devastating explosions of passion or Ilona's acerbic, demanding humor. He was sure now that Amparo María had moved definitively into the realm of his past. She had been the last opportunity offered by life to hold in his arms the inexhaustible miracle of a woman's body marked by the grace of the gods.

At the start of the precipices he removed the lead that joined the team of mules, and allowed each animal to move ahead by itself, calculating a prudent distance between them so that they climbed separate from the others. He knew that after awhile the mules would all move together again, but he hoped this would not happen until they had passed the walls of protruding rock. The animals, accustomed to the procedure on the previous climbs, behaved as the Gaviero had expected. The lead mule carried a crate of explosives, the next two carried the automatic weapons, and the last had the second crate of TNT. But when this one came to the sheer drop, it balked, digging all four feet into the ground. It was pointless to use the whip to force the animal to go on, for if the mule shied at all, it would bang into the rocky wall. In the end Maqroll had to carry the crate himself. He led the other three animals ahead, and the recalcitrant mule followed with no further resistance. Using the greatest caution, Maqroll began the climb, testing each step of the way, since the box in his arms prevented him from seeing the trail. The wind, forced into the narrow passes, gave a long sob and fled to the sierra, closely pursued by the fog that was also escaping to the mountain peaks. When he had crossed the dangerous stretch, the Gaviero set the crate at the side of the trail and leaned against some rocks at the base of the cliff to catch his breath. His heart was pounding wildly and a band of pain squeezed his temples with growing intensity. He closed his eyes, began to take in air, and tried to relax, until he lost all notion of where he was. Once again his years were making their presence felt with a brutal eruption of symptoms that still caught him off guard, as if he had never known them before. He thought that the real tragedy of aging lay in the fact that an eternal boy still lives inside us, unaware of the passage of time. A boy whose secrets had been revealed with notable clarity when Maqroll withdrew to the Aracuriare Canyon, and who claimed the prerogative of not aging, since he carried that portion of broken dreams, stubborn hopes, and mad, illusory enterprises in which time not only does not count but is, in fact, inconceivable. One day the body sends a warning and, for a moment, we awake to the evidence of our own deterioration: someone has been living our life, consuming our strength. But we immediately return to the phantom of our spotless youth, and continue to do so until the final, inevitable awakening.

The mules stopped next to him with the serene indifference of animals that do not know they are mortal. A distant sound, like the crack of dry branches breaking, came from the sierra. The mules all raised their heads at the same time. It took the Gaviero a moment to realize it was the scattered firing of automatic weapons. Immediately after that he heard intermittent bursts of fire, undoubtedly from the same source. Then two booming explosions echoed down the ravine. They sounded like bazookas or high-powered grenades. He stood up, loaded the crate of explosives onto the resistant mule, and hurried to finish the climb up the slope and reach the miners' cabin as soon as he could. An unexpected sense of relief lightened his step. What he had feared so much was finally here. Uncertainty had ended, and with it the anxiety that deforms and poisons everything. Once again men had begun the dark work of summoning death. Everything was in order. Now he would try to get out alive. He would not play their game. The firing stopped. At the top of the slope, not far from the cabin, he heard an explosion much louder than the earlier ones. There, at the summit on the Tambo Ridge, a thick column of black smoke was piercing the fog with sudden fury. Maqroll continued on his way. He had resolved to leave the crates in the cabin. The Tambo sheds had just been blown to bits and were being consumed by a raging, explosive fire. He would return immediately, even if he had to climb down the precipices in the dark. The mules were skittish and unwilling to continue along the flat trail that led to the shelter. Patiently, trying to quiet them with soothing words, the Gaviero managed to keep them going. He reached the cabin late in the afternoon. From time to time he still heard distant shots in the barrens. He arranged the crates inside the cabin, taking care that the explosives were far from each other and from the fireplace even though the hearth was dark and cold. He led the animals to the stable to feed them. When he opened the sack of corn that was always kept there, he found a piece of stationery with the letterhead torn off. A message was printed in purple ink: "Leave the crates here and go back to the river right away. Disappear." He was almost certain it came from Captain Segura.

Suddenly he was famished. The final effort of carrying the crate of TNT had left him exhausted. But he started out immediately to take all possible advantage of the afternoon light. Maqroll put the four mules on the same lead so they would all climb down together and he would not have to tend to them one by one. He began to gnaw on one of the yuca biscuits that the blind woman had given him for the journey, but could not produce enough of his thick, bitter saliva to soften what was in his mouth. The Gaviero did not swallow until he found a small trickle of water beside the trail, and then he sat down and devoured all the biscuits, which gave him the strength to continue the descent. His dry mouth and the verbena taste of the thick saliva he had to spit out constantly indicated the presence of fear. They knew each other very well. The symptoms were familiar. Again he felt a certain relief. Fear was his old ally, made to the measure of his astuteness and self-protection. Living with fear was routine for Maqroll, a challenge that returned him to times in his life when his strength still followed him with unerring obedience.

When they reached the precipices, the mules stayed in line and showed no reluctance to face the difficulties of the trail. But they occasionally twitched their ears as if they perceived a distant danger. The moon began to climb the clear, calm sky with serene, almost conciliatory slowness. Fatigue and hunger forced Maqroll to mount the mule at the end of the train in spite of the fact that riding it was extremely uncomfortable and his talents as a horseman were nonexistent. He constantly shifted position, trying to avoid the prongs meant to keep loads in place. The Gaviero began dozing for short periods of time, waking when the animal took a false step or started down a steep slope. His mind was a blank. Exhaustion and a longing for hot food anesthetized his memory. The road flattened and the mules began a hurried trot. They knew that the Álvarez Flat, the warm stable, and their ration of corn were waiting for them. The Gaviero decided to continue on foot. Riding the mule made his bones ache and caused a sick dizziness he had never felt at sea. He reached the ranch after midnight. There was no sign of life in the main house or in the tenants' shacks. He led the mules to the stable, and while he was feeding them, he heard a door squeak in the ranch house. He went out to see who it was and found himself face-to-face with Don Aníbal, who was waiting for him at the bottom of the stairs and holding up a Coleman lamp to light his way.

"I'm so glad to see you. I was worried about you. The shooting started up there yesterday afternoon and we didn't know where you were when it began." Maqroll was moved by the rancher's affectionate concern.

They went into the kitchen. Don Aníbal invited him to help himself to the supper that had been waiting for him for several hours. He ate with an appetite that made Don Aníbal smile. As Maqroll was drinking his coffee, his strength restored, he asked for the latest news.

"My people have left for the mountains," said the rancher. "Tomorrow before dawn I'll go to join them. Zuro is coming with me to bring up horses for the women and children and a couple of sick men who can hardly walk. You heard the shooting yesterday, didn't you? It's begun and it doesn't look good. The Army is trying to cut off the men who came for the weapons and explosives on the Tambo. Today they'll go to the cabin to capture whoever picks up the crates you brought yesterday. But something really worries me. The final explosion last night must have been in the Tambo sheds. Did you hear it?"

"Yes, señor, I did, and I think it came from the sheds too," replied the Gaviero.

"I don't like that at all," continued Don Aníbal. "It's a bad sign. If the smugglers blew up the sheds, it means they have enough weapons and can count on replacements from other areas where they're virtually in control. Segura's force isn't very big. They're very well trained but there are no more than thirty men plus a lieutenant and three noncommissioned officers. Maybe they'll finish off the foreigners and everything else on the Tambo, but if more men attack them, they'll be in trouble. All I can do now is hope the shortcut through the mountains that we plan to use is kept clear. If they came in that way to surprise

Segura, we're finished. But I have to take the risk. There's no other way out."

"Why don't you leave through La Plata?" asked Maqroll. "It's easier and closer."

"No, my friend, it isn't easier," explained the rancher. "If they ambush the Army, they'll attack the port and that'll be the end. Besides, I have no way to get my people out on the river. The two or three barges in La Plata aren't enough; they can carry only three or four people at most, and they're not in good shape." He looked at the Gaviero in silence, and then he continued: "Tomorrow at the latest you must get out of La Plata however you can. Preferably at night. Even if it's in a canoe and you only take what's on your back. Captain Segura will fight for at least two more days. They're very seasoned men, lots of battle experience. They've been fighting for years. You have time, and Doña Empera can help you. She knows the people in town very well, and they respect her. All right. Go to sleep now. Don't worry. You have no past here. You have nothing to worry about."

"I don't know, Don Aníbal. I transported those weapons, and that can cost me dear. I'm afraid the Army doesn't believe I'm innocent. As for the other side, they'll be very interested in keeping me quiet."

"Segura believed you. You can sleep easy. Tomorrow is another day. When you're tired, everything looks black."

Maqroll said good night and went to sleep in a room that the rancher said was ready for him. The bed was soft, the sheets cool and clean. It had been a long time since he had enjoyed such luxuries. He slept soundly.

At first light Don Aníbal knocked at the door. "Wake up, my friend. The coffee's ready and there's some reheated supper. You have to get to La Plata as soon as you can. The shooting began again this morning. It sounded as if it came from the miners' cabin."

Maqroll got up and ate breakfast with Don Aníbal. Then he went to the stable for the mules. When he led them out to the front of the ranch house, Don Aníbal and Zuro were waiting for him, mounted on horseback and leading two other animals by the halter. Few words were exchanged in an effort to conceal the emotion of a leavetaking so filled with uncertainty. The Gaviero thanked Don Aníbal for his friendship and help, and shook his hand warmly. He did the same with Zuro, and said, "I don't think we'll see each other again, Zuro. But I want you to know you were an exemplary companion. I know what you're worth, and I won't forget you. Good luck, boy. Say hello to Amparo María for me and tell her I'll always remember her. Don Aníbal, good luck to you, and thank you again for everything."

"It was a pleasure, my friend," answered Don Aníbal with a restrained, melancholy smile. "Good luck. We're all going to need it. God bless you." He spurred his horse and galloped off, followed by the mule driver, who led the other two horses. Maqroll watched them disappear up a narrow trail that ran from the ranch into the foothills of the sierra. He went down to the coffee groves and walked through them, overwhelmed by a sadness that was composed of longing for the girl with her air of a temple courtesan, affection for his two friends who were facing mortal danger, and nostalgia for the hotlands that he was perhaps leaving forever.

At the boardinghouse Doña Empera was waiting for him, her agitation revealed in the way she ran her hands through her graying hair and in the slight trembling of her head. The Gaviero recounted the events of the trip and his farewell to Don Aníbal and Zuro. Doña Empera let him tell his story. When he was finished, she sat on her chair and, constantly rubbing her knees—a typical gesture when she wanted someone to listen very carefully—said: "You have to leave. The sooner the better. I'll tell you how we'll arrange it. I talked to a compadre of mine who has a barge he wants to sell. His name is Tomás Izquierdo, but everybody calls him Tomasito. He used to have a lot of money, but he lost it gambling. All he has left is a shack along the river and a barge with a diesel motor. He used it to transport goods along the river to places not far from here, but the fever made him take to his bed, and he can't do anything now. I arranged things with him. He's ready to trade the barge for the mules and little cash. You still must have some of the money the Belgian gave you, and you have the two checks I kept for you. I think it'll be enough, and you'll even have something left over for the trip. Go see the barge early tomorrow. You have to check the motor because it hasn't been run for at least four months.

The hull has more patches than a hen, but it sails all right. You can get to the estuary with it. Tomorrow we'll find out what happened up in the barrens. For now, get a little rest and put your things in order."

The Gaviero accepted the blind woman's plan and said he preferred to go to see Tomasito right away and speed up preparations for whatever work needed to be done on the barge. "You can't go now," said Doña Empera, "because a nephew of his is with him and he can't be trusted. He's known to be an informer and it seems he works for both sides. But at dawn he's going back to the avocado groves he owns upriver. Don't rush. Everything will be taken care of tomorrow. We have a couple of days before things come to a head."

Inaction weighed on the Gaviero and made the trap he had fallen into seem even more deadly. He went out to the clearing that faced the river. The tavern was closed. He returned to his room and tried to lose himself in the letters of the prince of Ligne. The unfailingly elegant and intelligently sober prose of this great nobleman, diplomat, and lover, had an immediate tranquilizing effect. All his attention was directed to the early nineteenth century, when, as Talleyrand said, those who had known the sweetness of living in the twilight of the *ancien régime* still gave lessons in good manners, serene skepticism, and cynical judgment of the changes imposed by politics. No more effective balm for his current perplexities than the example of the great Belgian aristocrat who, with constant good fortune and an amiable smile, had escaped the Jacobin scaffold, the vigilance of the Vienna police and the black cabinet, and the deadly ambushes of the tsar's court. Maqroll's ability to enter fully into another time, a world so foreign to the present, had often saved him from succumbing to the tribulations brought on by his nomadic calling. The serenity he regained led to drowsiness, and without undressing he fell into a deep sleep on the bamboo cot, lulled by the flow of water beneath his room.

He woke very early the next day. During breakfast in the kitchen the blind woman said, "My compadre is alone now, and the barge is ready for you to look at. You remember, his name is Tomás Izquierdo but we all call him Tomasito. His shack is along the water in a banana grove, past the warehouse, where the

Duende stream flows into the river." The Gaviero started out, walking past the row of whitewashed houses with palm roofs that made up the shabby little settlement, built and named during the mining fever that lasted so short a time. Not a soul was on the street; all the windows were closed; no sound was heard in the houses, which were usually brimming over with the noise of children and the shouts of women calling to one another from one yard to the next as they washed clothes or prepared food. Everyone had to be awake: the heat got them out of bed very early. Fear hovered over the village, an imprecise, vague fear that was finally resolved into the silent waiting of those who know that a disaster is fast approaching.

When Maqroll reached Tomasito's cabin, the owner was waiting for him on a reed chair, leaning against one of the beams that held up the roof of the hut. There were no walls. A hammock hung inside, and under it slept a dog that woke when it heard a strange voice. "Quiet, Kaiser!" shouted the old man. The dog went back to sleep in resignation. Tomasito was a man of indeterminate age. He could as easily have been fifty as ninety. The climate had so weathered him that in certain places his skin stuck to his bones, and in others it hung yellow and lifeless. He rolled an unlit cigar with mechanical regularity from one side of his toothless mouth to the other. His eyes contained all the life that seemed to have withdrawn from the rest of his wasted, trembling body. Black, intense, inquisitive, with a restless, dizzying mobility of expression, they seemed to burn with a flame that flickered in the ashes of a dying fire. Tomasito invited the Gaviero to the river to look at the barge. They climbed down a muddy bank worn away by the footsteps of many people. The water slowed here, held back by a wall of reddish earth that extended several meters into the water. The barge, tied to a section of railing, was no more than eight meters long and three meters wide. The flat keel, covered with soldering and patches, rocked in the current with a monotonous splashing sound. Four rusted rods were fixed to the sides of the barge and supported two sheets of tin that were stained with bird droppings and the sap from a great mango tree growing on the riverbank. Tomasito explained that the fuel tank was empty and the battery was in his comadre Empera's house. They went for the battery and bought four gallons of diesel at Hakim's store. At first the Turk refused to open the door, but when he heard the blind woman's voice he hurried to let them in, although the look on his face was unfriendly. "If he wants any women, he has to wait on us. He knows that." Doña Empera's comment required no further explanation.

They installed the battery and filled the tank with fuel. The engine turned over after several tries. "The timing has to be adjusted. It won't get very far this way," said the Gaviero. The old man agreed and they began to work under a punishing sun. When they had finally tuned the motor, Maqroll realized that the propeller was not balanced, making it impossible to go downriver or control the barge in very low water. Tomasito said he had another propeller, but that was in Doña Empera's house too. They picked it up, and by the time it was installed, night had fallen, coming suddenly as it does in the tropics. The Gaviero returned to Doña Empera's house to pack his few belongings. As he approached he heard voices in the kitchen and knew from their tone that the subject was serious. He went in and saw a boy sitting on a rush chair, his eyes bulging, his body trembling as if he were suffering an attack of malaria. His shirt was stained with blood, his arms and knees covered with it. Doña Empera sat in her chair, her face turned toward the body. A marble pallor had frozen her features in an expression of the terror that only the blind can feel in the darkness of their impotence. The Gaviero asked what had happened. The blind woman could manage only a few words. "It's Nachito, Amparo María's cousin. Up there . . . in the mountains . . . all of them. Tell him, son, tell the man. You're safe here. Tell him . . ." But it was evident that the unfortunate child could not speak a coherent sentence. The blind woman told Maqroll that from what she could gather, the boy brought terrible news. The Gaviero's presence helped to calm her, and she was able to quiet the boy until he had almost stopped sobbing. The tears ran down his cheeks and fell onto the shirt stained with dried blood.

The boy's story lasted almost an hour. He would return to certain details and suddenly begin to tremble again, and his voice would break. Don Aníbal and his people had been ambushed in the middle of the forest; men were waiting, apparently with the kind of automatic weapons used by the smugglers, firing round after round until they were all lying in pools of blood. After the first rounds the women and children who were still alive were screaming. A final volley, from closed ranks, silenced them forever. Nacho was hugging the body of his father, one of the first to fall, his chest blown open. Terror paralyzed the boy, and he lay there for several hours, unmoving and silent. His father's death agony had not lasted long. He heard the sound of running feet that disappeared into the densest part of the forest, and distant, occasional words he could not understand. Hours later he fled, panic-stricken, through a pass he usually took down to La Plata. He had waited all afternoon on the outskirts of the village; he did not dare show himself by day looking the way he did. When it was dark, he resolved to come to Doña Empera's house; he knew her because he had carried messages for her.

When Nacho finished his story, Gaviero had the boy sit beside him. He stroked his hair, unable to say a word. He felt a crushing pity that centered on the boy's frail, thin body and then extended gradually, and even more painfully, to all his people who had been cut down with the cold, gratuitous cruelty of which only our species is capable. Faces, words, gestures, laughter, brief family histories of the residents on the Álvarez Flat, crowded his memory. The brutality of the pointless massacre was impossible for him to understand or accept. The intensity of the pain it caused him became physical, piercing his body like a stab wound, overwhelming him. The blind woman took Nacho away to change his clothes and wash off the dried blood that covered his body. She lay down beside him in the small hammock where the boy slept when he had to spend the night in La Plata.

Maqroll tried for several hours to come to a decision. It was unthinkable to leave now. He would wait until the next morning, when Doña Empera had regained some control of herself. The friendly presences of the people sacrificed in the forest encircled him again: Amparo María, with her air of a maja by Goya and her love without master or issue; Don Aníbal Álvarez, a nobleman on his land, loyal and just with his friends, resigned and fatalistic like the Knight of the Green Coat in *Don Quijote;* Zuro, intelligent, faithful, stubborn, independent, with his inexhaustible resources in the barrens. And so many other nameless faces of hospitable, amiable people: all slaughtered by anonymous men whose habit of killing had become their only reason for living. Demented jackals, ready to take orders from those above them who work the puppet strings of implacable greed. If he stayed where he was, Maqroll knew that his despair would increase. He carried his chair to the balcony and watched the river, its indifference to the age-old vileness of men and their calamitous vocation for sacrifice. The silence was broken from time to time by the sudden shriek of a bird that had lost its way, or the sound of water whirling around the eddies in the current. Only the stars tried in vain to penetrate the heavy fog. The moon had long since gone into hiding. Something mournful and funereal hung in the air. Or perhaps the Gaviero's spirit imposed on the night the taste of death and destruction knotted in his throat. He went back to bed before daybreak to try to sleep. The first stage of his journey downriver, filled with hidden, unpredictable dangers, still lay ahead of him.

He was sleeping soundly when the deafening roar of engines raged over the roof of the house. He sat bolt upright in bed, panic-stricken. He managed to control his terror and ran to the balcony; at that moment two gray Catalina seaplanes with Marine insignias on the wings landed on the river in quick succession. An orderly, silent line of troops wearing gray field uniforms and gray helmets were filing from two large Marine lighters moored at the dock. They were supervised by officers who barked curt orders at the men as they disembarked. The planes made fast beside the barges, the doors opened, and officers from various services climbed down: physicians in the uniform of the Medical Corps, captains from the Quartermaster Corps carrying briefcases and portable typewriters, men from Military Intelligence, unmistakable in their civilian dress of white guayaberas and light tan trousers. The Gaviero knew immediately that his plan to leave that morning had been ruined. But he decided to attempt it anyway. He gathered together a few things and packed them in the knapsack that Doña Empera had given to him. With a silent, close embrace he took his leave of the blind woman, who repeated like a sleepwalker, "Hurry, for God's sake, hurry." She blessed him, whispering incantations, calling on all the saints in an incomprehensible mix of languages. Maqroll left the suitcase with the rest of his clothing and papers, telling Doña Empera to burn everything in the event he was killed. When he reached Tomasito's shack, the old man was waiting for him, his eyes wilder and more feverish than ever. "Be careful, señor. You can't fool around with the Marines. They come here to impose law and order, and they know exactly how to do it." Maqroll gave him the cash they had agreed on as partial payment for the barge. The mules were in the stable and the blind woman had been instructed to give them to Tomasito. The Gaviero tossed his bag onto the deck and jumped in. The motor started up immediately. The old man untied the mooring lines and said goodbye with a wave that had in it something of a desperate blessing.

With the engine at half speed Maqroll moved the barge to the middle of the current and began an unhurried descent downriver, looking with feigned indifference at the opposite bank, as if he were letting it be known that he simply intended to cross the river. As he passed the military lighters, a voice came over a loudspeaker mounted on the roof of the bridge on one of the craft. "Where do you think you're going? You, on the barge, turn around right now! Here, alongside. Yes, you!" The peremptory tone was amplified a good distance in a brutal, paralyzing echo. As unhurriedly as before, the Gaviero obeyed the orders and moved alongside the lighter, where several soldiers who were waiting on deck signaled to him and helped him aboard. Two of them jumped into the smaller barge and took it to where the Catalinas were anchored—downriver, at the end of the settlement. A sergeant gestured to the Gaviero to walk ahead, pointing to a cabin with its door open, and following close behind without saying a word. When he walked into the cabin, the Gaviero saw an officer bending over some maps spread out before him on a small table mounted to the wall. For a few seconds that seemed like hours to Maqroll the officer took measurements with a compass. When he finally looked up, the sergeant saluted and said, "Your orders have been carried out, Captain." The officer took off a pair of rimless glasses as he answered, "You can go." Then he stared at Maqroll as if he were trying to focus his eyes. They were an intense blue that seemed to fade in the reflected light. His close-cropped, graying-blond hair was thinning in front and made him look more like a bank executive than a soldier. He wiped his glasses with a handkerchief, a purely reflexive gesture, and spoke to the Gaviero in a deep voice that in no way matched his appearance.

"I'm afraid you're the person who carried automatic weapons and explosives acquired on the Panama black market up to the Tambo Ridge. Your name is Maqroll, if I'm not mistaken, but you're also known as the Gaviero. You came here recently, and I don't believe all your papers are in order. Am I correct?" There was a distant courtesy in his words and movements, as if he wanted to establish a strict separation from Maqroll. It was probably his usual attitude, totally unconscious, acquired in officer-training courses.

"Yes sir. You're correct. But I'd like to clarify something with regard to what you said about the weapons." The Gaviero replied with a serenity that came from his resignation to what he had feared for so long.

"This clarification, as you call it, does not have to be made to me. The proper persons will interrogate you in due course. For now, I want to inform you that you are detained under the extraordinary powers granted the armed forces during the state of siege." When he finished speaking these words in a routine official tone, the captain gave an order to the sergeant who had brought in Maqroll and was waiting just outside the cabin: "Call the guard on duty." There was the immediate sound of hurried footsteps, and a soldier came in and stood at attention in the doorway. "Yes, Captain." "Take this man to headquarters. Tell Captain Ariza that I'll speak to him about this later." "Yes, Captain," answered the soldier, saluting again. He took the prisoner by the arm, and the two men left the cabin. They walked to the dock where the barge was moored, and climbed the slight rise to the embankment. The guard, a corpulent man of black and Indian descent who looked like a soccer player, was wearing an impeccable uniform and had the kind of indefinite face that no one can ever remember. He did not let go of the Gaviero's arm, but there was no trace of violence in his grip. It seemed, rather, as if he were guiding the prisoner along unfamiliar terrain. They came to the military post; the Gaviero had always seen it closed, but now the installation bustled with an extraordinary animation that made him think of an anthill. Soldiers and officers walked in and out; peremptory orders were given; weapons clanged and furniture and equipment were moved from one part of the building to another. Everything was finding its place in a quick, precise rhythm, a demonstration of efficiency and discipline that inspired both fear and respect. The air was heavy with the odor of recently oiled rifles and the classroom smell of newly sharpened pencils and rancid sweat.

The guard led Maqroll to the office of Captain Ariza, a short, dark man who had the thin pencil mustache of a 1940s Mexican movie star. He wore a sparkling white guayabera and tan trousers. On his lapel was an unobtrusive pin with narrow orange and green stripes. "Military Intelligence," the Gaviero said to himself. "Now the fun begins." Ariza listened to the guard's message and nodded without saying a word. He raised his hand to his forehead, sketching a salute, and signaled to the soldier that he could leave. Then he went to the door and called someone by his last name. A lieutenant, also dressed in a white guayabera and tan trousers, came in, stood beside Ariza to listen to a whispered order, nodded, and approached Maqroll, saying with a certain courtesy, "Come with me, please." Maqroll followed him without saying anything to Ariza. He was struck by the impersonal deference of the man who led him through corridors and offices filled with activity. That "please" rang in his ears. It was a sign that he was no longer among conventional soldiers. Although Intelligence served the military, their methods and language were those of the police, any police, anywhere in the world. This fact did not fail to produce a relative sense of relief. He could almost anticipate what lay before him. All he had to endure was the strain of playing mouse with the astute, tireless cat and trying to escape with his life from between those claws. It was not impossible, and he was ready to begin the game.

They crossed a courtyard where some Marines were mounting half a dozen machine guns, working silently in the sun as perspiration stains spread under their arms and on their chests, darkening their gray drill uniforms. Maqroll and his guide entered a corridor lit by high-powered bulbs protected by metal grates. He thought they must have installed their own electrical plant, since La Plata had no electricity. They were planning to stay for a long time, then. They walked past doors that opened and closed as officers and orderlies carried papers and document files from one

side of the corridor to the other. At the end of the hallway the
lieutenant stopped in front of a metal door with cylinder bolts
and a narrow peephole in the center, covered by grating. He
took a key ring out of his pocket, tried several keys, and found
the one that opened the heavy lock. He gestured to the Gaviero
to walk in and then followed him, locking the door after them.
They were in a cell lit by two narrow windows almost at ceiling
level and protected by thick bars. The light blue tiles on the floor
also covered almost three meters of the wall. In the middle of the
cell was a kind of cement table with a narrow groove running
down the center. It tilted forward slightly and resembled an elongated washboard. The mattress from his bamboo cot and the
knapsack he had taken with him in the barge were at the foot of
the table. In one corner of the room were two identical sinks
with soap; towels hung beside them. In the other corner a toilet
was only partially concealed behind a precarious curtain. Its tank
was located just under the ceiling, well out of reach even if one
stood on the toilet bowl. The officer ordered him to remove his
shoes and belt. Gaviero obeyed and handed them over in silence.

"If you need anything, you can bang twice on the peephole.
Somebody is always there. Meals will be brought three times a
day. It's the same food the troops eat. If you don't like it, they
can bring any food you want from the boardinghouse where you
were staying. They'll be calling for you soon. Things are settled
very quickly here."

The man's voice was flat, indifferent, almost soothing. But his
words were not, and the Gaviero gave himself over to every kind
of deduction. The officer, holding the prisoner's shoes and belt in
his hand, was about to leave, when Maqroll decided to ask him
what the table was for and what kind of cell it was. The lieutenant explained that for now the table would be used as his bed and
that was where he should lay his mattress. He said nothing else
and left, locking the door and running the bolts. All of this was
executed with a scrupulous patience that had something irritating
and stupid in it.

Maqroll spread the mattress on the table and lay down to rest.
The slight upward tilt of his feet made him feel like a corpse
ready for autopsy. In the middle of the ceiling a powerful bulb
behind a heavy metal grate shed a bluish light. He realized that

the light took its color from the floor and walls. It was an operating room atmosphere not likely to calm anyone. Clearly this was an interrogation cell that they were using temporarily as secured quarters for him. He remembered a similar place in the port of Piraeus. That one too had been furnished as a cell; the thought calmed him somewhat though it left room for hypotheses it was advisable to ignore for the moment. He could not sleep but did relax his body, which immediately brought him a sense of relief that was reflected in his state of mind. He recalled other occasions when he had become involved with that shadowy, alarming, faceless world through which the servants of the law move.

He remembered the time he was stopped on the outskirts of Kabul by a patrol of Afghan police. They insisted on inspecting the packs of rugs, made for tourists, that were on the backs of two emaciated camels he was leading to Peshawar. He showed the receipt for his merchandise and the corresponding permit to sell his goods. But a sergeant with a huge black mustache, its ends twisted and stiff, insisted on slipping his hand between the saddle and the blanket that protected the animal. There he discovered two goatskin bags full of uncut semiprecious stones. Maqroll spent two weeks in the jail of a nearby village, waiting for a decision by the authorities in Kabul. He was not treated as a prisoner, and he often went to the guards' houses for meals. They were people whose natural haughtiness was tempered by spontaneous affection and a sense of hospitality that was deeply moving. He heard the most stupendous, unforgettable stories of encounters between caravans and mountain bandits who came down from the snows to spread terror along the craggy routes of the central plateau. He was told of the false dervishes who took advantage of the women who went to the river for water, subjecting them to prolonged, complex erotic manipulations that left them practically insane. This stay in an Afghan jail allowed him to come to know one of the most indomitable, admirable peoples in the world. The authorities required him to pay a fee for taking the stones out of the country and for the cost of the food he had eaten during his detention. With a resounding kiss on each cheek his companions and guards said goodbye with such warm friendship that he felt he was leaving the country where he could have ended his wandering and lived among men he truly considered his brothers; they were inhabitants of a world he often evoked as an ideal he had lost all hope of finding again. There it was, and he had left it forever.

Then he remembered the two months he had spent in prison in Kitimat, British Columbia, charged with abducting an Indian girl. They had met in a store in town and he had struck up a conversation with her, attracted by the intensity in her dark, startled eyes and by her tobacco-colored skin, which he guessed was beguilingly smooth and velvety. She told him a complicated tale of a drunken father and prostitute mother, of endless beatings and attempts to sell her to the captains of whaling ships anchored in the bay. Maqroll allowed himself to be caught up in the story, and he took her to the cutter he used for trading at nearby coastal towns, where he dealt in animal skins and, when the occasion presented itself, in hunting weapons smuggled out of Alaska. The girl conscientiously controlled her sensuality, and this had the charm of an artful eroticism that concealed its simulations behind an exceptional aesthetic sense. The alleged orphan turned out to be the wife of a gigantic Pole who searched frantically for his wife's abductor in order to strangle him. His crossed, bloodshot eyes gave him a devastatingly ferocious appearance. He waited for the Gaviero beside the cutter; fortunately, the police intervened before Maqroll was killed at the hands of the madman from Warsaw. Maqroll had to spend sixty days in prison for adultery with intent to deceive, a crime that he thought was invented by the judge at the moment he passed sentence. The magistrate was a partially paralyzed dwarf who for some reason had taken an immediate dislike to him. Maqroll would have remembered his months of confinement in a Canadian prison as a pleasant vacation had it not been for the cold he felt at night because there were not enough blankets. The other prisoners came from every corner of the globe. Almost all of them had committed crimes against property and were, in fact, the elite of their profession. What he learned there could have filled an encyclopedia on thievery and all its variations, although he never dared use it even at his moments of direst poverty. The cold was unbearable, and the prison authorities insisted on providing each prisoner with only one regulation army blanket. "I don't doubt these blankets come from the army," said a Chilean who was serving a sentence for stealing fish from the freezers in the port, "but it's the army of His Majesty the Emperor of India. If they were Canadian blankets, the soldiers would have frozen to death long ago."

When he was released, the Polish giant was waiting for him outside the prison. With tears in his eyes he told Maqroll that his wife had run away again, this time with a Russian harpooner. There was no way to get her back because the ship had already sailed for Petropavlovsk-Kamchatski. He invited Maqroll to have a vodka with him so they could console each other for the loss of a woman of such outstanding erotic accomplishments. With extreme caution the Gaviero declined. He knew the matter would end in another exceedingly unequal dispute, and he did not want to run the risk of freezing in prison again. The Pole accompanied him to his cutter, and as Maqroll made preparations for his departure, the man stood on the pier and continued to enumerate the catalogue of delights lost because of that damned harpooner who, to the husband's even greater shame, was Russian. As the cutter pulled away from the pier, the Pole waved goodbye with a tear-soaked handkerchief. His final request was that if Maqroll ever ran into the Indian on his travels, he should tell her that her husband was waiting, without rancor and with the firm intention of giving her a good life.

It began to grow dark in La Plata. The rattle of dishes at the cell door brought Maqroll back to the present. The meal had that unmistakably bland, slightly bitter taste of barracks food. He scarcely ate, but asked for a second cup of coffee, and the guard returned immediately with a large cup of watered coffee that the prisoner nonetheless drank with pleasure. The tilt of his bed, and the ghosts awakened by the light blue tiles and the surgically white ceiling, kept him from sleeping peacefully. Very early the next morning breakfast was brought in: the same tasteless coffee and two small rolls as hard as rocks. Two guards came to take away the dishes; one was carrying Maqroll's belt and shoes, and the other, who picked up the pewter tray, said, "They're coming soon to take you to Captain Ariza. Please put on your shoes and belt. You have time to wash up. It's better to be fresh and wide awake during interrogation."

He was not certain how to interpret these relative courtesies: the constant "please," the second cup of coffee, and now the guard's comments. He could not imagine that they were acts of simple compassion. In the armed forces that is the first quality eliminated in a recruit. It could be an attitude peculiar to the Marines. But courteous words and actions should not lead him to harbor any hope for pity or indulgence in the men who were now going to decide his fate. He washed his face with the mud-colored warm water that came in a meager, intermittent stream from one of the faucets. None of the other taps worked. He was drying himself when the door opened. The same guards who had brought breakfast led him to the office of Captain Ariza, who stood waiting for him, examining some papers on his desk. The guards withdrew and Ariza asked Maqroll to sit down. The captain began to pace up and down, holding the papers in his hand. He put them back and placed both hands on the desk, leaning slightly toward the Gaviero and staring at him intently. He was wearing a different guayabera, as impeccably white as the first. His Mexican movie star face was impassive. For a moment Maqroll thought he would never speak again, but the rather sharp, uninflected voice disabused him of that idea.

"Well, to begin with, we have some identity problems with you. They aren't the reason you were detained, but they are unsettling. You're traveling with a Cypriot passport. The most recent visa, dated Marseilles, expired a year and a half ago. Earlier ones were obtained in Panama City, Glasgow, and Antwerp. Your stated profession is sailor. Place of birth, unknown. This is not the kind of passport that brings peace of mind to the authorities in a country that is in a state of virtual civil war. What do you have to say about the matter?"

"Captain, this is the first time I've heard anyone take exception to my passport," replied Maqroll with a serenity that was quite convincing. "I've sailed the Caribbean and its islands for many years. Before that I was in the Mediterranean and the North Sea. No one has ever raised objections to the document. But I see now that, given the circumstances here, a passport like mine might arouse suspicions."

"All right. As I said, that isn't our primary concern. Let's go straight to the point: You used your own mules, purchased at the Álvarez Flat, to transport smuggled weapons to the Tambo Ridge. The deal was made in Panama City and Kingston. The three smugglers captured by the Army were carrying passports very similar to yours, with consular stamps from cities that also appear in your passport. The act of supplying weapons to any group attempting to undermine the stability of our institutions carries a penalty that you are surely aware of. I'd like to hear what you have to say."

Point by point, the Gaviero told the captain about his meeting with van Branden, the Belgian's proposition and all the subsequent events related to the transport of the crates up to the ridge, his dealings with the two foreigners on the Tambo, and what he had deduced from their behavior. He insisted, emphatically and firmly, each time it was relevant, that he had absolutely no knowledge of what was in the crates until he found a piece of label at the bottom of the ravine where the mule had gone over the edge, and then at his subsequent meeting with Captain Segura. The coincidence of the same cities appearing in his passport and those of the arms dealers was simply that: sheer coincidence. He had never been in the arms business or had contact with anyone who was. In British Columbia he had sold some hunting rifles he had bought at a very low price in Alaska, but that wasn't enough to trouble a county sheriff.

Captain Ariza seemed to discount the Gaviero's explanations, and in the same tone as before he said: "Hasn't it occurred to you that it's inconceivable, to say the least, that you were in no way suspicious of a story as clumsy as the supposed construction of the railroad, or Brandon's appearances and disappearances, or the look of his pals on the Tambo? Didn't you ever think there might be something going on behind a pack of lies that not even the most naive boy running around the docks would have swallowed?"

"Of course, Captain," Maqroll went on in the same tone, "van Branden, or Brandon, always seemed like a fairly shady character, and his friends in the barrens even more so. But I thought they were probably swindling the contractors; by the way, I did see sections of track that had long since been abandoned. The fact that they were starting the project again didn't seem suspicious to me. I just took the money and let them go about their business. All my conjectures were very vague, and experience has taught me that many people who look very untrustworthy turn out later to be perfectly honest and ordinary."

"Answer yes or no to my next question." The intelligence officer's voice had sharpened, betraying some impatience. "Did you have any idea of what you were carrying up to the Tambo Ridge before you talked to Captain Segura? The slightest hint, the least suspicion? Up until the time the mule went over the cliff, did you really think it was equipment for laying the track?"

"Here's the trap," thought the Gaviero. And his life depended on his answer. Again, in a calm tone, he reiterated his absolute ignorance of the crates' contents, and the fact that his natural suspicions of the foreigners had leaned toward the assumption that they were cheating the contractors. He described, this time in complete detail, his meeting with Captain Segura, who had told him the truth and asked for his cooperation in making a final climb with the crates that were still in La Plata and whatever might come in on the boat. He mentioned identifying the crates as TNT because of his mining experience. Ariza interrupted several times to ask for even more precise details concerning certain aspects of his meeting with Captain Segura and the participation of Don Aníbal Álvarez, "a person who has our complete confidence," the captain added in passing. When Maqroll finished, Ariza was silent for a few minutes that seemed eternal to the Gaviero. At last Ariza spoke, this time with a hint of relief, which could be detected more on his face than in the voice that had been trained for so long in military procedures.

"I don't know if I should say you're a lucky man or a doomed one. We'll see. Captain Segura's confirmation of what you've said would clarify your situation completely. But Captain Segura, whom we all admired and respected for his bravery and esprit de corps, was killed along with all his men during a siege of the Tambo sheds and the miners' cabin. Just as the middlemen came to pick up the load of weapons, and Segura achieved his objective and blew up the sheds, a much larger force attacked. Their superior weapons and overwhelming numbers were too much for our troops despite their heroic resistance. At the end of the fighting Captain Segura was hit by a fragmentation grenade. His last remaining men died with him. All right. That's all for now.

I'll have to make certain inquiries into what you've told me. You'll be interrogated again."

Captain Ariza stood up and went to the door to call the guard on duty. When he was back in his cell, the Gaviero began to weave a net of consequences and deductions designed to hold his newly acquired hope of escaping the trap he had fallen into. He spent the afternoon reading pages from the life of the Poverello of Assisi. The evocation of the proportion and harmony of the Umbrian landscape, the perfect frame for Francis's miracles, which occurred with the simple naturalness used later by Giotto to depict them in his frescoes, helped the Gaviero to recover his serenity and establish a healthy distance between his current misfortune and the inviolate, hidden part of his being from which there always flowed a stream of confidence in his true destiny. That night he placed the mattress on the floor in order to sleep more comfortably. The sinister table produced the darkest forebodings in him.

When they brought breakfast, the guard asked why he had put the mattress on the floor.

"I can't sleep with the table tilting that way. I'm more comfortable on the floor. Is it against regulations?"

"No," replied the soldier. "The table isn't for sleeping." Maqroll asked what it was really for. The man only smiled in disbelief at the prisoner's feigned ignorance and left without saying anything. And Maqroll did not want to know more. It had all been said.

The next day he was taken to the courtyard to help raise a crate of ammunition to a storage area on the second floor of the barracks, which was less humid. He thought, as he worked, of the ironic fate that obliged him once again to carry war matériel. That night he was informed that in the morning he was to go to headquarters. They came for him after breakfast and took him to an office with windows overlooking the river. They asked him to sit down and left him there alone. After a time a major came in, wearing an impeccably clean and pressed olive-green field uniform and an olive-green cap that was similar to a baseball hat. He was a heavy man, somewhat short of breath and congested, with a graying mustache and an arrogant air. He smoked incessantly and his hands trembled slightly. He looked like a member of a country club masquerading as a soldier. In a deliberate, rather hoarse voice he made some routine inquiries similar to the questions Captain Ariza had asked. When he was finished, he put on a pair of gold-rimmed glasses and looked over the papers in a bright red folder on his desk. Then he signaled to the guard who had come in to pick up some documents to take the prisoner away. He did not even raise his head, and continued to read as if the Gaviero did not exist.

Maqroll had noticed that some of the papers examined by the major were handwritten pages, stained with blood and mud, that had been torn from a notebook. The writing was clear and round and easy to read. Back in his cell, the uncertainty and anguish he thought he had overcome tormented him again for the rest of the day and a good part of the night. In dreams the major came to him in a parade uniform and explained, in a very cordial, worldly manner, a series of increasingly complex and tiresome military maneuvers. In the morning he was awakened, as always, by a noise at the door. They were bringing his breakfast. The guard informed him that he would soon be taken back to the offices of Military Intelligence. An overwhelming weariness, a deadening of all his limbs and a bitter taste in his mouth, sapped the forces he had vainly attempted to gather during his days in prison. It was clear that his hour had come. Unfortunately, it had caught him when his guard was lower than ever and his body had become a bag of aching bones that refused to support him when he needed it most. He waited all morning for them to come for him. After lunch he lay dozing in an oppressive stupor. The footsteps of the guard who opened the door woke him. He had slept in the heaviness of an afternoon that threatened rain and made the atmosphere like a Turkish bath. Even the smallest noises were muffled by a thick, damp cloak of unbreathable air.

"The captain wants to talk to you," said the guard. "Get dressed and come with us."

Another guard was waiting at the door. The Gaviero wiped his face and part of his body with a towel soaked in warm tap water. He put on a clean shirt and a pair of Bermuda shorts, sent to him by the blind woman, which he had kept since his days as a sailor. He pulled a comb through his graying, rumpled hair and walked out between the two soldiers. As he crossed the courtyard, his legs moved somewhat more firmly. Knowing that he was going to face Ariza helped to sharpen his wits. His fate would be decided, and he began to feel an uneasy wariness, like a gambler about to play a complicated game in which each wager may be conclusive. He walked into Ariza's office. The guards stayed outside and closed the door behind him. There was the man from Military Intelligence twisting his graduation ring from the base at Corpus Christi, Texas, with his thumb. The same insignia was still on the lapel of his impeccable guayabera. The straight mustache, very prominent on his recently shaved face, emphasized a faint smile, but the Gaviero resolved to have no illusions whatsoever regarding its sincerity.

"Have a seat, friend. Make yourself comfortable." Ariza pointed to a swivel chair that had been brought in from another office. It tilted dangerously from one side to the other at Maqroll's slightest movement, and he attempted to sit as quietly as possible in order to keep the diabolical seat in some semblance of equilibrium. That "friend" had appeared in the captain's vocabulary toward the end of their previous interview. He said it with a certain tone of complicity that roused the Gaviero's suspicions, and Maqroll made ready to play the game and to control each of his responses and replies.

"Well," Ariza began, "here we are again trying to clarify what, to be perfectly frank, is as clear as water to me. No one can convince me you're innocent. I can't believe you didn't know what you were carrying up to the Tambo Ridge. And we've collected reports about your past: arms smuggling in Cyprus, tampering with signal flags in Marseilles, trafficking in gold and rugs in Alicante, prostitutes in Panama City—it would take hours to read the entire list. A man with a past like yours isn't going to transport weapons and think they're engineering instruments for a nonexistent railway. What I can't understand is your settling for so little money when you could have gotten thousands of dollars."

"With all due respect, Captain," the Gaviero replied in the calmest, most civil voice he could muster, "you can't imagine how it happened simply because you don't know me. All those activities you've mentioned from my past are true, but there are hidden aspects in all of them that can't show up in the kind of summary catalogue you've just read. Believe me, given the situation here, if I had suspected even for a moment what their business was, I would never have become involved with those so-called Belgians. They're not the kind of people I usually associate with. I suspected them from the start, but I was almost certain they were using the story of the railroad to swindle the government."

"Well. I don't know. In any event," Ariza went on, "the General Staff obtained a report written by Captain Segura on the same night he met with you and Aníbal Álvarez. In it you appear fully exonerated and perfectly willing to cooperate with us. Everything confirms and corroborates what you've told us. And if that weren't enough, the Lebanese government has requested your freedom through its embassy and has offered to guarantee your conduct for as long as you're in the country. There are, apparently, a number of complex factors that oblige us to be responsive to this request by the Lebanese diplomatic mission; we need their vote in some United Nations commission or other. That's the way things stand, and despite my serious reservations regarding your innocence, I have to give a properly closed file to the General Staff. Your being alive complicates the issue."

Maqroll could not understand exactly what the officer meant. But his unadorned discussion of the matter sent a chill down the Gaviero's spine. It seemed they needed him dead rather than here, creating unnecessary confusion. He could barely manage a shrug, as if he were begging pardon for still being alive.

"You'll get out alive. It can't be helped. But don't stick your nose into any more problems; just disappear. The sooner the better." The captain began to return to a folder all the papers he had been examining while talking to the prisoner.

"Does this mean I'm free?" asked Maqroll with an incredulity that had something pathetic and childish in it.

"Yes, señor. That means you're free from this moment on, and you ought to leave La Plata right now if you can. Your barge is waiting for you at the embankment. Try to get out of this area. It's under military control, and if they pick you up at another post downriver, there's nothing we can do. They're not going to wait for communiqués from the Middle East; do you understand? It's not their style. Is that clear?"

"Yes, Captain. I understand perfectly," replied the Gaviero, trying to hide the euphoric relief that washed over him. "But I'd like to wait until nightfall to leave. I think it's safer. That won't be a problem, will it?"

"Not at all. Do whatever you want," answered Ariza brusquely, wanting to bring the interview to an end. "There's your barge. Here's a safe-conduct for traveling through our area. I hope it works. Things are very chaotic. Leave as soon as it's dark, and I hope we never see each other again." The captain handed him a paper with his signature; it was stamped by post headquarters. He extended his hand to say goodbye, and the Gaviero shook it. He walked toward the door, and when he was about to open it, he turned to ask Ariza a question.

"May I know something?"

"Yes, what is it?" answered Ariza impatiently.

"If Captain Segura's report hadn't arrived, and if the Lebanese embassy hadn't become involved, what would have happened to me?"

"To you?" A laugh strangled in the officer's throat. "Man, you would've been dead a long time ago. You can leave now, and remember what I told you: be careful, this isn't a country for people like you."

Maqroll went to the cell to pick up his things, unaccompanied now by any guard. As he placed his clothes and other gear into Doña Empera's knapsack, he thought about his friend and one-time companion on his wanderings, Abdul Bashur. From his place in eternity, even after his death in a plane crash in Funchal, he was still taking care of him through relatives and friends in every corner of the globe. Not a day went by that Maqroll did not think of him with irremediable affection and nostalgia. Now, once again, he had saved his life. A sob caught in his chest. He struggled to regain control of himself, and left the military post under the indifferent eyes of the guards who had watched him so closely before.

As he made his way to the blind woman's boardinghouse, Captain Ariza's words continued ringing in his ears: "This isn't a country for people like you." He thought perhaps there really was no place for him in the world, no country where he could end his wandering. Just like the poet who had been his companion on long visits to countless bars and cafés in a rainy Andean city, the Gaviero could say, "I imagine a Country, a blurred, fogbound Country, an enchanted magical Country where I could live. What Country, where? . . . Not Mosul or Basra or Samarkand. Not Karlskrona or Abylund or Stockholm or Copenhagen. Not Kazan or Kanpur or Aleppo. Not in lacustrian Venice or chimerical Istambul, not on the Ile-de-France or in Tours or Stratford-on-Avon or Weimar or Yasnaia Poliana or in the baths of Algiers," and his comrade continued to evoke cities where he perhaps had never been. "I, who have known them all," thought Maqroll, "and in many have turned life's most surprising corners, now I'm running from this shit hamlet without knowing exactly why I let myself be caught in the most stupid trap that destiny ever set for me. All that's left for me now is the estuary, nothing but the marshes in the delta. That's all."

An anxious Doña Empera was waiting for him. "I'm so glad they let you go. Nachito told me. He saw you leave the post and came running with the news. I sent him to the Turk's for more diesel and told him to take it to the barge. It's important for you to leave as soon as it's dark, and with enough fuel so you don't have to stop for at least three days. You should stay away from the posts where the Marines are now." The woman thought of everything. She seemed to have aged. Her hair looked whiter and her shoulders more bent. He was moved when he thought that without saying a word, with the deep resignation of the blind, she had taken on the burden of her guest's uncertain fate, the doubts as to whether he would leave the barracks dead or alive. There was something maternal in her loving vigilance, and a good deal of affectionate solidarity with a man whose contrary, uncertain life bore no resemblance to her own buried existence in a corner of the cordillera, on the banks of a muddy river, with no companion at her side.

She invited him into the kitchen for coffee prepared the way he liked it. The Gaviero's things were already there, ready to be taken to the river. He only had to add what he was carrying in the knapsack. When Nacho returned from the embankment, he would put it all together and take it to the barge that Tomasito was watching as he waited to take his leave of Maqroll and give a few final touches to the motor. The two enamel cups, filled with dark, steaming coffee that had a strong, almost woodsy aroma, were in front of Doña Empera as she began to tell the Gaviero what she had been saving since the moment she first met him.

"There's something I've been wanting to tell you for a long time. I didn't do it before because it would have meant more worry for you, more bitterness on top of what you already had with the mules and the devil's load you were carrying. Now it's time for you to know: Flor Estévez was here some years ago. She stayed in this house and we were good friends."

A silent blow deep inside, in the center of his chest, left the Gaviero breathless for a moment. Never, not for an instant, had he forgotten the woman who had sheltered him in the barrens, in The Snow of the Admiral, her little shop beside the highway, where he had come with his leg almost gangrenous from the bite of a spider on the Okuriare. Her dark, wild hair, her silent, intense, almost religious, almost vegetative lovemaking, her immense rages that devastated everything around her, her docile tenderness that could put everything in order again. Flor Estévez. How could he forget her? When he returned from his journey up the Xurandó, he went to the mountains to look for her and found nothing. Just the abandoned shop in ruins. The trucker who drove him up to the highest part of the road, where Flor lived, said something about La Osa Gully. He went there and could not find Flor anywhere. He had even sold women's clothing at a ford on the river, hoping she would pass by one day. And now here, suddenly, a sign of her appeared as if by miracle. Choking with inconsolable sadness, he asked the blind woman what else she knew of his friend.

"She spoke about you all the time," said Doña Empera. "That's why when I first met you, I knew you as if we had been old friends. Flor told me she had to leave the shop because the security police came and confiscated her house to use as a watch post. Then it seems they left too. After that came a terrible winter. Avalanches closed off the highway and they had to build another road somewhere else. Nobody went back there, and the place fell apart."

"I went back, Doña Empera. Nothing was standing."

"Flor Estévez," continued the blind woman, "left to try to

earn a living. She asked for you everywhere. In the big port along the estuary she set up a dressmaking shop—party dresses and bridal gowns. Little by little the business changed direction, and the police began bothering her. Flor sold everything and started upriver, stopping at every port. When she arrived here, she was sick with fever. She didn't have a cent. For a time she lived with me and helped me in the boardinghouse. We became very good friends. In the morning I untangled her hair; it was so wild, but very beautiful. She recovered from the malaria and became attractive again. Finally she left with the captain of one of the boats that worked for the oil company. I never heard from her again. You can't imagine how often she said that the only thing that tormented her in life was that you would think she had abandoned you and didn't love you anymore. 'I'll die bearing that cross,' she would say. 'If I could only see him one day, just for a minute!' Now you know the story. If she's still alive, she carries that hopeless sorrow with her."

Maqroll did not know what to say. Or rather, he realized there was nothing to add. Night had fallen. They talked a little while longer, both of them pondering his departure and the feeling of farewells when everything suddenly rushes toward the past, and the present is emptied of meaning. Finally Doña Empera said: "It's time to go. Be very careful. You'll always be remembered here with much affection. Too bad we didn't finish the books you were reading to me. At night I talk to Saint Francis. You don't know how he comforts me. It's a gift from you, a memento that I'll keep until I die. That's how we blind people settle our accounts with life, and we win out over the dark by remembering those we love. It's not so bad being blind, you know. I don't believe there's all that much to see. What do you think?"

"You're right, Doña Empera," the Gaviero answered, very moved. "There really isn't much to see, and sometimes it's better to forget what little there is."

He walked toward the blind woman, who had stood to embrace him. She hugged him in silence, without tears or sobs. The woman who knew everything felt that the man leaving her arms was saying goodbye to life.

Maqroll went down to the dock where Tomasito was waiting

for him. Nacho had insisted on carrying his suitcase to the barge. The motor was running, purring with an occasional cough, a symptom of its great age, provisional repairs, and ephemeral adjustments. When Maqroll said goodbye to the old man, he thought he saw a fleeting spark of warm affection in his eyes. Nacho, his face serious and his hair carefully combed, was wearing the new clothes Doña Empera had given him. The Gaviero caressed his cheek and jumped onto the barge without saying a word. The boy's eyes were wet. Maqroll thought about Amparo María and her air of an Andalusian maja. The old man pushed the barge away with his foot, and it moved at half speed to the middle of the river. Carried by the current, the barge sailed into the night as if it were entering a lethal, unknown world. The Gaviero, without turning around, waved goodbye with his hand. Leaning on the tiller, he looked like a tired Charon overcome by the weight of his memories, on his way to find the rest he had been seeking for so long, and for which he would not have to pay anything.

APPENDIX

T here are several versions of the Gaviero's last days. The oldest one bears a title too pretentious to be taken seriously: A Recounting of Certain Memorable Visions of Maqroll the Gaviero, Some of His Experiences on Several of His Journeys, and a Catalogue of Some of His Most Familiar and Oldest Objects.[1] *The death of Maqroll as narrated in this brief and certainly apocryphal work is too literary to be credible. Then, in a slightly more probable piece of prose, some have thought they have found a description of the death of our friend. The fragment in question is entitled "Dwelling place" and appears in* A Report on Overseas Hospitals,[2] *a book that is almost unobtainable today. Finally, the version that seems closest to a reality that conforms to certain circumstances narrated in* Un Bel Morir, *and which is transcribed below, has been met with the greatest skepticism by friends and companions of the Gaviero such as Ludwig Zeller, Enrique Molina, and Gonzalo Rojas. The latter has even threatened to take the case to court and challenge the disappearance of his old comrade and accomplice in countless escapades that are more bacchanalian and amatory than anything else. With these reservations, whose authority we are far from disputing, we transcribe the testimony in question. It appeared some years ago in* Caravansary,[3] *a book containing other experiences of Maqroll that are certainly*

[1] *Summa de Maqroll el Gaviero,* p. 63, Barral Editores. "Insulae Poetarum," Barcelona, 1973.
[2] *Reseña de los Hospitales de Ultramar,* p. 151, idem.
[3] *Caravansary,* p. 55, Fondo de Cultura Económica, México, 1981.

reliable. This document, written in somewhat longer periods than usual, is entitled In the Marshes, *and reads as follows:*

Before penetrating the marshes, the time had come for the Gaviero to review the moments of his life from which there had flowed, with regular and gratifying constancy, the reason for his days, the sequence of motives that had always overcome the gentle call of death.

They were sailing down the river in a rusty barge that had once been used to carry fuel oil to the uplands and had been retired from service many years before. An asthmatic diesel engine struggled to push the vessel along to the catastrophic clang of metal against metal.

There were four travelers on the barge. They had been eating fruit, much of it still green, which they picked on the bank when they pulled ashore to repair another breakdown in the infernal machinery. At times they consumed the flesh of drowned animals that floated on the muddy surface of the water.

Two of the travelers died in silent convulsions after devouring a water rat that, as they killed it, stared at them with the fixed wrath of its bulging eyes like two demented, incandescent carbuncles confronting a painful, inexplicable death.

The Gaviero remained, accompanied by a woman who had been wounded in a brothel fight and came aboard at one of the ports in the interior. Her clothes were torn and her dark, unruly hair was flattened in places by dried blood. Her scent was bittersweet, fruity and feline. The woman's wounds healed easily, but an attack of malaria left her prostrate in a hammock that hung from the metal supports of the precarious tin roof protecting the tiller and controls. The Gaviero did not know if the sick woman's body trembled with attacks of fever or because of the vibrating propeller.

Maqroll sat on a plank bench and steered the barge in the middle of the river. He let the river carry them, not trying to avoid the whirlpools and sandbars, which became more frequent as they approached the marshes where the river began to merge with the sea, extending silently and effortlessly into a horizon of saline swamp.

One day the motor suddenly fell silent. The metal parts had

*been vanquished by the unrelenting struggle to which they had
been subjected for so many years. A great quiet descended on the
travelers. The bubbling water against the flat prow of the barge
and the faint moaning of the sick woman lulled the Gaviero into
tropical somnolence.*

*Then, in the lucid delirium of implacable hunger, he was
able to isolate the most familiar, recurrent signs that had nourished
the substance of certain times in his life. What follows are some of
those moments, summoned by Maqroll the Gaviero as he drifted
into the marshes at the river's mouth:*

A coin that fell from his hands and rolled down a street
in the port of Antwerp, until it was lost in a sewer drain.

The song of a girl hanging clothes on the deck of a
freighter as it waited for the sluice gates to open.

The sun gilding the wooden bed where he slept with a
woman whose language he could not understand.

The air in the trees announcing the coolness that would
restore his strength when he reached La Arena.

His conversation with a peddler of miraculous medals in
a tavern in Turko-Limanon.

The roar of the torrent in the ravine drowning out the
voice of the woman in the coffee groves who always came
to him when all hope was lost.

The fire, yes, the flames licking with implacable urgency
at the high walls of a castle in Moravia.

The clink of glasses in a sordid bar on the Strand where
he learned the other face of evil that dissolves, slowly and
with no surprise, at the indifference of those present.

The feigned moaning of two old whores who, naked
and entwined, imitated the ancient rite of desire in a dingy
room in Istanbul whose windows overlooked the Bosphorus. The performers' eyes stared at the stained walls
while the kohl ran down their ageless cheeks.

A long, imaginary dialogue with the prince of Viana and
the Gaviero's plans for an action in Provence designed to
save an improbable inheritance of the unfortunate heir to
the house of Aragón.

A certain sliding of the parts of a firearm when it has just been oiled after a meticulous cleaning.

The night when the train stopped at the burning ravine. The din of water smashing against the great rocks, almost invisible in the milky starlight. A cry in the banana groves. Solitude corroding like rust. The vegetal breath coming out of the darkness.

All the stories and lies about his past accumulating until they formed another being, always present and naturally more deeply loved than his own pale, useless existence composed of nausea and dreams.

A crack of wood waking him in the humble hotel on the Rue du Rempart and, in the middle of the night, leaving him on that shore where only God is aware of other people.

The eyelid twitching with the autonomous speed of one who knows he is in the hands of death. The eyelid of the man he had to kill, with repugnance, with no anger, to save the life of a woman whom he now found unbearable.

All his waiting. All the emptiness of that nameless time used up in the foolishness of negotiations, proceedings, journeys, blank days, mistaken itineraries. All that life, from which he now begs, as he slips through the wounded dark toward death, some of the leftover scraps he thinks he has a right to.

Some days later a customs launch found the barge run aground among the mangroves. The woman, deformed by extraordinary swelling, gave off an unbearable stench that spread like the limitless swamp. The Gaviero lay curled up beside the tiller, his body dried and sere like a pile of roots withered by the sun. His wide-open eyes were fixed on that nothingness, immediate and anonymous, where the dead find the rest that was denied them during their wanderings when they were alive.